DOWN THE VALLEY OF THE SHADOW

AN AMERICAN NOVEL

The story as told in
Over the Mountains of the Moon
continues…

MARY RAMSTETTER

C Lazy Three
PRESS

Golden, Colorado

DOWN THE VALLEY OF THE SHADOW
An American Novel

Ramstetter, Mary
ISBN 0-9643283-1-3
Library of Congress Catalog Card Number 2001-129344

Cover and interior design by Troy Scott Parker, Cimarron Design, www.cimarrondesign.com

Ⓐ PRINTED ON RECYCLED PAPER

Printed in the United States of America by Thomson-Shore
First printing February 2002
5 4 3 2 1

Published by
C Lazy Three Press
5957 Crawford Gulch
Golden, CO 80403

With the exception of actual historical personages, the characters are entirely the product of the author's imagination and have no implied relation to any person in real life.

Dedicated to all

those historians

whose dusty,

windblown notes

make this story

possible

THE UNITED STATES AND TERRITORIES
1857

OREGON TERRITORY
1846

MINN
T

UTAH TERRITORY
1850

NEBRASKA TERR
1854

KANSAS TER
1854

NEW MEXICO TERRITORY
1850

South Pass

Fourth of July Rock

Fort Bridger

Fort Laramie

Scotts Bluffs

Chimney Rock

Court House Rock

Ash Hollow

New Fort Kearney

Platte River

Salt Lake City

Provo

Sacramento

San Francisco

Mountain Meadows

Parowan

Cedar City

Santa Clara
Indian Mission

Kaibab
Plateau

Colorado River

Bent's Fort

Arkansas River

San Bernardino

N
W · E
S

Houlton ·
Abacotnetic ·
Camp
Molunkus
· Bangor
Montreal ·
· Portland
Fort Edward ·
· Marchion Farm
Albany · Troy
· New York
·TORY
Allegheny River
Hudson R.
· Economy
Wheeling ·
uncil Bluffs
ble Creek Landing
· Nauvoo
Ohio River
St. Joseph
Fort Leavenworth
Missouri River
Independence
Mississippi River
Fort Smith

Over the mountains of the moon,
Down the valley of the shadow,
"Ride, boldly ride," the shade replied,
"If you seek for Eldorado!"

– EDGAR ALLEN POE, 1849

PROLOGUE

ONCE UPON A TIME, a long time ago, a farm boy from the Hudson Valley journeyed west in search of adventure and brought back a wife. This wife had an Indian son but did not care to live with Indians. For her, the marriage proved to be the best of all possible worlds.

Her husband, however, soon grew restless with the farm and the woodlot. Perhaps even with this wife. And no longer came home every night.

The year was 1849.

The saga of the Marchion and Harris families as chronicled in the first novel of this series, Over the Mountains of the Moon, continues.

Walker and Katherine live on a large wheat farm near Kingston. Deeply involved in the politics of women's suffrage and the temperance movement, Katherine is the perfect foil for her melancholy, self-absorbed husband.

Dinky Marchion, 15 years old and dazzled by the political movements sweeping the country, dreams of traveling about America on the lecture circuit.

George Harris, the Mormon elder who led a train of Saints from Nauvoo to the Willamette Valley in 1846, has been elevated to the rank of bishop in Salt Lake City. As an example to other husbands, George has taught his second wife, Phoebe, to read and write. But she prefers to spend her spare time painting. Ellen corresponds regularly with Phoebe, thinking of her as a sister.

Conrad Uergin, the Oregon Trail guide hired by Harris in 1846, has bid Mexico and his wealthy Chihuahua widow adieu and is once more advertising his services as a trail guide.

Charlie Reeves, the U.S. Army sergeant who led Ellen south down the Taos Trail when she abandoned the Harris train in Fort Laramie, only to lose her in the desert, has quit his job as a civilian teamster and reenlisted in the Army.

Those consummate carpetbaggers Nathaniel and Daphne Laffite are in the Canterbury region of New Zealand pedaling railroad stock to British cultural notables.

Jed and Ellen Marchion have remained in New York, losing their investment in the sawmill on Snook Creek when fire destroyed the mill, but managing to pay off the Betty place.

Halloween 1849. They'd drunk too much pumpkin wine and were driving home in the dark with no lamp on the buggy, laughing and asking each other what did it matter? there were no lions or bears or wild Indians anymore.

And Jed said, "God, I'm bored!"

"Leave," Ellen said.

"What would you do?"

"Get a teaching position," she answered. "I'm not the one who's bored. I love it here." Such casual words to mark the parting of the waters. No face-saving accusations: *I warned you marrying a woman four years older with a ready-made family wouldn't be easy. I make it as easy as I can. I stay away from*

Katherine's craziness, and I do my share of the work—more
when you're off up Snook Creek in the Indian camps.
 The truth was, she'd seduced him and it didn't work. She had
her safe harbor, all he had was a harness. They still reached for
each other in the night, but there was no touching for the sake
of touching. That saving grace had escaped them.
 He had a right to more children, probably secretly wanted
them, but she didn't. She'd been taking stoneseed with cold
water for years to prevent contraception. They both knew it and
didn't talk about it.
 "Maybe if you wore more clothes," Jed observed, poking fun.
Inside the house she went naked as temperature permitted, it
was like living with an Indian.
 "I can do that," she teased. "Maybe we just better buck up
and go on."
 "We can sell the Betty, give us both a boost," he offered shyly,
feeling like a calf unexpectedly encountering an open door.
 "We aren't the first two people in the wrong place at the
wrong time," Ellen linked her arm in his and squeezed it
"particularly you—you have the damnedest time sowing your
wild oats."
 The holidays came and went—the remembered Halloween
conversation backlighting the Yule festivities like a worn candle
flickering inside an old pumpkin. Spring was coming and with it,
good-bye. But March came first, bringing its own closure.
 Suddenly both of them were adrift, their anchor on the
Hudson gone. Jed disappeared for three days, making Walker
furious at the abandonment of their mother and sister. Furious,
but not surprised.

◈

FRIDAY, MARCH 15, 1850.
Red-faced, eyes tearing from the cold, the minister closed his bible. "We shall now bow our heads in prayer." The young woman across the grave continued to stare dumbly ahead, and Electus favored her with a wintry scowl.

> *I thought Walker's frizzy-haired wife was mule-headed, but you, you shamefaced whore, are worse. Every Sunday it's the same, sitting there waiting for me to come forth with some convenient revelation that will make it alright for you to have an Indian child. You didn't like that sermon, did you? about red men being upright beasts of the field. Christianity is a harsh and painful reality. I refuse to help evil shade its cunning face by pretending otherwise.*

> – REVEREND ELECTUS AMES
>   FIRST CONGREGATIONAL CHURCH OUT OF
>   SARATOGA, NEW YORK

The little boy dressed all in black let go of his grandmother's hand to kick at a centipede wiggling through the fresh dirt. Christina smiled wanly down at him.

> *Poor little Jeremy, whatever will happen to you? Why don't your mother just tell people you're French? No one'd ever know different. She's the one wants to be Indian. What she did out in the dark, that was Indian.*

> – CHRISTINA MARCHION,
>   WIFE OF THE DECEASED

"Are you tired of standing?" the gentleman with his hand hooked under his mother's arm asked in a whisper. A rather short of stature, important-looking fellow, black neck cloth wrapped around a white stand-up collar, dark coat open on a figured-velvet waistcoat. Christina shook her head, and Walker resumed his stern scrutiny of the proceedings, his eyes inviting his sister-in-law to share his agony even as his heart shrank away.

> *You are truly Eve. Wicked. Wicked.*
>
> *Last summer when I came on you lying in the grass, I wanted to tell you how you make men feel. Does Jed hit you? I wish I could see your arms. Did Jed cut you?*
>
> — WALKER MARCHION,
> ELDER SON OF THE DECEASED

The fleshy woman in the long fur cape drew the cape close and, through silk-lined pockets, smoothed the deep vee of her bodice with splayed fingers. A black cashmere babushka edged with heavy silk fringe lay lightly over her black hair. Cold nipped her cheeks and brightened her eyes.

> *Good Lord, Jed! you are beautiful, like a Greek warrior. How I would love to touch your face. Does she even see you? I loathe and despise her! She's like a cat, always looking past me. I wish Walker would stop staring at her!*
>
> — KATHERINE MARCHION,
> DAUGHTER-IN-LAW OF THE DECEASED

Two children in woolen coats scramble to restrain the little boy kicking dirt over their shoes and are themselves restrained by an older girl. In the scuffle the girl's knit hood slips from her head, exposing a strangely splintered thatch of brown hair. She bravely suffers the draft to give the youngsters' clothing a hard yank and, straightening, glances obliquely at her sister-in-law, her own tear-swollen face filling with the sweetest kind of sorrow.

You are so brave, I could never make skin sacrifices. It's bad enough wrecking my hair. I truly wish you wouldn't leave. You'll never come back.

–EDITHA ANNE MARCHION,
DAUGHTER OF THE DECEASED

Worn greatcoat lifting slightly in the cold draft, the hatless figure at the foot of the grave was thinking about the man in the casket. And about the family. How the sometime lumberman, sometime farmer, was never really anything more than a wild voyageur gone to ground—one of those great Canadian geese dropping out of the sky for reasons of its own to settle and die on the Hudson waterway.

Jed and Editha Anne are their father's children. I wonder what happened to Walker. I remember how he couldn't eat his school treats without curling his arm around the plate. Whether it was apple crumble or bastard wings, it didn't make any difference.

The schoolmaster glanced at Jed and the woman.

I always knew this would happen. What's surprising is how civilized they are about it. Look at them...leaning against each other like two old plow horses, totally unaware of the people around them. The West has changed them in ways they don't even realize.

– JOHN RELIABLE HOGAN,
RURAL SCHOOLMASTER
TROY, NEW YORK

Thoughts over an open grave on top of a viewless hill under a slate grey sky.

Obituary, Troy News, New York, Sunday, March 17, 1850, Upriver Section:

Passing of a Pioneer
Shocking Death of Jean Paul Marchion

Born 1783, Died 1850

Seldom has a farm community received a greater shock than was given to the neighborhood of Batten-Kill upon the receipt of the news of the sad and sudden death of Jean Paul Marchion.

Mr. Marchion started for Fort Edward early Saturday, March 9, with a load of apples. He drove a team of colts and a spring wagon. He had made the trip many times before, was an expert horseman, and no fear was entertained by his family as to his safety. The terrible news first came to his wife by way of a neighbor that the lifeless body of her husband had been found on the road about four miles south of Fort Edward. Bearing up bravely under the shock Mrs. Marchion at once drove to the scene of the tragedy and from there to Fort Edward where the remains had been taken.

The accident happened near a grist mill, the miller being the first to discover the body lying in the road. The miller immediately drove to Fort Edward and notified the coroner, who drove out to the place where the body lay. The dead man was lying on his face with his arm underneath. There were no marks to show that he had been dragged. The appearance indicated that he had fallen from the buggy without any unusual cause, and many are of the opinion that he was attacked with heart trouble, else he would not have fallen out of the vehicle.

Mr. Marchion was 67 years of age... After a short service at the home, the remains were conveyed to the Congregational Church where the Reverend Electus Ames performed the last sad rites. The body was laid to rest in the old pioneer cemetery on Spring Hill.

The day after the funeral, Ellen stopped by the one-room school east of the Batten-Kill bridge. And in hushed tones in the anteroom told Master Hogan they were selling the farm. Jed was leaving the valley, she was applying for a teacherage.

The news came as no surprise to the schoolmaster. With the exception of both being leggy, handsome people, the Marchions were a complete mismatch. Not only had the unfortunate Indian encounter left Ellen slightly daft—as witnessed by the torn hair and the rumored mutilation (the night of Jean Paul's death, she'd cut herself, her arms, her hair, seized by a wild grief)—but she was also totally devoted to her half-breed son. And all but oblivious to her husband.

As was his habit when hearing a weighty confession, Master Hogan whistled softly behind his fingers.

Too bad you're not a man, his eyes said. *Men are allowed their bastards. But then, they don't have to raise them. What a shame the boy was brought here in the first place.*

"I plan to make enough to send Jeremy to West Point." Ellen finished her recital with a small boast.

Shifting his weight, the teacher leaned against the wainscoting, fingertips together prayerfully. *Why lie to yourself? You cannot seriously believe they would consider an Indian.* And said aloud, "I'll gladly give you my recommendation. But if you remain alone, you shall have to be very frugal, and fortunate indeed, to be able to afford the Point. There are cheaper universities."

"A military degree gives Jeremy a lot of clout."

"What if, as an officer, he's sent to remove the western Indian?"

"That will never happen."

"Forgive me the argument, but I believe it's only a matter of time."

"Well...I don't know. I guess we'll cross that bridge when we get to it."

"Cross it now. The Point will. They don't take Indians. For good reason, there are none to take. Look in there." The school master gestured toward the classroom, the children huddled around the stove giggling amongst themselves, lunch boxes balanced on their knees. "We don't educate Indians. If we start, it will be in their own schools, as with the northern Negro. I suggest you discuss your plans with the officers at the Point, in the meantime you might want to consider Utah Territory. The Mormonites claim a strong predilection for Indian culture."

"I'm no longer a Saint." Ellen made no effort to keep the annoyance out of her voice.

"That shouldn't make any difference. Are your parents there?"

"No. Jeremy's people aren't either. Those are Utes, he's Cheyenne."

"An Indian is an Indian..." *I sound like Electus,* the school-master chided himself. *His soap box is hell and damnation, mine's Indians.* And added aloud, "...the way you and I are both Americans."

A poor olive branch at best.

Later at home, Ellen told Jed, "I changed my mind about staying here." They were standing by the kitchen stove, their coats on, waiting for the room to warm. "I'm going to Utah."

"Why there?"

"They love Indians."

"I thought you didn't like sharing a husband."

"I already do...share a husband."

Jed grimaced. "That's not the same."

"Of course not, 'cause you're with squaws. Never mind, I really don't care."

❖

Troy News, New York, April 7, 1850, Upriver Section:

Mr. Jedrich Thomas Marchion was in the city yesterday to file divorce papers on Ellen Marchion on the grounds of desertion. He was accompanied by his sister-in-law and his widowed mother, who signed as witnesses.

The runaway purports to be the daughter of Hiram Scott, whose disappearance named the landmark bluffs on the Oregon Trail. She had made her home in the bosom of the Marchion family since 1847, after a gallant and brave rescue by her husband from a fate worse than death at the hands of the western Indians.

She is of the Mormonite persuasion and is reported to have fled to Utah where she hopes to raise her native son, a product of the Indian encounter. "Get thee to the hinterlands" would appear to be her motto, and we would agree.

We understand that J.T. Marchion has accepted employment in the wilds of Maine, and that his brother is looking to relocate so as to take over the care of their mother and sister. If this be true, our farmers are indeed fortunate. Walker Marchion is well known in Kingston circles for his willingness to experiment with Peruvian guano and Chilean nitrate. He has had remarkable success replacing his herd-grass with clover and oat grass, and it is hoped he can be persuaded to tackle a similar experiment in this region.

ONE

SUNDAY, APRIL 28, 1850. Table Creek Landing on the Missouri River. The day is mild and breezy, trees bowing this way and that, showing sweeps of pale underleaf. The Mary Blane, up from St. Louis with 400 California emigrants, eases alongside the wharf. From the decks the ladies wave their long, bright scarves.

Two saddle horses poked in the last minute on the Westport Landing follow a lean, middle-aged man across the gangplank. Onshore he pays a boy a nickel to hold the horses while he works his way through the crowd gathering around a crude, three-sided shelter. Notices paper the shelter's walls. One such notice, in large, carefully blocked letters on lemon-colored stationary, reads

HEDRICK PARTY, ONE MILE UP CREEK

A woman in a filthy print dress and grimy head rag wrestled a burlap sack out through the rock-ribbed doorway into the bright light. Her sleeves were rolled up, dirt smeared her hands and face. Easing herself upright, she tugged on her blouse collar and blew air between her breasts. A tall woman in her late twenties.

"Hello, easy money." Dark against the sun, a man with a quiet voice.

She started. "Mr. Uergin?"

"S'me, in the flesh."

"You're the guide we're waiting for?"

Uergin swung out of the saddle, took the woman in his arms and kissed her soundly. "That's in case I ain't," he said, releasing her.

She closed her mouth over a smile. "I never thought you interested."

Uergin's eyes widened at the faint reproach. "Saving myself. You with Hedrick?"

"As far as the salt lake."

Shuffling his thoughts, Uergin studied the angular features. The missing Ellen Harris. Only Harris wasn't her real name, at least it wasn't when George Harris was passing her off as his third wife. That was four years ago. She'd lost her coltishness. The dark green eyes had lost their visionary sadness. She used to look like a weeping willow, now she looked sturdier.

Uergin wondered if Hedrick were Mormon. He wondered a lot of things that had nothing to do with what he asked.

"What's going on in there?"

"Squatter sold us some potatoes." She'd reached the sunlight itching with the hurry of earwigs through her clothing and longing for a dipper of cold water. It was a wish forgotten.

A small, wispy-looking man, shirttail out, appeared in the doorway of the root cellar, blinked uncertainly, upended a sack of potatoes, and returned to his labors.

"Your husband?" Uergin asked.

"I don't have a husband, just a three-year-old son." It sounded of an invitation.

Uergin grinned with a small boy's delight and pulled her close. "I guess we'll be seeing a lot of each other, huh?" His hands slid lower on her hips.

"I guess," Ellen agreed, with a warmth that teased another kiss. She was a long time from New York, a long time from anyone's arms, and this man felt tough as a hickory stick. But she didn't remember the dark hair being so shot through with grey, or the face so deeply furrowed.

That he was fresh-shaved and wearing a new hat and shirt tickled her funny bone. He'd left Independence all gussied up that way back in '46, this after having met with the Harris party the previous afternoon looking like a tramp and smelling like a goat. Everybody had laughed to see the sudden change in his spots.

Watching the guide ride off, Ellen felt a mooring slip somewhere deep inside. What a flood of memories seeing him against the skyline brought back. How he'd anchored their days—the little knot of people in the Harris train like a kite being tugged against the wind over the boundless prairies. Anchored their nights—the evening camps placed just so, like a skipping stone flung across dark waters. How terribly good it was to know that he'd be the one leading the Hedrick train.

Undone by a fierce, sudden loneliness, she began to run—a joyful gallop, skirt held high over bare legs, bare feet sliding on the grit in the sloppy-fitting boots.

"Are you like it was before?" she called. "You aren't married?" Reining his horse around, Uergin was silent. But when she said, "Jeremy sleeps in a wagon, I sleep alone on the ground," the habitual watchfulness in his face died, replaced with a quizzical expression at once familiar.

"I'll look you up come dark," he promised, hiding his surprise.

Riding through the wallow of canvas roofs, Uergin counted 61 wagons. A small train as trains went, probably less than 50 families. Pilgrims generally underestimated their final numbers. But Hedrick, in promising no more than 65 wagons, had been high. Uergin could see why when he caught up with the captain. Hedrick was a Scotsman in store-bought clothes. The usual crop of ne'er-do-wells wouldn't be welcome on the train of a prosperous Scot.

The wiry man, legs braided, plate balanced on the point of knee, was perched on a stump eating his dinner. "Conrad Uergin?" he sputtered. "Conrad Uergin, did ye say?" The red face, framed in ginger sideburns and white hair, got even redder. "We been on tha ground tae days! Where tha hell ye been?!"

"What's your hurry? There ain't enough grass out there to wad a shotgun."

"Hell no! ye fool, not with what all's on it!"

"What's your loose stock?"

"Eighteen standardbred mares, 20 oxen, Holstein crosses."

"How'd you come?"

"Steamer. *Melodean*. She was clean." The veins purpled under Hedrick's eyes. By god, who was skinning this cat anyway?! "We fly this coop first thing taemorrow!"

"Balance is $300," Uergin said, dismounting.

"Nae sae fast!" The force of the objection jerked the captain to his feet. The tin plate flipped its soft pile of stew in the grass. "I dinna ken you from Adam's off-ox. Ye're as good as ye toot, ye get ye money."

"You owe me a meal."

"Eh?"

"I come 150 miles for nothing."

Bouncing back and forth, making himself taller than Uergin, the blistery man swooped sideways, picked up the overturned plate and smacked it down on the stump.

"Truth is, I'm otherwise-minded now. That there's a regular parade out there. Ye seen it."

"I seen it," Uergin agreed stonily. One-room houses on wheels choked the road up from St. Joe on the Iowa side of the river. At the Table Creek Landing steamboats were shucking out emigrants faster than turtles shucking out eggs.

Hedrick leaned forward like the prow of a ship, indecision pounding in his temples. That's what came of knowing how to read—an educated fool! Two long years he'd studied on the journey and already he'd made two bad mistakes.

Insisting on northern Illinois wagons and work cattle, as spelled out in *The Emigrants' Guide to California*...

> Take no horses unless of the Indian breed;
> the common horse cannot stand the road...
> Oxen upon the whole, are the best; they
> need no shoeing, as the hot sand of the
> plain renders their hoofs so hard as to super-
> sede the use of shoes....

only to find everyone else using mules and horses and big-wheeled freight wagons.

And hiring a fancy $600 guide—advertised in the St. Joseph Gazette as "highly esteemed by travelers everywhere"—only to find no one else using guides, not with Fort Kearny relocated on the Platte and American soldiers occupying the old Laramie trading post.

Eyes squinched shut, Hedrick rubbed the heel of his hand against his head. A short, round woman in an unbelted tent of a dress hurried from behind the wagon and, with a sniff of disapproval, retrieved the tin plate.

Finally, Uergin just got on his horse and rode away, but not before feeling an unfamiliar jab of self-pity. Guides were getting as useless as tits on a boar hog. Several minutes later he heard "Hi! Hi up there!" and saw the Scot splashing through the scummy green water of the marsh.

It was sure everybody's day for second thoughts.

Uergin in tow, Hedrick collected his party in the center of the camp and climbed into a parked spring wagon.

"This here's our fella," he blustered. "Ye all ken tha terms— $300 left owed, $6.67 cents a family." Making rather a ceremony of it, the captain plunked his share of the money in the skillet on the wagon seat. "Got anything to say, Mister Uergin?"

Uergin shook his head.

"He's gonna let us be surprised," someone yelled.

"Empty can makes the most noise," Uergin replied.

Nearby, a man built like a blacksmith looked blank, then laughed explosively. He was the only one laughing. That they had once been so afraid of the road now so plain before them, embarrassed the Virginians. Even more embarrassing was their beholdance to this peripatetic dentist passing himself off as a trail guide. The eye of the eagle, the cunning of the lion? Ha! not here. As for that knife under the belt, it wasn't even a Bowie!

The man who laughed opened his purse. Hedrick plastered a smile on his face. Uergin didn't notice. He was thinking about the rolling stock—it looked good. About the grass—it didn't.

"No traveling on Sunday," a woman called from the back of the crowd. Hedrick stared fiercely in that direction.

"A day of rest don't hurt no one," Uergin said.

Late the following afternoon, 13 miles upriver, Uergin pulled the train off to the side on a little-used trace—the military road opened by the Missouri Mounted Volunteers traveling west from old Fort Kearny in 1848. In a fan of fine sand he drew a long, narrow plow point.

The point represented Grand Island on the Platte. The base, the Missouri River. The X at the top of the base marked Council Bluffs, the jumping-off place. The bottom X marked the train's present location. Swing west here, up the military road, and the train would save a good three days.

Eyes narrowed against the sun, the Virginians considered the empty westward trace. Truth was, they enjoyed the pike. Frail buggies bobbing merrily behind high-stepping, hot-blooded thoroughbreds. Quality folks jousting the air with parasols and top hats. Big, boat-shaped Conestogas, cloth walls bellied-out boasting GOLD HUNTER, THE ROUGH AND READY, OLD BOURBON WHISKEY SOLD HERE, HO FOR CALIFORNIA, OREGON OR DEATH, WILD YANKEE. Gaily pennanted Concord springs packed full with picnic goers. Everybody happy as if they had good sense. Even the peddlers, junkyard horses already used up, drove by like kings of the road.

But then, who didn't drive by the slow moving oxen with their little bitty prairie schooners? Damn that old-maid Hedrick anyway!

The Virginians were chewing on these bones—asking themselves and each other why, if the shortcut was such a good idea, no one else was using it—when Uergin doled out another piece of gristle.

"I been watching your teams, you're too heavy. Lighten up here while you can."

Now they squealed like stuck hogs.

Who's gonna buy?....Folks already got ever'thing they need!....We might as well a'gone overland at Panama or around the Horn if we wasn't gonna haul anything....I thought that's what we bought big cattle for!....I'm pared to the bone now.

"You'll see things different on the desert," Uergin promised the chorus of complaints. He pointed at a young, round-faced coppersmith standing beside a heavily pregnant woman. "And you there, lower the canvas on that wagon, it's high as a goddamn shit house."

"That's so my wife can stand up comfortable."

"And your cattle can wear theirselves out pulling against the wind."

The party met in private and voted to keep the goods and shitcan the guide. Hedrick argued for the military road.

"We dinna carry grain like tha horse wagoners, we need tha idle grass."

That wasn't the real reason the captain threw in with Uergin. He'd read about the dangers of overloading back in Virginia, but no one would listen. Four yoke of oxen and a light, hardwood wagon could handle 6,000 pounds in the short haul, but over the long haul the poundage *must not exceed 2,000!* The carefully researched orders had been ignored, as near as Hedrick could tell, by every member of his party, including his own wife!

Whistling a dark, old tune about death and glory, he pulled the 8-foot grandfather clock from his wagon. Propped upright against a bush, the heirloom grumbled for a time and fell silent.

Heavy arms akimbo, half-moon of mouth turned down, the missus turned her back and began to cry.

"I feel bad as ken be about ye papa's fine clock," Hedrick breathed against her ear.

The train camped beside the river road till noon of the next day, parting with plows, stoves, forges, and furniture for 10 cents on the dollar. And done with concessioning, the unhappy emigrants dug in their heels and voted against turning west.

"I done what I could, Mister Uergin," Hedrick said, wringing his hands. "Ye'll have to settle for half a loaf."

But the last dog wasn't hung yet. Something ugly was coming up the road—large droves of barefoot Negroes sidelined with chains run through loops attached to leg irons. Black men carrying willow switches and riding mules tended the cotton pickers. Black women and children followed behind.

Now wasn't that a pretty picture to tie to! Swear and be damned if freedmen would follow slavers anywhere! That understood, the Virginians chased the sun west.

Up the divide between the Little Nemaha and Salt Creek watersheds. Over into Big Blue country and up that watercourse—a sparkling stream some 30 yards wide with a narrow skirt of timber on both banks. Good stands of oak and elm and high banks of plum bushes in bloom. Good grades and the ground hard, except for deep sand in the ravines. No grass to speak of, the spring holding off as it did.

The fork was reached, the trace growing fainter every day. On the northern bank of the west fork all sign of previous travel disappeared, in part because of showers that freshened the pastures.

On the southern bank of Beaver Creek the camp killed a turkey and several deer, fried the fresh meat with a mess of wild onions, and ate until their stomachs hurt. The creek was abandoned for a slough-like runoff that barely watered the stock, the scanty water adding considerably to Hedrick's stock of worries.

Adrift in the eerie treelessness of unfamiliar hills, growing increasingly fearful of encountering the skulking Pawnee, Hedrick posted an all-night guard and assigned a two-hour shift to Uergin, who slept through it and was promptly relieved of the duty.

The Virginians imagined their guide lost, or worse, in cahoots with cutthroat runagates. But the sun kept rising at their backs and setting in their faces, so they kept their counsel. And concentrated their suspicions on the harpy sharing the wolfer's blankets.

SITUATION WANTED, the ad in Harper's Weekly read,

> Passage overland to Utah Territory for New York school mistress and son in exchange for tutoring emigrant children. Health excellent. References. All inquiries promptly answered. Mrs. J. T. Marchion, c/o Postmaster, Troy, New York.

"A little learning is a dangerous thing," Hedrick had pontificated, arguing for the exchange, lest the long tramp idle the minds of the train's 46 school-age children.

But he knew he was looking at trouble that cold day in April when Miz Marchion stepped off the Wheeling train. Trouble with its hair bobbed short under a little red feather of a hat and a face that made the proud owner of Hedrick's Elegant Shoes for Elegant Feet overlook what he never overlooked in a woman— her footwear!

Not that she hadn't minded her Ps and Qs out of the gate. But that hadn't stopped the men in the party from falling all over her. The ensuing pack of loose-jawed, jealous wives had turned the hiring of Uergin into an unexpected boon—thank god for loose morals and a guide willing to take up the slack— but that beachhead, too, was fast eroding.

The fools making the biggest goo-goo eyes before Uergin showed up, were the ones crying loudest now about the schoolmarm's morality. Something had to give, and Hedrick didn't want it to be his captaincy. Nor did he wish to fire the guide, not as long as the wagons rolled west.

"We've nae choice but tae relieve tha techer of her duties in tha face of moral turpitude," the worried Scot informed his lieutenants, with a sad shake of the head. The red herring worked, but Hedrick didn't feel at all good about it.

Two hours after sunrise, 14 days west of the Missouri on a poor, high ridge of prairie, the train reached what a guidebook called

> the Great Pawnee Trail, the route taken by them in visiting Comanche country

Eight wide, deeply beaten paths curving out of the northeast and disappearing into the southwest. Fortunately, except for hundreds of mule-eared rabbits, the Indian roadway was empty.

The ridge bellied out, and by midday the entire Nebraska coastline was falling away.

"Ho for the Platte!" cried the Virginians, spying a long, thin line of river timber shimmering in the heat.

For Ellen, that first sight of the desert river the Indians called the Moonshell for the pink shells found in its water-washed sands was a coming home. She had no idea she'd missed the desert so much. Her heart sang.

"We don't camp with no one or stop to visit," Uergin told Hedrick. "You can visit at the forts."

Hedrick dutifully relayed the instructions, much to his eventual chagrin. No sooner did his train reach the river, then a surge of ground-covering Percherons and mammoth jacks, up the road from Council Bluffs, was passing it by—manes brightly beribboned, hides shiny with sweat, footfalls striking the earth like hammers. A most unfortunate happenstance, loosening as it did no end of caustic remarks on the captain's poor, old white head.

T W O

IN ADDITION TO THE USUAL horse companies, the Oregon Trail
was full of droll curiosities. The six Dutchmen driving packed
cows, the lads in white dusters whizzing by on their spindly
Swift Walkers, a Hoosier with his wheelbarrow, the four emigrants hitched to their cart like dray animals. Even the horse
companies themselves were worth a second look, accompanied as
they often were by bold women striding manfully along, tanned
and leather-gloved and wearing britches.

Yes sir, an amazing pike—easily the worth of 8 or 10 roads
Stateside and smooth as a race track. But the surrounding
countryside was horrible, good for nothing but windmills. The
hard bursts drove one wit to observe that the large number of
trees in the East was undoubtedly due to their having been
blown there from the west.

Made braver by all the traffic, the Virginians next looked
forward to seeing Indians.

A large white blossom that, on closer inspection, turned out
to be 67 bleached horse skulls arranged in a circle whetted the
appetite for sight of the nomad. As did the structures seen the
following day—33 white circular lodges standing out clearly in
the bright sunshine across the river. And then, there he was!
Lo, the poor Indian, in all his glory.

The Indians were lolling in the shade of the nearer trees.
Now they got to their feet and, accompanied by a thin chiming

sound, wended their way deliberately toward the wagons. Apprehension changed to laughter as the queer procession drew near.

The bucks were large and well-formed with the true eagle-beaked face of the noble savage. The squaws were not so noble as old, their features heavily corrugated. No Hiawathas here. Piled upon each squaw's head was a stack of sunbonnets. Layers of skirts and tops smothered their bodies. The braves sported frock coats, vests and cummerbunds, and trousers that ran the gambit from long red underwear to shrunken green wool pants.

About one dandy's ankles flopped the tops of ladies' shoes. Propped on the dandy's ears was a stovepipe hat full of holes. Another displayed a yellow rubber hat hanging basket-like from its ties around his neck. What appeared to be a pet fox peered from the basket. A would-be musician carried over his shoulders long strings of brass cartridges that, shaken, gave the band its music.

Uergin had to see the hand raised to the shoulder to know the walking clothes pegs were Pawnee. He hated these encounters—the Indians wanting a piece of the big parade, the white men taking them for fools—and ordered the wagons be kept moving.

The emigrants began pitching their worn-out clothing on the bushes, setting off a mad scramble. Uergin ignored the fracas, damn nincompoops could go naked for all he cared.

An old man with a face like a peach pit and cloudy eyes came close to Ellen. He whined and rubbed his well-padded stomach. *"Kiyuksa Pani!"* Ellen hissed and spit on the ground, exploding in a fury that caught her completely off-guard. "Where is your corn? Have you forgotten your mother? Where are your eagle feathers and your bear claws? Tirawa will not know you! Where will you go, you will not meet death? It is better to be ready!"

Frightened, the beggar ran back to the village and told his wife the Otter had entered into the skins of the white devils.

Several of the children witnessed the unintelligible outburst and told their parents, who were astonished to learn Miz Marchion spoke Indian. That night the camp's women accused Hedrick of cutting off his nose to spite his face. Why weren't they using their teacher? She was very smart, and with California little more than a hop, skip and jump away, those children needed their basics!

Striking while the iron was hot, the captain reinstated Ellen, who resumed the duties gratefully, weak with relief that her foolish anger had not caused trouble. Refusing to suffer the Pawnee's lazy ways, she had behaved as if she herself were wearing hides. A stupid mistake and one she wouldn't repeat.

A plume of dust signaled the junction of the road up from Independence and St. Joe with the Platte River Road. Descending the gentle slopes, the incoming outfits were fanning out across the wild pastures, jockeying for position through a scatter of gravel and loose livestock. Making the turn directly ahead of the Virginians was a string of 90 ox teams from Kentucky.

"Virginia spots Hardbooters!" the coppersmith yelled. A Kentuckian hooted and shot his pistol in the air.

"Don't worry about the loose stuff till we get away from the junction," Uergin told Hedrick and rode back to walk with Ellen.

"Such a commotion!" The dishtowel over her nose muffled her words. "It's exciting, isn't it. The whole world's going to market."

"The only exciting thing about it is you."

Loosening the dishtowel, Ellen kissed the guide's bearded cheek.

The relentless push of men and animals retreated. Underfoot, the churned dirt felt like a deep, warm fleece. "I could get used to you," she said with a grin.

Uergin made a wry face. But he did feel the magic. It was like being suspended in space with nothing pushing or pulling. It was like being drunk.

A big emigrant horse plodded by carrying a terrified pint-sized youngster howling at the top of his lungs, and Uergin rode away after the youngster.

Tiring of the dust, Ellen climbed in the Hedrick wagon and huddled with Jeremy and Elvira Hedrick under a makeshift tent fashioned from one of Elvira's cotton petticoats. Hedrick trotted past on horseback, yelling about moving the line over.

"Slow down, Herbert!" Elvira hollered.

She said it all the time. As near as Ellen could tell, the command never seemed to do a whit of good. But maybe it did. Maybe the constant scold greased the captain's skid through life.

Jeremy poked his mother and opened his fist to reveal a squished fly.

"You are very fast, Jeremy," Ellen said, blowing the fly away. Jeremy bobbed his head and laughed soundlessly.

"Black is the color of my true love's hair," Ellen cooed, touching a damp lock. "His eyes are something wondrous fair. His grandpa's hair and his papa's eyes, but I don't know where…" she pushed her head against the round little belly "…he learned to catch flies!"

Hedrick would hemorrhage if he knew the truth.

Oh by the way, Mr. Hedrick, did I happen to mention I've been here before?

I was on my way to Oregon Territory, and my people kicked me out because I wouldn't marry the elder, who already had a wife. So I stayed in Fort Laramie in the room the whores used and served whiskey in the bar.

Then I ran off with a soldier, and the Indians caught me. That's where Jeremy came from. His father was a Cheyenne warrior. Very fierce he was. His name was Hunumpayohos, the Grizzly. I called him Whonow for short.

Sometimes he wore a skull on his head and did a lot of things you wouldn't approve of. Mexican traders killed him, and Jed Marchion came along and made an honest woman out of me. And that's how I got to be a schoolteacher who talks to Indians. I do hope you don't mind.

The Cheyenne had reduced her world to dirt and dog stew and put it back together their way—their need for endless ritual forever blotting out her own. Given her a name, Mis'tai, ghost woman. Occasionally she told Uergin the stories, invariably putting him to sleep.

That the Hedrick train wouldn't be encountering Jeremy's relatives on the overland journey was a great relief to her. Tobacco's band was forbidden to visit the Moonshell and the wicked road that ran beside it, on account of the whiskey peddlers. Thank goodness, since that part of her life was done.

Done. Never mind that the great ocean of softly-colored prairie kept gnawing at her. That the more she saw of the far-flung mesas, particularly off to the south, the more she wanted to see. That walking out to escape the wagon dust, she found it harder and harder to turn back.

Never mind that crossing a broad, dry wash, she could forget completely where she was, the soft, sliding sound of wheels in sand becoming the sound of moccasins and travois poles. So much so that when the jingle of harness intruded, along with the sound of bending tie-rods, she had no idea what she was hearing.

Around the fires at night the feelings of déjà vu increased. She constantly saw ghosts in the shadows and heard Indian voices in the soft Virginia vowels. It was Jeremy who kept her on the straight and narrow. If it weren't for Jeremy, she'd leave, drift south. The People would find her.

In New York she'd told everyone Jeremy was part Indian. This despite her mother-in-law's protests.

"It won't work," is how Christina put it. "Don't ever let that cat out of the bag."

"Why not? I can't lie to my son, and I can't ask him to lie. There's nothing wrong with having a Cheyenne chief for a father."

Recalling her high-mindedness made Ellen cringe. There was something very wrong with being even part Indian in America. "Little fella's smart for an Indian," that's how the small talk went.

Which was why, traveling with the Hedrick train, Jeremy was now a Frenchman. He could be an Indian in Utah. If that didn't work out, they'd go on to California and he could just go on being French.

T H R E E

ATURDAY, MAY 18, 1850. New Fort Kearny at the top of Grand Island, gateway to the true plains and the real mountains beyond. The national flag dancing red, white and blue atop the horizon, the heart leaping to see it. But what was going on over there? Oh, good Lord, look at that!

Two men dressed in black, jackets flapping open to reveal snowy white shirts, and a woman in red velvet, the heavy cloth like a bloodstain on the sandy pasture—all three dead as doornails. How sad, sad.

Hedrick talked with men at the edge of the crowd. Whooping cough, one thought. Another said cholera.

The new fort righted itself in a mournful assortment of soddies, small tents, and one unpainted frame house—a wistful-looking, two-story affair. A scatter of dust devils attended the sorry collection.

A soldier rode out. The regulation blue, sun-bleached coat lacked buttons, the Irish face was scabby with sunburn. Everyone was to register, wagons were to be left outside the gate.

The storehouse that served as the emigrant registry smelled sweetly of stacked foodstuffs. One by one the party gave their names, former residences, destination. As captain, Hedrick reported deaths, livestock used, and road conditions. With his own questions, the Scot learned that better than 17,000 people had passed up both sides of the river, most using horses and mules, most bound for the gold fields.

In a shady bower thrown up against the sutler's room, two ladies counting their money at a knife-scarred table were startled to Uergin join them without so much as a by-your-leave. The tough cuss sucked noisily on his whiskey and leered menacingly. Scooping up their coins, the ladies disappeared into the crowd.

Sunlight on sailcloth walls honeyed the room in a soft glow. Dried leaves wafted off the cottonwood branches piled overhead on the roof poles. A bottle hit the table.

"How's it goin', friend?"

Uergin pushed up the brim of his hat with his empty cup.

A heavy-set, black man with pock-marked features was easing himself into the further chair. Joe Deroin, the half-breed Otoe who worked as the fort's Indian interpreter.

"You know how it used to be in the old days with pilgrims," Uergin said. "It ain't like that no more." He took a pull on the Otoe's bottle, shook his head and blew air between his lips. "I used to be their hero, now I'm just their nigger."

Joe grinned, yellowed teeth rotting off at the gumline. "I ain't noticed no difference."

"You always was lucky." Uergin gave a huge, satisfied belch. "How's come this fort ain't called Childs no more?"

"*General Childs don't die!*" The Otoe sounded an indignant note. Both men laughed, the laughter erupting in easy little pieces.

"A lot of cholera in the trains?" Uergin asked.

"Over a thousand dead between here and St. Joseph. How'd you come, for chrissake?"

"Straight across out of the old fort," Uergin said.

"Damned Injun, you was smart."

"Last summer I was in Chihuahua." Uergin pressed his hands against the table and pushed himself back against his chair. The whiskey was making a roar in his head, his hands and feet jingled. "That's when I was really smart."

A large wooden sign directly beside the main gate proclaimed

Fort Kearny, U.S. Army Reservation
Off Limits to Unauthorized Camping

Assuming their guide to be obtaining the necessary permission, the Virginians waited with the patience of people who have no choice. And no liking for what they saw. The new Army post was as big a waste of taxpayer money as the new suspension bridge across the Ohio at Wheeling. What good was a fort without granite walls and cannon? Those rambling mud walls wouldn't keep out a jackrabbit!

Truth to tell, the whole damned road was wearing powerful thin. Nothing but buffalo grooves from morning to night. Dirty old flood runoff for a river. Dreary old plains to either side. Seldom a stick of timber except for the sticks of driftwood in the river.

In the late light a long string of pearls inched caterpillar-like toward the fort. Ox wagons. Poor bastards.

Uergin staggered through the sod portals of Valhalla, climbed on his horse and, sagging like a sack of meal, led the wagons into the hard, red sun. Two miles later, immediately outside the second boundary sign, on a dry, wind-blown slope well above the river, he signaled a halt and put himself down for a nap.

It was not a camp to gladden the heart. Done with keeping up appearances, Hedrick determined to salvage what he could of his costly mistake and cut the belligerent employee loose. If the problem with the school mistress returned, he'd cut her loose too, let her catch another ride.

He shook the guide awake. But before he could work up the spit to give the man his walking papers, he changed his mind.

Uergin was wanting to go back for a little hair of the dog that bit him. That'd be the better place to lower the boom.

In the sutler's shed the smells of horse, tobacco, cottonwood powder, and hot lamp-oil mingled queerly to produce the scent of furniture polish. An incense of fine dust wafted off the hard dirt floor. The canvas walls puffed in and out, causing the shadows to crawl up and down. Flies droned, glassware clinked agreeably.

Reminded of civilization, Hedrick reminded himself that the worst of the trip was over, knocked back two shots of red States' whiskey, and joined his guide.

"'Tis a good crowd on tha road," he laughed heartily, "puts tha bit in tha teeth, it does."

Uergin fixed the captain with a humorless stare—the business of the watering hole was different than the business of the trail—and went back to staring at nothing, soaking up the smells and sounds of the room, pulling them into the marrow of his bones.

"My folks nae like tha way ye ride herd on 'em," the Scotsman confided with a shake of his head, "like tae night. Thay was o' a mind tae camp lower."

"With the 'squitas?" Uergin asked, incredulous.

"Sae I decided, being captain and all," Hedrick's long face said Uergin would understand, "tae hang it up." A knowing nod. "We'll let tha Lord take us from here."

Leaning forward, Uergin rested his head in his arms.

"Sae what d'ya figure?" Hedrick rubbed his hands together briskly. "Tha Missouri tae here?"

"Six hundred dollars." The words could barely be heard.

"That's wha' we give ye tha whole way! Dammit man! d'ye ken what I say? We scotch it here! Ye know nae more about guidin' than a hog knows about Sunday!" The captain had worked himself to the edge of his chair. Now, taking a deep breath, he slouched back and called on sweet reason.

"We come a sixth of tha distance contracted for, we'll pay four/sixths for ye trouble. Give us tae back and go about ye business a fra mon."

"Six hundred dollars."

"Look at me, ye long-headed gillie!" Hedrick blistered up like a rat caught in a corner. "This ain't tha Sacramento!"

Uergin lifted his head, the vagueness in his eyes dissolving in woebegone acceptance. "Ain't that the shits."

Hedrick swaggered back across the room and threw himself on the mercy of the watchers propped against the bar.

"Tha poor mon begged for another chance. He's got nae family out here, nae way tae make a livin'. Tha poor mon, he knows he's gang agley. Look at 'im 'ide his head wi' shame! We'll let him lead tha row a wee bit longer."

The next morning, awash in rosewater perfume and swathed in gowns of sheer summer fabric closed at the waist with ribbon belts and shaded by large Sunday straws complete with ruched facing and wide strings, the ladies took on the sutler's store.

Hearing that they were too late for Congregational tent services occasioned barely a sniff from these good Calvinists, who happily whiled away the hours shopping and visiting with other travelers. And armed with the luxuries of lotion, syrup, soap, and a stove-lid wheel of moldy cheese that skinned the tongue, strolled home across the prairie contented, the wind lifting their unhooped skirts and their unbound hair and making them laugh.

For the men, the day proved no less entertaining. Catching up on much-needed repairs at the government shop and walking around inspecting in general, they learned what the world was up to. And, in the process, what a smart fellow their Leather-stocking really was, keeping them off that Council Bluffs road the way he did.

Feeling guilty that she hadn't written Jed since arriving in Wheeling, Ellen spent the morning beside the river with her writing box. It'd been a good marriage. With Jed she'd known real freedom. Far from the rigorous rules of the Indian camps, further still from the paranoia that smothered her childhood.

Jeremy went to sleep on his back, rolled over and got a mouthful of water.

"Why get mad at the river?" Ellen teased, shaken from her wool-gathering by the little boy's complaints. "It's the water spirit's fault." And making herself comfortable on the bank, dutifully uncapped the little ink bottle.

> Sunday, May 19, 1850
> My dear Jed,
>   I am sorry for not writing sooner. We are thriving.
> Remember where the livestock ran away in that terrible
> hail storm? That's where we are now. New Fort Kearny. You
> will be surprised to learn Uergin is our guide. The Virginians
> don't like him any better than George did. Guides seem to
> be as outdated as codpieces. Roads on both sides of the river
> are very busy, the whole world has caught gold mania.

She put down the pen, as last seeing him clearly in her thoughts, the lean, honest face so serious, the tall slender body without an ounce of fat, the unruly light-brown hair. The Troy courthouse had wanted a reason for the divorce, and rather than accuse the other of anything, they chose desertion.

"I don't mind being deserted," Jed had told her, saying good-bye at the train station. "You been deserted, now it's my turn." He made it sound funny.

Daydreaming, her eye fell on an odd shadow—a wooden bowl the size of her fist wedged between an exposed tree root and a river rock. "You're like me," she told the bowl, wiggling it free. And sang as the little bowl bobbed away, "Where are we going? we don't know, when will we get there? we don't care."

Placing the unfinished letter in her pocket, she offered a prayer. "Dear Jed, you are so sweet, may you have all the bells and whistles."

Three days above Fort Kearny, at Plum Creek, the republic vaulting a continent in search of the promised land began purging itself. Soaking up the dirt under a pile of glass shards was enough whiskey to make a man rich. Strewn away from the wreckage like the tail of a comet were tables, chairs, barrels of dishes—broken and splintered by perhaps the same churlish hand on the ax.

Further along, two huge Percherons lay dead, stripped of their harness and shoes, black hides scored with whip marks. A tumble of iron stoves and blacksmith anvils cast a shadow gravestone-like across the brutes.

The bitter distress signals increased. Feather comforters bled themselves dry in the wind that was like a blast from an open furnace door. Massive claw-footed bureaus spilled fine linens into the dust. Trunks lying popped open made enormous bright bouquets of expensive ball gowns. Paintings and fine gold-leaf books waited unattended in the hot sun like pagan offerings to an illiterate god.

Varmints peered proprietarily from piles of green slimy pork. Delicate china nestled humpty-dumpty fashion amid heaps of rope and soap and scythes and little iron toys.

Witchcraft was everywhere. Seen through the wavery heat ahead of the wagons, Uergin and his horse puffed up 20 feet tall. Crows walking on the ground looked like men. Buttes sprouted battlements and waved flags. Wolves danced by on stilts. Mountains rose purple and grey and flattened into nothing. Basins spread with silvery lakes emptied themselves into thin air.

And on and on the silty river ran, like hammered gold on top
of the sand.

The buffalo grass went to seed without growing. What did
grow near the road was quickly erased by the heavy traffic. Four
o'clock of every afternoon, the distances smudged in heat and
haze, found Uergin veering off across untracked sage in search
of the withered clumps that passed for fresh graze.

Gone from the Platte were the large herds of wild animals
seen on the military road. Guidebooks to the contrary, deer
showed themselves only in the distance and elk never.

Cooking pots remained as uninviting as the landscape. Sage
hen, rabbit, prairie dog, badger, eagle, rattlesnake, goat—what
kind of food was that? The only thing worse than the road
pantry was the damned eternal cod—flat and rubbery from its
salting down in the barrels.

The large army of coonhounds accompanying the train gave
chase to whatever moved. But Hedrick, chary of someone's
getting lost—particularly so since hearing at Fort Kearny of a
Texas company, supposedly familiar with treeless land, losing
five good men off hunting—firmly discouraged all talk of riding
to the hounds.

A buffalo wandered alone out of the breaks. Shot and
skinned, it hung in thin strips along the wagon sides, the coarse
red fringe collected a powdery coat. The marchers cut the meat
off in chunks, chewed the moisture back into the morsel until
it filled their mouths and made their jaws ache, and spit it out.
Hedrick asked Uergin if guiding shouldn't include providing
fresh meat for the commissary.

"Nope."

It truly was a sad world. Never had the Scot suffered a land
with so little purchase, so dry the progress of far-away trains fore
and aft could easily be charted by the dust raised. Adding to the
melancholy landscape were the miseries suffered by the poor

animals. Trains jockeying for position made a Roman chariot race of the road—teams running flat out in the terrible heat. Wasted beasts left to die reeled drunkenly over the parched prairie. Carcasses of dray animals and of the scavengers shot for target practice littered the road.

By day Hedrick's eyes ached from searching the distance for timber and water. At night in his bed, finding the endless web of gullies awash in blow sand and scanty sunburned grass, all crooked and stiff, still behind his eyelids, he struggled to recall knobby green hills drowning in mists, velvety grasses streaked where the cattle walked through the rich frosts. Once he dreamt he heard the wool carders singing,

> Sing my bonny harmless sheep,
> that upon the mountains skip,
> bleating sweetly as ye go,
> through the winter frost and snow....

and woke as usual to the sounds of an ancient, echoing place where he had no business being—the wind singing so violent in the riggings and the wolves crying like fiends of the infernal regions. Oh, if only he had it all to do over!

A dismal cadence of graves started up, singularly and in groups—two, three, four to a mile—freely pawed over by loose stock and dug into by wolves and dogs. The freshest graves, fragile markers yet in place, were the most hurtful to see. The porcelain doll face-down, arms outstretched. The black-beaded rosary swinging gently from its bough of sage. The red straw hat caressing its stake with long, white silk ribbons.

Were it not for the nights, blessed nights, the sojourners would have gone stark, raving mad. As it was, letting the dark wall out what it would, they sedated themselves with old music and dreams of a new land.

As did the guide and his lady.

"How come you never say anything about their dogs or the target practice?" Ellen asked, both of them naked, the weariness in their bones making the ground soft. "You never gave poor George that kind of slack."

The guide sounded a note of disgust. "What Hedrick's doing ain't a drop in the bucket. I'm tired of fighting it. This is my last time out."

He was opening a bawdy house in San Francisco. She was marrying a rich Utah bishop. He furnished his house with beautiful decorations and beautiful women, and everything came down to money. She saw herself in a mansion overlooking the salt lake, and everything came down to Jeremy.

"That's the good thing about Utah, Jeremy's Indian blood won't matter. He's only half anyway."

He was only half in America too. Uergin closed his mouth over the words.

She confessed to being glad that she couldn't see the Cheyenne, likening their camps to leaves blowing over the prairies. Uergin didn't tell her what he'd learned from the Otoe at Fort Kearny—that cholera raged on the high plains. Instead, he entertained her with the wildest stories, losing himself in the telling and laughing open-mouthed against the stars.

That by day he rode chiseled dark and cold on the skyline, and by night became *heyoka* the clown, delighted Ellen. Sometimes they talked about marrying each other, the way people talk about finding the pot at the end of the rainbow.

A day above Brady's Island, stiff blasts of wind coated the train a ghostly grey with the shakings off saltpeter and saleratus beds. Dipping his head to pull up his nose rag, Uergin glanced idly around at the wagons and the hair stood up on the back of his neck. *Today.*

Toward noon, the party passed a message tied to a human skull. "This ain't us," the scrap of paperboard bragged, "were still clicking and ticking."

The Virginians smiled to read the boast. But Uergin didn't. Dead ahead, something waited.

Midafternoon. A horse wagon abandoned in the road, traces empty. The oilcloth cover was painted with mountain scenery. Above the blue points of mountain was the motto THE ROUGH AND READY. Resting in the shadow of a wheel, a man swelled out of his clothes, a halo of flies about his head. Using a stick, Uergin held back the canvas flap. A woman with wheat-colored hair sprawled inside, face-down on a jumble of bedding, her arm flung over a child laid out in a long white dress. Both bodies swollen and crawling with flies.

Breathing through rags, the Virginians looked in on the abomination. And came away gagging. Parking their own wagons upwind, they walked back and piled brush against the wheels and fired the canvas.

"I'm taking you across to the Mormon road," Uergin told Hedrick.

The news rang like a hosanna in the ear. "Quicksand and a relentless current make the Platte deceptive," the guidebooks warned, "...dangerous...deadly." But the wide stretch of muddy water with its usual sprinkle of naked sandbars paled in comparison to the horror going up in smoke. Girding their loins, the Virginians turned their teams toward the Platte and didn't look back.

With caution went order. The train disintegrated into streamers of goaded oxen followed by madly rocking wagons. Loose horses and cattle swept past the wagons. In the excitement of the race nobody paid the least attention to Uergin's hoarse cries. Waving his hat, he tried turning the lead yokes aside. But the brutes, having caught the spirit, stayed the course.

And pulling with a mighty effort, bellowing, sticking their tails in the air, took the bank as they found it.

Three wagons mired 50 yards out. Nine floundered on to reach a small island deep in the heart of the river. Six circled round and returned to where the remaining 43 wagons teetered virtually on the brink of destruction.

In 10 years of guiding pilgrims up the Oregon Trail, it was the worst crossing Uergin had ever seen. He couldn't move fast enough, or get anyone else to move fast enough, to save the oxen on the mired wagons. One of the wagons broke up, its passengers simply stepping off onto a sandbar and walking to safety. Pounding past on horseback, Uergin caught a glimpse of dazed, uncomprehending faces.

The two wagons still intact in the river began to tilt sharply, anchored by their dead cattle. Fearful of becoming entangled in the wagon sheeting, the occupants ripped the sheeting from the bows to perch ingloriously under their naked arches.

Uergin wanted the people brought in. Nobody heard him, everyone was giving different orders. He collared Hedrick and told the captain if they lost daylight, they'd lose lives.

Hedrick shot a rifle in the air and yelled for order. A meeting was what the captain wanted. RIGHT NOW! BEFORE SOME-BODY GOT KILLED!

The emigrants were mad and scared, but they stopped arguing amongst themselves.

"Catch up what horses are still here," Uergin yelled. "And you men that can swim ride out and start bringing people in off the wagons in the river. Swing wide and use your sandbars.

"The rest of you fellows, give me two bull lines and four ropes long enough to get out to the wagons. I'll need eight husky fellows for the wheels. Everyone else stay out of the water. That's an order."

In short order there were 10 riders in the water, the balance of the loose horses having crossed over to the island.

The bull teams were hurried into place and four piecemeal ropes fastened to the skid chains.

Curving against the bank where the wagons had sailed off into the river was a 20-yard stretch of fast, deep water.

"Don't come in till we get these ropes tight," Uergin warned the wheel men and, trailing the ropes behind his horse, headed for the mired wagons. Along the way he met the returning emigrants—some riding double, others being towed holding onto a horse's tail.

"Can you get my wagon out?" one man called above the river's voice.

"Gonna do our damnedest," Uergin hollered.

Out at the wagons, he concentrated on unhooking the drowned oxen and fastening the long ropes to the running-gear rings on the wagons. That done, he waved his hat.

Onshore, the long strings of oxen took up the slack. And stopped. The wheel men entered the water holding onto the taut ropes. When they reached the submerged wheels, Uergin told them, "These wagons are coming out one way or another, so don't make the mistake of getting in front of a wheel thinking it's gonna stay stuck. If a wagon goes over, don't try to save anything. That's an order."

He waved his hat a second time. Onshore the bull lines stepped up. The mired wagons lurched backward, grabbing at one pothole after another, the men in the water straining to lift the wheels.

An axle broke, and one of the ropes snapped. A second rope held, and the lopsided wagon kept coming, water washing over the lower sideboard, scooping out the contents. As both wagons neared the shore, men working with shovels and crowbars pared the bank down to water level.

With the wagons once more on dry ground, Uergin ordered the riders who had rescued the emigrants, out to the island with enough bridles and saddles for the rest of the horses.

And entering the river a second time, ordered the captain in no uncertain terms, "Whatever happens out there, you stay put." Nodding, Hedrick ate his humble pie.

Out on the island, nine wagons and 36 oxen bunched like downed pelicans. The arrival of the horses from the south shore, together with those horses already on the island, gave Uergin more than enough mounts to get all the women and children out of his hair. The sun lurched lower over the brown, rolling river. Seen from the south shore, the returning horses silhouetted against the rusty sunset appeared to be walking on burnished copper—a real regal parade on any other day.

Astride a fresh horse, Uergin explored his options. The island stretched northward for several hundred yards and ran for another hundred just beneath the water before reaching an open channel. The current here looked to be faster, leaving the bottom better scoured out. Mind made up to cross the north channel, the guide returned to dry land and, riding past the coppersmith's wagon, saw the coppersmith's pregnant wife sitting like a barrel on the wagon seat.

"What the hell!" he shouted hoarsely.

"I figured her safer with you than on a horse," the coppersmith confessed grimly. Leaving Uergin to stare open-mouthed.

The sun was behind the willows. There were enough horses left on the island to put two men in the river downstream of the wagons, all that was needed now was a little luck. Uergin placed a rope over the horns of the neigh leader of the biggest ox team, wrapped the loose end around his saddle horn, and headed down the sandbar. The Virginians followed and, through clenched teeth, urged their oxen into the water.

An hour inched by. The long string of wagons disappeared in the dusk. The stars came out, the river sighed and creaked, night-birds cried, in the distance a cat screamed.

Another hour. Hooked over the edge of the world, a thin moon poked up like a distant bonfire.

And then…what was that? There on the north side, a light. Are you sure? can't see it. Yes! over there, a fire! and another! Three now!…five!…eight!…………..nine!

That night the Hedrick train was a camp divided. "Today we saw the elephant and felt the brush of its tail," Hedrick noted gloomily in his diary, embarrassment so sharp-edged (he'd burned the wind hard as any) that he added no further details, except to say that two mired wagons were successfully retrieved. And that his stock of ladies hand turn boots and shoes, boarded over beneath his wagon floor, was still dry as the sand.

Exhausted and cold under damp blankets, his barked hand wrapped in a rag, Uergin counted coup. His worst troubles on the Oregon Trail always came on the Platte Road. It was a rule—the necessary evil that was his good-luck charm. They'd make it now, all the way to the coast.

FOUR

IN 1838, DECLARING THE WEST to be a vast, worthless land, United States Senator Daniel Webster refused to vote one red cent for its acquisition. Twelve years later the Hedrick company found every reason to agree. It was a worthless land.

At Ash Hollow, emigrants fleeing the cholera were crossing to the Mormon road by the hundreds, bringing the plague with them. Burial parties were out on both sides of the river. The Virginians stayed shy of the camps and, approached by strangers, tied rags over their faces.

Uergin planned to salvage enough lumber here to see his party through the next 75 miles to Scotts Bluffs, but the groves of cedar and ash were overrun with emigrants. Abandoning the idea, he kept rolling, the wheeling heavy in the deep sand.

At the evening stop Hedrick wrote in his diary

> The ash hollow has a charnel air about it. The earth everywhere is the color of ashes except for a wee bit of common greenery made uncommon by its absence elsewhere on this bleak road.

Sadly, the captain left his writing box on the convenient rock used for a table, and it was awhile before he could bring himself to resume the chore. In the meantime, Courthouse Bluff, Chimney Rock and Scotts Bluffs came and went like thieves in the night.

A day west of Horse Creek—a shallow hollow in the darkness.

"I *need* a Mormon wife, someone who don't mind sharing."

"You're not an elder."

"So what's an elder got I ain't?"

"Money."

"Just the old ones, and it's already spoke for. They drive around Salt Lake in big carriages stuffed full of women."

"A rich man'll make room, and he'll make Jeremy a bishop."

"Puttin' kind of a burden on the little shaver, ain't you? What if he wants to be an Indian chief?"

"All little boys do." Ellen blew in Uergin's ear and worked herself against him. "Didn't you ever play Indian chief?"

"What happens when you're all comfy, cozy in your big nest," Uergin squeezed her buttocks, "and a dandy comes along wants to do this?"

"I'll handle it."

"What if you like it?"

"I won't."

"You won't like hell. How many husbands was you plannin' on? If you want a travelin' man, I'll get back often as I can."

"Women only have one."

"That's the way it should be." Uergin pulled the blanket aside to dislodge an offending rock.

"One's enough, as long as he's rich," Ellen said, and added with an air of resignation, "The sharing does bother me...the first time I went into the water with the squaws, they all jumped out and ran off. My white skin scared them. But they wanted in the water, and I wasn't budging, so pretty soon here they came back. Now I'm in their moccasins. Polygamy's a cruel thing for a woman in love with her husband, but I don't intend to fall in love, and Salt Lake's where I want to be."

She pulled Uergin's legs apart to kiss the inside of his knees. "Actually it might be nice, having someone to share the work with, along with the bedroom chores. You know why there aren't so many graves this side of the river?" she smothered a giggle against his thigh, "'cause God takes care of the Saints."

She was the only woman Uergin ever met who could hump and talk religion at the same time.

Tuesday, June 18, 1850. The junction of the Platte and Laramie rivers. A hazy evening sun spilled golden cream across the seared hills, letting the hungry imagination make what it would of the Fort Laramie Military Reservation.

Steeped in the West of Francis Parkman, the Virginians saw the outpost as a respectable step forward in the hugger-mugger. Even the Indian tepees on the hillside appeared pastoral. For Uergin, the military presence was a reminder of things gone to hell in a handbasket. In the sutler's store, with its orderly posting of rules against disorderly conduct, nobody ever got gloriously drunk.

Smoke bannered the poor scraggle of trees. Empty campsites were as scarce as hen's teeth. Uergin wedged the train into a narrow alley and called a halt. Freed of their yokes, the oxen blew over the bare ground and stretched long tongues toward the tree limbs. That foliage, too, was gone, chewed off high as a tall horse could reach.

"Send someone upriver into the breaks tomorrow with the livestock," Uergin ordered, turning his horse toward the Platte. "Tell 'em to keep their eyes peeled."

"How's 'bout a fella going over there wi' ye?" the captain called peevishly.

"It's a free country."

The sky flared crimson and faded. At the fort a lone drummer beat "The Retreat." The evening gun was fired. Reassured by the civilized sounds, Hedrick decided to catch up a horse, but then he heard a closer drum with an uneven pulse and recalled the Indian tepees.

Dawn's early light brought stackings of rusting machinery whiskered with for-sale signs. Dogs and Indians poked furtively through piles of abandoned bacon and hard bread. Broken and burned wagons were everywhere pitched to earth, never to rise again. A Chinese puzzle of ropes strung on bushes and tree limbs served for a clothesline.

At sunrise the fort's gun was fired and the colors set. "Reveille," the signal for the men to rise and the sentries to leave off challenging, was beat at 5 a.m. "Peas Upon a Trencher" was heard at 7 a.m. and "The Troop" at 8 o'clock, calling the men to duty and inspection at guard mounting.

Such reassuring sounds.

By the time morning parade was sounded at 9 a.m., the Virginians, were ready for their own sight-seeing parade. They were headed out of camp when Uergin rode up, pie-eyed and smelling of spittoon emptyings.

"Ferry a wagon across for provisions," he ordered and, after thinking on it awhile, added, "throw in whatever you got for the smithy." He reached for the horn, missed, and fell out of the saddle.

"Anything left over there for us," Hedrick asked sarcastically.

Uergin got to his feet, someone handed him his hat. "Indian snatch," he said and limped away.

The government ferry was a crude contraption requiring the labor of its users in addition to a dollar toll. A long line of mule-drawn Army wagons heavy with cedar posts and quarried rock waited at the landing. Out of sight, a sawmill shrieked with the bite of metal into wood. Errant breezes carried the whiff of burning limestone.

The explorers hurried across the rude footbridge and up the

hill for the fort, while Ellen went in search of Ruth, the little Sioux girl met four years earlier.

Indian children were everywhere playing their games. Like Ruth, the only English they knew was profanity. But they were not as shy as Ellen remembered, nor as poorly dressed. All wore articles of civilized clothing, most had learned to beg—approaching with smiling faces and outstretched hands.

Ruth would be about 12 now. Afraid she wouldn't recognize the girl, Ellen asked again and again in English, "You know me?" "You are Ruth?"

An older boy with an outsize head and shriveled trunk and arms rose from where he was sitting on the ground and began to follow. Ellen turned a questioning face in that direction, and the creature moved closer and fingered its mouth. The large bloodshot eyes steadied, rolled about and steadied. The large mouth opened. "Horse," it said hollowly.

Ellen shook her head.

The mouth turned down. The poor pretender shied sideways and began circling at a trot.

"Firewater," Ellen called.

The circles got larger.

"HORSE!"

Wheeling, jumping, throwing its head, the curiosity came close and threw itself flat on the ground. Ellen squatted and lifted the boy's head by the hair and made her own face fierce. "What do you give for a horse?"

"Ruth."

Ellen hurried back to camp. Uergin was nowhere in sight. A lantern-jawed woman, faded hair blowing girlishly about her sun-ravaged face, had collected the camp's smallest children under a mosquito netting for a story telling. Upended like a duck over the Hedrick hindboard, Ellen listened to the fairy tale about the royal princess who could feel a pea under 20 mattresses.

"What a perfectly royal ninny!" she snarled, recalling how she herself used to pray she would be able to pass the pea test.

Uergin kept his things in the back corner of the wagon beneath a little shelf of wooden boxes. Ellen wrestled the bedroll free and groped for his possibles sack. The bottle stashed in the bottom was cool to the touch. Held against the sun, it was the color of dark honey. Satisfied, she went looking for a horse.

The squaw loading a liver-spotted mare with pieces of wood torn from an abandoned wagon could scarcely believe her eyes. She unloaded the mare, handed Ellen the jaw string, and dragged the leather panniers away on foot, stopping occasionally to toast her good fortune.

When the goblin saw the horse, he worked aside the breech-cloth to relieve himself.

"Where is Ruth?" Ellen asked, looking away.

The Indian eased close. Petting the coarse mane as if it were a butterfly wing, he mouthed a series of unspoken words, finally stringing together "San-der-son."

Ellen was amazed. Major Sanderson was the fort's commanding officer! Skirt hoisted well above her knees, she crossed the river easily.

Peppercorn braids wrapped the head of the woman behind the screen door. A gold wreath pin glinted dully on the white lace collar. In the shadows Mrs. Sanderson looked to be deplorably thin. She was also very sorry. The girl who called herself Ruth? left a week ago. Or was it two weeks? She asked the sentry posted at the edge of the porch, and the sentry thought two. For a native camp, she said, and the sentry agreed. "A real shame," she observed, "the girl was trainable. She's to be the bride of Little Boom."

"Thunder, ma'am," the sentry said. "Chief Little Thunder."

"She's just a child!" Ellen protested, reminding herself that it happened all the time in the camps. "Didn't you feel some responsibility?"

Checking to be sure the latch was locked, the major's wife retreated to the far side of her small sitting room. Eastern do-gooders had *absolutely no comprehension* of western customs! She took a fan from the top of a china cabinet and snapped it open under her chin.

Through the cabinet's glass curve Ellen saw a large bronze teardrop hanging from the pitcher spout. She pressed her face against the warm, rusty-smelling screen. "That's Ruth's medal. It has the seal of the United States on one side and President Washington on the other. I gave it to her."

Mrs. Sanderson sidled back to the door. Perhaps she should clarify her husband's position with regard to the medal. "Major Sanderson collects artifacts of historical significance. That's one of his orders. I hope you're not asking to have it returned." She opened and closed the fan and said pleasantly, "If you know the family, you must know her brother, a most piteous freak. He traded her for a horse."

"Two horses, ma'am," the sentry corrected. "But one was lame."

Late that afternoon Ellen took pen and paper and dutifully finished the letter started at Fort Kearny.

> Wed. June 19. 1850. We have reached the Laramie healthy which is a miracle considering the cholera in the trains. The traffic is very heavy. Fort Laramie is full of soldiers, you wouldn't know it. Their buildings have swallowed Bordeaux's little white-walled kingdom. The old buildings are in deplorable condition. On the corners of the pole roofs the wind has ferreted the dirt from the sod coverings and the tangled grass flaps like worn toupees. I saw your treaty medal in the commanding officer's china cabinet. Now your father would have loved that story! How are you there in

your wild north woods surrounded by your wonderful trees that shut out the sun? Better not show the white feather. I miss you. I miss trees. Travel gently. Love, Ellen.

And backed the letter

Jed Marchion, Care of the Post Master, Aroostook Valley, Maine, America

The following day, returning from where the mountain men operated their own version of a sutler's store up the Laramie, Uergin did not look like a man to trifle with. Eyeing the ripped coat and bulbous blue nose, the Virginians made no comment, but went quickly to their tasks.

The train was a week above Fort Laramie, at the far end of the 80-mile pull through the Black Hills, before its guide wanted a woman. Ellen wasn't interested.

"You jealous?" Uergin asked.

"Of what? an Indian?!"

"One minute you're talkin' like they hung the moon, the next minute they ain't shit."

"That's not true. I went after Ruth, I didn't find her."

"I could of told you that." He would have told her more, but she was crying.

"Ruth kept her name…" hard jerks punctuated Ellen's words "…she was learning English…it's so awful out here, so ugly. Her brother sold her…and he tricked me."

"Tricked you?"

"Into giving him a horse."

"Whose horse?"

"One I traded your whiskey for."

"My whiskey?…" Uergin sat up. "MY RUM? you traded my rum? You're right, it *is* ugly out here! Well Jeeesus Christ! Goddamn! You never said you needed a horse!"

"You were gone, but I did replace it. At the sutler's. They put some in a little jar for me."

"Well, thank you very much! That's Mexican mule! You're a thief. You're a goddamn thief. Well, shit!"

"You didn't even miss it. It's the devil's brew anyway."

"I was saving it for Bridger. Owed him. And it ain't the devil's brew, it's mine."

"I'm sorry."

"That's a big help. You tell Bridger that, make him feel real good." Mumbling, swearing, Uergin lay back.

"Something else happened," Ellen whispered.

"Oh, Jesus!" Uergin ground the words through his teeth. "You got the clap."

"I walked through Bordeaux's old drinking room. The bar's torn out, it's all empty now except for some crates in a corner. I sat on the floor in the whore's room and thought about how hard I used to pray for the Saints to come. 'My people,' I called them. Isn't that something? How I end up living with Indians who call themselves *the* people.

"Anyway, I'm sitting there and I hear a mouth harp clear as clear, and I hear Bordeaux laugh and whiskey glug-glugging. Isn't that spooky?"

Uergin didn't answer.

"You don't believe in ghosts? I do. Bordeaux himself told me the fort was haunted."

There was no answer

"The name the Indians gave me, Mis'tai, that was supposed to be a ghost. Was she a good ghost or a bad ghost?"

"Neither, according to their lights. Just a harmless nuisance."

A coyote sounded a weary late-night note. Eastward the ground fog wrapped the rising moon in bluish gauze. The cool night air carried the faint perfume of a far-off alpine blooming, a reminder that the road, although having settled once more on the long arm of the Platte, was climbing into the mountains.

Ellen took a deep breath and blew it up over her face. "I *am* sorry. I was afraid if I went up to the fort after whiskey, the boy would be gone."

No answer.

"Doesn't anyone ever get to tell you how the boar ate the cabbage?" she asked, nudging him.

"What?" He was drifting off. He blinked at the paling stars, pulling himself against them.

Ellen eased herself onto his stomach and sucked gently on his earlobe. "When I get rich," she worked her leg between his, "I'll buy you a dozen cases of rum."

"That's nice." He smoothed her breasts with a rein-callused hand.

F I V E

WHEN HEDRICK LEFT THE NORTH PLATTE below Fourth of July rock and began the long upgrade haul for South Pass, he realized at last the soundness of his investment in oxen. The dozens of poor, faithful dobbins dead or standing sadly off alone, heads down, too weary to pick, was beyond reason. Whereas his teams, lean and hard, continued on like stamp mills, patiently crushing out the miles.

Leaving the heartbeat of the Platte, Ellen made her prayer to Jeremy's great grandfather, the Cheyenne Dog Soldier Ohkumhkakit. "We are here, Ohkum," she called over the lighter song of the Sweetwater, "on a trail of the Sioux. Come find us here. Guard us."

Fort Bridger. Saturday, July 20, 1850. A mean huddle of mud-daubed poles hopelessly lost in a sea of sage. Abandoning the basket traps they were using to catch army crickets, a handful of squaws ran to set out trade goods. A gaunt-faced Frenchman strolled over to mind the traps, and Uergin rode that direction. Later he told Ellen, "Gabe ain't here, lucky for you."

"Too bad," she answered archly, realizing they were talking about Bridger. "We could have worked something out."

"Ain't you the sassy one. You must be smelling that salt water."

A sail of small blue butterflies, dropping over the top of a wagon, dipped above Ellen's head and changed direction in an explosion of sapphire. Deep inside, Uergin felt something catch. His beautiful *mariposa* should be wearing sapphires. That's the world she belonged to, the safe, cool world of high-ceilinged rooms overlooking shaded streets running past green-grass yards and sidewalk water fountains—a world musty with the smell of banks and courthouses and schools.

Made uncomfortable by the silent scrutiny, Ellen looked away. But Uergin continued to stare, thoughts turning inward. He'd tried changing his life once, down in Chihuahua. The money was good, but not that good, and he and his Spanish señora parted strangers.

He breathed a small whistle and walked to where the squaws were squatted beside elk hides weighed down with beaded leather goods and blue-stone jewelry. No trade goods were being accepted, Bridger's traders having more than enough of emigrant fixings. Instead, the Virginians were tossing coins at what they wanted. Satisfied, a squaw picked up the money and the exchange was made.

Uergin caught the eye of a rouge-prettied girl and made sign talk and they smiled at each other with understanding in their smiles. Her earrings, rifle caps strung on loops of copper wire, jingled like delicate bells when she leaned forward to slip the biggest blue-stone necklace back out of sight.

The Virginians were done with the Oregon Trail. Now it was the Salt Lake Trail that would take them better than 100 miles south and west over two mountain passes.

Hedrick left two trail-worn oxen at the fort, and did not look back to see the Indians fall on them. Slowly the desert sage gave way to low, scraggy cedar. Mornings were cold and clear, followed by afternoons pitted with violent, brief showers. Densely clouded skies spitting miserable, cold rain hastened the evenings. A thunderstorm of immense power rumbled through the hills, loosing a massive bolt that killed an ox and carved a trench a foot wide 50 yards through the brush to knock down a horse.

Five days out of Bridger's the wagons reached the Bear— swift, rocky-bottomed, 40 yards wide and three feet deep. The next morning, rolling easily along, they crossed the further grassy valley, skirting high stone buttes the guide called the Needles. The terrain grew increasingly difficult. Tempers grew short. Something about being in the true mountains made the company chary, as if, having come to terms with the desert, they resented its being walled away.

On a long, steep hill into the valley of Lost Creek, a lost wind, finding itself in spurts, tipped a wagon over, badly laming a wheel ox and ripping the canvas. Bedding and clothing boiled high into the sky. The ensuing layover triggered an hellacious argument when the party decided to go fishing. The futile lines became entangled, and rods and all were hurled angrily into the trout brook.

The next morning the sun came up as always and the wagons rolled out as always.

Up over the rim into Echo Canyon and down to the Weber— the steep mountains opening and closing like a stone accordion. Never had the Easterners seen so many rocks and mountains piled one on another. Serviceberries were everywhere. Gathered for pies and compotes, the acid fruit proved as dear as rhubarb itself to sweeten, but for people hungry for fresh fruit, no berry ever tasted better.

The Weber was the worst of nightmares. Swampy timber and brawling runnels choked the narrow passageway. *Remember the Donners*, became the watchword. *See where they blazed the trees. They were the ones had it bad.*

Water-worn boulders as big as barns bent the trace this way

and that. Bogs obliterated it completely and riddled it with root snares.

Remember the Donners. Snow got those poor bastards in the Sierra, but it was these mountains here that brought them down, chewed the heart right out of their summer. They were the ones had it bad.

Men pulled with their teams, going to their knees with the brutes. Axles disappeared in mud and snapped in unseen potholes.

At least they didn't have to open the trace, the Donners did that, cut away the heavy underbrush step-by-step, used it for the road bed.

Wallowing through the chewed-up mud and rocks behind the lurching wagons, the women and children bore their own miseries of wet clothing and bruised bones and feeding insects.

Remember the Donners. For all their struggles, they never had a prayer. They were doomed from the minute they left Bridger's.

Three oxen laid down and died. A man caught his foot in the rocks and snapped his leg. A woman miscarried.

Remember the Donners.

Hedrick lost his brass pendulum odometer, smashed to pieces against its wheel. He would buy another in Salt Lake City if the Mormonites had such a clever thing.

Four years ago there was no supply depot waiting. Poor Donner party. They were the ones had it bad. Twenty-one days it took them here in this canyon alone, 21 days of frantic, back-breaking labor. And all for naught. Eating each other the way they did in the Sierras.

Seven days through the Weber the Virginians reached the foot of a steep mountain. They put all their teams on 30 wagons and struck out for the top. And from the broad, open pass over the Wasatch, through a fluttery yellow curtain of hundreds of wild canaries, caught their first glimpse of the valley of the salt lake.

So this is where old Brigham went to ground. A peculiar people, the Mormonites, thinking their own laws better than the democracy. But what the hell, let 'em have their dead lake. The men unhitched their oxen and put the teams back on the slant for the rest of the wagons.

Last Creek Canyon, the last night out. Ellen wiggled face-down against the unyielding earth and, unable to get comfortable, rolled over. Tomorrow. Tomorrow. Uergin patted her flank and murmured something. She woke to see pale dawn in the depths of the narrow canyon and Uergin saddling his horse. Seized with a queer reluctance to let the day impose its duty, she called the guide over to the blankets and kissed him again and again. "Stay with me while we're in the city, we'll hire a buggy and look around."

"Ain't that gonna put a crimp in your style?"

"Gentile husbands aren't anything."

"At least they try," Uergin observed dryly. "That's all a steer can do."

"How come you never kiss me anymore?" Ellen asked. But he rode away without answering.

Slowly but surely the dark corridor opened on a bleak bench ground. Beneath the bench the steep slopes of grass and shrubbery fell precipitously away, revealing the Holy Valley of the West in all its splendor.

Ellen's eyes filled with tears. Nor was she alone in her emotions. The Virginians, too, gazed in awe so quiet that the faint metallic tolling of a distant bell could be heard. The largest lake seen since leaving the States bounded the northward horizon. Feathery marshes occupied what could be seen of the shoreline, while the greens and browns of pastures and fields dotted the higher ground. Below the wagons, gathered to the foot of the lowering slopes like small adobe footstools, were hundreds of homes. Switzerland-like pinnacles rose in the distance.

Mormon town. Friday, August 2, 1850. Civilized as any in the States. The usual assortment of people going about their business, the usual assortment of business. Checkerboard streets eight rods wide edged with crystal streams. Sidewalks 20 feet across. Ten-acre lots outlined in staked saplings. Flowers every-where—the red French bean and the rose, geraniums, nasturtiums, tansies.

The astounding order of things wiped out whatever reservations the Virginians entertained regards doing business with the Holy Joes. Uergin led the wagons to an emigrant park by a river, where Hedrick cheerfully paid the $5 per wagon. After 97 days in the wilderness, the wooden bathhouses and long row of privies over the water looked real nifty.

S I X

LLEN CHANGED HER BLOUSE and walked uptown alone. She was reading the rate sheet posted in the window of the Salt Lake House when she heard the funny squeak of a familiar voice.

"They do talk about it, but they don't make fun of it."

And turning around, came face-to-face with Irene Pomeroy and her mother, Ursulia Hascall. Both women wore white day dresses and carried parasols. Irene's hair hung down in ringlets of spun gold.

"Good Lord, have mercy!" cried Irene. "I heard you died in the desert!" She hugged her school chum warmly. "I am so glad to see you!"

Ursulia eyed the prodigal good-humoredly. "Ellen Wausau. Come back from the dead."

"My husband and I are here with a train from Virginia. I'm looking for rooms," Ellen explained, acutely conscious of her own hank of hair, tied in a mop, and her burned skin and filthy skirts.

Digging a pencil and paper out of her handbag, Irene scribbled furiously. "Oh dear, this is so exciting. Sister Jackman's house is empty. I'll draw you a map. And you have to come for supper."

Uergin was in the dram house scaring up a card game when Ellen found him. He objected loudly to leaving and, having made sure no one missed what a looker she was, followed her out the door.

Small and stout, with a loose roll of caramel-colored blonde hair and guarded eyes, Mrs. Jackman wanted two dollars a night for her rental house, in advance. Uergin handed over a $10-dollar gold piece, Mrs. Jackman clamped an eye tooth on it, examined the bite, and led the way through a gate overhung with flowering red French bean.

In addition to the usual barn and pens, the back lot was home to numerous chickens of all colors, a clothesline, and an outhouse marked PRIVATE. A narrow plank walkway, beginning at the street, led past the main house and out the back-lot gate to a clay-covered structure with diminutive casements.

A small, uncovered porch anchored the front of the building. The skinny, rectangular pole structure attached to one side turned out to be a shower. Further down the pasture, at the end of a path mashed through the grasses, a second outhouse tilted backward alarmingly.

The flooring inside the house sagged. In the middle of the sag a large cookstove with a warming oven served as a partition of sorts—iron sink and badly weathered table on one side, slatted double bed on the other.

Uergin stretched out on the bed's thin mattress and was sound asleep when Jeremy's cries woke him. The little warrior had lost everything and was sitting in a dishpan on the table.

"I hope you ain't thinkin' of takin' me anywhere tonight," Uergin muttered, turning his back to the noise.

"You've got to go, you're my husband."

"Izzat so? Then be a good wife and come to bed."

"Conrad."

"Ain't it enough I give you my name and my money?"

"I need a stalking-horse."

The streets smelled sweetly of roses. The gardens throbbed with the shrill of locust. The setting sun, raining fire on the high peaks of the Wasatch, turned the lead-colored houses bronze.

"So what's your plan, my little gold digger?" Uergin asked.

"Get work and settle in. I'm in no hurry, and I'm not a gold digger, I'm a businesswoman."

"That's a new word."

"Think of me as a gambler. It's a good gamble, isn't it?"

"That depends on what the Mormons hold. What d'you hold?"

"Hold?"

"The cards you're not showing."

They walked aways in silence, comfortable with the cadence of their boots. "I'll use my confession. Saints love a good confession, and they love secrets. When I pick my new husband, I'll confess the truth."

"What's 'the truth'?" Uergin asked. She had some odd quirks. She hated to hear him talk Mexican, and yet, aroused, breathed Spanish so coarse he was sure she didn't know the meaning of the words. She refused to watch him sharpen a knife.

"That Jeremy's half-Indian," she answered.

The Pomeroy house boasted flat roofs and low shady verandas well trellised and supported by pillars. The yard reeked of simmering peppers. Uergin took a deep, mouth-watering breath.

"I should of told you to follow your nose," Irene called from the doorway. "Once you learn to cook this way, you forget white cooking."

Unusually wide windows and archways lent the rooms space and light. Canvases made heavy with white paint covered the walls. Attached to the canvases, like unframed paintings, were bright red, black, and white woven-rug tapestries. Similarly colored rugs patterned the red brick floors.

Uergin was speechless. The last thing he expected to come

across in Salt Lake City was a rich man's hacienda. The usual mattresses folded against the wall and covered with Navajo blankets were gone, but that was the only difference. Except for the bizarre collection of metal, wood, and stone statues. Nude dancers with bird heads, bare-breasted bald women with multiple arms, goat-headed men with unreal penises.

Studying the art, Uergin's amazement grew. It had never occurred to him that a man might go out of his way to live with things that came from somewhere else—things he didn't need and would never use. The awareness struck him in the same manner as learning, when he was 15, that his word had any value. It was like opening a door on something waiting for him.

"My husband designed the house," Irene explained, her hand resting affectionately on a garishly painted high-backed chair. "He spent two years in South America and hasn't been the same since. If he had his way, we'd be burning horse droppings to keep the mosquitoes out, but there I draw the line. It's a horrible smell." Reading Uergin's fascination with the art, she blushed prettily. "It gets worse, but we keep that part in the bedroom."

Francis Pomeroy, a shy man impeccably dressed in a dark suit and white shirt, managed to join his guests in the dining room and fall to eating without so much as a single word. He was not, however, oblivious to Uergin's wolfing down three pieces of hot pork tamale pie well ladled with red chile pequin. Excusing himself immediately after supper, Francis returned shortly to place several maps on the table being cleared by the kitchen help.

"I'm a water engineer, and I was wondering if you're familiar with the Pima villages down along El Camino de Nuevo Mexico."

In the steamy kitchen, Irene dismissed the colored help. "We can busy ourselves and visit at the same time. Mother and I want to hear all about you."

Drying dishes, Ellen dutifully trotted out the details of her decision to leave the Harris train. "I didn't know, when I left Nauvoo, I'd be expected to marry Elder Harris. When I wouldn't, I was voted out of the train. I met my husband at Fort Laramie. He has family in New York." She hesitated, the lies plugging up her ears.

"What's New York like?" Ursulia asked.

"Mostly farmland and big rivers. The women push babies in little carriages and fasten the diapers with pieces of wire called safety pins. In Albany they sell silk thread wound on spools, and there's a new candy called gum. You chew it like pitch, only it lasts forever." The stories edged closer to Batten-Kill. Jed's family became Uergin's family, the blurred interleafing growing easier.

"But you couldn't forget us, could you," Irene gloated knowingly.

"Nobody can. Your Kingdom is always in the newspapers."

"I bet it is," Ursulia cooed.

Irene's mouth tightened noticeably, and Ursulia winked mischievously at Ellen.

"Francis only has one wife," Irene snapped, popping a plate in the cupboard. "I'm sure you're dying to ask."

Ellen gasped. "It really never entered my mind."

"I don't mind talking about the polygamy." Irene glanced defiantly at her mother, who made a pickle face. "Everybody else does."

"All I said was," Ursulia shook out a dry dishtowel, "'Joseph must of been buried a bald man.' Now, wouldn't you say so, dear?" She looked askance at Ellen, "If you were sitting in a room full of women and every one of them wearing a lock of Joseph's hair in an amulet on their neck chain?"

"That's not all you said, mother," Irene shot back. "You said proxy husbands were porch climbers."

"Well, I, yes…yes, they are. But if that's what God wants…"

"You mustn't talk about it the way you did this afternoon. Just because you and I aren't involved in spiritual wifery, who's to say it's wrong?"

Spiritual wifery.

Ellen stared unseeing at the pastoral scene embroidered on the table linen. When she was 14, the Prophet and Brigham came to her house. They sat in her darkened bedroom—she on the bed, they on chairs—to counsel with her about the need for unquestioning obedience to the great Jehovah. She could even become a spiritual wife, Brigham whispered, taking her hand. Joseph took her other hand and whispered that the peepings of his heart told him she could be his for time and Brigham's for eternity.

She was aware of a tension in herself, a not unpleasant tension of being close to a wonderful secret. The churchmen sprinkled her with holy water and left her alone to pray. They never came again, and gradually the fervent hope that they would, particularly in times of stress, diminished in the light of Rubin's lusty pursuit.

When she told Rubin of her desire for their return, her sweetheart announced happily that women were always following the important men around. He looked forward to the day when women would make themselves a problem to him, showering him with goodies and requesting private cleansings.

Irene fed the stove and put the chocolate water on to boil. Roused from her reverie, Ellen glanced through the doorway into the next room. The men were leaning over a large map, Uergin talking with his hands Indian-fashion. He looked up and for a few fleeting seconds was alone with her outside the game.

"I do apologize, dear," Ursulia told her daughter, sounding more amused than sorry.

Irene was wiping off the pots and pans with the stove rag.
"You have to be careful." Bang! went a pan into a nest of pans.
"The Society ladies are very political."

"It's a free country."

"You could cause Francis trouble, mother." Bang-BANG!
"And we don't want that. It's like you're attacking Brigham."

"Now, how could I be attacking Brigham?"

"How do you think? He approves all the marriages."

"Learn anything?" Uergin asked walking home, Jeremy
drowsing on his shoulder.

"Brigham approves the marriages. That hadn't occurred to me."

"So now you gotta see him?"

"Absolutely not! My husband can do that."

"What if he gives me the bum's rush?"

"Not you." Ellen kissed him soundly on the cheek. A carriage
passed by with a loud clip-clop of hooves on the packed road
dirt.

"You're a hard woman in a hard church."

"A funny church. That Ursulia's a stitch. She has the face
of an angel, but she's full of the devil. She and Irene had a real
knock-down, drag-out over the polygamy. Ursulia makes fun of
it, and that makes Irene mad. Irene thinks it's alright, but not in
her house, I'm sure."

"Holy shit! So that's why that woman didn't eat with us."

"Conrad! The kitchen help?"

"Maybe Francis wants to change his luck."

"Be serious."

"Hold on. I think I'm onto something here. You can tell Irene
you took the second thought about being a Gentile's wife and
decided to share her husband instead." Jeremy stretched, waking
up, and Uergin put the boy on the ground. "That Francis is sure
no afternoon farmer, that's a nice house."

"You would think so—all those obscene things." Ellen bumped his shoulder affectionately. "I asked about Phoebe. Irene says Phoebe's way too good for the likes of her husband. She says he's is a tyrant."

"She say that? Against poor old George?"

"She never gets to attend ladies' meetings, for taking care of Constance. I guess Constance hasn't been out of the house in years. The neighbors are never invited in." Velvety thunder floated out of the southern mountains, overhead the night sky was brilliant with stars.

"He's a bishop now, the tax collector and chief tithe collector. His inheritance has been apportioned in property fronting on the Temple Block. Also, he's one of the directors of the church mint. I didn't ask about wives, Irene's so touchy about that."

Forced down on a convenient stone bench by the laughter making a fist in his stomach, Uergin managed to spit out, "George Harris? is he your candidate? Godalmightydamn! it'll serve him right!"

"What do you mean? I'll be a good wife."

"You're damn right you will, or he'll know the reason why."

"What's so funny?"

"I'd like to see the look on his face when you break the news."

"I'll have to check it out, you know, the situation and all, see what I think."

"Well, damn right! And if he still ain't up to snuff," Uergin shook with laughter, "give him the boot again!"

"He may not want me back."

Uergin could see her chin lifted against the starlight. By god, she wasn't kidding! He got to his feet and, wrapping his arms around her, kissed her warmly. "Ellen Wausau, daughter to Hiram Scott, wife to the Grizz, mistress to the Great Scout, George Harris ain't got a prayer."

S E V E N

An accidental meeting? No. His home. No appointment, nothing to forewarn him. Late afternoon, the light fading and evening company not yet arrived.

Lying beside Uergin in the darkness, Ellen smiled, a small cynical smile. George was no prize—almost 60 and a bully. He used his size—over 6 feet tall and perhaps as much as 300 pounds—to intimidate people. When that didn't work, he hit them. She could break him of hitting her, but there was no breaking him of his preacher's other-worldliness. The insufferable bastard. She sighed deeply. She'd earn every penny of that money.

"What's wrong?" Uergin asked. He could do that—sleeping, be instantly awake.

"I was thinking about George. I wonder if he beats his wives."

"Lord! I'd hate to be married to a woman I had to beat up to get along with." The next minute he was asleep again.

I'm going to miss the stars, Ellen thought, staring into the total darkness of the ceiling, and made herself concentrate on George's wives. Constance hated the sin but not the sinner. How fair was it to add to her woes? As for Phoebe, did Phoebe love George? How could she? Still, with her parents dead in Winter Quarters and her brothers and sisters living back in the States, Phoebe's only family was George. And Constance.

And you, Phoebe, are my only family, the closest thing I will ever have to a sister.

In her letters, Phoebe had relayed the news that Ellen's father was buried in Illinois on land owned by Emma Smith, who had married a Lewis Bidamon. And that Ellen's mother, Jane, was troubled with inflammatory rheumatism and in the care of Emma. Ellen wrote both her mother and the Prophet's widow, addressing her as Emma Smith Bidamon, but never got a reply.

You're right, Uergin, Ellen kissed the sleeping man lightly on the shoulder, *I am a hard woman, and it is a hard church.*

The next morning, buying eggs and milk from Mrs. Jackman against the $10-dollar gold piece, Ellen asked about Sister Phoebe Harris. The fishing expedition netted an address, which Ellen already knew, but nothing else. Except for Mrs. Jackman's pointing out a painted tin lid hanging on the wall—a fuzzy flock of chickens in a barnyard.

Puzzled, Ellen examined the tiny PT in the corner. Taggart was Phoebe's maiden name.

Over a breakfast of eggs scrambled in boiled milk, Ellen made Uergin promise to stay sober and come back by 4 o'clock with groceries. As for herself, she intended to lie low, not wanting to spoil her surprise. Confined to the back lot, she unpacked her only dress, a heavy, dark blue cotton, blotted out the mold with hot teakettle water, and hung the dress on the line. Later, she and Jeremy read stories and helped themselves to snap peas and a cucumber.

And then it was time for the paint. Crouched in front of the mirror *(Mrs. Jackman is short, the mister must be too),* she rubbed lip rouge on her cheeks and powdered her face with wheat starch. The ritual reminded her of Whonow's sister, Sasha—of the squaw's poking at her little paint pots in preparation for the ceremonies.

Satisfied, Ellen wadded her hair into a loose topknot and

looked again into the mirror. And unable to meet her eyes,
turned her attention outside the window. Several chickens were
busy scratching near the front step. The geese were making long
curving lines across the sky toward the lake.

*What I'm pecking at the edges of tastes like shit. It's too bad I
can't just make like a goose and go away and leave them alone.*

The scene, her mood, brought back a song her mother sang.

> Birds of a feather, they flock together,
> that's what's my grandmother said.
> They swoop and they dive and they sleep in one coop
> with their feathers over their eyes.
> Men worth their salt do what they ought,
> that's what my grandmother said...

I wonder what my grandmother would say about me.

Uergin returned that afternoon with bread and a ring of
cured sausage, and he and Jeremy fell to. They told Ellen she
looked beautiful. That she better eat. She barely heard them.
The sky was coming right. She dabbed on the last of her perfume
and sallied forth.

Situated as it was on a slight elevation of grassy knoll at the
far end of Fourth South Street, the Harris mansion looked like an
over-large brown shoe box. The windows were tall and narrow,
but pleasantly numerous. No gables to speak of, no porches,
but all in all a certainly suitable house. A half-dozen scrawny
saplings spiked the front yard. In the back lot, two skinny barns
sticking up like jack-in-the-boxes supported a clutch of smaller
sheds.

The front walk was lined with white stones. The thick plank
steps that made up the stoop smelled strongly of creosote. The
door gong—a fancy affair, large black dome topped with a plain
bronze rosette—set off a loud bell.

"George, how are you?"

Stunned. He was stunned. He had answered the ring only after it became apparent Phoebe was indisposed, and then only after pulling on his suit coat and painting a smile on his face— one never knew. Now he stopped smiling and there was a kind of wildness in his eyes. He was bigger than Ellen remembered, an imposing bulkiness pressed the seams of his clothing. His thick beard had been reduced to a carefully manicured fringe of salt-and-pepper whiskers, exposing unfamiliar soft, full lips and pink veined cheeks. The pale forehead loomed, the hair thinning away. Dark circles overshadowed the once startling greenness of his eyes.

"Do I know you?" he asked stiffly.

"Yes, of course. Ellen…Ellen Wausau. I thought you'd…" she broke off, covered with confusion.

"What do you want?"

"May I come in?"

The door closed slightly, leaving only the voice, heavy with authority. "My office is at the corner of Main and South Temple. The hours are posted outside."

"Please, just a few minutes."

There was no answer, the door remained ajar. Ellen leaned forward, intent on putting her foot in the crack when, abruptly, the door swung wide and the churchman was walking briskly away. She followed down an uncarpeted hallway, past a spill of dark polished stairs into a sitting room lined with a stiff offering of straight-backed chairs, and through the sitting room into a small, windowless sanctuary.

A chain, descending from the shadowy ceiling, held a lantern shaded so as to drop its light over a large desk. Making a throne of the swivel chair behind the desk, George pinned the unwelcome visitor in the judicial severity of his expression.

"What do you want here?"

The room's other chair was tilted backward in a corner. Buying time, Ellen wrestled the heavy chair around over the braided rug while George watched dispassionately, glad for once for Phoebe's carelessness in straightening a room.

"I was in the city," Ellen said warmly, positioning herself at the edge of the light. "It's lovely, a real miracle."

George pressed his hands flat on the desk in a gesture of dismissal. "I'm very busy." He didn't remember the apostate's face being so angular, the mouth so loose. What in the world had he ever seen in her?! Her perfume profaned the sanctuary, and he despised her for it.

"I came to visit Phoebe...and you," Ellen said shyly.

"How thoughtful," George sneered. How old was she now? Twenty-seven? Against the shadows, her hair looked black, as did her eyes. It was the sun that gave her color. Without it, she looked coarse, very coarse. And gaunt as a starved dog. "Why are you really here?"

"Oh, please, George."

Her irreverence grated on him. "Come, come," he demanded loudly, shuffling the papers. "What do you want?"

Ellen kept her own voice soft. "I know how difficult this must be for you."

George made a snort of laughter. "You flatter yourself to think these circumstances difficult. Our business was finished long ago."

"How could I forget? I was the one who finished it."

"Why are you here?" The question curled with hate. "You want a handout?"

"I came to see Phoebe and to ask your forgiveness for what happened back there on the Trail. I was young and foolish." Chirpy words with just a hint of hesitancy.

"There is nothing..." George shook his head and started again. "You are nothing. Am I supposed to forgive a snake because it's a snake, or a maggot because it's a maggot?"

"You don't wish me ill?"

"Wish you ill?!" his words lunged at her, "for using me and running away? No. I survived that nasty piece of testing."

"You have no idea how many times..."

"...get out! Your apostasy, your evil ways, make you ugly in my sight." Ellen made no move to obey, and George realized that the Lord was once more using the woman's deceit to test him. He took a book from the drawer and, making of it a shield, showed its spidery gold title—*The Book of Mormon*.

"By the authority vested in me by the Council of Fifty," the bishop leaned back, leaving the book in the lamp's golden glow, "your name has been taken off the membership rolls and you have been turned over to the devil to be buffeted in the flesh. No one who walks in the Lord shall know you."

"George..." Ellen moaned as if struck a death blow. In the silence that followed, the sitting-room clock could be heard sonorously winding down. "George, please..."

"Go! NOW!" Keeping to the shadows, George watched the Jezebel push herself to her feet and slink away.

And shut the goddamned door, he crowed silently. The door stayed open. The footsteps, retreating through the sitting room, faded into nothing. All that remained of the encounter was a lingering scent of wild mint and beneath it the smell common to all people newly arrived from the States—mold. Seized with a light-headed exuberance, George rested his forehead on the holy book. How sweet it was!

"ELLEN, IS THAT YOU? YES, IT IS!" The horsey squeal bounced off the walls of the sanctuary like a shriek gone mad. "WELL AIN'T YOU A SIGHT FOR SORE EYES!"

Up came George's head with the force of a spring trap. *Lord have mercy!* He closed his eyes and lowered his head once more, this time with a bang.

The woman who greeted Ellen in the hallway smelled of green onions and fresh dirt. Wrenched from Nauvoo when she was 13 and hauled off across the prairie—a little girl in a big, turnip-shaped body, gap-toothed, eyes hidden behind thick glasses—Phoebe had grown into her weight and squared off solid as a gum-tree post.

"You're pretty as a picture!" Ellen cried happily. "And all grown up!" She tousled the curly topknot, seeing the cropped curls as a very good sign. Short hair was the one thing that, crossing the desert, Phoebe kept of herself in the face of count-less rules. The little girl had insisted her light blonde hair wouldn't grow, snipping it off surreptitiously, and George made no fuss, perhaps suspecting something he didn't want to know.

"WELL, AIN'T YOU A SIGHT FOR SORE EYES!" Phoebe exclaimed joyfully, reared back, hands on hips.

Why don't you tell her again, Sister Phoebe? Maybe you can drive her deaf. Realizing that he was cowering, George straight-ened his shoulders. Phoebe had a mind like a cornpopper. God only knew what would fall out. He had to get rid of Ellen. That's when he heard the thump seeping through the house, cutting through the timbers with a ghostly heartbeat.

He threw himself around the desk and out through the sitting room into the hallway. Too late.

Phoebe was taking the stairs at a gallop, Ellen hard on her heels. George caught a glimpse of worn boot under a swish of dark blue material. The bogus lament, "Poor dear Phoebe, you have your hands full, don't you," fell on his head like slop thrown out the window.

He stomped down the hall to the kitchen. The ashdoor was open on the cookstove, the lids red hot. Swearing, he kicked the door shut and pulled the damper, noticed that the beans were in danger of boiling dry and put that pot in the warming oven.

The thumping was picking up speed. In the pantry the noise was awesome. Searching through the dim light for the whiskey jug, George felt as if he were standing under a clay pot that was being wacked with a big stick.

"Ordinarily there ain't no hurry," Phoebe explained over her shoulder. They had reached the upper landing and were walking rapidly down the narrow corridor that ran the length of the house. "But Mr. G. don't want Sister Constance thumping when we got company." She whirled to give Ellen a quick embrace, "not that you're company," and resumed her stride.

"Is Constance bedridden?" Ellen whispered.

"When it suits her." At the far end of the corridor, Phoebe pushed the door open on a cavernous room. A four-poster double bed occupied the middle of the room. Sitting on the edge of the bed, pounding the floor with a heavy walking stick, was a small bald figure in a night shift.

"Fe fe fe, be be be," sang the elf on the down stroke, "light the lights for me me me. Fe fe fe, be be be…"

"…look who come to see you," Phoebe broke in.

The thumping stopped, the head snapped around bird-like, the eyes, pale brown marbles, widened.

Waiting for Constance to say something, Ellen's attention wandered. Bleached feed-sack curtains over the windows gave the room a yellow gloom. A child's vanity overflowed with clothing. A table near the bed held a lamp and a row of tallow dips in hollowed-out turnips, the turnips dried and shriveled.

The glass hit the doorjamb and shattered, leaving a long track of water across the bare floorboards. Ellen jumped back into the hall.

"George!" Constance screamed, casting about for something else to throw. "GEORGE! GEOOOORGE!!"

Downstairs, braced against a kitchen counter, the wanted

man raised his whiskey cup in solemn benediction. "Enjoy your cow pie, my dears."

The storm ended as quickly as it began.

"What'd you let that whore in for?" Ellen heard Constance ask. The bump-bump-bump started up again, and stopped almost at once.

"Where are you going with my cane?"

"I gotta catch Ellen an' I don't want you thumping."

"She's right outside the door, listening," Constance rasped.

"Oh," Phoebe said, having discovered that for herself, leaning around the doorjamb into the hallway.

"Bring her back, you dumb cow!" Constance raged.

Ellen stuck out her tongue and crossed her eyes and waggled her head. Phoebe laughed.

"Come back in here! both of you!"

Now it was Ellen who leaned around the doorjamb.

Constance made a sly, knowing smile and hopped under the covers. "Fix the pillows, you nincompoop," she ordered Phoebe without taking her rheumy eyes off the intruder. "You're here for George, ain't you?"

Somewhere in the marrow of those old bones the wind-blown woman who stood between the rain and the cooking fires still lived. Saluting that woman in her thoughts, Ellen stepped free of the door. "No."

"You're lying," Constance trumpeted. "I always knew you'd come, but it won't work. He hates you." With its thin smattering of wispy hair, her skull looked shiny, as if waxed. Of a sudden Ellen identified the smell in the room. Oil of almonds. Mixed with strained tallow, it made the tallow an acceptable sun lotion.

"Phoebe likes you," Constance revealed. "She don't have no brains. She likes everybody. Tell her." The older woman poked at Phoebe with the cane. "Tell her how many he's got. Is it three? Is that how many's out there? I forget."

Done with the pillows, Phoebe busied herself with the broken glass.

"PHOEBE!"

"Five."

Constance's stick fingers cupped her egg-white cheeks and flew apart in mock surprise. "Five! What a busy little boy!"

Recalling the closed doors on both sides of the gloomy hall, Ellen could only stare in horror. The room's thin light pinched away.

"They make him feel manly. Ain't that so, Phoebe. You make him feel manly."

Phoebe's face brightened in a rare shame.

"You don't have to put up with this, Phoebe," Ellen said sharply. "You're nobody's jigger." Immediately she was sorry.

"Phoebe's a jigger," Constance sang out. "Phoebe's a jigger. I don't know, but I been told, jiggers eat chiggers, ain't that so? I don't know…"

Ellen left the room in a blind fury. Phoebe followed, pleading, "Don't leave. I'm sorry."

"You have nothing to be sorry about!" Now it was Ellen hurrying down the hall, talking over her shoulder. "And don't worry, I'm not leaving Gomorra without you. You're going with me to California."

"Wait!" Phoebe wailed, grabbing Ellen's sleeve. "Stop! It ain't so bad. Constance and me, we take care of ourselves. We got plenty."

"Plenty of nothing is still nothing!" Ellen shot back, no longer whispering, wanting to be heard in the closed-off rooms. "Why didn't you tell me about the other wives? Are they bedridden too?"

"We ain't supposed to write nothing outside the Valley about it. Mr. G. says the only reason he's got us is that it's the law, he has to take what he can afford. He says we're expensive as slaves to keep."

"You *are* a slave, don't you see?"

"Just to Constance. The rest got their own houses. We get one lot and one farm acreage for each wife." Phoebe put her arm across Ellen's shoulders, slowing her friend's retreat, wanting her so much to understand.

And Ellen did understand, at least she was beginning to. "You have six more houses besides this one?"

"Five. I gotta live here on account of Constance. But we're thinking about building another one, just like this one. Mr. G. don't like clay houses."

The bed creaked. Constance's dry voice, lifting in song, joined them. "Nobody likes me…"

"Stay for dinner," Phoebe pleaded. "So we can visit. Constance don't come downstairs."

"…everybody hates me…" The voice, strengthening, rattled down the corridor with the clang of a stove lid.

"I can't." Ellen reached the head of the stairs. Turning back, she took Phoebe's rough hands in her own. "I promise, one way or another, I'll see you again."

"…I'm going out in the garden and eat worms…"

"How many children?" Ellen asked.

"None. He don't even try anymore, leastways not with me."

"…great big fat worms. Little, bitty skinny worms…"

George was waiting when the harlot came downstairs, his face full of sneering condemnation. Ellen reached the lower steps and, standing there taller than the churchman, sneered back. When George saw the hard dislike in her eyes, a sudden anger filled him. What'd she expect? He grabbed her arm. "I don't want you back here."

"Then let me go." She could smell the liquor on his breath.

"I want it understood," his fingers were like spikes, "that you are not to see my wives either."

"What I cannot be, I do not wish to see." She pulled away and he shoved her, harder than he meant, against the stairs. She landed on her back, slid down several steps to the floor and got to her feet. Except for the rouge, her face was white.

"Don't ever shove me again," she threatened, the way a man threatens when he has a knife or a gun to back it up—in a whisper. "Never, you hear. *Hijo de tu chingada!*" She walked to the front door, yanked up the latch and left the house.

Pulling a stick, making a rap-rap-rap on the plank walk, Jeremy materialized out of the darkness. When he met his mother, he turned and followed, rap-rap-rapping. Uergin was sitting on the rental stoop, the tip of his cigar aglow.

"Seven," Ellen said, settling beside him.

"Seven! Good Lord, I didn't think he had it in him!"

"Six houses. Constance and Phoebe live with him in one, the others have their own houses. No children. I can see why. He's fat and mean and loud. He's driven Constance nutty as a chinquapin."

"How's Phoebe?"

"She looks healthy as a horse, probably works like a horse, but says she has everything she wants." Ellen sounded dubious, then amused. "She calls George, 'Mr. G.' It could be a new rule, but I have a feeling it's just Phoebe."

Uergin stroked her fingers. "You still interested?"

"It's a big house, probably the nicest of the houses he owns, wouldn't you think? Phoebe won't be jealous, I can tell. Constance is very abusive, but seems to be confined to her room. Yes, I'm still interested. It is peaceful here, a good place to raise children, particularly if they have a rich father."

Uergin quashed his cigar in the dirt under the porch.

Peaceful? He wasn't sure. Mormon country wasn't called the Valley of the Shadow for nothing. Main street, GSL City, wasn't like any other main street he'd ever ridden down. There was something different about it, something slightly off-cant, as if it were a mask for something else entirely.

"Wish me luck?" Ellen asked.

"I do that," Uergin promised. She probably could set Harris to sniffing around again, but she could be wrong about the preacher's willingness to accept a half-breed. Damn few white people Uergin ever met liked Indians.

"But what...? What do I hear in your voice?"

"Maybe you should ask yourself why George don't have kids. Maybe he don't like 'em."

"He'll like Jeremy."

"What if he don't?"

"I'll kill him."

E I G H T

T HE NEXT DAY BEING SUNDAY, Jackmans went to church.
Early arrival was everything. Tying up next to the Bowery,
seeing and being seen. Which is why Mr. Jackman, in the
process of harnessing his team, became instantly concerned about
the delay (to say nothing of the terrible burden) caused when one
of his pets planted a bucket-sized hoof on the toe of his well-rubbed
boot.

Crowded against the stall wall, the apple-round Mr. Jackman
swore mightily and banged the Belgian with his fists. Busy with
its grain, the brute paid no attention, and several excruciating
seconds elapsed before Mr. Jackman was able to free himself and
hobble over to a pile of feed sacks.

By the time he recovered sufficiently to get the team into the
hitch, his good wife was hiking down to the barn in her good
clothing to see what in the world was the matter! Foot smarting,
Mr. Jackman loaded the anxious woman and himself. And hearing his name, looked around to see the renter and her child.

"Why, Mrs. Uergin!" Mrs. Jackman's surprise soured in open
displeasure, "where on earth is your husband?" *To help you into
the seat,* her tone said. Grunting loudly, Mr. Jackman crawled
back out of the wagon.

"I'm afraid he's indisposed," Ellen confessed with an air of
resignation, hoisting Jeremy over the edge of the box. "He's not
yet seen the true way. I am hopeful, of course, always."

"Yes," Mrs. Jackman agreed impatiently. "Always."

Head down, Mr. Jackman took Ellen's elbow.

The wagon started up, the team dawdled. Beset by a sudden perversity, Mr. Jackman refused to hurry them. A rooster crowed, a hundred roosters answered. The early morning air keeled under the climbing sun, the smell of salt water evaporating in the sharper smells of sage and sand.

A swoop of wind down the dusty avenue threw gravel in Jeremy's eyes and lifted the flimsy vail on Ellen's hat. Rising in the distance, the whitewashed walls of President Young's house brought Ursulia's words to mind, "We call him a Prophet 'cause he's a profit to us."

The wagon was nearing a confusion of horses and vehicles outside a large, long shed-like structure roofed over with boughs and dirt. A tall, well-groomed man with beardless face rode by, and Mrs. Jackman swallowed her silence to explain, "That's General Wells, one of our lawyers," she shielded an exaggerated wink with her hand, "a real swordsman."

Ellen smiled shyly at the lawyer, who tipped his hat, his glance lingering. The Belgians swung in toward the ditch curb, and four young men dressed in dark wool suits hurried over to catch the bridles and assist the passengers. Another team approached in a jingle of harness, the driver steadying the animals with a loud urgency.

Dour face straight ahead, Mr. Jackman swung his empty wagon into the traffic. It was some time before he reappeared, limping and out of breath, to be favored with a wintry stare from his wife.

Husband and renter in tow, Mrs. Jackman elbowed herself into the floodtide of English and Scandinavian immigrants. The unruly horde, calling out in thick, unfamiliar tongues, funneled down the Bowery's center aisle, depositing Mrs. Jackman a good 30 rows shy of her accustomed perch. With a swish of crinoline, she dropped into place and sat stone-faced.

A stiff breeze through the open doors sounded a pleasant murmur in the roof's withered branches. Finches wandered aimlessly overhead. Belly pressed against the back of the bench, Jeremy considered the faces collecting in front of him like leaves in a windrow.

A bell chimed. Small boys, having climbed the roof supports like scouts on a whaling ship, shinnied back down. Church officials began taking their seats on the platform. Bible in hand, long black coat billowing, a reader mounted the pulpit steps. Except for the shuffle of people continuing to wedge themselves along the edges of the Bowery, the congregation fell silent.

Craning her neck, Ellen studied the platform.

"President Young and his party are off visiting the Sanpete settlement," Mrs. Jackman said, misreading her renter's scrutiny.

"First we shall make a gladsome noise onto the Lord," the reader intoned. He lifted his hand, affecting a ragged uprising that slowly came together. The hand swung wildly, the worshippers broke into joyful song, the words pouring forth with glorious fervor. Jeremy's mouth flew open. The uproar increased, the dirt floor rumbled. The hundreds of teams tied outside on the street pricked their ears.

Made homesick by the racket, the Gentiles downtown reminded themselves that if there were a real church in the city, they too would be attending services. In the cavernous storage room of Holladay & Warner Mercantile, Uergin was counting the cards.

"Read 'em and weep, gentlemen. Read 'em and weep."

The singing ended. The sermoning began.

"Thanks be to GOD...," the reader paused briefly to allow his listeners time to collect themselves, and took off, "...for this Kingdom here in the middle of the naked desert. Thanks be to

GOD for our Saintdom, that we are not Gentiles fallen out of the ark of safety and floundering in heathen darkness.

"Thanks be to GOD for Joseph. JOSEPH! Whose home is in the sky and who dwells with the Lord far from the furious rage of Zenephi's lawless armies. Dear brothers and sisters, when we meet with our martyred Seer in heaven, do you know what his first question shall be? WHAT DID WE DO TO PRESERVE THE KINGDOM? Did we pay the faithful tithe due on our property? Did we donate every tenth day of our labor to the church? Did we give an honest accounting of our produce and stock?

"Remember, we were not sent here to build a Kingdom, we were sent here TO PRESERVE A KINGDOM. Those of you who live your religion, and you know who you are…"

Good nature wilting, Jeremy sighed and rubbed his eyes. His hair was damp. His New York shoes felt stiff and hot. He worked them off, and his mother poked them in her purse, wishing she could do the same with her heavy dress. It felt like a blanket. The sermon felt like a blanket. She was getting slightly sick to her stomach. The day was too beautiful to be wasted in listening to rambling, loose-jointed harangues.

She glanced up and down the rough pine boards, seeing mostly women. With few exceptions, Mrs. Jackman's being one, the faces bore the indelible marks of hard labor and poverty. With what grave sincerity they attended the reader's every word, as if needing only to know what was expected in order to heave themselves anew into their worn harnesses.

The ominous drumroll of mutinous babies grew louder and louder. Folded against his mother, Jeremy sat up with a jerk and made a long "whooo" call.

Ellen shook her head and touched the little boy's chin. *Count your blessings, my little tatanka. Americans can only single-hitch to get where they're going, but here the Saints can double- and triple-team. Thanks be to Joseph indeed!*

Glancing over her shoulder, seeing more people than she'd ever in her life seen together in one place, she thought of the thousands more on their way, strung out ant-like across the desert.

And thinking thus, remembered the time she and Whonow were playing on a sandhill, running and sliding in the loose sand. A skunk, tail raised, strolled in front of her, followed by an armada of miniatures.

"Jump!" Whonow yelled, laughing. "Jump, Mis'tai!"

"The Lord works in mysterious ways." The reader's words broke into Ellen's thoughts.

"Whoooo," Jeremy called loudly. "WhooooOOOoo. WhooooOOOoo."

"Now, Mis'tai!" Whonow cried. "Jump!"

Ellen stood, head bowed in embarrassment and, lifting the little owl singer against her shoulder, started down the long row of shifting knees.

"She's staying with us," Mrs. Jackman confided, surrounded by sotto voce inquiries. "Her husband's a Gentile."

On the platform, an apostle rose to his feet to point a commanding finger. "Do NOT let that woman leave! If we can't make ourselves heard above a baby's feeble cry, by Jesus, how are we ever going to make God hear us?"

Seated in the front row, wives flanking him like a heavenly host, George twisted around to see what the racket was about. A huge farmer in bib overalls caught his eye. The man was giving up his place, and mother and child were sinking behind a sea of heads. Stupefied, George righted himself. So that's why she was in the Valley!

After church, working his way more quickly than was his wont through the crowd, he kept one hand firmly clenched on

Phoebe's arm. "If we see the Wausau woman," he ordered, "you are to ignore her."

"Ellen's here?" Phoebe looked around excitedly.

"No, she's not. Now do as I tell you."

They reached the buggy, and Ellen separated herself from the crowd. George refused to lift his hat. There was absolutely nothing the harlot could do to redeem herself. Nevertheless, he entertained the thought, truly unbidden, that she was more beautiful than any of Brigham's wives.

That crown of molasses-black hair, those dark green eyes, that firm (although hardly pious) face. It also occurred to him, for no particular reason other than that the assessing of people's finances was his business, that she hadn't much money. Poor shop-worn piece of goods, she was more to be pitied than scorned, wearing the same dress she'd worn the night before, the same trail-worn boots.

Phoebe picked up Jeremy and plopped the boy, stiff with surprise, in George's arms. Standing off aways, Sister Jackman lifted a limp hand and wiggled her fingers girlishly in George's direction.

With a loud hurrumph, the bishop stood the child on the ground, took Phoebe's arm and propelled her roughly into the buggy. And wasted no time untying the lead rope from the hitching rail. Unfortunately, waiting for traffic to clear, he was unable to prevent Phoebe from talking.

"Maybe you could come for supper." Phoebe leaned around her husband's considerable girth. "We got lots of cookies at our house for little fellas named Jeremy." She pointed a finger at Jeremy. "Ain't that your name? "

George shook the reins and wedged the buggy into the street traffic.

"Jeremiah George," Ellen called.

"I thought I told you to ignore her!" George fumed.

Phoebe nodded as if agreeing to what a nice day it was.

"You can't cook, you can't keep house. The very least you can do is keep quiet!"

"I thought…"

"…you can't think! The child's a bastard, she's looking for a husband."

"Ain't he a little toughie, he's only three."

George twisted his head back and forth, pulling at his collar to scratch his neck. Nothing made any impression on Phoebe. Nothing at all…but paint. He smiled mirthlessly and, wanting the simpleton to know he hadn't been gulled, said, "The child's part Indian."

"Yep," Phoebe agreed happily. "I told you that."

Maybe she did, George thought. She was always babbling on about something.

"We need more boys in the Valley," Phoebe declared. "Most of the kids are girls."

Most of the children are girls? How does she know that? A herd of untended goats filled the street, kids bouncing about as if on springs. "The apostate is forbidden in my house," George yelled over the bleating and the bells. "If she comes when I'm gone, sack something for the boy and send them away immediately. They are not to come inside."

Not wanting to linger at the Bowery, Ellen waved at Mrs. Jackman and strolled off hand-in-hand with Jeremy. A tall, graceful woman enjoying the company of her good little boy. Observing the pair, who would suspect, on this day so beautifully warmed by soul-stirring sermonizing, that the mother's thoughts moved like angry seas of buffalo.

How far she'd come from the crackling mysteries of the church! The years spent away had reduced it to a glass paperweight she could see into quite clearly, but couldn't return to.

And without faith, she needed Phoebe to hide behind. Making George her only choice if she wished to stay in the Valley.

The churchman would want revenge, claiming it was for God. The more desperate her appeals for reinstatement, the more severe would be the conditions of her return. He must not set those conditions. That left only curiosity. Here was the path he must be turned onto—narrow, ugly trace that it was—the details of the punishment meted out by the heathen Catholics, enough to keep him coming.

Jeremy plucked a hollyhock from a stalk angled through a pole fence and offered the blossom to his mother. Ellen crushed her face against it, forcing herself to smell and feel the petals. The time would come soon enough to dish up memories of the Cimarron Trail, along with her head, on the platter.

N I N E

U ERGIN WAS DRUNK. Rather than navigate the plank walk, he walked beside it. And reaching the stoop, considered what to put down, the flour sack or the Valley Tan. But then he realized the door was open. The room was hot, buckets steamed on the stove.

"Pickled meat, fresh cherries, bread." He hoisted the lumpy sack onto the table and wobbled toward the bed.

Ellen took the bottle out of his hand and smelled it. "How can you drink this awful stuff?"

"It ain't easy." He sat staring at his boots, wishing them off.

Having anticipated drawing out the details of her day, Ellen groaned inwardly. "How do the Virginians like Salt Lake City?"

"More now than they're gonna later. Your Mormon brothers are soaking 'em good."

"I don't suppose Hedrick wants your advice on anything."

"Dogs," Uergin drawled. "Wants to know what'll survive the mountains." He closed his eyes and fell back.

"'Thirty of tha finest hounds ever bred, all lost tae tha rigors of tha trail,'" Ellen parroted Hedrick's honest-enough lament. "What'd you tell him?"

"To ask the Mormons," Uergin told the ceiling.

"You shot 'em, didn't you. Every last one. How come you hate dogs so?"

"I don't hate dogs." He wished she'd be quiet, he was feeling too good to start feeling better. "Don't want 'em chasin'."

"There's wild animals everywhere. What difference does it make?"

"A lot...to the one being chased."

"'Uergin.' What's that? Swedish?"

"Be quiet," he mumbled,

Ellen sat down beside him. "I've been thinking about you, about things I never got around to asking. Pretty soon it'll be too late. You're a nice person, you know that? I'll miss you...Conrad?"

"Hmmmmm? Oh yeah. Swedish. That's it. Good as any." He went to pat her leg and patted the bed instead. She was a nice person too. "Ma married a man hated me. Every time I come in the house, he's saying, 'you again?' My little brothers took to calling me that. 'You Again.'" This last with a whine.

"It sounds like a real sad way to grow up."

"Agggh, shit...they's worse. Got a last name out of it. Spelt it like the man I worked for...spelt it." The words sounded sloppily. He'd soon be asleep.

"Phoebe, bless her heart," Ellen cut to the bare bones of her story, "with no thanks to George, invited Jeremy over for cookies."

"George gonna get his cookies too?"

"If he's good. Are you jealous?"

"Goddamned right," Uergin said sincerely, although he'd already forgotten what they were talking about.

She pulled off his boots and rubbed his feet. "Jeremy's not going with me."

Uergin groaned like a mashed cat. Ellen poked the bed's one pillow under his head, smoothed his temples, and wrapped a curly lock of hair around her finger. Beneath the smells of whiskey and rank cigars was the faint odor of vomit.

"I can't run after two rabbits at once. I'll get everything

nailed down tonight, one way or another." There was no answer. She sat a minute longer, fussing with the threadbare coat collar. It was his good coat. He wore it on the Laramie when he went off to visit the trappers. Now here in Salt Lake.

How many miles have you packed this around, she asked in her thoughts, *wanting to look nice when you got where you were going?* She kissed his ear, his cheek. *I love you, Conrad, You Again. I will always love you. May God, wherever He is, go easy on you wherever you go.*

She filled the wash basin with hot water and unfolded a small wad of cloth. A chunk of soap scented with apple blossoms rolled free—a gift from Dinky, carried all the way from New York. Jeremy was asleep under the table, the leather scrap he carried everywhere, tangled in his bare feet, a serene thoughtfulness on his face. In his sleep, particularly, he was Whonow. And he was in Utah. Exactly where the Cheyenne said he would be.

How did they know?

Undressing next to the stove, Ellen studied what she could see of the city through the further window. The multitude of little adobe houses squatted like blue blocks beneath their haze of wood smoke. The two-story wooden houses, not so many in number, looked like factories, high metal chimneys spewing smoke and dying cinders. Which of these were George's? She made herself concentrate on the tax collector, setting her traps, thinking how they would go.

"What's that all over you?"

She started, knocking the basin. The water popped angrily on the hot stove lids. Uergin had gotten to his feet, a shocked look on his face. The white scars that criss-crossed her breasts and trailed back and forth over her stomach and down her inner thighs shone with a luminous flatness in the soft light. Uergin had never seen her naked in the daylight. Crossing the desert, she'd steadfastly refused to swim with him. It was bad enough that she slept with him under cover of darkness, she'd argued, without rubbing the train's nose in her lack of decency.

Now he knew the truth—her modesty had nothing at all to do with modesty. How careless of her to opt for a spit bath with him in the house, rather than haul the buckets around to the bath house. She grabbed for her clothing, and Uergin grabbed her wrist.

"How'd it happen?" He touched her stomach lightly.

"Jed didn't find me with the Indians, the way I let you think." Ellen closed her eyes, not wanting to see her lizard skin reflected in Uergin's expression. The guide liked beautiful women, liked talking about how much money beautiful women could make him in a bawdy house.

"He found me in New Mexico." Shame made her whisper. "After Whonow died, hide hunters took me there. This is how one of them entertained himself."

"Marry me," Uergin said, holding fast to her wrist.

"No! leave me alone. You smell like a saloon." She was crying.

"How do you know what saloons smell like?" Uergin brushed her cheek with the question, drawing her toward the bed. She pulled the blanket up, but he pushed it aside, his breath warm against her flesh, and kissed the scars, following the colorless tracks around her nipples, down between her legs.

"I honor you, brave Mis'tai, beautiful Mis'tai."

The stove wood cracked, the basin water boiled, dissolving the soap and filling the room with the smell of hot apple pies.

T E N

E VERY SUNDAY MORNING, George's hired man hitched the draft horses to the break and picked up the outside wives for church. After services, the driver returned the wives to their respective residences. Two hours later, he picked them up again, this time for dinner in their husband's home, where the women showered the table with delicacies, all the while indulging in obsequious pleasantries that added immeasurably to George's sense of well being.

Life in the Valley had not always been so pleasant. Constance refused to suffer what she called Brigham's "fixins" in her home, except for Phoebe, who had a function. This selfish obstinacy left George in a quandary. Men suspected of failing to hold complete power at home did not long hold power in the church.

To hide his inability to make his first wife be civil, George found it prudent, as wives three, four, five, six, and seven arrived upon the scene, to find a way to keep them at bay. Which is why each wife had her own house. The huge investment of time and money was finally beginning to show a profit with the rental of guest rooms—a windfall the bishop would like to have trumpeted but did not, fearing Brigham would reward him with another wife.

Never happy, Constance continued to insist that the extra wives sit behind her and George at church. Publicly, George pretended the seating arrangement was his idea, while every night going to his knees to ask God to make the first wife accept the Lord's obligations.

Then, will wonders never cease! Constance, claiming the Bowery reminded her of a rat hole, quit attending services. Thus was George finally able to move his obligations into their proper places.

Would it be too much to ask, he next asked God, to include just one more blessing? Could the outside wives sit at their husband's dinner table?

God told him to lace Constance's Sunday morning coffee with 30 drops of laudanum. Which George did. The burdensome first wife fell immediately into a deep sleep. By that evening she was still asleep, causing her husband considerable consternation. But when she woke Monday morning bright-eyed and sharp-tongued as ever, George knew his problems were over.

Assuming, and rightly so, that Phoebe was as grateful for the peace and quiet as he, George never discussed the weekly dosing with the second wife. Instead, he went out and bought a large, leaf table.

For over a year now the outside wives had been taking their rightful places at Sunday table and afterward assembling for the required work session in the parlor. In addition to the usual prayers and sermonizing, the session enabled George to get through Brigham's latest pronouncements on female behavior—the color of the hair ribbon, the turn of the stocking, the number of petticoats, whatever happened to have crossed the President's mind—in one fell swoop.

By fortuitous coincidence, the session also ruled out entertaining Sabbath walk-about company, the politics of which George hated.

Only in recognizing the importance of his wives did George break with the President. Brigham put his favorite wife at his right elbow. George, in strict observance of the order of marriage and unable to put his first wife on his right, put Phoebe there, the third wife on his left, and so on down the table. There was no particular order at the work session—the women, with the exception of Phoebe, who did not attend, vying with each other to sit in a semicircle at their husband's feet.

Every Sunday evening George met alone with a different outside wife. The purpose of these meetings was to collect rent monies, review housekeeping skills, and hear confession. Each visit was duly recorded on a paper attached inside the front door of the house being visited.

The wife so honored prepared an artful meal and appeared quite happy at first. But then she began to make teary little confessions and air petty grievances. This was particularly true of the older ones. Often they asked for money for personal items— Jersey knit-ribbed drawers, rubber douche bags. Invariably, George found himself eating too much and using God as a wedge to pry loose the intimacies.

He did not have sex with any of the outside wives. One was 66, ten years older than Constance. One had bad teeth and smelled. One, George had married simply as a kindness after her husband abandoned her. One was some relative of Joseph's and, in addition to being extremely vain, had a laugh that would shatter glass.

This is not to say George was not a true Saint. He liked looking at pious females every bit as much as Apostle Heber Kimball, who boasted of being married to 33 of them. And, like Brigham, George had a favorite wife—a virgin made pretty by her youth.

While he saw each of the other outside wives alone only once every five weeks, his virgin he saw privately every week, stopping by her house after Sunday-evening duties elsewhere. She was the only one allowed to entertain him in her bedroom, where, singing home-made church songs, she cavorted in various stages of undress. Anticipation of these late-night tête-à-têtes made what preceded them elsewhere bearable.

That he would not sleep with this particular wife, George told himself, was due to the enjoyment of keeping a vestal virgin. But deep down in his heart of hearts he knew differently. The sex act with anyone other than Constance was immoral. Constance was the woman he had vowed to be true to. In the hereafter he would have to answer for his unfaithfulness with Phoebe, but no one else.

Fortunately, his passions had diminished of late. At first he blamed the virgin. She was pretty, but not at all talented. Then too, there was his terrible workload. This dark night of the soul led ultimately to the truth—he had risen above lust. The church, by making him rich and powerful, had become his real mistress. His life could not be more perfect and still be mortal.

The break arrived in front of the Harris residence at 5 p.m. sharp. Carrying their empty dishes, the outside wives departed in a line down the walk. As usual, the youngest held back, George pinching her uncorseted waist, enjoying her blushes. At this moment, Ellen came through the open yard gate and, standing aside, looked down her nose at the passing parade. Her expression so grated on George that he sent his virgin on and, blocking the steps, asked belligerently, "Where's your son?"

"With Conrad Uergin," Ellen answered cheerily.

"Uergin?"

"He's leading the train I'm with."

"He always was after you." George sneered. "I don't want you here. Go away."

"I came to see Phoebe. To ask her to visit me in California."

"Phoebe? Leave the safety of the Valley?!" The absurdity of the notion made George laugh. "She may be dumb, but she's not stupid! She has everything she needs here." *Which is more than you can say,* he sneered silently. The sun-faded skirt and thin, slightly yellowed shirtwaist with its ruffled collar were hardly acceptable Sunday wear.

"You're afraid she'll leave, aren't you."

"Afraid? I'll ask her myself." George stuck his head inside the front hallway and called loudly, "Phoebe, Mary Magdalene is here."

Sunday was Phoebe's favorite day. Having neither to cook nor serve nor clean up after Sunday dinner, nor to attend work sessions—George's private household expenditures never being discussed in the presence of the outside wives—Phoebe painted. Glorious masterpieces that transported her far beyond the Valley's summer heat and winter drearies. Painted outside, weather permitting, inside otherwise, until the last of the day's light was gone.

This day, anticipating her visit with Ellen and Jeremy, she was almost too excited to paint. But persisted nonetheless, producing a bright object flying shawl-like through the air. She was adding the finishing touches when she heard her husband call. And found him seated beside the cleared dinner table, Ellen standing nearby at loose ends, and no little boy in sight.

"We have a strange request to consider," George explained patronizingly. "Let's have a bite to eat."

Phoebe glared at her husband, at the swollen jowls sagging over the coat collar, the puffy, slightly greasy fingers sticking out like sausages. "Ain't you eating at Zilpha's?"

George acted like he didn't hear. Phoebe marched into the kitchen, yanked plates and cups from the cupboard, marched into the dining room and slammed the heavy china on the clothless table.

She had as much trouble making conversation over the meal as she did serving it. But persisted, as she had earlier with the sail.

Ellen spoke but little, wading into the cold mashed potatoes and sliced meats. George ignored the light-minded talk altogether, until it led, as he knew it would, to painting.

"I'm trying to do a ship," Phoebe lamented. "But it's real hard. I ain't never seen the ocean."

"Then why do it?" George asked.

"I wanna look at the ocean!"

"Where are your paintings?" Ellen glanced around at the bare walls.

"What don't fit in my room has to go in the kitchen, or else outside to the barns." Phoebe turned a wintry stare on her husband, and on the wall's timepiece.

George didn't notice her snit. Picking at his food, he was thinking about Ellen, about how he favored the narrower jaw that marked the better bred. That she refused to meet his eyes came as no surprise. He had that effect on lower-ranking people, particularly women.

"Our deserter thinks you should go to California, Sister Phoebe," he revealed sarcastically.

"Alright."

George was dumbfounded. "YOU ARE NOT GOING TO CALIFORNIA." Food dribbled from his mouth, he wiped at it with his coat sleeve. "Go clean up the kitchen."

Phoebe left the room sniffling, Ellen kept her eyes on the table, hiding their smile. George gazed about petulantly and buttered another roll. If he went off and left the witch alone with Phoebe, he could well return to find his second wife gone. And what would Brigham say about that! Not bothering to hide his irritation, the bishop cleared his throat and rang the table bell, a cleverly converted silver sugar caster.

"It's time, Sister Phoebe," he called. Ellen looked up timidly, and George added a stern command—the words setting the blue cheese caught in his beard to quavering—"I have an important appointment, I'll leave you at the Jackmans on the way."

Moving at a sedate gait, Phoebe returned bearing three goblets and a pitcher of red wine on a tray.

"What are you doing?" George asked heatedly.

The answer, equally heated, matched Phoebe's blotchy face. "You wanted wine." She placed the tray on the table carefully.

"I WANT THE BUGGY SENT AROUND, YOU DUMB COW! You know I have inspection every Sunday evening." Why was she acting so strangely? She was always so docile. It was Ellen. The apostate's very presence was poisoning the house. "Go do as I say, Sister Phoebe. And stop gulping that wine!"

"Come with me," Phoebe begged, taking the words out of Ellen's mouth.

Reaching the safety of the hallway, Ellen whispered, "Don't be in a hurry to order the buggy."

"Oh," Phoebe waved the air with her hand, "I ain't."

In the women's absence, the clock's voice took over. George glanced in that direction and sipped half-heartedly at his wine.

A motley crowd of roiled, thickly painted landscapes jostled each other for space on the kitchen wall. Sooty grease clung cobweb-like to the rough swabbing of paint.

"Well…well," Ellen remarked, moving from picture to picture. The strange outbursts of color, some as large as three feet square, were overwhelmingly ugly. She stepped back into the hall, trying for distance, and bumped into George who, when he didn't hear the screen bang, realized the women had stalled themselves.

"Whoops," Ellen said, grateful for the distraction. "They're just beautiful, Phoebe. You wrote you were painting, but I had no idea…just how much. Shouldn't you get them out of here, though? It's so dirty."

Phoebe lifted a shoulder toward George. "Ask him."

As George had earlier seen the outside wives through the eyes of a Gentile, he now saw his kitchen walls through the eyes of an outsider. And what hideous walls they were! The paint globbed up like mold! Figures with no faces, hands with no fingers, clothing with no buttons, flowers with no stems, mere spills of color for distant scenery. The only thing the blurry mess was good for was fire starter.

Phoebe was telling the stories behind the scenes.

"Get yourself to the barns," George ordered.

Phoebe went on talking, walking about, pointing.

George stomped over to the screen door and opened it. "NOW!"

The artist hustled outside, but not before screwing her face into a bodacious wink.

E L E V E N

IMAGINING THE LOOK on Uergin's face at the pandemonium swirling around her, Ellen slipped away to the dining room to stand at the uncurtained window. George came in flourishing a cigar. When his unwelcome guest failed to look offended at the smoke being blown in her direction, he explained, "I don't smoke in front of ladies, but you aren't one."

Ellen continued to study the high bank of clouds reddening in the last of the light. Sprawled back in his chair, George rubbed his groin and let his eyes drift over the line of shoulder under the thin material, the provocative puckering of fabric at the breast. At one time he would have done anything to have her. Anything, even to leaving his church. He must have been demented.

"Are you still nursing?" he asked with mock coziness.

"No, and I'm not some horse for sale." The tone cool and blank.

"Don't worry," George said with amusement. "I'm not buying, whatever you are."

Phoebe returned and, in the silence, gulped the contents of her goblet and filled it again. "Sit down," she ordered Ellen. "You ain't in no hurry."

"When do you leave?" George asked, gesturing to Phoebe to light the lamps.

Ellen took a chair at the far end of the table. "I'd like to stay and teach. I have a certificate from New York."

"There aren't any Gentile schools here. Besides, I doubt you want a job."

Ellen was watching Phoebe, who was having some trouble lining up the match with the wick.

"Look at me!" George barked. "I think you want a home for your son."

"Of course I do," Ellen observed sweetly, meeting the bishop's gaze briefly. "What mother doesn't? But if I wanted the church to pick my husband, I'd of traveled here with Saints instead of Uergin."

"Uergin's with you?" Phoebe cried.

"Yes, he's with me. It's very comfortable, he doesn't have a wife that hates me." The words sounded of self-pity.

The shriveled cast-off in her lonely upstairs bed laid a withered hand on the table.

George's smile twisted his heavy face. "You are no longer the rose I so foolishly plucked out of Nauvoo. There's nothing I envy Mr. Uergin for, and that includes sleeping with you." Tired of the game, he got to his feet. It crossed his mind that supper was waiting elsewhere, and that he wasn't hungry. "The buggy should be ready."

Phoebe poured herself another drink. "Send it back for Ellen when you get where you're going. Gimme your glass, Ellen."

Ellen quickly offered the glass along with a brave smile. *Ah dear Phoebe, what would I ever do without you to spread the leaves?* She lifted the full glass toward George, her face loose and sharing. He thought she was going to offer a toast. Instead she said, "Will you be late? I have a favor to ask, but it can wait."

The audacity galled him. He glared at Phoebe, that simpleton was like a loose cannon. If he didn't separate the two women soon, there'd be real trouble. "You're leaving with me," he snapped. "Phoebe, go to bed."

Sauntering out of George's sight, Phoebe turned and gave her husband an imaginary kick in the seat of the pants.

George was straightening his tie. He heard Phoebe say, "Come back tomorrow," and heard Ellen answer, "Right after I see General Wells."

Wells! He jerked on the tie and had to loosen it. Why? What would she say to the lawyer? What could she? She was an apostate, for god's sake! It was her word against his.

Watching the churchman struggle to control himself, Ellen winced inwardly. She'd wanted to count coup, not wound.

"What are you seeing him for?"

"To ask for a recommendation."

George stared at her as if she had snakes coming out of her mouth.

"I thought if I could say I'd spoken with you," she said, wishing she'd never mentioned Wells, "that it would help."

"And what do I say when asked?" George asked. The fears were like mosquitoes. Even after he identified the paranoia, the whine remained. He drew on his coat. "That you are weak-willed? You ran away? You have a bastard son, a Gentile lover?" Attacking her, he gained his balance. "You are hardly a virgin, not that Brother Wells will care."

"If Uergin were my lover, I wouldn't be here. As for Jeremy, he's not a bastard. His father and I were married in the Indian way. If he were alive now, I'd be with him. He was a kind, gentle Lamanite."

"What happened?"

"The Mexicans killed him and sold me to a Catholic priest for gold."

"I thought Catholic priests were eunuchs."

"He never touched me."

George made a fist of his hand and blew through it. "The Mexicans did?"

"Yes." Ellen's lips trembled. The yellow light from the nearer lamp tangled itself in the red lights in her hair and lifted the planes of her cheeks. "One of them had a knife, he liked the sight of blood, particularly on the woman he was raping."

George stared down the length of the table, his mind clear as crystal. He knew a game when he saw one. But she was good, very good, he gave her that. And wondered what Wells had given her.

"And now you want to teach our children?"

"Are you suggesting that I am unfit because I know how to please a man?"

"You would learn that I suppose," he said with a knowing leer.

"I had no choice, you've seen the way Mexicans treat their horses. A woman is no different. They expect her to respond to the slightest touch."

George had a mental flash of Mexican riders in paintings— horses white with lather, necks arched, hooves dancing, mouths foaming red from the cruel bits.

"I was a foolish girl when you courted me," Ellen continued slowly, her eyes filling with tears. "You offered me everything, but I didn't know until I dwelled in the house of the Gadiantons how generous your offer was." She leaned forward, hugging herself. "A woman is a vessel, she is made to serve and in service lies her strength. She needs only to be appreciated, as you once appreciated me."

George licked his lips, his hands gripped the arm of his chair. It was only a game. He stared at the shirtwaist, at the ruffled front.

"I will bear the marks all my life," Ellen whispered, lowering her head.

George walked around the table. "Did you say marks? Let me see." His mouth felt cottony.

Ellen hesitated and, unbuttoning the shirtwaist, untied the camisole, the garments slowly opening on the fruits George fully intended to never see again, the nipples appearing at last like large dark cherries. He slid the table lamp near and studied the swollen flesh white as marble, the grotesque designs. At that minute he wanted her so desperately he was sick.

"Put your clothes back on," he said, holding onto the edge of the table with a death grip.

"Now you know," she was redoing the clothing, "why I'm not about to offer myself to anyone. I merely want gainful employment."

George walked to the window. Not seeing his carriage lamps in the darkening street, he resumed his seat and stared at the glint of candlelight on a silver serving spoon.

Ellen thought he'd want to know more about the Mexicans. She was fully prepared to tell more. When he didn't ask, she quartered abruptly. "I never got over the fact you were married. Now you are thrice that and twice more." The pitch grew slightly hysterical.

George shifted his melancholy gaze to the pool of light mottling the pine flooring beneath a wall lamp.

"Why do you hate me?" she asked.

"You are weak and foolish, my dear. I never hated you. I forgive you your sins. And…" the churchman sighed deeply, forgetting what he was going to say next, his gaze still on the floor. He was very tired. After he dropped her off, maybe he'd just come back, forego the evening inspection. He frowned, trying to remember which wife was scheduled.

Ellen hesitated, unsure which of her carefully measured lines to pursue. "It's too late anyway, I see that after meeting with Constance."

"Constance?" George snapped to attention. "What's Constance got to do with this?"

"She's still the first wife."

"She's ill and bedridden! Why are we talking about her?"

"Then Phoebe is the first wife?"

So that was it. George felt himself getting bristly and squeezed his eyes shut. The back of his neck felt as if it were in a vise. What a petty little maneuver! Ellen complained to Wells of Constance's treatment of her, and Wells went straight to Brigham with the gossip. Now Ellen was to be used to remind the bishop of Phoebe's dereliction to duty.

It never ended. The President didn't like it that Phoebe didn't attend the Ladies Aid planning sessions or the sewing circles that met in the Beehive. More than once he'd ordered George to raise Phoebe's presence in the community.

A bottomless sadness eddied through George. How contemptible of Ellen to pass herself off as Phoebe's friend. Was there no one they could trust? Not that he'd trusted Ellen, not for a minute. But Phoebe did. She called Ellen her sister. Poor Phoebe. She hadn't an ounce of guile in her heart. They'd pick her to shreds. *Over my dead body!* he reassured himself. *I'll leave the church before I let that happen.*

"Who do you confide in?" Ellen breathed. And realized immediately the game was over. George's hand above the sugar caster was shaking. He was going to throw it. Her face widened in surprise.

"Get out! Now!" George growled. "You rooked me, you snide little witch. My wives are not your concern and never…"

"…neither is the number, but I would have to be first."

The churchman wondered if he'd heard right. He stilled his hand by resting it on the caster.

"I will live here with you and Phoebe," Ellen said, blindly

pursuing the chase, instincts screaming. "Constance will be sent away."

"What are you talking about?"

"My presence here would kill her."

Now what was happening? George wondered. Did Brigham actually think he could force his bishop to marry this stained woman? Was having a spy in the Harris household *that* important? "You lived too long with the savages. Isn't that what they do, send their old people off?"

"Constance will have someone to care for her, whoever you pick."

"How generous of you. It so happens I've already picked Phoebe, or didn't you notice?" George pushed himself to his feet and walked out of the room.

Ellen heard the back screen door bang and sat hands laced behind her neck. She was having trouble remembering her ground. It was the wine. George's glass was half-empty. She refilled it with the contents of her own, Uergin's words about the cards the Mormons held turning over in her mind.

George found her sitting where he'd left her, hands clasped together on the table. Ignoring his chair for one nearer, he took the badly chapped hands in his own.

"You are not my keeper, you are not my wives' keeper. General Wells is not my friend. I want you to tell me the truth. Where did you get the idea to send Constance off and be my first wife?"

"I'm not about to marry you and live somewhere else, like the others do."

"I'm not asking you to marry me." He pushed his thumb against her forehead in a familiar gesture of benediction. "I could have you arrested right now for attempting to corrupt Church Authority. I'm not going to do that. I'll give you enough money to get you safely away on the coach to California, on condition that you don't come back. Believe me, you must not pursue this madness. You will not be allowed to wander loose in Zion, as you did in Nauvoo. You will be watched every minute of every day, and when you are no longer of any use, you will simply disappear."

Ordinarily he listened to his voice—such a fine voice, heavy, authoritative, full of knowledge and self-discipline. But now, deeply aware that he himself, not Phoebe, might be the target, he concentrated solely on the face of the woman before him.

"It is important that I know who sent you and how much you were paid."

"As God as my witness, no one."

"Where did you get the idea I would marry you?"

Ellen stared at the tin ceiling, feeling as if she were up to her neck in muddy water. "My son is meant to be in Utah, it's prophesied by the Indians." She was completely off the pace. Even in her own ears the words sounded like a highfalutin' lie.

"That's marvelous!" George exclaimed, entertained despite himself. "By the Indians. Mmmmm."

Angry at herself, Ellen struck viciously at a gnat that settled on her neck.

"But why me?" George asked. "The Valley's full of younger men who'd be glad to overlook your nasty indiscretions in the interest of saving your soul."

"I'm not a believer anymore. I need Phoebe. She would never betray me."

"'Betray.' Mmmm, that's an interesting word. Who would she betray you to?"

"Whoever it is you're afraid of."

"I'm not afraid of anyone." He felt better just saying it. "What exactly did you tell Wells?"

Yes, you are afraid.

As a child in Nauvoo, she'd been aware of a deep distrust in all the houses, not only of the outside world but of the neighbor behind the curtain. Now it was as if she herself stood behind that curtain. "I didn't talk to Wells. Mrs. Jackman pointed him out today at church. She called him 'a real swordsman.' I thought telling you would make you jealous."

"What else did you and Sister Jackman talk about?"

"Not about anything that amounted to anything. I asked about Phoebe…"

"…what about Phoebe?"

"…the address."

"You have the address. You've been writing her for years."

"I was just fishing. I was trying to find out something about you, but I never told her I knew you."

The confession felt like the truth to George. And if so, then it was a pretty amazing story when he stopped to think about it. He was old and fat. He didn't even pick his virgin bride. Brigham did that.

This talk of sending Constance away, it could have come from Ellen's having lived in New York. As a matter of fact, it probably did. Not only was she selling herself, she was negotiating the terms like some damn Yankee peddler!

George felt a tinge of unworthiness as a Saint in passing so quickly from judging to acceptance. But remembering Joseph's words—"that which is wrong under one circumstance may be, and often is, right under another"—felt immediately better. And why in the name of all that was holy hadn't it occurred to him to send Constance off to another house?

He relaxed and, keeping his face closed, let himself feel the nearness of the sinner. She smelled cleaner than she had earlier—like apples. The clothes she wore now she'd probably worn out on the prairie in the sun. She'd come all the way from New York. For him? Surely not for him. Yet here she was, insisting it was so. After all these years, after all the other men. He wondered how many men, but didn't really want to know.

"You were going to seduce me with the Mexican story."
Needing some distance, George rose and retreated to the end of
the table where he finished his wine. "And then remind me of
church law, that adultery is a sin."

"Yes." What was that in his voice? Ellen closed her eyes
briefly, trying to relax.

"Why did you run away from me in the first place?"

"Constance said you took a vote and decided I was to stay at
the fort."

George wasn't surprised. He'd always suspected something
like that. Constance was afraid of Ellen, and why shouldn't she
be? She must have known, for all his talk of obeying religious
orders, that what her husband was really doing was falling in
love. Of a sudden he felt very old, and too timid.

Carriage lamps drew up, glowing faintly in the evening mist.
Getting to his feet, George closed the shutters against the night
air and considered Ellen. She was sitting stone-faced, staring at
the table, waiting, he realized, to be dismissed.

Barren women were the curse of his life. How many times
he'd prayed for children! Was God sending this woman back in
answer to his prayers? Brigham liked to chuck pregnant women
under the chin and say, "Give me a son to match my mountains."
Well, by god! here was a woman to match those damn mountains!
Her professed lack of faith was probably a sincere enough confession. Women, once given an audience, were likely to confess
anything. They were natural pretenders and often deceived
themselves. All this wild goose really needed was a real home
and a firm hand, and there'd be nothing to confess at all.

He wasn't afraid of her. That was silly. Sometimes his thinking fogged up like that. She wasn't Brigham's foil. She was his
own doing. He'd approached her when she wasn't ready, and
scared her. Now she was back, looking for his protection. She
had more courage than he did—good Lord! that's for sure—to

think they could take up where they left off, just like nothing had happened.

Those who sow generously shall reap generously. She had one child, she could have others.

"Don't ever tell me the Mexican story," he said, and he meant it.

"Never." She was totally unprepared for what happened next.

He was walking around the table. "You were going to seduce me." Now he was chucking her under the chin. "Do you know other ways? Show me."

"Conrad! Wake up. I've come for Jeremy."

Uergin rolled over, reaching for her. "You got everything you want?"

"Everything! Jeremiah will be his son. I will be the first wife."

He could hear the triumph in her voice. She was laughing and kissing him.

"George get everything he wants?"

"Not yet. He will. It's the least I can do." She jumped up and began packing Jeremy's things, the candle on the table flaring wildly in the rush of her skirts. "The buggy's waiting, I have to hurry, before he changes his mind. He's gotten old, Conrad, and afraid of his shadow."

"Remember what I told you," Uergin warned. "You marry for money, you earn every penny."

"I know, sweetheart, I know. But I can't be afraid to win. You told me that too."

Uergin yawned mightily and sat up. "Wear that fancy I give you, for good luck."

"It's too gaudy," Ellen protested and was appalled at her thoughtlessness. Throwing open the traveling bag, she located the turquoise necklace and sat patiently for Uergin to hook it. When he was done, she kissed him again and rushed outside with the bag.

Jeremy was half-awake, watching his mother. Uergin uncovered a foot and smoothed the small instep. "Don't ever forget where you come from, Little White Bear. Whatever's out there, it's in you too, remember that. Every time you see the eagle spread against the sky, remember he's your brother."

Ellen came back and leaned close. Uergin could feel the elation, the soaring circling. "So long, easy money," he kissed her, a slow, lingering kiss, wanting it to last a lifetime, "don't take any wooden nickels."

T W E L V E

F IVE YEARS LATER, AUTUMN 1855, Molunkus, Maine.
Fraud Shoch was deaf as a post. Fifty-nine years he'd
lived in the woods and never heard a tree fall. He never
heard young Tufts tell him to step back inside the store. The
coroner said he never felt the bullet. But Fraud heard the tin
cans hit the wooden porch and roll away, and they sounded just
like he always thought tin cans would.

No one else appeared on the street, and the three bank
robbers rode away without firing another shot. In a lonely cabin
five miles above Molunkus, at the northernmost tip of the lake,
a rat explored the floor in nervous starts and stops. The yellow
tail hanging from the windowsill flicked, and the cat went back
to sleep.

Dawn the next morning the sheriff took 12 men out, among
them an ax man—a bean-pole youth with a thin braid of light
brown hair who had ridden into Molunkus the previous evening
looking for Fraud. The posse caught up with the thieves in
Mattawamkeag, routed young Tufts from a gin's bed and filled
him full of holes.

The renegade Ottawa who rode with Tufts disappeared on
foot into a tract of heavy timber recently felled and burned over.
The trees lay like burnt matches, helter-skelter behind grey slats
of slow-moving smoke. The sheriff took one look at the deadly
maze and went home.

Three hours later the Ottawa broke through the smoky silence to a tote road and made off at a dogtrot for the Wytopitlock. Midday they shot a red squirrel that, dying, wedged itself in a high fork of a linden tree. The Indian who climbed to retrieve the bloody meal hooked his arm over a limb and swung around to study the countryside. That's when he caught a glimpse of the man approaching on foot.

Near the tree where the squirrel died, the Indian sign disappeared.

The ax man made a circle, another larger circle, and realizing he'd been spotted, took out at a stiff walk. The road reached a large clearing drained of all but crooked and young trees. Here the ax man felt fairly safe. Indians were too much in awe of their rifles, and ammunition too dear, to learn how to shoot quickly and accurately at any great distance. When it came to dispatching an enemy, they favored the short broadside in black timber.

On the far side of the clearing, the road dropped off through low, water-worn boulders into uncut pine. The ax man entered the trees and folded himself against a mossy outcropping hollowed out by an ancient, unrecorded river.

The Ottawa, seeing the white man leave the clearing, circled around to wait further along the road. And tiring of waiting, went looking.

The hours sifted by. In the shadowless light at the edge of dusk, a crab-like sound scraped the rock above the ax man's head. An Indian made himself comfortable, bare feet dangling over the ledge. A soft hoot-owl cry floated up and was answered in the distance. Night was in the trees when the second Indian stepped into the open. On an unseen lake a loon was laughing.

The second Indian looked at the rock, and the surprise on his face died away in the roar of gunfire. The ax man rolled free, turned and fired again.

It took the ax man a day to walk back to Mattawamkeag, get his horse and ride around the burn to retrieve the renegades. Three days later he was in Molunkus. The village was quiet as a graveyard. He dumped the bodies by the jail and led his horse over to the livery. His squaw's horse was there and the squaw snugged down in the hay waiting. She didn't ask if the hunting were good, and he didn't say.

The next morning the sheriff handed over $50 in reward money and a crudely-carved, four-inch wooden crucifix on a leather string. "Lookee here on the back," the sheriff said. "Ain't that how you spell your name? It was on one of them bucks."

The ax man studied the crucifix. He'd noticed the ornament, but hadn't paid any attention. Now the letters M A R C H I O N, carved the length of the wood, jumped out at him. "Where are they?" he asked.

"Behind the junk pile."

The bodies under the wagon canvas were starting to smell. Jed took a good look at the dark, frozen faces and dropped the canvas.

Outside the public house, a squaw wearing a Mackinac blanket around her shoulders and baggy man's pants beneath her leather skirt, was making a show of studying the Treaty Day posters. Big pieces of paper meant celebration, celebration meant dancing. Jed walked by, and she backed up, bumping into him. She'd lost a front tooth, and the grin she turned on her husband looked jack-o-lanternish.

"We dance."

Ignoring the woman, Jed took a table in the public house and ordered a cup of tea, which was served with the usual scoffing smile. He and Fraud had spent the better part of their summer

searching the north woods for a suitable blossom of white pine.
What they found wasn't tip-top—not the giant 160-foot King's
Arrow pines Fraud liked to remember as measuring six feet
through at the base—but a vein of 130-footers easily worth $80
in the log at the Bangor boom in Oldtown.

They had the necessary permit made out to Shoch and
Marchion with the contract price set at $3/1,000 board feet.
They had good men lined up with oxen and supplies. What they
didn't have now was each other.

Staring absently at the grainy alcohol, the ax man swore
softly. Damn Fraud's fuckin' one-eyed cat for running off at the
last minute. "Need some extra canned goods," Fraud had stalled.
"Got to go to town."

The squaw took a nearby chair. Jed gave her the same unseeing stare he gave the tea. He would need extra choppers now, to
free him to run the crews, along with a good dose of damn good
luck.

Mouse looked down shyly, pleased by his jealousy.

They went to the dance and got roaring drunk and whooped
it up. Jed hired two extra choppers and roostered around and got
in a terrible knock-down, drag-out. At 4 a.m. Mouse towed him
back to the livery.

The bleary-eyed men from New Brunswick, who claimed to
have worked on the Woolastook, showed up a couple of hours
later. Taking their measure in the daylight, Jed figured he hadn't
hurt himself. He and Mouse were saddling their horses when the
livery boy came in and began wiping down the funeral wagon.

"Gettin' pretty fancy for a couple of renegades ain't you?" Jed
asked idly.

"It's for the parade. 'Sides, some Injun come and got them
bucks. Said they was his brothers."

"Brothers?"

"You know how it is with Injuns."

"Which way'd he go?"

"Toward Macwahoe."

Jed bought a dollar blanket from the general store, took the blanket and Fraud's horse to the undertaker, where he wrapped and loaded the body, and sent the grisly load off to the cabin above Molunkus Lake with Mouse and the choppers. This unpleasant business done, he rode out the east road at a lope.

His head pounded. One of his eyes was swollen shut. Four years he'd worked with Fraud in a partnership where he kept the books and Fraud ran the crews. Now the whole fucking load was his—Fraud's 30 years experience as principal in charge of lumber camps in New England and Canada gone like smoke up the stove.

And what was he doing about it? Already three days behind the calendar? Chasing after a goddamned redskin! that's what! He was as bad as Fraud with Yellow Cat.

Arguing with himself, he came up on a thin grey horse heavily blanketed and weighed down with the dead renegades and a pile of empty sacks.

The outfit stank to high heaven of fish dried with fox grapes. Leading the horse was a barefoot Indian. The Indian's military-issue shirt and black leather cap had seen better days, as had his leather britches, held up with a rope over the shoulder. His hair was bobbed off, and he wore his cap at a rakish angle. A slight man who, moving aside for the road traffic, paid no attention to that traffic until finding his way blocked.

Jed stared intently into the shrewd, patient face. The man was one of those people his pa called the *métis*, the half-breeds.

I'll be go to hell! you really could be my brother. Jesus! you look more like pa even than Walker. Now what do we do?

The Indian was a patient man. But the sun was hot. He led his horse around the white man's.

Jed didn't know whether to claim kinship or ride off. As a

little boy, he'd prayed for Indians to sneak out of the woods and scalp Walker. Eventually, through his father's stories, it dawned on him that his own father had Indian children. From then on, he'd kept an eye out. Believing, not believing.

He rode in front of the Indian a second time and slid out of the saddle.

"Your brothers had this." Mixing rough pidgin English with sign, Jed handed the Indian the cross. "See the marks, this is my father's name. His name was Marchion. He was a trapper and a trader."

The Indian considered the scratches and placed the object's leather string around his neck. That he knew a little English he didn't let on, not wanting to be bothered.

"You want work in the timber this winter?" Jed asked. "At the top of Molunkus Lake is my cabin. I leave tomorrow morning for the Penobscot. From there we go upriver by boat. I supply food and tools."

Again the Indian led his horse around the white man's horse and walked on, walked on with the same rolling gait that marked every Marchion Jed ever knew.

Aches and pains vanished, Jed watched him go. Holy shit! Come next summer, they'd have to do a little fishing, a little hunting, get to know each other. "So long," he called in English.

The Indian did not look back. The white man was young and arrogant in the way white men were. Did he want the Indian to buy the cross with work? It wasn't clear and it wasn't important. The Indian would not work for a white man, particularly now that he was so rich.

Not only had he traded his fish for heavy winter blankets, but also the labor of his sway-backed horse for a handful of silver coins. The Molunkus magistrate, recognizing him for an Ottawa, had paid him the coins to take the renegades back to their tribe as a lesson to would-be thieves. Hauling the dead men did not trouble the Indian. These men were lost a long time ago, running like wolves who hunt only for themselves.

He fingered the cross tentatively. It was once owned by Round Stone, a great Ottawa chief. As the owner of the sacred object, Round Stone ignored insult and danger because of the greater responsibility of letting the power of the cross work through him. Tiring of the responsibility, the chief chose a successor who was obliged to pay heavily for the honor. In this fashion had the cross been owned by many brave men. The renegades must have stolen it.

The sun beat down. The smells of the empty sacks and the dead men pooled like incense around the Indian's head. His shoulders began to ache. He took off the cross and tied it to the horse's bridle. Still, he could feel its nearness, and his thoughts, like his shoulders, grew heavy.

Once upon a time a long time ago, far beyond the setting sun in a distant, cold land, over 100 Ottawa families banded together to follow the ancient trail through the eastward mountains. These families were drawn by the stories heard of the good life enjoyed by the people to the east, the people of the dawn. The ancient trail took the Ottawa into the low, swampy ground of the Allagaskwigamook and down that little river into the fish-spearing-stream.

The coming-to-a-new-land-day held sad surprises. The much-storied people of the dawn did not display warm clothing, there was no welcoming feast. The Abnaki confederacy had grown blind and sore-footed like an old camp dog kicked away from the fires to starve out in the darkness.

Even so, keeping to themselves, the Ottawa made a good life in their new country. This is where Yam was born, beside a lake so big that as a boy, traveling around the lake with his father, it took all the summer moons. He was 10 years old before he saw a

white man. But by the time he was married, there seemed
nowhere that the smoke from the white men's campfires was not
drifting through the trees.

The years went by, the Ottawa grew lonely and ill. No longer
did they sing and dance. The deaths of their warriors were
covered in silence. Even in summer, food was short. With the
white men living amongst them, the Ottawa learned the white
man's ways. But this caused more problems than it solved.

Walking along, drowning in sorrow, the Indian mourned the
loss of his mother, whom he had never known. Mourned also
the lost of his old wife, who died leaving him with no children.
A restless man by nature, but not a melancholy man, he decided
to thank the sacred object for such as he did have—a new,
young wife who was good to him, new blankets, and silver coins.

It was with great relief that the Indian reached his village.
His wife was happy to see him. The renegades went off with
their relatives to be buried in the woods under stones, and the
sacred object went off to the story teller.

"The white man wanted nothing for it?" the story teller asked
wonderingly. An old man with no teeth and cloudy eyes, blowing
softly on the cross and polishing it with his spit.

"Nothing." The Indian sidled away.

The story teller called him back. "The spirit that lives in the
wood is leaving our people. The journey is long and difficult."

The words made the Indian's neck prickle. "I am not going
anywhere," he replied.

"Maybe not, my friend." The old man shrugged and gave
back the sacred object. "But two men are dead. You must ask
Great Father Above why."

And that is the story, simply put, of how the brothers
Marchion came to go into the lumber business together. It is a
story easier told than lived. Not only did it take a white man

crazy enough to claim kinship with an Indian, it took an Indian more afraid of Great Father Above than of white man's work.

When the Indian told his new wife of his decision to take the winter work, the wife, her parents and aged grandmother prepared to accompany him. Early the next morning the rag-tag band and their pack dogs walked through the forest wall out into the clearing that held Fraud's cabin and a fresh grave.

Jed was putting a rope on the milk cow that was to be exchanged for the horses' keep through the winter. He had completely overlooked the possibility of the Indian's showing up. Much less with a family. He tied the cow to a post and felt in his pocket for Fraud's poke. The poke was half-full of gold nuggets, the company's hedge against low prices at the boom.

"I made a mistake," he said, offering one of the nuggets. "This will see you through the winter."

Having no tobacco of his own, the Indian had hoped to learn of the white man's work with smoke from the white man's calumet. Hiding his disappointment, he put a finger in the air reprovingly and began to speak in a polite, earnest way, his hands filling the spaces between his words.

"I am an honorable man. I will send my wife home. It will be easier if she has the cow." He made no move to take the nugget.

Jed's amusement gave way to irritation. "No, I'm not doing that. Now you go home."

The loud words, the pointing at the trees, puzzled the Indian. Yesterday this boy offered work. Today he didn't. There was no understanding white men.

Checked by a familiarity in the other's expression, Jed turned away and kicked a stone against the sky. For crying out loud! he'd offered the fellow a job. Pocketing the poke, he gestured at the cow.

The Indian spoke softly with his wife. A brief argument erupted. The squaw walked over to the cow, untied the rope, and led it off. The Indian gave the cottony call of a mourning dove as the woman neared the trees, but none of the Ottawa looked back at the man who had traded a cow for his freedom.

Jed and the choppers were loading the horses. The Indian wandered into the cabin. A movement on the wall caught his eye. He backed up and looked into the mirror, seeing the whole of his face for the first time—a dark, angular face with a broad nose made uneven by a scar. He touched the knotted flesh, remembering a bad fall and a torn nostril.

A shabby-hided, one-eyed yellow cat brushed his leg.

The Indian sucked in his breath. A white man with a bad eye, a cat with no eye. The signs were not good.

Jed's squaw came in, picked up the cat and stuffed it into a small willow basket. She carried the basket outside, and the Indian followed.

T H I R T E E N

IS NAME WAS YELLOW APPLE. Jed called him Yam. There was no talk of wages and very little talk of anything else. Near the junction of the Little Salmon Stream with the Penobscot, the farmer anticipating the milk cow got his pick of the company horses instead. Jed sweetened the pot with $50, and the farmer stopped grumbling.

The company transferred their goods to a bateau and a birch canoe and set off up the Penobscot towing the birch. At the fork they took the west branch. Seven days later, having crossed Seboomook Lake and followed the curve of the river in a northerly direction, they reached the mouth of the Abacotnetic. Jed climbed a tall pine easily visible to the upriver traveler and, chopping the trunk in half, laid over the top 20 feet.

Turning up the Abacotnetic, they came at length to where Fraud's crude scarecrow waited—a hacked-up cedar draped with the deaf man's blanket. A second tree top was laid over here, and the boats stashed upside-down in the undergrowth.

On foot, the company followed up a northwesterly brook to where, three miles above the Abacotnetic, a dying spruce rose rich red against the dark pine The spruce marked the spot where the brook came closest to the timber vein.

In the nearby woods, the men measured their campsite, removed the mat of forest floor, and felled and measured the trees. The shelter came together in a tin baker of a cabin—eight feet high in the front wall, less than three feet in the back.

The crevices between the notched logs were chinked with tree moss, and the pole roof overlaid with slabs, then boughs. Foot poles strung string-like on the dirt marked off the kitchen, dining room, and common sleeping area. The only privacy was in the corner of the kitchen behind the blanket that curtained off Mouse and Jed's bed.

The oxen's hovel was next. Walls and roof plastered over with clay and manure to keep the beasts warm, a flooring of small poles laid tightly side-by-side and smoothed with the adze to keep them dry.

The last thing to be engineered before winter was the most difficult—a pond wide and deep enough to carry the harvest down to the Abacotnetic. A mile downstream of the cabin, the brook made a short, steep drop into a marsh a good half-mile wide. The trees at the edge of the marsh were timbered, and the timber used to built a dam below the marsh. By the time the dam's uprights were in place and fitted with gates, the forest's leaf trees were bare and the daily rains were becoming snow showers.

The crew hired by Fraud showed up—eight farmers from around Cold Stream Pond with their oxen. Jed set the choppers and Yam to swamping out a twitching path from the camp through to where the first cut would be made, and took the farmers up to look over the vein.

Yam was in camp skinning a moose when Jed returned. "I can not make roads to kill the standing people," the Indian explained haltingly. "I will hunt and feed the animals.

"Shit! my cook takes care of the livestock," Jed said angrily. "And we got all the meat we need, hanging. Now, by god! you'll do something 'sides hunt. If you don't wanna chop, you can bark or swamp, I don't give a damn. But you gotta pull your share of the load if you wanna eat in this camp."

Clouds drifted over the sun, tiny balls of snow dusted the ground. Jed went up to inspect the twitching path and came back to find Yam, white with snow, sitting in front of a small fire in the cabin clearing.

An unexpected melancholy flooded Jed's senses. He didn't make friends easily. Uergin in '46 along the Oregon Trail. Fraud, whom he went to work for in '50. That was it. In taking up with Yam, he realized how much he wanted a brother that didn't hate him. And they *were* brothers, there was no denying it. Yam had their father's face, his build, his rolling gait, even the same way of pulling at his chin. But Jesus! it was no good.

Hunkering beside the fire, Jed lit his pipe and handed it over. "You are my brother. We have another brother. His name is Walker. He lives to the south a long ways down a big river. We have a sister. Her name is Dinky. Our father, my father, your father, lived in the woods a lot. He liked Indians. He died alone on the Fort Edward Road. He was taking apples to market."

Yam knew differently. He had seen his father die on the hides in a rock shelter. That he himself did not look like a full-blood Ottawa was because his mother was Seneca. She died in childbirth with her second child. He started to speak of these things, but Jed was getting to his feet.

"Take the birch and go home while the river's still open, our father will understand." Jed threw a pitch knot on the fire, raising a scarf of black smoke, and went in the cabin. "Yam is leaving," he told Mouse. "Fix him some food."

As soon as her husband was gone, Mouse went out to sit bareheaded in the storm with Yam. "If you leave, brother, I'll be sorry."

"I can't cut down the trees," Yam answered, staring grim-faced at the ground.

Mouse put her shoulder against Yam's shoulder. Snow prickled their faces. "If you stay, you can tell the standing people what's happening." She slid a branch of burning wood deeper into the flames. "They'll listen to you and not be afraid to travel down the river and see many new things."

Yam laced his long fingers together and began to talk in words Mouse didn't understand. Out of respect, the squaw rose and went through the slanting curtain of snow to the cabin. It was good for brother to be alone, it was hard for an Indian to pray in a white man's camp. White men never prayed. Late that afternoon, Jed saw an extra man working with the barkers, the cutting spade moving with hatchet-like awkwardness.

The chill and dark damp grew steadily worse, the storms more intense. Like beetles, the choppers burrowed into the vein, taking every tree above 80 feet. Leaving the false-hearted behind on the ground. Two and three at a time the white pine came down—tap, tap, tapping the sky, spilling veils of snow from the upper boughs in a death dance that ended in glorious explosions of white powder.

Behind the choppers came the barkers, strewing deep carpets of green finery in their wake. Preparing the base of the trees for a smooth drag, Yam promised each of the people-no-longer-standing a safe journey with new things to see.

Deeper and deeper grew the cushioning snow, easing the drag down the twitching paths to the road that led to the landing. On the landing, the trees were cut in 16-foot lengths and piled in rows. The snow drifted over the rows, tucking them in.

The end of December, and all that could be seen of the cabin under the white overhang was the door. The deeper the snow, the warmer the shelter. The warmer the shelter, the worse the food. Overcooked meat, undercooked potatoes, doughy pies, gravies that tasted like jelly.

Plainly the cook wasn't happy. Mouse couldn't keep her eyes off Yam's face, her hands off his shoulders. Yam ignored her, and she took to washing and mending his clothes.

Plainly the cook was sleeping with the wrong man.

Speaking privately with their employer, the Cold Stream farmers suggested a swap. Jed did nothing. Tokens began appearing under Yam's pillow—a pretty stone and the next night a feather. The following day the Indian came in early from the woods.

"You're pleasing to look at and your temper is good," he told Mouse. "But you can not have two husbands." He held her wrist as he spoke, preventing her from crowding against him. "If you don't behave, I'll leave this camp."

"I come too," Mouse moaned.

"I'll tie you and bring you back," Yam promised grimly and, having spoken what was right, returned to work. This was not easy. It was a long time since he'd had a woman. Trudging through the snow, he fell into a wonderful plan.

Jed was with the ox teams repairing a chain when Yam approached. "I want to buy something of great value from you," the Indian said. Removing his hat, he pulled the leather thong over his head. "The Malicite woman for the sacred object that belongs to your father. This will give you strength to live with the insult."

Jed worked a frozen glove off with his teeth and palmed the worn wood with great affection. The Indians thought there was something magic in the cross. Maybe there was. It was enough for him that his own father had carved it in the mysterious magical days of his father's youth. He made his face indignant.

"What am I supposed to do for a cook?"

Relieved that there was no mention of love, Yam answered, "She can work for you."

"I paid a good horse for her."

"The sacred object is worth more than one horse." Closing his eyes, Yam made a little prayer of good-bye to the wood spirit.

"Keep your cross, I'll take $30 out of your wages."

Yam's face opened wide. *But I do not want the cross!* Fear of being struck dead kept him from speaking thus aloud.

That night Jed found his blankets folded neatly on the fir boughs of the common bed and, looking around, realized Yam had retired early to the privacy of the kitchen's blanketed-off room.

Outside of missing a woman, Jed had few regrets. He didn't need that kind of tension in the cabin, and Mouse needed to get her mind back on her cooking. It couldn't be easy at best for Indians to follow the white man's way. Not that he himself had much first-hand knowledge of Indian life, but Ellen did, after living a year on the prairie with the Cheyenne.

He thought a lot about Ellen. Oh, not a lot at one time, just a lot of bits and pieces, chinking up the empty places. God! but she was hard-headed. Going to raise little Jeremiah to be a redskin in a white man's world come hell or high water. There were times, overhearing the crew talk about their families with real longing in their voices, he wondered that he didn't miss her more. Maybe Yam had something to do with that.

Would Yam stick with him? They were more alike than not. They thought alike and, insofar as they understood what the other was seeing, they reacted alike. But in all fairness, he should have given more thought to Yam's place in the scheme of things before offering the Indian work. Logging was a young man's game. What saved Yam's bacon was his sociability. The crew, all of them younger, called him "chief" and kept an eye on him in the woods, bringing him on as they themselves had been brought on by experienced loggers.

"Just how old are you?" a Cold Stream farmer asked one evening after a particularly hard day, the temperatures below zero and fresh snow fine as powder choking the main drag.

"I was born the year of no summer," Yam replied. The exchange surprised Jed who, thinking Indians didn't know their age, had never asked.

"That was 1816," the farmer said. "That makes you...39. I'd of swore you was older."

"I am now!" Yam cried and the whole room laughed.

Warmed by the memory, Jed slept.

Supper was the main meal of the day. The food, except for varying between salt fish and venison, was always the same— potatoes and bread sopped in pork fat, Dutch-oven beans sweetened with molasses, meat pies, dried apple pies, the whole washed down with coffee and tea.

Columns of knife marks advanced the days down the inside wall. Ten fresh cuts signaled a party. Mouse fried doughnuts, Jed uncorked the wine, and Yam made his inevitable speech, rising from the deacon seat, drink in hand, to announce, "I am Yellow Apple. I am master barker and loader. Inside this house, no fighting, every jack remember. Now please the party begin."

They polished off half a barrel of doughnuts, coined match songs, stretched stories, and danced crazily about like grasshop- pers—the excitement never failing to unleash in Mouse wild mumbo-jumbo war chants that could cause Yam to look at her in disbelief and Yellow Cat to run and hide.

Thus did the occupants of the tin baker, with the great wolves howling outside the door and the dark, torn woods drifted deep with snow, ease their minds of the long winter's gloom.

The last of March brought the first thaw. With winter's icy

grip loosened, trickles became freshets, then rivers. Behind its dam, the brook widened into a narrow lake that slowly but surely backed itself up. With each day's new offering of brook water the surface of the lake rose, freezing over at night to become increasingly lumpy and ridged. When the rising water reached the landing, a lane was chopped through the ice the length of the lake.

Like beached, snow-covered whales, the logs were dragged one by one across the landing and wrestled bumping and thumping down the chute. Hitting the water, choppy with broken ice, they bobbed up black and glistening—the brand, S M 34 for Shoch Marchion Camp 34, showing clear on the butt. Next they were herded into the lane, becoming part of a long line of logs being nudged along toward the front of the dam.

The brutal, dangerous work of clearing the landing went on hour after hour, day after day without let-up, the men working in the water beneath the chute having the worst of it all. Every few minutes they needed to be helped onto a log, there to thump and rub their arms and stamp their feet to bring back the circulation.

In eight days the entire surface of the lake was a rough, gently bobbing floor of timber. The harvest was ready, but that night the temperature fell like a rock. Encased in ice, the logs no longer bobbed.

For three days the bitter cold held on, then a feathery snow began to fall. Under its down comforter, the lake ice grew mushy. Jed waited two more days and, with the snow a foot deep on the ice, opened the gates. There was a sound like a squirrel chattering, and then the pines were breaking free with an enormous boom, boom, booming of smothered thunder.

That stopped abruptly.

A wadding of ice and logs, catching a corner post of the dam, blocked the channel. The water poured free, leaving its precious harvest behind. Drenched in icy spray, the men fought back, using heavy pries, hand pikes, and cant dogs, uprooting the dam's corner post and dodging for cover. With a mighty whoosh, the logs scampered free, this time for good. Bouncing, caroming, scooting down the brook's lower shoals, headed for the Abacotnetic two miles distant.

Tools in hand, the loggers followed, slipping and sliding over and around boulders, crashing through branches heavy with snow, pushing at the wash of logs to keep the water doing its work. Shepherds and their sheep.

When the last of the drive reached the Abacotnetic, the Cold Stream farmers turned back to put the camp together. They would take Mouse and the Marchion bateau with them as far as Little Salmon junction. Jed and Yam and the Woolastook choppers, packs stowed in the birch, would stay with the drive.

On the Abacotnetic, Jed offered Yam the birch, but the Indian choose to ride the logs, keeping near the bank where he could jump to safety. As a boy, he had ridden logs for fun—old, water-soaked logs, their broken branches catching on everything. These logs were different. Green and limbed, riding high in the water and rolling mindlessly.

The first of the Marchion cut reached the Penobscot, jousting and shouldering its way into the rumbling race. Moving like a water skipper across the writhing floor, Jed joined the crews making common cause of the driving operation.

When Yam reached the Penobscot, his preoccupation with his new occupation suffered a serious setback. The sight of the timber-bloated river so paralyzed him that he lost his footing and straddled a log. Before he had the presence of mind to get back on his feet, he was hit, first on one shin then the other, by the neighboring logs. Badly skinned, he forced himself upright and made his way back to shore.

On both sides of the river, men worked to clean the coves and bump the logs away from pinching up against the banks. But Yam, brooding over the terrible war going on between the white man and the standing people, stole into the woods to be alone. The standing people would all be gone from the woods! there would be no woods left!

What did white people do with so many trees?

That evening, around the fire, no one had missed him, and by the time the Marchion cut passed Chesuncook Lake, Yam's good nature had returned. He was again riding the drive, screeching and howling at the slippery logs, shaking them to keep them moving.

And almost dying.

A crevice on the lip of a 30-foot fall grabbed a log and held on. In a twinkling of an eye, hundreds, then thousands, of logs had jammed themselves together pick-up-stick fashion. For miles upriver, the open water vanished beneath a floor of stalled timber. Beneath the soaring breastwork, an angry waterspout shot upward like the spout on a coffee pot, before falling in a plume to the pond below the falls, turning the pond into a boiling caldron.

When Yam arrived on the scene, he walked out on the jam to argue with the trees. He called them old women afraid of under-water monsters. "I am not afraid to go on," he yelled, prodding with his pole. "Be brave, act with honor."

Seeing the Indian on top of the jam, Jed yelled at him to get back, but there was no hearing anything above the roar of the water.

Deep in the tangled web, a log five feet through at the butt snapped, freeing the whole of the river. Yam disappeared over the edge of the fall into the furious churn of white water and logs, shot up like a porpoise, and disappeared again, sucked away in the undertow.

Scrambling down the carry, Jed searched the mad torrent for a glimpse of the luckless logger. He saw the back of Yam's coat bounce through the foam like a piece of bark and spin out of sight into a whirlpool. Saw it shoot free through sheets of spray and disappear again. Then a long, crooked cedar, tilting sharply, flicked the coat high in the air. Arms and legs flailing tick-like, Yam sailed onto an island in the middle of the boiling race.

The watching men set up a cheer that the logger, face down on the rocks, couldn't hear. But the message from the people-no-longer-standing sounded loud and clear in his battered ears.

The jams happened over and over again, logs piling up six and eight feet deep. The worst was above Gulliver Pitch, where the drive jammed for over 10 days, and the logs had to be removed one by one to clear the channel.

The next jam, below the Soudyhunk, was more easily undone. Lowered by rope, Jed swung gently back and forth in front of the eerie wall of motionless timber. Below his boots, the river was forcing its way free with the whistle of a steam kettle. In front of his face, the logs were shining in the sun and dripping water. A beetle crawled out of a hole, spread its wings, and flew off. Five long minutes Jed studied the wall, before giving the signal to be raised. Passing a log caught only by a lip of bark, he shoved it hard with his boot.

The dam exploded, the log catching Jed as he was being jerked to safety, slamming into his hip and swinging him round and round. With a roar that ricocheted across the forests, the timber poured through the opening, the sound and fury of the sight igniting the river drivers in a wild hurrahing.

One day, with nothing but gentle rips and riffles to mark the powerful current, Yam blindsided Jed and set the log Jed was riding to spinning. Faster and faster the brothers went at it, howling, doubling back and forth, feet a blur. Then the log butted up against another, and Yam jumped free. A raucous jeering from the drivers floated across the water. Turning to Jed, Yam doffed his hat.

With the grin of a man who knows the truth when he sees it, Jed ducked his head.

F O U R T E E N

HOULTON, MAINE, Thursday, June 26, 1856. The Shoch home in Paddy Hollow was boarded up, Fraud's mother having died the previous winter. Jed burned Fraud's papers in the abandoned Hancock Barracks on Garrison Hill in memory of the man stationed there as a soldier, and Yam blew a handful of the warm ashes to the four winds that the paper might reunite with its spirit owner.

In the basement of an Irish boarding house on Kendall Street the wake continued with pot-still whiskey served in pickle jars. Two chippies, arriving long after dark and taking stock of the crowded room, descended on the strangers. The chippies' smiles cracked the powder on their faces, their shrill voices rose and fell with the cadence of hoarse meadowlarks. Musky perfume swirled like incense over the table.

Julia and Bettina. Young and beautiful. Knowing turquoise eyes in laughing heart-shaped faces. Blue-black hair hanging down in waves. Sisters obviously and very expensive if clothes were the barometer. Extravagantly flounced wine-colored taffeta dresses tilting and swaying provocatively over hooped skirts. Bodices open to the waist to reveal pretty white chemisettes. Wide, layered sleeves edged with black velvet over delicate wine-colored lace undersleeves. Smooth white hands aglint with bracelets and rings.

What a ladies man, Jed thought, watching Yam and the fancy women. *Am I like that?* It was a funny thing, this being around Yam. Sometimes the Indian reminded him of their father, other times of Walker or Dinky. Or himself. Like now, asking himself idly if he, too, could be a ladies man. If maybe he should lift his sights and quit settling for squaws and whores.

Julia was the more talkative of the pair. Inquiring after what the boys were drinking and ordering the same. Inquiring after their business pursuits and launching a broadside of ribald stories about boom rats.

"JULia!" Bettina protested again and again, feigning astonishment and dissolving in bright, quicksilvery laughter.

Several hours into the party, the night pleasantly drunk, Yam suggested they go for a walk.

"Oh, my! I couldn't do that!" Julia protested loudly, "I promised my dear, departed daddy…"

"…JULia!" Bettina chimed, "your daddy…"

"…never to get it on with a logger." Julia rolled her eyes heavenward.

"JULia," Jed made his voice as departed as possible, "you got it all wrong. I said never anybody but a logger." Everybody laughed and jostled each other, and Julia's eyes lingered invitingly on Jed's face.

The town crier stuck his head in the door to announce midnight.

Julia jumped up. "It's time, Bettina."

"What are you? Cinderella?" Jed asked.

"Yes. And my carriage is waiting." She was clutching the chair, resisting the impulse to sit back down, her rouged face a bright red above the table's candle.

"But your prince is here." Jed was stroking her leg, balling up the taffeta to reveal a well-turned ankle. "How much are we talking about?"

Julia gazed down at him, owl-eyed. "Too much."

And the lovely ladies of the night were gone. Never to return.

Not the next night nor the night after. Tiring of keeping his white brother company in Houlton, Yam went home. Jed wasn't sure if home meant Mouse or the Ottawa and decided it probably meant both. Yam knew next winter's timber was yet to be found, that he and Jed were partners, and that the camp needed a cook. But how exactly the Indian translated this information, Jed didn't know.

As for the chippies, when they didn't show up again and when the barkeep denied knowing their names, Jed figured them for cheating on their husbands. But he hadn't lost anything. Houlton was his kind of town. Buried in a wilderness of trees, busily going about the business of cutting and marketing those trees, happy as if it had good sense, as if the Saint John were right downtown instead of 20 miles away down crooked little Meduxnekeag.

Tuesday morning he walked out the Bangor Road in the lazy sunshine to Cary's Mills to tour the new building for making and planing clapboards. There was something about sawmills he particularly loved. The noises, the smells, the sight of the lumber sliding into the blade and the clean boards falling free.

In five years he'd have his own mill. He'd made some bonehead mistakes this past winter—left behind too many false-hearted trees instead of sawing around the rot, left logs too long, causing a good deal of grumbling amongst the river drivers. Next winter would be better. But he had no complaints, he'd been damn lucky. Nobody killed, no broken bones, no injuries what wouldn't heal. Paid every man $700 apiece and the Cold Stream farmers $300 extra for the use of their teams. And deposited $1,860 in the Bangor Eastern Bank with Yam as beneficiary.

Moseying back to town, Jed decided he'd had enough horsing

around. The cabin roof needed patching, and he needed to locate next winter's cut. He was headed for the Snell House in Market Square to get his things together when the display in Tenney's variety-store window caught his eye. John Rider's new self-cocking revolving pistol. Fifteen dollars.

Assessing his finances, he remembered that Yam still owed him $30 for Mouse. In Bangor, the Indian had dressed himself to the nines in a wool suit complete with white turned-down collar, red bow tie fringed at one end, plaid waistcoat, and wide-brimmed, flat-crowned "wide-awake" hat. And probably didn't have a red cent left.

Wool-gathering, Jed almost overlooked the reflection dancing before his eyes in the glass.

An open Concord was coming up Main Street, and sitting beside the driver... Jed turned around. Yep. That was Julia, alright. In a pale green dress with long sleeves and a neckline low enough to catch a whole school of fish. The chippy's black hair was pinned up under a white off-the-face bonnet, and she was holding a dainty white parasol she waved about baton-like.

Jed slapped his dusty hat against his heart. His lost love kept her nose in the air. He sprinted to the corner, hooked an arm around a porch upright and, leaning into the street, jammed his thumb in his ear and waggled his hand. The carriage pulled past, Julia frowned at the spectacle and stuck out her tongue.

With an invitation like that, what was a fellow to do but follow? keeping a discreet distance in the street traffic, of course, but still close enough to hear snatches of loud talk. From the chippy. The driver, old as Methuselah and barely in control of his team, had no time for idle chit-chat.

The Concord made several stops, Julia bustling in and out of first Woodbury's Grocery then Wilson's Grocery, and between stops entertaining the driver with numerous hugs and kisses.

Was she the old man's wife? using Bettina for a cover when

she wanted out of her gilded cage? or just his fancy woman. A half-mile out the Calais Road from the thickest part of town, the carriage stopped at a two-story, grey-painted house with diamond panes and a shingled mansard roof. A 40-foot sassafras tree, encircled by a wooden bench, stood alone in the front yard, its wiggly branches hung with brightly-painted bird feeders. *Wah-eh-nak-kas*, the Indians' smelling stick. Instinctively Jed tested the air for the scent, even as he realized it was too far into summer.

He had plenty of time to look around, the old man being anything but fast in getting himself and his lady off the high seat. The front stoop held several large pots of bright red flowers. Tethered goats clipped away at the lawn grasses. An old stand of red oak shaded the sides of the yard. The back yard was given over to two gambrel-roofed barns, drowning in their own shade. The weathered caribou horns above the open doorways looked like giant wishbones.

The old man tottered around and finally got himself headed for the house, Julie taking his arm like some grand lady. Watching her sashay up the front walk, Jed had to laugh. She knew he was back there, and now he knew they were having a party.

That night he put on his cleanest woolen work shirt, fastened on a wide, brand new, black bow tie, buttoned up his coat, wet down his newly barbered hair, and walked back out the Calais Road to survey the situation.

The house was lit up like a Christmas tree, buggies all but blocking the road. Jed hesitated and lifted the iron knocker. What the hell, it was the only game in town. He wasn't about to cuckold any man, much less one 80 years old, but he'd figure something to do. Maybe check out Bettina, if she was here.

Opening the door, a maid extended a silver tray scattered with small paper cards. Jed smiled and walked on by, expecting any second to be asked to leave.

The front room was empty, except for a large trestle table, sway-backed under its load of heavy crockery. Bailey cloth, decorated at the hem with American flags, overlay the table. Between the heaped food marched numerous wooden flagpoles, starched flags unfurled. Jed helped himself to a jelly tartlet from a painted bowl and was reaching for the stack of pigs feet when the fire bell went off in his ear.

"JED!"

"JULia!"

"What a surPRISE!" Free of powder, the chippy's guileless face shone with the translucence of pearls. Her lips were like red cherries. Her short, hoopskirted blue-and-white sailor dress revealed high-topped, white-laced shoes that hoisted her to Jed's shoulders. A bouquet of buttercups filled her hands.

"Now that you've crashed the party, bub," the whispered resignation was accompanied by a gig in the ribs, "ya might as well meet who's paying for it."

In the adjoining room, well-dressed diners wearing red-white-and-blue tricorner hats sat straight-backed, balancing plates on their knees and listening attentively to a young man reciting poetry. Crumpled like a sock doll in a corner armchair, the driver of the Concord dozed, party favor askew over one ear, a precariously tipped wine glass in hand. Julia retrieved the glass and prodded the senescent awake.

The old man looked up, startled. Liver spots mottled his skin. His eyes, overlarge behind thick glasses, were a watery hazel.

"Mr. Marchion, sir," Jed said, extending his hand. The soft, seemingly boneless hand that took his own displayed a wedding band. *I guess that settles that,* Jed told himself. Straightening, the thought in his eyes, he heard Julia say, "My father, Dr. Clare."

The doctor brushed at his ear, knocking off the paper hat, and sat up. "Julia tells me you are a lumberman."

Jed was speechless, features slack with surprise.

"You have an Indian partner," Dr. Clare added, putting it together.

Behind the bouquet, Julia doubled with laughter, the buttercups giving her skin a golden cast.

"Come! come!" the doctor snapped, wanting to be answered.

"I'm in Houlton on business, and Julia said to be sure and stop by." The words came out squeakier than Jed meant.

"Yes, daddy, I told him we were going to play pin-the-tail-on-the-donkey, and he insisted on volunteering."

Jed felt his face getting hot. "Only because I wanted to spare you," he replied, tight-lipped. What he really wanted to do was march out of the house as quickly as possible with whatever dignity he could salvage from the gulling.

Dr. Clare lifted his hand, waving both of them away. "I'm sure you children have better things to do than entertain me with your games."

"The real party is downstairs," Julia confided with a smirk as soon as they were out of earshot, and popped her chewing gum. "The one that separates the men from the boys."

Jed looked at her, his smile slow in coming, and tipped his head.

The real party, Jed soon learned, was to celebrate the independence of the Houlton Academy Class of '56. With a cellar worthy of the task. Over 700 bottles of Madeira, sherry, port both pale and brown, and muscatel.

"And you, darling," Julia blew a kiss off her fingers at Jed, "you may have whatever you want." The jarring chippie voice was changing, sloughing off its hard edges.

Bettina was there, a cousin as it happened, along with numerous other young people decked out in fanciful variations of red, white and blue. The male contingent took immediate exception to Jed's being downstairs, measuring their dislike in hard stares through the smoke of their short sixes—stares which Jed ignored in favor of Julia and the muscatel.

As for the young women, they found the stranger in their midst the most handsome thing ever. Tall, lean, the face of a desert sheik, and those eyes…!

"We're talking hot hazel here," Bettina intoned to a chorus of smothered shrieks.

Enjoying themselves, the celebrants ducked for apples, soaking themselves and the floor in the process. Played silly charades. And blindfolded and spun around, crashed into the wall in hilariously futile attempts to pin the tail on the donkey. And with everybody well into their cups and looking as disreputable as possible, took up poses both ridiculous and sublime in front of the new-fangled, collodion camera that was Julia's graduation gift.

After the picture-taking, Julia drew Bettina off alone. "I have never seen anything like him!" She swooned against the wall. "I am dying, Bettina! dying! do you hear me?"

Employing artful, come-hither glances, she coaxed Jed outside under the sassafras tree, letting him kiss and hug her, even going so far as to allow his hands on her breasts before running back to the house to tell Bettina that indeed her logger was an animal.

When Jed returned to the house, the graduates were upstairs dancing. The trestle table had been removed and musicians installed in the front room. He hung around awhile watching Julia waltz from room to room gaily flirting with a succession of partners, and aware that for himself, at least, the party was over, was moving toward the front door when the music leaped into the familiar "Yankee Doodle Dandy."

"You have to dance with me," Julia was beside him, pulling at his coat, "nobody else will, it's too fast."

"I don't dance."

"You can learn...or I can call Sheriff Doyle and have you locked up."

"Don't worry, I'm leaving."

"For rape."

He put his arms around her and galloped out on the floor.

F I F T E E N

SEATED ON HIS FRONT PORCH reading the weekly New York
Herald, Cyrus Clare heard the terrier bark and, taking off
his reading glasses, fumbling about for his driving specta-
cles, heard the screen door open. Julia was thumping down the
porch steps and greeting...the doctor held up the tortoiseshell
frames...Mr. Marchion.

He'd suspected her shenanigans from the jump. The minute
she opened her mouth about a party marking the start of
Houlton's Great Anniversary Festival, along with her class graduation. God forbid that her half-blind father and their spavined
housekeeper be the only ones in Houlton not to host the graduates. Complete with Bettina's hired maid.

Goddamn graduates! would they never move on to other
things? Not only must his name appear on invitations oozing
inane banalities, but he must also gallivant about Houlton with
his air-headed daughter preening like a plucked peacock. And,
adding insult to injury, host a party that transformed respectable
citizenry into village idiots.

The doctor put down the glasses and sat staring through the
paper into his thoughts. The whole thing—getting him out from
underfoot while Bettina d.e.c.o.r.a.t.e.d in her usual sieve-headed
style, that of gutting the front room by dragging everything to
the back porch—the whole thing was to coax Mr. Marchion
from hiding? A very serious game indeed, if so. Young women

were due some rites of passage, he supposed, but in whose home had his daughter met this Mr. Marchion? The man hardly seemed one to trifle with.

The housekeeper paddled by with a bucket of dirty water.

"Comes the hour, comes the man," the doctor offered by way of explaining the mess inside.

With an audible sigh, the housekeeper emptied the bucket off the side of the porch.

"Ah, my dear Julia," the doctor continued aloud conversationally, eyeing the couple strolling under the trees, "I'm afraid this time you've belled the wrong cat."

They walked and talked until they were out of sight of the house, then, easy as the unexpected fall of summer rain, Julia's logger was kissing her and she was letting him. Warmed by the brush fires that raced through her body even as she was warned by their intensity.

"I think we should stop," she murmured. Her breasts were cupped in his hands and his mouth was everywhere, tasting her cheeks, her neck, blowing in her ears. He drew away and she followed, her tongue locked against his. They were on the ground with the hardness in his groin pressed against her thigh before she made him stop.

"No, you're too horny. NO! Get off! I want to sit up."

Jed rolled away and propped himself on his elbow to watch his pretty woman straighten her shirtwaist and replace the combs in her hair.

"This is a lot of fun, I admit." Julia was careful not to look at him. "But maybe we should know each other first."

"That's what I had in mind."

"I'm not that kind of girl." She scrambled to her feet. "If you can't just sit and talk like a gentleman, we'll have to go back."

"Can this be my sweet Julia? from whose ruby lips I heard

about a certain young lady from Houlton *'whose dailies with men were forbotten, but when the boom rats came round she laid herself down, all for the logs they were totin'?"*

Julia flounced away and Jed jumped in front of her, hands high, suing for peace. "Alright, alright, let's walk and talk."

Strolling along, they came to a fallen oak and sat with a burl between them. Julia asked about Jed's business in Houlton and that question led to others, Molunkus and his business there. All the while she was recalling his mouth, the pressure of his body against hers, the knowing strength in his rough hands. One of his hands had a bad scar across the back. Studying the scar, she realized she was copying her father—the idle chit-chat the doctor made while considering other things like pulse rate and lung congestion.

"So what was you doing in the Micks' shanty?" Jed asked.

"It was just a dare."

He glanced at the cool profile. "You're pretty good for a beginner." Without powder she looked like a porcelain doll.

"You're going into the woods now, to cut timber?"

"No, just find it. We don't cut till winter. Been living in Maine long?"

"What with being a doctor's daughter and all, I've had other things on my mind. I make up most of my father's prescriptions, including ointments and poultices. I'm quite used to dead people and seeing men treated for the clap."

"You a nurse or something?"

"You could say that."

"Mmmm, I could use a nurse in my business…"

"…I bet you could…"

"…in case I got hurt so far away from a doctor."

Julia gave him a scornful smile. "Too bad you won't be here when I learn how to print my glass plates. You were the life of the party."

"I could come back."

"You could…" The problem with her daring sheik was that he moved too quickly. Since puberty, her parrying skills had been honed by bumbling advances, but Jed came on like a new ship down a greased way. He was kissing her again, and she didn't want him to stop.

"See you around." He had stopped on his own accord.

"How long will you be in the woods? Does anybody else go?"

"Three, four weeks. Probably Yam and his squaw."

"They could be our chaperones."

Bettina went into instant shock. "We're going to rough it? Oh, good Lord! I'll have to get new boots!"

"You can't go! Yam and his squaw are going."

"That's the same as no chaperons at all. It's too wild! Your father will forbid it."

Julia stared at Bettina in disbelief. But for once her holy-Jesus-what-now look failed to draw Bettina into the game.

"What if you get pregnant?"

"Bettina, you are so goddamn gloom and doom! What would I do that for?"

"You're going to have to be *intimate*, Julia. That's why he's taking you."

"Well, that's *not* the reason *I'm* going, stupid." Now she really was irritated. "It'll be more fun than a barrel of monkeys. Besides, I know how to handle men."

For her father she described a slightly different adventure, one having more to do with scenery, and concluded with a passionate plea to be allowed to take her life in her own hands.

"Julia, you're a caution. Where do you get such talk? Certainly you aren't serious."

"Oh, but I am, Father. I can't help but covet him."

"Today maybe, but tomorrow things will look different."

Julia's face tightened in that pretty pout the doctor knew so well, and he smiled despite himself. She was so like her dear departed mother. How it took away the years to visit with her. Of course he'd spoiled her, but the antidote for that was a good education, which she had plenty of, fortunately.

"Nothing is free. You think this isn't going to cost you? Folks'll have no opinion of you."

"Oh, I should just hate that!"

"Julia! remember your station. The words, 'Come grow old with me, the best is yet to be,' were not spoken of women who marry beneath themselves. In whose home, did you meet this fellow?"

"Who said anything about marriage?"

"And no one around here ever will, should you persist in this foolishness. People will always suspect the worst." He smiled at her engagingly, refusing to take her vapors seriously. "How old is this Mr. Marchion?"

"Twenty-eight. He's very responsible, I've interviewed him thoroughly." Drawing her chair close to her father's rocker, Julia folded her hand into his. "I'm the only girl in my class who's never, ever roughed it in the depths of Maine, but I never, ever minded because I knew the patients had to come first…"

"…we have relatives in Winn, whom I'm sure…"

"…it's just the thing to do in the summer, and this way I'll have my own personal guide. They cost a sight otherwise…"

"…will be glad to have you. As for a guiding service, your uncle…"

"…NO! That wouldn't be any fun."

In the end she won. It would have been a surprise to both of them if she hadn't.

"My intellect may totter now and then," the frustrated doctor complained, refusing to allow the retreat to become a complete rout, while at the same time thinking how ironic that he, a doctor, should have failed to overlook his own daughter's glands.

"And I may be shaky in one of my legs, but I am not so old that I've forgotten what comes of such foolishness. I met your mother at a wedding in the old Houlton home. All Major Clarke's officers were invited. She was a Putnam and of excellent English stock, and I was a callow youth fresh out of Bowdoin with a degree from the Medical School, who thought he was the cock of the walk. Whatever in the world she saw in me..." His voice broke off, and resumed.

"Good land, child! Shouldn't you be getting ready for the continent?" It was his graduation gift to her, and to himself, although he worried about the boat and old diseases. But the thought of not going was totally unacceptable.

"We'll do it next spring," Julia promised with a dazzling smile, her eyes misting. He was such a dear. "I never get tired of hearing about you and mother and the old days."

"Well, no. I courted her at picnics, at parties, on sleigh rides, at croquet. Croquet! that was the worst. A man in love should never have to negotiate a croquet course. Then, all at once, she was ready. Oh, there were bans, everything had to be done properly, but still you came early. Two months early as I recall."

The confession caught Julia off guard. "Two months...?" She looked away, keenly embarrassed.

"So you see, the best of plans go awry. Of course, a forced miscarriage was never considered, and I want you to promise me, on your mother's grave, that the same will hold true for you."

Julia shifted uncomfortably. Why did he always have to make such a big deal out of everything? The back screen rattled. She jumped up, and the doctor caught her wrist.

"Promise me, Julia, and I won't say another word."

Rattle, rattle went the screen.

"There's nothing to promise...oh, of course!" It always

annoyed her to have terms extracted. It also annoyed her to be interrupted. Temper up, she hurried through the kitchen and saw her cousin peering into the back-porch shadows. "What do you want, Sigvald?"

"I've just this minute heard the most preposterous rumor. Dearest, you must tell me it isn't true."

Julia flung open the screen and pointed at a dining room chair that, having grown rickety, had migrated to the back of the house.

"Sit!" Standing with arms folded, she listened to the heartfelt outpourings of her willing slave. And taking pity on him, bestowed numerous baby kisses on the throbbing brow.

"Mr. Marchion," she explained sweetly, "is merely a guide whose services my father has employed. And now, ta, ta, must run." She planted a wet, lingering kiss full on Sigvald's mouth, made him promise to be faithful forever, and hurried upstairs to pack.

That night, seeing clearly the price one paid for asserting one's self she cried herself to sleep and, rising at dawn, carried two large canvas sacks filled with clothing and toiletries downstairs one at a time and placed them on the front porch. She next walked out through the wet grasses with grain in a bucket for her pony.

Chimney smoke layered the meadow mists. A red fox, trotting along a deer path, froze and then trotted on. Down by the river a whistler duck sounded a romantic note. The horse called Socks made no objection to the iron bit, which it hadn't tasted in years. Nor did it object, later in the barn, to Julia's gingerly testing her weight in the Two-Horn Somerset Side Saddle with its fancy carpet seat and round skirts of imitation enameled leather.

She tied the readied pony at the house railing and, slipping through the still-quiet rooms, returned upstairs to her bedroom.

The strains of the Cornet Band practicing "Hail Columbia!" wafted through an open window as she stood before her mirror dropping rose water mixed with sulfate of zinc and tincture of opium in her eyes.

Over breakfast, which she barely touched, she poured out her heart to her father, the torrent of words managing somehow to fashion of the doctor's stormy silence a blessing on the sweetest boon of her life.

As previously agreed, Jed came promptly at 9 o'clock. His new coat and hat, his businessman's approach to the business at hand, and most particularly his sturdy white charger, swept aside whatever small doubts Julia may have entertained as to the adventure.

First her guide saw to the canvas sacks by tying them together to hang down on either side of his saddle. Next, he checked the pony's saddle cinch. A true gentleman, he glanced decorously aside when she flung her leg, well encased in new Equestrienne Tights, over the double horn and readjusted the folds in her gray mottled Mackinaw Skirt.

"I do believe I'm ready," Julia said primly.

At which time the stern-faced hireling handed up the pony's reins and got on his own horse.

(Thanking his lucky stars all the while that he'd a horse to get on. He planned on walking the 30-some miles to Fraud's cabin until it occurred to him that his lady love might pack more goods than could be carried on her pony. The farmer downriver on the Meduxnekeag had wanted an arm and a leg for the plow horse, horses being dear this time of year, and an extra $10 for the weathered saddle and bridle. And all of it worth every penny!)

The front porch remained empty. Tapping Socks with her parasol, Julia called loudly, "Good-bye, dear father, good-bye. Don't worry about anything."

It was the Fourth of July, Houlton was primed with merry-makers. Vibrating with the aftershocks of her own declaration of freedom, Julia paid no mind. The greased-pig scuffle, Sigvald's first appearance as a new fire laddy, the baseball contest, the pole climb, the monster clambake, the parade, the bells, the bonfires—all so eagerly anticipated—now dismissed out of hand.

Following her tall logger down the street, Julia neared the post office in Market Square. The Glee Club was assembling there. Bettina began to wave, and the singers to sing the ode to the Class of '56.

> …Listen children! Youth is fleeing
> Toward the zenith mounts the sun.
> Conquer! do not be out run.
> Leave behind vain, idle, dreaming, school and joys, without
> a tear.
> Greet the world with bright eyes beaming, strong in purpose,
> scorning fear.…

Breast filled to overflowing with the need to scorn fear, Julia acknowledged the recognition with a small, tragic gesture. And clad (more or less) in the homespun garments of her ancestors, face preoccupied and chin in the air, bravely followed her destiny up the Soldiers' Road.

Yam was at the cabin along with Mouse, much to Jed's relief. Julia slept that night with the squaw, who, every time she looked at the white woman, giggled. Jed slept outside with Yam, who didn't bother to hide his astonishment at what he insisted on calling a raid.

The next morning—horses turned loose in the large pasture fenced on one side by the lake— the company loaded two canoes and floated down the Molunkus to the junction, there to begin the journey up the Penobscot into the interior.

That night the moon turned full, rising golden in the east

even as the sun sank in the rosy west over an endless black
sierra. A fitting introduction to the woods of the poet—woods
lovely, dark and deep. Full of stately moose and roaring waters.
Full of whispering rains and ghostly mists that rolled and rose
through winding sheets of long grey moss on long-dead cedars.

Julia embraced it all—the lost-soul lament of the loon, the
muddy portages with their ancient footholds, the scarred trunks
echoing the concerns of men long in their graves, the sunlight
streaming through the overhead foliage to lie in golden knives
on the forest floor, the spotted trails twisting away in the undergrowth, the lakes so smooth as to give wings to the birch gliding
straight and swift, the pale green light lingering at the edge of
dawn, the water glowing blood-stained ebony in the light of the
evening fire—the sights and sounds flaking off in one magnificent canvas after another, pulling her to pieces and pounding
her senses numb.

Where Jed went, she went. The deserted wongens that served
for their camps would have been just the place on a rainy day
to curl up with a good book. She'd brought along Lord Byron's
Stanzas to Augusta and Thoreau's *A Week on the Concord and
Merrimack Rivers*. But no! rain or shine, she must be off, tromp-
ing through emerald vaults serenaded by robins, craning her
neck to watch squirrels perform their acrobatics from hanging
balcony to balcony.

She kissed her woodsman shamelessly in front of Yam and
Mouse, and was ultimately persuaded to go skinny dipping with
them all—a terrible embarrassment at first, but one soon overcome with Yam's wide-awake hat. She must have it, she insisted,
to cover herself. Eventually it wound up on top of her head,
where it stayed, more or less, the whole of the time.

When Jed rolled up his sleeves on his lean, brown arms, she
thought she would swoon. When he fed her frizzled salt pork and

touched her lips with his fingers, it was all she could do to look away from his smoldering eyes.

Much less keep in mind that a woman was most fertile on the 10 days immediately preceding onset of menses, during which time she must avoid intimacy, wet feet and cold bathing, and remember to take her aperient pills.

S I X T E E N

T HEY RETURNED TO HOULTON in early August to stand
dusty and disheveled in front of Cyrus. Except for that
first, flushed-face stare, the doctor would not acknowledge
his daughter, horribly as he had missed her. On hearing the couple
wanted to be married, he said to Jed, "As least you are prepared to
make an honest woman out of her."

"I love Julia very much."

"That would be easier to believe if I knew more about you.
Since I'm not to have that opportunity beforehand, you'll
forgive my lack of enthusiasm."

"I ain't hard to get along with," Jed answered with a grin,
oblivious to the other's anger.

"Perhaps, but it is my sense that we have not changed your
life so much as you have forever changed ours. Be that as it may,
my daughter appears to have no regrets. I hope, for your sake,
this continues to be the case."

Both men looked at Julia, who favored the room with a vague
smile and settled herself, utterly exhausted, on the sofa.

The item Julia posted to the Bangor Herald appeared in the
next "Down Easter" column.

> THAT enormously popular Miss Julia Clare
> of Houlton, Maine, having recently re-
> turned from summering with friends in the
> wilderness above Moosehead Lake, is

> rumored to be engaged to her dashing
> timber magnate, Mr. Jedrich Marchion from
> New York. We look for an official an-
> nouncement soon.

Followed a week later by,

> Dr. Cyrus Clare, highly-esteemed Houlton
> physician of forty years, recently retired,
> announces the marriage of his beloved
> daughter, Julia Cordelia Clare, to Mr.
> Jedrich Thomas Marchion, Esq., of New
> York. The wedding is to be in September
> and all fortunate enough to receive an invi-
> tation are sure to attend.

The setting sun crowds close to Mount Katahdin. The
verbena have stopped flowering, and the house smells of thyme
and sage and oregano, their iron pots having been moved to the
back porch out of the heavy rains. The light is thinning and,
with it, the lush greens of summer. The highest branches of the
maples send out flares of red, orange, and yellow, and the high
bush cranberries, not to be outdone, turn from orange to deep
red. The translucent eggshell-winged butterflies that lifted by
the thousands from the undergrowth only last week, are almost
gone, banished by the chill in the shadows.

In a conciliatory gesture, the good doctor plants the tradi-
tional elm trees on either side of the front walk. He also
purchases the eight-foot, carved-oak letter **J** that has for years
adorned the Andrews Jones barn, paying good coin for the
carving to be braced upright in the Clare yard, where Julia's
friends wrap it with blue and gold bunting.

The afternoon of the wedding, Sigvald Proulx, in his cups,
barred Jed's way up the front walk and, in a loud voice, demanded
the truth of his religion.

"My religion, brother," Jed spoke in a louder voice, pointing his finger in Sigvald's face, "is half the road and four pecks to the bushel."

No one let on as to having heard the rebuke. But Cyrus, chin jutting forward, felt a small measure of vindication. At least the whippersnapper had a ready wit.

Julia's great aunt played the spinet for the occasion, fulfilling the family obligation. A large, grim woman, she cared not a whit for her niece, whom she described as having far too much brass. And less anyone think her taken in by the bride's virginal dress and simpering modesty, preceded the wedding march from Lohengrin with clever variations on "The Logger's Boast."

The wedding party assembled in a semicircle in the front yard—Bettina and Jed and somebody's little boy who was the ring-bearer. Yam and Mouse shared a front row with several of Julia's academy classmates, including Sigvald. Taking their seats, the older people of Houlton went out of their way to greet the well-liked captain of the rowing team and the lead in the school's spring play "The Last of the Saxon Kings." And to inquire as to Sigvald's rumored appointment as an aide to Maine's congress-man in Washington.

When the soloist began singing "Won't You Come Along?" the grin on Mouse's face crinkled up the red circles painted on her cheekbones. She was expecting fireworks, at the very least a loud boom. Yam was wearing his wide-awake hat. Jed made a furtive gesture and Yam put the hat in his lap. There was another song, "Joyful Be Thy Day." The squaw looked around restlessly.

Jamming a straight thumb against the itch in the small of his back, Jed remembered himself and returned to attention. The second-hand suit smelled faintly of moth balls. Then Julia was approaching on the arm of her father, and he forgot about the wool suit. Forgot about everything except how unreal she looked, like an angel in a painting. He'd had a good feeling

about Maine from the jump, but he never could have anticipated this.

*I wonder if this woman knows what she's doing? Good Lord!
Julia, you are beautiful! Ma would be proud of me. She'd like
this house too. But you know who wouldn't believe this is my
pa, never in a thousand years.*

Cyrus gave his daughter away and slowly made his way to a
facing row of wooden chairs, there to sit amidst others of his
vintage.

Next came a little sermon on sanctity, and then the minister
was saying, "If anyone here knows why this man and woman
should not be joined in holy matrimony, let him speak now or
forever hold his peace."

A disturbance broke out in the second row. One of the boys
had Sigvald's sleeve wadded in his fist. Sigvald's Viking features
were cold and hard. There was a spate of angry whispering. Now
everyone was noticing, except Julia, who refused to countenance
the foolishness.

Jed swallowed a smile. *Hey, hey what's this? A little jealousy,
my friend? Be careful there, whoever you are. My brother'll lob
knots on your head and dare 'em to rise.*

The moment passed, the ceremony went on.

Space permitting, the Herald finally got around to reporting
on the lovely fall wedding

> ...held in Houlton, Maine, Sunday, September 7...in
> the front yard of the Clare residence with the Reverend
> Augustus Wetherall of the Unitarian Church officiating...
> Not even the rain dared to fall on such a perfect setting...
>
> AFTER the ceremony, supper was served in the Aaron
> Putnam Mansion...The sunshine that warmed the polished
> oak floors was reflected in the sunny faces of the guests, par-
> ticularly those of the happy newlyweds who will be
> receiving at their home on Calais Road. The former Miss

Clare is a graduate of the Houlton Academy. Mr. Marchion attended school in the Hudson Valley and is currently engaged in the lumber business in the Caucomgomoc pineries.

Yam returned immediately to the woods, along with Mouse and two choppers from Houlton. Jed delayed until late October and went in with the Cold Stream Pond farmers. A departure dutifully noted in the Herald as exciting deep trepidation in the breast of the new Mrs. Marchion for the safe return of her devoted husband from the winter's venturing.

Left at last to her own entertainments, Julia dutifully opened the writing desk.

> October 23. 1856
> Dear Mrs. Marchion, It is my happy lot to inform you that you have a new daughter-in-law. Your wonderful son and I were married this past September and now my dear husband has just this morning returned to the woods to resume his winter work and already I miss him terribly.

She glanced over at the cat sprawled upside-down, all four paws in the air, on her father's lap. There they slept, like two old friends. Her father, who hated cats. Perhaps he felt sorry for this one, it was so ratty. And so unclean—forever overeating and leaving a pile of barf beside its food pan. Julia made a face. Yellow Cat was Mouse's wedding gift, what an intelligent idea that was!

> I am nineteen, nine years younger than my husband, which I believe to be the perfect age difference for the duties we shall assume.

With a noise of disgust, she stopped again. His mother would know how old he was! but she was *not* starting over.

> We shall make our home with my father, my mother having passed way some years ago.

How terribly boring! For no reason, she recalled the night in the woods when Mouse tore her hand open on a broken knife. Jed insisted she doctor the wound, leaving no choice but to admit that her knowledge of nursing came from peeking through keyholes. The confession sent Jed, half-drunk, to rolling on the ground, and Yam, when he could finally be made to understand the story, to prancing around peeking through his circled fingers. By the time they were done, she was in tears.

She shifted her gaze to the wind-whipped trees outside the living-room window. In the worn light, the remaining leaves looked like dark birds banging about a cage. Remembering Yam made her remember the swimming parties. Whatever was she thinking, to let him see her naked? The dirty little savage. There was no way he and Jed could be related. There must be something more to it, he must have saved Jed's life or something. She refilled the pen. Jed wanted his family to know of Fraud's death, but she would do that later. This *was* a wedding letter after all.

> I hope you will come to see us as soon as possible. I hope my
> new sister and brother will also come with their families. I
> look forward to hearing from you and trust this news will
> not in any way distress you.
>   Love, your obedient new daughter,
>   Julia Cordelia Clare Marchion

The winter of 1856-57 was the worst winter of Jed's life. When he wasn't missing Julia, he was thinking up inventions to get ahead in the world. Whole trees crashed on him, logs rolled over him. He tumbled 40 feet off a dam and twice set the cabin afire. He fought with the timber, hurrying it to fall and be dragged away. Fought with his crew, everyone except Yam, who gave the unhappy man a wide berth.

Adding insult to the injury of shortened days and long, lonely nights was the light snowfall. The logs were hard to drag. The cabin, without its deep insulating drifts, impossible to keep warm. In February winter got its back up, the temperature fell to 35 degrees below zero and shattered the thermometer.

A bitter wind blew steadily out of the north, pressing a numbing cold into the bone where it stayed like a deep toothache. The noses of the oxen bled, their splayed feet broke open and left crimson splotches in the snow.

Cruel hard as the winter was for the logger and his crew, it was twice as hard on his sweet wife. Julia was bored TO PIECES!

Showering her friends with the beatitudes of wifedom, she turned her back forever on the days of entertaining them with liquor and tobacco and ribald stories garnered from eavesdropping on her father's chats with old men.

No more smoky grog shops, rank with the earthy smells of cheap alcohol and perfumed cigars. Where ungirdled women made maudlin by Stephen Foster songs gathered under prim signs—No Liquor Served Here. No Vulgar Language. No Dancing. No Loose Women—to be wooed by sloe-eyed men with careless hands and bodies that arced like reeds in the wind.

Never again.

Well, maybe one last time for old time's sake. Wracked with nostalgia, she persuaded Bettina to spend an evening in a corner of the tavern on White Settlement Road. A terrible mistake. The smoke clogged her sinuses, and she threw up the whiskey. She was sick again the next morning and went right on being sick every morning afterward. The morning sickness of pregnancy. So much for aperient pills. So much for youth.

The nausea, over in six weeks according to the medical books, lingered. Her feet and gums swelled. The Christmas holidays, always so gay, were a nightmare. The customary blizzard of cleverly wrapped caches of delicacies provoked no interest whatsoever as to their contents, and the rich spice flavors in the winter posies turned her stomach. None of her pretty clothes fit, the cranberry wine tasted like soap, and an allergy to celery, discovered after she made a pig of herself on the turkey dressing at Christmas dinner, sent her to bed with a damp cloth over her face, eyes swelled shut.

The New Year's Eve Ball in the Joseph Houlton hall on the hill felt more like Halloween. The only man who danced with her was her father, while that turncoat Sigvald took evil enjoyment in waltzing all the pretty girls right over her toes.

Not only was she deathly ill *all* the time, but her meager entertainments didn't amount to Hannah Cook. Studying out the charades in the weekly paper, memorizing *Godey's Lady's Book*, and sewing, sewing, sewing...baby clothes, maternity clothes, elaborate decorations for cradle and toilet table, countless Yule decorations. On and on *ad nauseum*.

She organized a new scrapbook that grouped all the "Down Easter" clippings together on pages enameled with hearts and sprinkled with flowers twined from tiny braids of her hair. The not-very-interesting chore, it was really Bettina's idea, took a long time.

The postponement of a visit to the European continent in the foreseeable future was a great discouragement to Dr. Clare, one which he partially overcame by anticipating the pleasures of being a grandparent. For Julia, there was no such out. She had not grown up around babies and most certainly never desired one of her own.

Crying against the cheerless pillows of her lonely bed, she terrified herself with dreadful imaginings—what if her husband didn't come back? he had such low associations—and consoled herself with considerations of a second husband. Handsome and rich, of course. And not chary of a widow with a prattling child. But always in her dreams she was with Jed, the two of them alone in the woods, floating like swans.

The days and nights plodded dumbly by. Accustomed to sleighing and skating, she was now housebound, walking no further than the end of the shoveled walk and, if the sun were warm, a short way down the ribbons left by buggy wheels in the boil of muddy road.

Occasionally a fox walked with her, dancing over the snow's icy crust. The fox was red and plush and snapped up the table scraps she tossed it. And Yellow Cat and the old terrier chased the fox, who ran in circles, laughing.

But then the snows got too deep, and she was truly housebound.

That's when the letters came—little epistles like bright points of light in the suffocating dreariness of early February—fleshing out Jed's world and drawing her inside.

Dinky had been visiting her mother in New York when the wedding announcement arrived.

> Dec. 1, '56
>
> My dear new sister, what a fine ring that has to it. I take pen in hand for both mother and me to let you know how thrilled we are at your news. We haven't heard from Jed in years, thank goodness he took a wife that can write.
>
> This summer the children and I are leaving the States, I have twin girls age 3 and a son age 1. We are moving to California where we can be nearer my husband's work. He is a deputy surveyor with the General Land Office. So if we come, it will be soon. Then you shall see me just as I am, a short, plain, matter-of-fact-looking person.
>
> I'll try to bring mother with me. She hasn't been out of this valley since she came here 41 years ago with pa. I'm dying to know more about you. I was a part-time teacher in Ohio but this winter I'm being lazy and getting fat. Mother is German Presbyterian and I am Agnostic. Write soon.
>
> Lovingly, your new sister,
>
> Editha Anne (Marchion) Miller
>
> postscript, I am 22.

The next letter, dated Dec. 11, 1856, was from Jed's sister-in-law, who, after making polite introductions, bared her soul.

> ...You lucky girl! I've been in love with Jed all my life but we were young and foolish and those sweetly remembered days are long past. However, I shall never put aside my admiration for his fearless determination to accomplish any goal he sets his mind to. Thank goodness he finally set his mind to taking a wife. I hope you do not intend submitting to him as your liege lord and master, but rather as a partner. As a token of this hope I have ordered a copy of Women in the Nineteenth Century for you as a gift. Everybody here is talking about it.
>   With love, Katherine, <u>A FREETHINKER</u>

Then, on the last day in February, like a slow star descending, came the unexpected—a frayed manila envelope hand-stamped "Great Salt Lake City, Great Basin, Territory of Deseret, North America," and addressed, "Jed Marchion, Post Master, Aroostock Valley, The State of Maine, The United States."

Salt Lake City was where Jed's first wife lived. The wickedness of the story fascinated Julia—the third wife of a Mormon elder running off with an American soldier, suffering a fate worse than death at the hands of the Indians, being rescued by Jed and running off again. It was all so damnably romantic!!

Jed had insisted she hear him out about the liaison before announcing their wedding, but the confession only made her that much determined to have him. Not once did he admit to having loved the Lorelei. Nonetheless, Julia had poked and prodded enough to know that the measured recitations came not from indifference but from scar tissue.

She put the mysterious letter away, spent two delicious days tantalizing herself with imaginings, and fished it out.

The first thing she noticed was that it had been opened before and sealed back together rather carelessly. The second thing was the handwriting itself. Bold, unwavering strokes, beautifully formed, the penmanship of a woman neither timid nor…Julia glanced out the bedroom window. Yes, "afraid" was the word that came to mind, oddly enough.

Carefully she smoothed flat the coarse, dull grey sheets.

> Mon. Nov. 3, '56
> Dear Jed,
> Another Christmas is drawing close and still we don't hear from you. Jeremiah is growing like a weed. It's hard to believe he's almost 10 and will soon join the Aaronic Priesthood. Nancy Jane is 5 now and the apple of her father's eye. Phoebe sends her love.
> Zion is very beautiful, not at all the barren waste it used to be. Even after unfortunate crop losses due to black crickets a year ago and then so many cattle dying in the deep winter snows we are still able to find many reasons for rejoicing. Just this past summer we had a bounteous harvest. Recently a company of Saints from the Baltic countries entered the city pulling handcarts. Such a sight. I am busy learning our Deseret alphabet so we can all talk to each other. George sends his warmest regards. His hours are long and responsibilities are many but his faith in the Lord and Brigham refreshes him.
> We miss you and hope to see you before you get too long in the tooth. We have a big new house on State Road and plenty of room, bring your family and come see us.
> Yours in the Reformation.
> Ellen

Julia read the letter twice, leaving fragile first impressions to settle undisturbed. It had been written for two people, Jed and whoever opened it. A jealous husband? She refolded the sheets with a shiver. What quaint mumbo-jumbo—Aaronic Priesthood? Deseret alphabet? Reformation? And just who was Phoebe?

S E V E N T E E N

S ALT LAKE CITY. JANUARY 1857.
"George, how could you allow it?"
"What was I supposed to do?"
"Buy them of course! Five dollars?! They were masterpieces, there was nothing like them in the hall." A hot-water bag appeared from beneath the blankets and, before George could grab it, dropped to the floor. "Never mind," Ellen barked. "It doesn't help anyway. That stupid committee, they couldn't paint a barn."

"They're all apostles' wives."

"Don't give me that crap! They put their shoes on one at a time same as me. Maybe we should could buy a domestic, that would give her more time."

The man seated on the vanity bench winced. Only last week Apostle John Brown had valued his African servant girl at $1,000 on his consecration form. "I don't think Phoebe's got anything to complain about," George offered mildly. "She just…didn't paint the right things, that's all."

"I've told you and told you, Phoebe…" A painful coughing choked off the words.

…will make us all famous. He knew the little sermon by

heart. Only Phoebe wouldn't. She was too careless. Ellen used to think so too, until she read an article in a Gentile paper about great art and decided to send for a home-schooling course. The course never came, the request probably never made it past the censors, but that hadn't stopped her from encouraging Phoebe. Now she had Phoebe thinking she was going to be famous.

A sobbing sound issued faintly from the bowels of the house. Poor Sister Phoebe. She was a lot happier not thinking.

"I don't suppose you could possibly buy them back?" Grey light, seeping around the drawn drapes, lent a marble sheen to Ellen's features. A braid had come undone, the dark curl against her cheek making her younger than her 32 years.

"I'll see what I can do." Leaning down, George brushed the dry, cracked lips with his own. His fierce wife. Slim as a ferret she was, and every bit as wild. That she could fill him with even a ghost of the majestic bonfires of his youth was only because she was so totally whorish. A man would never sell his body the way a woman did. Particularly this woman. Using her teeth and her tongue until he was like a rooting hog, made mad with lust and agreeing to anything.

He shook off the thought, feeling dirty.

She had this mistaken idea that he was some sort of raging bull, restrained but barely by her commands—he must not take another wife, he must not sleep with the wives he already had.

For her part, she'd agreed to go to church every Sunday and to not turn up her nose in public at Brigham's pungent speech. At least he'd kept his share of the bargain! He ought to move her out of their new house on State Road, make her live with Sister Zilpha out on City Creek Road. By god, that'd take the starch out of her!

Why did she have to be so mulish? Why couldn't she be like other women and behave herself? Here he was, a Presiding Bishop of the Church, Recorder of Documents of the Consecration Movement, Treasurer of the Temple Block Public Works, Assistant President of the Perpetual Emigrating Company, Assistant Trustee of the General Tithing Office, and probably several other titles he'd forgotten. But at home he was just plain old "George, I've told you and told you." The very name he himself had coined to describe Christian preachers, fit him like a glove. Pussy-whipped, he was pussy-whipped.

Buy a domestic? Piss on that!

The New Year's Day craft fair was his idea. Phoebe submitted three paintings—"Brigham in Shirtsleeves outside the Temple in Nauvoo," "Wagons Descending a Cliff," and "Children at Play." Visiting the hall during the judging, George had been mortified to see Brigham portrayed with a cowlick loose over his forehead, the rest of the features obscured in what may have been a beard or a shadow. There was no telling, Phoebe having never mastered faces.

In the second painting, several women were walking down a hill in the sunshine. The woman looked radiant, like angels. Below, in the darkness of canyon walls, was a stew of wagons and men and animals. The third painting was of two children (Jeremiah and Nancy, according to Ellen) with no historical backdrop.

All the paintings became the property of the church. The winners were hung in various church offices, the rest were put on display in the Salt Lake House and sold to Gentile buyers for $5 each. As an added incentive for entering the contest, the winners were allowed to sign their entries with their full married name. None of this seemed unreasonable to George. Not everybody could win. The whole point of the craft fair in the first place was to raise money.

Well, maybe now Sister Phoebe would take up knitting.

He grunted aloud in self-agreement and made a stab at joviality. "Sister Phoebe's efforts were certainly appreciated. I over-heard the judges say…"

Like the swipe of a cat's paw, the tendered olive branch snapped back in his face. "…those goddamn women made her write on the back, 'LDS—Only for the money, Phoebe Taggart.' Whoever picked that Selection Committee's a fool."

By god, that is it! I'll turn her over to the Reformation Committee. Let the Danites drag her to the river and re-baptize her, let Brigham put her under the ban.

Evening came on. George heard Phoebe go downstairs to start dinner. Still he lingered, hoarding his emotions against the gloom.

Times were hard. Life in the Territory was becoming pure hell on earth. The summer of '55 pinched the Saints with drought and bugs to see if they were worthy. The winter tested them with deep snows that killed over a thousand cattle. Last summer the crickets destroyed yet another harvest. Now, this winter, starving Indians were thieving what was left of the shrunken cattle herds. Would the trials never cease?

And what did his wives know about suffering? Nothing! Nor did they care a fig about his. That he was working like a whipped slave to set aright the calamitous events of the past two years was no skin off their teeth. All had comfortable houses and large wood piles and good milk cows. All lived better than Brigham's wives, stalled like horses under the same roof.

Last summer he oversaw the construction of seed drills as an alternative to broadcasting by hand, and drew up circulars putting mechanics and artisans to work raising food. This summer he organized over 300 missions to keep the city's idle young men off the dole. But even with the extra December tithing, there was hardly enough to make a life of it. Now

Brigham was wanting fast-day offerings combined with share-the-wealth programs.

Brigham was getting even, that's what.

That George's extraordinary burdens were the result of George's own incompetency was made perfectly clear at Brigham's Pic-Nic Party at the top of Big Cottonwood Creek the previous July.

"Bishop Harris has taken it upon himself to lead the charge for the Lord," the President had shouted joyfully. "Bishop Harris is the sword point that shields all of Zion from the evils of Babylon."

See what happens when Bishop Harris gets out of line.

It started in the early 1850's.

Worried that the church was losing control of the Territory's finances due to the large gold discoveries in near-by California, George persuaded the Council of Fifty to go into the freight- and passenger-hauling business. The Kingdom of Deseret was fast becoming the wagon-hub of the Far West. Gentile wagons crowded the public roads, Gentile stores cluttered the city. The church *must* spread the blanket. Spread the blanket and hold up the corners.

By pegging the overland rate at 12.5 cents per pound, 4.5 cents below outside competitors, the church could monopolize on the freight business. This monopoly would enable the church to buy blooded livestock and heavy farm machinery, resulting in large surpluses for export. Profits from these exports would, in turn, trigger an industrial explosion that would give the church a powerful voice in shaping the future boundaries the State of Utah. It was all so very simple.

At George's urging, the Great Salt Lake Valley Carrying

Company was born. Agents were sent out, wagons built and teams collected. But the company, jauntily referred as the "Swiftsure Line," carried not a single gold miner to California, nor a single piece of Gentile iron west from the States.

Immediately after the company prospectus appeared in the Missouri Valley newspapers, Orson Hyde killed the idea. In a business meeting of the bishops in Provo, the head of the apostles preached against using merchandise purchased in the Christian world from Gentile manufacturers. The warning had Brigham's fingerprints all over it. Let Brigham sneeze, and Orson was ripping up his temple garment for snot rags.

George had no choice but to go straight to the President.

It was early in the morning. Brigham was taking his usual morning stroll. He was hatless, his light-colored hair lifting slightly in the breeze. In his grey baggy coat and grey baggy pantaloons stuffed inside well-oiled Wellington boots, he more resembled a merchant than the most powerful man in the whole of the Territory.

Disdaining the actions of men who groveled at their Prophet's feet, George nevertheless felt his own shoulders round in supplication. Somewhat taller and heavier than Brigham, he leaned forward and stuck out his hand jerkily, ashamed to find himself so grateful for the other's cheerful greeting and affable smile.

Not until that minute—the power of the Lord's Prophet, Seer and Revelator flooding about him—did George realize how much he wanted to succeed. It wasn't just the personal vindication. If the church was to take over world government, as foretold in the writings of Joseph, it *must* be able to compete with the Gentile in the transportation of emigrants and manufactured goods.

In the intensity of his feelings, George saw the smallest details magnified. The sharply pointed nose and close lips that gave Brigham's stolid farmer's face its New Englander's cast. The half-curl of the wheatened hair just below the ears. The broad eyebrows with their thin line of color, the reserved grey-blue eyes, the well-made ringless hands.

Painstakingly reviewing what Brigham had already been told by the Council, George gathered momentum as they walked   . along.

The church was providing only enough goods for its own enterprises. The only thing it exported were horses and work cattle. Merchant Saints like John and Enoch Reese were too few and far between. The bulk of the city's trade was in Gentile hands. Gentile freighters like Holladay & Warner and Livingston & Kinkead—by hauling in their own merchandise and running their own stores—were making tremendous profits.

With his own eyes, George had seen brass kettles full of gold pieces under Gentile counters. Seen outbound Gentile wagons loaded with more gold dust than came into the church mint in a year, along with boxes of silver that required three men to lift them.

They had reached Brigham's office—a large, airy room, high walls adorned with maps and paintings of prominent Saints. There was a salt shaker and a basket of hard-boiled eggs on a table. Brigham closed his fist over one, cracking the shell, and handed it to George who, peeling the food as he talked, plunged deeper and deeper. (Even though he knew better, knew Brigham liked simple explanations, simple plans that took the church where the President wanted to go. Which was exactly why George seldom involved Brigham with the complexities of running the Tithing Office.)

Pegging the gold and silver leaving the city at $20,000 a month, the bishop outlined how to best plug up the drain. Breed mollies out of Mammoth Jack donkeys and Belgian mares. Mollies were capable of carrying 400 pounds apiece and could use the shorter mountain trails to reach some of the more remote settlements. The extra mollies would find a ready market with the Gentile traffic, which would, in turn, increase demand.

Slowly, unfeelingly, a corner of George's brain began to register something he'd never noticed before. Alone, the Lion of the Lord did not roar. Alone, Brigham was conciliatory, even sympathetic. Timid almost.

"This is no time for faint-hearted entrepreneurship," George concluded forcefully.

Then Brigham was showing his bishop the door and thanking him for his devotion, the egg shells crunching under their boots. And George knew, he just *knew*, that Brigham was with him.

The next day, in a secret meeting in the bath house, Brigham accused the leaders of the Council of Fifty of trading with the Devil. For over an hour the President harangued the Council. How soon it forgot Joseph's teachings! Hadn't Joseph said, back in Nauvoo, that the church could not keep a store and be a merchant? Hadn't Brigham pledged himself to Joseph's dream of an independent nation WITHOUT GENTILE INFLUENCE? The Council's brains were rotten as an old pumpkin frozen in the field seven times and then melted in the harvest sun.

The Saints were already too willing to pay cash to the whoresome Gentile merchants. While at the same time borrowing money, cattle and grain from the Tithing store. The stupid, short-sighted ungodly plan put forth by the Council of Fifty would only add to the Saints' problem—driving the frivolous spenders amongst them even deeper into debt. Winter would find them with nothing set by, and they would apostatize rather than pay their tithes.

"It is unSaintly to buy so much as a thimble from a Gentile!" Brigham roared. "Not only does the Council want the church in the mercantile business, they want the church supplying INFER-

NAL MOBOCRATS WHO WOULD SEE ALL ISRAEL IN TOPHET!"

The following Sunday, Brigham announced in the Tabernacle that the Council of Fifty had kindled the wrath of the Lord against it. As a result, home industry would now produce every article used in the home. Saints who ignored the Lord's teachings would be punished accordingly.

George suffered the bitter public embarrassment in silence. Later, at home, Ellen pronounced the order totally unacceptable. She was *not* doing without pins and needles.

George wouldn't say anything.

She prodded him. What exactly *did* he think?

"Gentile merchants," George forced the words through his teeth, "will make more money than ever before. The opportunity for a strong balance of trade will be lost."

"Brigham's an ass," Ellen hissed.

Well, maybe that's why he told her, so he could hear her say it.

That was six years ago and Brigham was still turning the screws, still insisting on domestic manufacture and home industry, still plastering over his own lack of foresight by demanding miracles of others.

Every morning and every night, with Ellen and Phoebe and the children gathered around him on their knees for the required prayer…

> Jehovah bless Brigham in his basket and in his store, and open the heavens to him, that the angels visit and instruct him and clothe him with power, to increase him in wives, children, flocks and herds, houses and lands and make him very great…

...George added the private plea that a way be found to bring the President to his senses. Hells bells! it was 1857! The Gentiles weren't going away. Why not, by all that was holy, do business with them?

His wonderful idea would have worked. The problem was he didn't let Brigham think of it.

Ellen was asleep. George could smell onions frying and the smell made him hungry, but he didn't want to leave. He eased himself off the hard vanity bench and sat on the rag rug, his back against the bed, the sound of Ellen's breath like a comforting hand on his heart.

Lord, God, how I thank you for this woman, sick or well, happy or unhappy. How very much I love her, my little Attila the Hun. Please don't ever take her away from me.

From the very beginning she'd breathed fresh air into his world. Showered him with blessings he'd despaired of ever having—a son to call his own, a beautiful daughter that was his own.

Put Constance in the care of his other wives and taken over the weekly visits with those wives—reviewing their books and regularly reminding them how fortunate they were to live in nice houses and have a provident husband who loved them enough to care for them in their old age.

And never, ever invited them to the home on State Street, except on special occasions, where they sat properly on chairs.

Said things he would never say and needed to hear. Things like he worked too hard and was smarter than any of the apostles, that Brigham wasn't God. The words became little shields, making it easier for him to go to work every day.

Best of all—she gave him back the Sunday outings he'd thought lost with his childhood. At least once a month they went up to the mountains on a picnic—played ball, took walks, explored. Invariably he had an afternoon meeting, invariably Brigham heard of his absence and asked about it, invariably he made up something about having forgotten the meeting or misunderstood the time.

That he didn't feel too guilty about lying had to do with the picnics themselves. Such beautiful disasters. One time the chicken was forgotten, another time the utensils. Once the horses ran away, chased by bees. Another time a herd of cattle plowed right over the picnic linen. One way or another, the account always got squared.

E I G H T E E N

A HOLLERING AND THUMPING NOISE rose through the floorboards. George smiled, shaken from his melancholy meditations. If Ellen were awake, she'd make him go downstairs and put a stop to the rough-housing. But he liked the sound of children tearing around like wild Indians. He never wanted them to grow up and go away into the world outside his door, the frightened world that after dark came knocking—a soft knock he never answered with a lantern.

It began in Kays ward with Apostle Jedediah Grant, Brigham's second counselor in the First Presidency and the Mayor of GSL City. The mayor was a well-liked man, tall, thin, with an acute, vigorous intellect. That he would make the drive up from the city to preach at the local conference was much appreciated. While there, he was joined by a large group of elders who also drove up from the city, among them George's good friend, John Henry, who borrowed Jeddy's mule for the occasion. That evening, the GSL elders having delivered themselves in their usual style, there was much comfort and good cheer in the meeting hall when Jeddy rose to speak.

But the apostle's bitter rain of accusations soon dissolved the splendid feeling. The elders had pushed their animals too hard in covering the dusty 25 miles from Salt Lake City. They didn't sustain the Holy Priesthood. What right had they to talk about good works or faithfulness when hypocrisy and thoughtlessness were their stocks in trade? They were not worthy stewards. The Kays ward bishop and his counselors were no better. Lazy, careless, wicked shepherds with a flock to match. Shame on the elders, shame on Kays ward, the Ammonihah of the northern settlements. SHAME! SHAME!

Following his outburst, Jeddy stomped outside to his buggy, slept there the night, and in the cold, drizzly dawn started off alone for home.

"And the rest of us just as glad to be shut of him." John Henry chuckled, enjoying his story. "He went berserk, George, berserk! Spittle flying from his mouth, eyes bulging out. I do believe a part of his brain fell away. If I'd of knowed he'd get so hopped up over his goddamned mule, I'd of walked."

Several days later, collecting taxes from another in John Henry's party, George asked casually about the Kays ward conference.

"A wonderfully gladsome evening!" the elder replied warmly. "The spirit burned in Brother Jeddy like a living fire."

George went immediately to the old bath house with its new HENRY TANNERY sign. The proud owner was standing in the street, head cocked. An erect, thickset man with grave eyes. "What d'you think, George? Is it straight?"

"Yes. Who else did you talk to about Kays ward besides me?"

"Only Heber." John laughed. "That crazy old fart. He said Brigham wouldn't give Jeddy any more chalk 'til he proved hisself."

George wasn't laughing. "There are cards under the table. Keep quiet."

Two weeks later Jeddy returned to Kays ward with an ultimatum. The Reformation was at hand. The Saints would do their first works over and be rebaptized, or God's judgment would overtake them. The elders earlier abused by Jeddy's tongue were there at the apostle's side to echo his warning. All except John Henry. That same day John Henry met with Brigham in the Library to discuss expansion of the southern colonies.

After the meeting, John stopped by George's office. "Brother Henry is being sent down the chute," the tanner announced grandly, hand over his heart. "Yes, sir, going down to Dixie."

Alarmed, George hastened to shut the inner door.

"It has become the happy lot of Brother Henry to determine what of the southwestern lands will be suitable garden spots for cotton. He is to sell his improvements next to the Twentieth ward bench and use the money to relocate." Broken not by forces he sought to subdue, but by those forces he thought fought with him, John collapsed onto a chair and buried his face in his hands, muffling his next words. "God bless Brother Henry."

After his friend left, George penned an invitation to Jeddy and his wives, the Grant sisters, to come for Sunday dinner. The note applauded Jeddy's call for the Reformation and pledged the full support of the Harris family. Returning the pen to its glass well, George ground the point so savagely that well and all fell to the floor.

The new Henry home and cobblestone barn weren't the first of the vastly improved inheritances to be sold and the owner uprooted to break new ground for the Lord. And no one with more money to spend at the auction block than Brigham himself. For good reason. Who else was able to discharge his obligations to the church by demanding credit in like amount for services rendered? Two hundred thousand dollars alone wiped off the books in '52 against the President's account, and the debit growing again into the thousands.

Prior to hatching the ill-fated Swiftsure Line, the Council of Fifty had been able to curb the President's excesses, but that was no longer the case now that Brigham had rubbed the once powerful council limber as a tallow rag.

George called conversationally to his clerk. When there was no answer, he went looking. The boy was asleep at his desk. Thanking God for small favors, the bishop swept up the glass splinters.

John Henry's banishment was business as usual in the Valley. What was unusual, and ugly, was the shadow from which it sprang—a Reformation of all things. The perfect blotter for Brigham's mistakes. George was scrubbing at the ink stain when the blotter analogy popped into his mind. Covered with shame, scrubbing away vigorously as if on his own soul, the bishop prayed for forgiveness and enlightenment.

But enlightenment, in the weeks to come, only served to strengthen conviction. Brigham's glorious plans for industrializing the Territory were going down a rat hole. The Sugar Works drained $100,000 off the church coffers before being abandoned as a total fiasco. The Iron Mission met its doom in low-grade coal, cold weather, and lack of skilled management. The Wool Factory sheep produced a poor crop and then got eaten by wolves.

Again and again in the Tabernacle, Brigham blamed his managers for being weak in the faith, calling their failures self-serving. He railed at the Gentile equipment manufacturers, likening their offers of help to shit shining in the sun.

Nevertheless, the Prophet was thankful. "I feel like shouting hallelujah all the time when I think how the brethren are strengthened by these trials!"

But he went to the Lord's well too often. Under the Sunday pulpit poundings, the Saints began to shift their feet. Natural disasters and Gentile avarice were one thing, bullheadedness was another. Did Brigham think he was the only one God talked to? Why not let the managers make some decisions? Why not get help from the Gentile manufacturers? they built the equipment for chrissake!

The thoughts welled up in a river of discontent. Brigham could feel it and, hating the people for what he saw in their faces, gave them the Reformation. George was sure this was so.

The city was full of converts fresh from the dank slums of London—converts consumed with a blind and burning zeal. Brigham had only to bend his little finger, and these unlettered, superstitious people would follow wherever he led. So he led them on a inquisition in the Lord's name and used Jeddy as his point dog. "Brigham's sledge-hammer," the Saints called their mayor, with good reason.

Poor Jeddy, a sad loss. A bright young man, fiercely dedicated, as George himself had once been. Wanting only a little time and the patient guidance of reasonable men, Jeddy could have become a great leader, perhaps even First President. Instead, he was to be wasted in a sacrifice that not even Brigham could call back.

The flaming arrow in Brigham's bow was dying.

Jeddy came alone to dinner, his wives staying home to clean and mend his vestments. The apostle had just that afternoon returned from Fillmore and was leaving the next day to spread the gospel of blood atonement in the newly formed Cache and Box Elder counties. His sunken cheeks had a yellowed, transparent tinge. His eyes radiated a spiritual intensity that bespoke death and damnation.

He smiled only once during the course of the evening—at Ellen when she seated him near the fire. The ascetic fare—baked potatoes with no butter, buttermilk with no salt, boiled goat with no seasoning—seemed to please him well enough, but he talked only to his plate and to the floor.

The Reformation…all his time…many sinners…willingness to die…smoking incense…hard medicine. The haunted voice labored and jerked, the fork trembled, the coffee sloshed from its heavy cup.

His listeners watched silently, as they would a broken snake.

A most distressing evening. Except for the actions of George's wives, all six (Constance having but recently died) behaving piously as nuns. Hair pulled severely back under lace prayer caps, grey homespun dresses cinched in by narrow white aprons, chins tucked, voices soft and pleasing. George could *not* get over it. Even Phoebe's extravagant pictures were gone from the hallway and dining room, leaving only a bloody-handed Christ standing alone in the gloom of the desert. The painting hung across from where Jeddy was seated, and was not, George was sure, done by Phoebe.

Immensely pleased at having his domestic affairs so firmly in hand, the bishop relaxed and grew expansive, even going so far as to offer Jeddy wine. Christ looked down on him, Jeddy rolled his eyes, all the grey wives lowered theirs. Overwhelmed, George recorked the bottle and settled back. His own home had somehow become a church!

After their guest left, followed shortly by the outside wives, Ellen told George, "I suppose the next time he comes, we'll have to burn incense."

"That's not what he's talking about." The energy was seeping back into the house. Throwing off the evening's mantle of pious reserve, George was helping to clean the table. "I don't want to scare you, but you know how, when you butcher on a cold morning, the blood steams? Well, that's the smoking incense. Sinner's blood."

Ellen gasped, sliding a stack of dirty dishes into the sink.

"It's just this Reformation thing. I told you he wasn't well."

The next morning in the Tabernacle, Jeddy called Brigham "God" and offered the President his wives and children.

Immediately, Heber threw in a couple of his wives. Stiff with shock, the congregation laughed gingerly. Trust that irreverent old Heber to salt down the brine.

But Jeddy, a dark spirit shaking inside his body, would not be stopped. "I say there are men and women here today I would advise go to the President and ask him to appoint a committee to attend to their case."

He hovered over the pulpit for several long seconds, resting his forehead as if overcome with a great weariness. And making a loud noise, coaxing the air back down his throat, looked up. His thin, hollowed-out face gleamed ghostly white, his dark eyes burned.

"Then let a place be selected, and let that committee shed their blood."

One by one The Twelve rose to second Jeddy's calls. After The Twelve came the president of the stake and his two counselors, then the chief bishop and his counselors. By the time Brother Brigham ascended the pulpit, many in the congregation were as wild-eyed as Jeddy himself.

"Strong doctrine," Brigham whispered harshly. "Strong doctrine, but necessary, if you are for God. ARE YOU FOR GOD?" The Prophet paused, rocked back on his heels, waiting for the ragged chorus of acceptance to come together. And leaning forward, promised, "if you are not heartily on the Lord's side, YOU WILL BE HEWN DOWN!!"

"YES!" Jeddy struggled to his feet. "Oh Lord YES!! Let the sword of the Almighty be unsheathed against Uncle Sam and the Gentiles, not only in word but in deed!" The apostle began to sing. The song had only recently been written and was not well known, so he sang alone. As a young man, he'd possessed a clear, sweet voice, but now it cracked and bled over the words,

> Remember the wrongs of Missouri,
> Forget not the fate of Nauvoo.
>
> When the God-hating foe is before you,
> Stand firm and be faithful and true.

"We're caught up in a nightmare!" a thoroughly shaken Ellen complained after the service. "We've got to get out of here!"

"Close your eyes to it," George warned her. "This madness will pass. We can't leave anyway, not for awhile. I can keep us safe." And he truly believed he could.

In the weeks that followed, Jeddy became a bright comet streaking across Israel's sky—a grim, spell-binding shower of hate and bigotry. Drawn by dreaded fascination, or by the loosening of some curdled wellspring of animal ferocity, crowds attended the apostle's every appearance, there to be charged with all manner of sins and crimes. Becoming caught up in the frenzy, they began to accuse themselves, speaking more and more warmly of blood atonement.

Again and again in Sunday services, Brigham assured the brethren that the throat-cutting, blood-spilling medicine was unavoidable. NO! More than that, much more! Meritorious, glorious, and soul saving! Only by shedding their own blood, that the smoke thereof might ascend to heaven as an offering for their sins, would true believers be saved.

> There are sins that can be atoned for by an offering upon an altar as in ancient days; and there are sins that the blood of a lamb, of a calf, or of turtle doves cannot remit. THESE ARE THE SINS THAT MUST BE ATONED FOR BY THE BLOOD OF MAN!

Fanaticism blind and dangerous poisoned the very air. Weekly meetings devoted solely to the Reformation were held by the high priests, the Seventies, the bishops. Schemes were mooted, plans adopted.

Everything obnoxious to the interests of the Kingdom was to be plucked out. Learning, eloquence, and reason, when used against sustaining authority, were to be denounced without mercy. Attempts at self-improvement were charged with pride, conceit, and wickedness. Parents were told that giving their children anything more than the basics of reading, writing, and arithmetic for the boys, and a knowledge of household, dairy, and farm work for the girls, was an abomination to God.

Keeping to the back rows of the meeting houses, wallowing in abject shame and guilt at his cowardice, George spoke out only to cheer. To be perceived as shaking the dust of the Reformation off one's feet was to place one's own households under the searching eye of God. That his friends wrestled with similar feelings was little consolation to the bishop.

The First Presidency—Brigham and his two counselors, Jeddy and Heber—drew up a list of questions to be asked the faithful. Armed with this catechism, cruel and remorseless spies were set loose in the land like bloodhounds to excite people to confess their most secret sins.

Teachers were appointed for every block in every ward and exhorted to poke and pry into the most indelicate of matters. Family members were separated and questioned alone, and once isolated, told repeatedly that trust and loyalty were the hiding places of the darker angels.

The truthful and simple replies thus ferreted out revealed more than was expected. The church's General Authority became drunk with power, the spies' reports working on them like an aphrodisiac. Confessions became public property, the more lurid the better. Words were noted, actions watched, and expressions—a tone of voice, a whisper—reported with malicious exaggeration.

People who refused to confess were threatened with disfellowship. The only safety lay in studied ignorance. But for the true believer, the thrill of weeding the Lord's garden proved a temptation few could rise above.

The doctrine of blood atonement raced through the outlying communities faster than a grass fire in a high wind. Even as the faithful, exhausted by weeks of acrimonious soul-searching, struggled to put their lives back together, new fears were raised, calling for new commandments.

The Kingdom must be increased, the stronger the Saints, the less mischief Uncle Sam would be able to work. Polygamy, long the providence of a select few, became the responsibility of the masses. A woman foolish enough to let it be known that she did not want to share her husband was openly taunted with "desiring a man to herself."

A man unable to feed extra children was urged to take an additional wife anyway, and withhold his seed until the Lord saw fit to improve his circumstances. Moved by the Spirit, the Legislature provided for the legitimate marriage of boys at age 15 and girls at 12. A son might, if he preferred, marry his half-sister. Twice blessed was the man able to marry a Rachel and a Leah at the same time. Marrying a woman with children, the new husband was encouraged to include the daughters as soon as age permitted in the celestial mysteries of spiritual wifedom.

Young unmarried women were remanded to the care of the society known as Elderly Mothers in Israel. In secret holy meetings, the young women were counseled to avoid young men not yet tried in the Kingdom. In order to be truly saved, these women must accept instead the holy attentions of older tried men. Engagements were broken, the young men sent off to earn the right to full salvation, and their sweethearts sealed with all the power and authority of the Holy Priesthood to gratify a bishop's preference or a great elder's desires.

And every night, school girls, kneeling by their virgin beds, prayed fervently for that ultimate proof of God's love—an invitation from the Lord of the Lion himself to live in his Bee House.

NINETEEN

A SUDDEN CRAMP stirred George's misery. He flexed his leg and rubbed the charley horse, willing himself to think pleasant thoughts, to let God take care of the mess in the Valley. This year he would get out in the yard more, get his hands in the dirt, replant the winter-killed bushes.

He thought about the park in Iowa. Families coming with their food and their blankets, playing ball in the afternoon, building their dinner fires and unrolling their blankets on the pavilion to stay the night. The undulating waves of fireflies with their flickering patterns.

He made a soft moan of complaint—for all the church's big brag about its accomplishments, there wasn't one park—and tried thinking about his bushes again. The leaves were so pretty in the fall, especially the cherry bushes.

But his thoughts, scattering, insisted on collecting themselves under a darker gridiron.

Sunday, November 23, 1856. From a distance the grid of faded leaf trees gives the four-square city the tranquil dignity of an old plaid blanket. Ice crystals, falling from a clear sky, mute the sunshine. The smell of chimney smoke mingles with the smells of bread baking, wet streets, and roasted meat.

In the sheltered places on the adobe brick of the Tabernacle, the ivy is still green. The service overflowing as usual, the double doors are propped open. On the top bench overlooking the congregation—the bench normally occupied by the President and his counselors—sit three gaunt Danes. The Danes have just the day before entered the city with the last remnant of the summer's handcart companies.

Brigham stands at their feet. In their ordeal, he says, the Danes have seen the face of God. Those unfortunates chosen by God to perish in the deep snows while trying to reach their new home, he explains, are part of a divine plan and will never be forgotten.

Understanding no English, the handcart survivors content themselves with staring out on the vast sea of Saints.

Brigham fished a little piece of cardboard out of his pocket. His palms were damp. He glanced at the cardboard, gripping it so hard it crumpled, his fingers smudging the ink. Scalded by humiliation over the ill-fated handcart parade, he wanted to shift the blame to the apostles involved. Franklin Richards, who launched the immigrants from Liverpool. Daniel Spencer, who joined them in Iowa City.

He had his little list of penances to tick off, starting with the vanity and wicked pride that led to the terrible and never-resolved arguments over who would be chief of the companies and, ultimately, to the fatal delay.

"Hereafter, any elders not starting the emigration in season…" He hesitated and plunged on. "…can be thankful if their heads are not found wallowing in the snow." His dizziness mounted. The words blurred.

He took a deep breath and, afraid to start something he couldn't finish, shoved the crumpled card back in his coat pocket.

"Listen, I want you to hear what I say!" he blustered, hanging his hat on a more familiar theme.

> No man cometh to the Father except by me. And he has PROMISED ME that those of the faithful who are beset with gross sin will, by the shedding of their own blood, be saved and exalted with the gods.

Crowded in beside George on a lower bench, Heber crossed and recrossed his legs. "The eighth time in as many Sundays. Goddamn, George, ain't he got nothing better to talk about than shedding blood?"

George smiled—a man would be hard put not to like Heber—but was careful not to seem too agreeable. Spoofing the priesthood and cracking jokes in the Tabernacle were Heber's province and Heber's alone. The littlest sneer from anyone else was sure to light, courtesy of Heber, right in the President's ear.

"Spilling blood," Brigham revealed, gaining momentum, "would be loving ourselves even unto an eternal exaltation."

"There's another $50-dollar word for you," Heber groused. "Make a note."

> Will you love your brothers or sisters likewise when they have a sin that cannot be atoned for without the shedding of their blood? Will you love that man or woman well enough to shed their blood? THAT IS WHAT JESUS CHRIST MEANT!

"Gettin' a little windy, ain't he, George? I wonder what he's got in mind, a firing squad?"

> I have known a great many men who have left this church for whom there is no chance whatever for exaltation, but if their blood had been spilled, it would have been better for them. THAT IS THE WAY TO LOVE MANKIND. Light and darkness cannot dwell together, and so it is with the Kingdom of God. Now brethren and sisters, will you live your religion? WILL YOU LIVE YOUR RELIGION?

The congregation responded with loud cries of "GO IT! GO IT!"

Turning to his guests of honor, Brigham opened his arms wide in welcome.

The Danes stood and began to clap, as did, belatedly, the congregation. Brigham beamed and bowed. The Danes clapped harder, hearts overflowing.

At the President's nod, Heber unfolded himself and mounted briskly to the pulpit, a bald-headed, raffish man with long sideburns and a beard under the chin. He frowned at the congregation. The front rows tittered and sat down, setting off wave after wave of lowering. Heber's face got sourer, the smiles got broader.

Careful, as usual, not to restate Brigham's position, the apostle began by cartwheeling over the earlier sermonizing. Thin voice squeaking and cackling, he explained that just as the Holy Ghost was to Jesus, so he, Heber, was to Brigham. God had revealed this to him.

"And just between you and me," the string-bean prophet confided, leaning over the pulpit, "the Holy Ghost don't want no fiddle-farting around when it comes to understanding The Word. You got to weed out your own patches and hew down the trees that don't produce. God ain't doing your dirty work for you. Not by a damn sight." Heber lifted his eyes heavenwards and nodded firmly, enjoying himself as only a bawdy, rakish man can.

My wives are barren, George thought defensively. *What am I supposed to do, quit feeding them? Even my Ellen could only give me one child.*

Catching himself, the bishop pressed his fingers against his eyes. What horridness he was being sucked into! Insanity! Insanity! His stomach in knots, he twisted to look over his shoulder, seeing in the forest of heads the frozen faces of the children. The sight shocked the bishop. He so loved children, so wished his house could be full of them as other houses were.

Overcome with remorse, he stood and, bumping into knees, hardly giving the worshippers time to shift aside, moved down the row to the center aisle.

Later, he let it be known that he had become ill. But Brigham, as it turned out, had already left.

Bitterly as George resented the profanity and calls for violence that passed for Sunday worship, he resented even more what he himself was becoming.

The shiver in the faces of friends and neighbors met on the street was undeniable. Their greetings, once warm, were fakey with a continuing smile that said he, their own bishop, was the spy at their elbow. And why shouldn't they think that? Look how he denied Jarvis.

Poor Jarvis. George cringed with self-loathing every time he recalled that hideous night.

Dazed and badly beaten, Jarvis, supported by his two wives, had come to beg God's representative in the Endowment House for protection. The shrill voices told a terrible story of being attacked after dark by elders in disguise and dragged by the hair of the head into the street, their store of fine goods robbed and their parlor set afire.

And what did their bishop do? Holy, brave man that he was, standing in the safety of his own front door? What did he do?

Answer loudly with the gossip heard on the street, that's what!

"You spoke evil of Authority."

"I never did so," Jarvis mumbled through smashed lips.

"You had Gentiles to supper in your house."

"That's my right if I want to."

"Sanctuary denied. Denied!" George's answer was immediate. "Israel was at work." Then he leaned close and whispered, "I regret this abuse." And leaning close, smelling the fear in Jarvis and the women, added "I'll see to it that it doesn't happen again."

But except to pray that the Reformation, like the sands that leapt up spinning in the desert, would disappear as it had come, he did nothing. Nothing! No one suspected the depth of his insidiousness—things turning out as they did, the Jarvis family being neglected in favor of fresh, unsuspecting targets—but he knew. Yes, he knew.

The honorable Bishop George Harris was as craven as the Judas goat.

On the first day of Christmas month, 1856, the Apostle Jedediah Grant, barely 40 years old, died. Some blamed his death on lingering too long in the baptismal waters in Kays ward. Ellen said God just got tired of hearing Jeddy talk about cutting people off and cut Jeddy off.

In Jeddy's place, Brigham appointed Apostle Daniel Wells to the Presidency and, troubled with the continuing problem of blood rising to the head, stopped attending services—leaving Heber and Daniel to spur on the Reformation apace.

Everything not sanctioned by the priesthood was denounced as leading to apostasy. Stimulants, particularly, were to be avoided. Evil thus identified sent out bizarre tendrils. Swept off the table of Zion along with alcohol, tobacco, and caffeine were light-minded thoughts and facial hair. A beard must remain under the chin. Bright colors were forbidden, especially red, the color of rebellion. Red barns were repainted, and the marching band's red tassels replaced with white.

All dancing stopped. Three popular fiddlers, rebaptized in a public ceremony, were sent out as missionaries to witness to the Reformation spirit. Their raucous cries of "wake up," "repent," "obey counsel," "pay tithing," "consecrate your property to the church," "get more wives," "give us a good collection," punctuated Tabernacle services.

Moving serenely in the eye of the storm, the President hosted a Christmas Eve entertainment in his new residence, the Lion House, for a few select brethren and a large number of missionaries recently returned from foreign missions.

George's relief at receiving an invitation was so great that he wept with despair at losing his soul.

Enlivened by harmony and the thrilling accounts of the sojourners, the evening passed with real enjoyment. Freely interpreting Brigham's invitation to enjoy themselves with singing and conversation, or with praying and preaching, not a few of the men became quite loud and suspiciously tipsy. Brigham himself drank considerable tithing wine and visited boisterously, even to urging those of his wives present to indulge in a sip.

At one point, a fatherly arm about Ellen's waist, the President noted what a shame it was that there could be no dancing. Hair tumbled, cheeks aglow, he looked boyishly handsome.

Made giddy by the attention, Ellen leaned briefly against the grey frock coat with its gay Christmas decoration. No wonder the Prophet's wives boasted of erasing a chalk mark on one door and redrawing it on their own in order to have an extra helping of their husband's teachings.

Afterward, walking home through snowy streets serenaded by the sleigh bells on the passing sleds and by Christmas hymns sung in the tongues of far-away lands, the partygoers talked of the Reformation as if it were a thing of the past. Brigham's illness was turning out to be a blessing in disguise, giving the Prophet time to reflect on a kinder, gentler Zion, one more in keeping with truth, liberty and love.

Content with singing and light-hearted reunionary conversation, Brigham had not spoken of blood atonement all evening.

T W E N T Y

GEORGE FISHED THE TIMEPIECE out of his vest pocket, but couldn't read the face in the gloom. Dinner should be ready. Without Ellen, Phoebe tended to dawdle. A slow draft of dry, cool air moved through the overlarge room. The bishop fished a stick from the brightly decorated woodbox and poked it in the potbellied stove. Resuming his seat on the rug, he wondered if anyone else in the city painted their woodboxes. His thoughts slid sideways, back to the office.

On the 31st day of January 1857, a Gentile, a cheerful fellow (*how different things look from the other side of the bible,* George reflected) brought to the General Tithing Office a letter spilled from a mail pouch. The letter, dated that morning in the President's private office, was addressed to Apostle Orson Pratt in England.

The clerk off on an errand, George was alone. Curious, the bishop hefted the envelope. Since Jeddy's death, Brigham had limited his public contacts to a few general instructions in the Social Hall. Although still in control of the church, the President no longer seemed in command.

Rumor persisted that Brigham was ashamed of the Reformation, but too ill to wrest it from the hands of the reformers. If this were the case, the President could be calling on Orson for help. The Apostle Pratt was a splendid, manly fellow. Quiet, modest, neither a firebrand nor an echo. His presence would shame the others into returning sanity to the pulpit.

Seduced by wishful thinking, George took out his knife. It would be useful to know how Brigham thought Orson should proceed.

> Judgment has begun in the house of the Lord, and sinners are being looked after.

The peculiarly rough penmanship jumped out at the bishop, condemning the invasion of privacy. A chill washed down his spine.

> ...arousing...people...from habits of lethargy...salutary influences are already perceptible. We have appointed... home missionaries to each ward in this city, and drawn up a list of questions to be asked.... Those missionaries go from house to house, and examine every individual therein separately...much honest confession and restitution have been made...
>
> The saints here are awakening...to live their religion, and do right...
>
> The bread and cup we have withheld from the Saints for some months, to afford them space and time for repentance, restitution and preparation for a renewal of their covenants...
>
> We have had no dancing—no theatrical representations, this season; and the peace and contentment among the Saints is greater than you have ever witnessed; they appear more willing to do as they are told—to abide counsel...

George read quickly, not wanting to believe. Peace and contentment? when counsel consisted of being dragged to the river Jordan and beaten? when the bread and cup being withheld was the bread of life and the cup of human kindness? when the home missionaries were Danites and the stronger food meant death for sinners?

The man who urged Yule candles be hung in the winter trees to give Europeans a taste of home, the man who hosted a Christmas party with wine and fine food, and himself led the singing, had changed his stripes not a whit.

The clerk returned from his errand. George scattered papers over the usurped letter and busied himself. A crude drawing entitled "Prophet, Seer and Revelator" stared up at him reproachfully from an old newspaper not yet clipped of its market reports. Beneath the drawing was Brigham's sermon on frugality dated January 27, 1856.

> I tell you honestly that I do not know when I have been more thankful, in all my life, than I have to see the pinching hand of want compel every man and woman to pray to God our Father to give us this day our daily bread. It makes me happy, inasmuch as the people will not otherwise understand that the Lord does feed them...

Strangled with rage, George stared at the newspaper. The brethren were better off then, with starvation nipping at their heels, than they were now with the loathsome dogs of fear and revenge.

The droppings of the Sanctuary were polluting the city. The President and his men were deliberately destroying the warm affection the people had for each other—affection that came from having shared the same hardships.

George's own neighbor had taken to keeping her living-room curtains drawn, the better to watch the Harris household and run to prayer meetings with such tidbits as Phoebe's hanging red rags on the line and the roses wanting pruning. The old lady's craziness was harmless enough (*certainly my wives think so,* George reminded himself), but what if he were not a high priest with a title? Would he find himself spying on the neighbor in self-defense?

He took out a clean sheet of paper and, in a hand deliberately made shaky, told Orson

> You are needed here. We are taking to killing apostates to save them. We are destroying Zion. Come home.

He folded his letter inside Brigham's and, sticking a finger in the glue pot, resealed the envelope and dropped it in the Endowment mail pouch. Afterward, making out a receipt for a consecration form, he noticed that his hand still shook.

His worst fears were for his family. Brigham stored old grievances the way a man hoards good silver. The President could very well choose to remember Phoebe's outburst of four years ago when she stopped to buy ribbons from Elder Smith.

Smith was speechifying on a public street about the spirit of Mormonism, when a handful of younger Saints took issue with a point of doctrine and attempted to move the elder's wagon. Protecting the old man, Phoebe drove his attackers off with a stick.

The following Sunday, in a sermon on apostacy, Brigham referred to the incident, noting that a "certain picture-maker" had become violent with the boys. Brigham concentrated his attack on the Smiths, newly come from St. Louis with Gentile trash in their wagons and on their minds. But after service, privately counseled George that Sister Phoebe had been ignorant of the Smiths' apostasy and shown her ignorance by speaking out, which was against scripture.

What kept Ellen's sins from catching up with her, George had no idea. She thought Brigham profane and a bully, and every Sunday she went to church (which was not *every* Sunday), George had to caution her against showing too full a face. He had gotten her clear of the Literary and Musical Society barely in time, his alarm triggered by the abrupt resignation of the poetess Eliza Snow, who pronounced the weekly meetings "a little too arty."

"It's become too dangerous."

"You can't be serious, George! Brigham's just jealous of his talented wife."

"I know that."

"Brigham's never read a book in his life. It's important, if the church is ever going to amount to anything, to have leaders who read, who want to improve their minds. The Society people recite literature and poems and have music. There's nothing in the offerings to offend anybody."

George agreed again. With that and every other furious assertion. Nonetheless, and he was very firm about this, Ellen must stay away from the meetings for the time being.

Ten days later the group was dissolved and, in an orgy of public humiliation in the Tabernacle, charged with pride, ambition, big-headedness, conceit, and sins. Immediately afterward, eight of the Society's most talented and well-known men were sent from their seats to be keepers at the door.

The memory grated on George like a potato ricer. He began to rock back and forth, kneading the edge of the rag rug with the heel of his hands, knocking his head against his fears. His very own Ellen had come that close to being publicly shamed!

"Mr. G....MR. G.! DINNER'S READY," Phoebe called from the bottom of the stairs.

The worried man patted the limp hand on the counterpane and struggled to his feet. He could hardly walk, he was so stiff. Years ago he'd installed a heavy railing that ran the length of the upstairs hallway for Constance, never dreaming that he himself would someday need it.

Depending on the dish, dinner was either burned or under-cooked. It didn't matter to anyone else, so it didn't matter to George. The children argued loudly with each other—Phoebe taking sides and adding fuel to the fire. George didn't care about that either, liking the noise, wanting his own arguments out of his ears.

After supper, the knock came again. He pulled on his woolen coat and stepped outside. At the onset of the Reformation the voice from the shadows used to sound incredulous and a little breathless, as if its owner had just come from a bad accident. But more and more the whispered words sounded of frustration and angry oaths.

Brother Wilson had been taken to the river Jordan and bru-tally beaten, his hands broken. His wife sought Brigham's help, but the Prophet refused, calling her weak in the faith.

The woodcarver who shaped the lion on Brigham's new house was forced to flee in the night with his wife and children, leaving behind all his fine furniture and tools.

Salter, the watchmaker, when asked about having Gentiles to supper, told the ward clerk he'd as soon have Gentiles at his table as elders who wore pillowcases over their heads after dark. The Missouri and Illinois Danites got him for that, whupped him good.

There was a long silence. George cocked his ear, hearing the retreating crunch of boots in the snow.

Late that night, in the darkness of his own bedroom, the questions, like little bats, settled again in the bishop's ears.

Could a church born out of persecution not live without it? Were the Saints bored with living in such a remote part of the world? Was this to be the end of their labors, a corrupt prophet who insisted that life and death were in the hands of the priests? who called his tirades holy sermons and egotistically ordered them scribed in the official "Journal of Discourses"?

In 1851, right after Nancy was born, George had given a speech he called "Looking to the Future."

> ...Born among mobs and cradled on the billows of persecution, we have learned to appreciate the banquet of peace that we enjoy in the valley of Ephraim. We have left Nauvoo and what happened there to the history books. We know that vengeance is God's and His alone, and that our little children must grow up looking to the future...

The speech was well received, but it didn't seemed to change anything.

Thinking about Nancy led to thinking about polygamy. Children marrying their half-siblings for god's sake! That Brigham would countenance that sort of allowance made George nauseous. By all that was holy, *his* children would pick their mates the Christian way or he *would* leave the church.

But where to go? He'd soon be 65, just an old fat man. Could he still find work in the Lord's vineyard? And what to do with Phoebe. She'd need to be Ellen's sister, or the children's nanny. Oh, there'd have to be all sorts of lies. All sorts. His poor children. He felt hollow at the core and began to sob, the covers wadded against his mouth.

Willing the soul-scouring storm to pass, he thought about the Temple.

Ah, the Temple. More than once late at night, weary and ill at ease, he'd put himself to sleep with thoughts of that white edifice—so wonderfully depicted on the drawing boards—rising against a blue sky. But here lately he seemed to be sinking into a morass. Would he live long enough to see so much as a doorway or a single spire? Ever since April Conference 1851, the church had been collecting temple funds. Six years later there was nothing to show for the monies but an unfinished public-works wall around unbroken ground.

What was Brigham doing with all that money?

He shifted his thoughts to the millennium and, wonderfully sedated, drifted off to sleep.

And to dream.

The first thing Christ did was to raise the Temple. Four stories high the great walls rose, anointed with towers and magnificent stained-glass windows. Strains of heavenly choirs filled the air, broad stairways climbed upward toward tall, arched doorways. Bookcases filled with scrolls lined the walls. Polished floors reflected massive hardwood tables and chairs.

A celestial current lifted him up and bore him away to a garden where the kindly Christ waited. Peach trees bloomed and bore fruit. And here came Brothers Harrison and Stenhouse, Pratt, Henry, Godbe, Tullidge, Kelsey and Lawrence and others—gloriously tenacious friends all, uncompromising in their generosity, courageous in their beliefs—come to eat the sweet fruit and talk.

Would the Son of God put as much emphasis on good administration as on the issue of children? George asked.

Yes, came the firm answer.

The bishop woke before dawn and, recalling the dream, smiled. It was closer to a revelation. How could any man be vain enough to believe his place in Heaven depended on the fertility of his wives? If that were the case, Heber already had so many descendants no one would ever catch up.

A stray truth, like a hard, green lime, rolled into George's mind, shattering his tranquillity. Of all the important churchmen in the city, he was *the only one with more wives than children.*

TWENTY-ONE

> Here is the church
> and here is the steeple.
> Open the door…annnnnnnnd…
> here's all the people!

LYMUND SQUEALED AND PULLED the toffee from his mother's finger. And found himself suspended above her head. Giving deliberate thought to what he was about, he opened his hand and let the gooey wad fall straight into her mouth. She made a surprised face. Lymund made a face to match. But the candy didn't reappear. To his loud dismay.

"Dinky! Stop teasing that baby! C'mon, Lymund, come to grandma."

Grabbing his grandmother's ear, Lymund pulled himself toward the bonier, friendlier embrace. Christina poked a piece of toffee in his mouth, "poor baby Mun, gotta stay home, don't get no fun," and eased herself into the rocker, a stern-faced, colorless benefactor.

Lymund played with her beads and happily dribbled melted candy down her dress front. In the sunshine the old iron toys on the side cabinet looked warm and rubbery—teams stretched out, drivers leaning forward, safely on their way to nowhere.

A puff of air through the open front door set the wallpaper curtains to swaying woodenly and stirred the house smells— Lymund's violet powder, boiled sugar and butter, mutton roasting, Brother Jonathan furniture polish.

The floorboards creaked and sighed, sighed and creaked—the old Seth Thomas clock keeping time from its rack on the wall. Lymund's head drooped, silken hair brushing his grandmother's chin. Folks said Dinky's children had their father's hair, but Christina remembered her own Jed being every bit as towheaded.

"Ma!" The tone curled up and down in amazement. Dinky and the twins were bringing the clothes in off the line and spilling them on the couch.

Christina planted her feet flat on the floor.

"Is this your only robe? They'll think you poor as a church mouse."

"Here!" The older woman pushed herself upward, sliding Lymund onto the rug where he cried out and went to sleep. "I'll take care of my own things." Upright in her heavy shoes, she tilted backward, as if determined to avoid being bent into a half-circle by old bones. "Besides, I haven't made up my mind yet."

"You gotta go!" cried the twins in unison.

"But of course you're going," Dinky said. "It's the only way we'll ever meet Jed's wife, he's never going to bring her here. What a stick-in-the-mud he's getting to be, just like Walker."

"It's just not practical."

"I'll pay for the rooms. That only leaves your fare—50 cents for the HR to New York, $2.00 for the morning train to Boston, $2.00 from Boston to Portland, $2.50 for the carriage to Houlton." A smiley little dragon intent on being understood, Dinky ticked off the amounts on her fingers. "That's $7.00 each way, plus a travel hat."

"And food."

That's not such a much. Walker doesn't need to plow all your money back into the ground."

"So what are they supposed to think when they see me in a hat as big as a dishpan?"

They'd purchased the hat on a shopping trip to Troy, where Dinky had dubbed the shoppers "the Maine Brigade." Anne and Emily had been using the name ever since. It was enough to drive anyone crazy.

"You'll look just grand." Dinky answered absently.

Christina grimaced. Here she was, an old lady in her seventies who asked nothing more than to wake up in her own bed and eat at her own board. Not run around like a silly goose with a borrowed traveling bag and a headdress that looked like wilted hollyhocks on a plate. Her only daughter was really her own father, Thomas Locke, whom she'd forsaken years ago to marry Jean Paul. Behind Dinky's lovely, chocolatey eyes was a blue-eyed, iron-willed German farmer bent on revenge.

Shorter and heavier than her mother, with a quick smile and enormous energy, Dinky had moved home from Ohio at Thanksgiving and lollygagged away her time since, visiting about the neighborhood. Now, tricked by the unseasonably warm winter the same way the trees were, she was on pins and needles to have everything done and to be packing for California instead of Houlton.

"I forgot when I was in Troy to order up some of those new parlor lamps," she mused, lifting the etched-glass table chimney off its stub of tallow to rub idly at the nicked rim. "Kerosene is perfectly safe and gives so much more light. And Walker can rock in the fireplace and nail down a carpet, you'll be warmer. God, the paint in this room is awful!"

"Dinky! don't get your Dutch up! I don't want you painting. And don't swear. Ladies don't swear."

"Walker can have it painted while we're gone. Treat yourself."

Wednesday, February 25, 1857. Half-past ten in the morning. Walker should be arriving any minute. Christina put her hand on the stove lids, straightened the table linoleum, tested the backdoor latch. She didn't check upstairs. It was getting harder and harder to come down the worn, crooked steps. With Dinky home, she didn't have to.

Killing time, she pulled out her sewing box and snipped off the peppermint-striped follow-me ribbons on her hat. And heard an errant honey bee bump against the kitchen window, a victim of its own persistence. Having taken up housekeeping under the eaves, the bees occasionally followed a wrong corridor through the wall. Lifting the window, she brushed the miscreant outside.

The front-room floor, scrubbed the day before with Fuller's earth and rinsed, gave off a mustardy patina. Mirrors, newly dusted with fine-powdered chalk and rubbed clean with leather, sparkled like diamonds. One never knew. People died all the time on trains. Boilers burst, bridges broke, rails snapped, draw-bridges were left open. The least she could do was leave the house clean.

Going down, they would stay the night with Jean Paul's brother in Albany. It would be the nicest part of the journey, Theodore looked and sounded so much like Jean Paul.

Dinky's room smelled of mint potpourri from the open sack hanging in the wardrobe. It had always been Dinky's room, added on the side of the house by Jean Paul, whose genuine astonishment at her arrival—"but I never have daughters!"—still rankled when recalled. The room felt like spring, the morning light filtering through the sway of new buds on the red oak, the window ajar on a wood chip, yellow gingham curtains tied back.

Christina removed the chip and, lowering the glass, saw Lymund. He was standing on his fat little legs considering the pile of luggage out by the gate. Frowning, hands on hips. It was such a sweet little stance, his own funny habit when perplexed.

She might never see him again, or Walker's youngsters. A wave of homesickness swept over her, so strong it nauseated her.

It had been her idea to leave Lymund behind with his aunt. (Whatever Katherine's faults, she wasn't lazy or mean.) Poor little tyke, he was barely two. Too little to go gallivanting around, be it Maine or California. Actually, the twins shouldn't be going either, they were only four. But Dinky was her father's daughter.

Jean Paul liked to tell how he walked down into William Penn's country and never stopped till he found a bride. Dinky wasn't going to stop until all three of her kids stuck their feet in the Pacific Ocean.

A *M'Guffy's Fifth Reader* and several heavier volumes with heavier names, *Social Destiny of Man*, *Cyclopædia of American Literature*, wrinkled the dresser cloth. Dinky called them the tools of her trade.

Christina lifted a corner of the books and smoothed the linen, wondering what was it about young women nowadays that made them want to sound like men. Stacked on the floor were other books—*Moby Dick*, *The Scarlet Letter*, *Walden*, *Leaves of Grass*, *The Blithedale Romance*—the winners in a sifting out that had taken place the previous evening. They'd had the best time, she and Dinky and Katherine, trying to decide what books Dinky should ship around the Horn.

"Take this book," Christina had begged, digging through buttons and balls of thread in her Housewife's Friend to pull out

The Lamplighter and read aloud of little Gerty's meeting with Mr. Flint. "Don't you think that's sad?" Tears filled her eyes. "Poor Gerty. Without Mr. Flint to shelter her, she'd have a terrible life."

"Little Gerty was able to hitch her wagon to a star alright," Katherine declared.

Having recently become a Transcendentalist, hitching a wagon to a star was her favorite saying. She was sitting on the floor, black stockings rolled down, skirt (as usual, without petticoats) hitched up over her hairy legs and piled between her knees.

Christina had a fleeting, distressing picture of her daughter-in-law sitting down that way at home to play jacks with the youngsters. Poor Walker. Katherine had as much class as a cowflop. As a girl, she'd been pretty in a hoydenish kind of way, but always rowing upstream was leaving her loud and mannish. Her thickening shoulders and black bushy eyebrows didn't help any.

Christina made a small sound of resignation and opened *The Lamplighter* to another passage, this time having to do with how hard Mr. Flint worked.

Taking her turn, Katherine quoted Harriet Beecher Stowe from the heart, her usual challenging expression smoothing mournfully.

> Eliza made her desperate retreat across the river just in the dusk of twilight. The grey mist of evening, rising slowly from the river, enveloped her as she disappeared up the bank, and the swollen current and floundering masses of ice presented a hopeless barrier between her and her pursuer.

Katherine folded her hands prayerfully. "Slavery is so *utterly evil!* I can not believe we've allowed it to go on this long. Did you read *Uncle Tom's Cabin?*"

"I don't care for books like that," Christina answered, entertaining herself with the possibility that Katherine's dark curly hair was really kinky hair. "There's nothing we can do about it."

Dinky was leafing through a book by Whitman. She *absolutely could not exist* without this book.

> I celebrate myself and sing myself,
> And what I assume you shall assume....
> I loaf and invite my soul....
> None has begun to think how divine he himself
> is, and how certain the future is.

Why was it, Christina puzzled, listening to the passage, that the only time her daughter sounded religious was when she was reading goofy things like that?

"That just makes me want to cry!" Katherine wailed.

"I'll give you something to cry about," Christina said and read an excerpt having to do with little Gerty's being raised in an orphanage with no schooling.

"That's just as well," Dinky said firmly. "'The child should be prepared to take his place in society, not stuffed drum-tight with useless facts.' Pestalozzi. He's a philosopher, ma."

"Oh, he's so dumb," Christina pulled her glasses down her nose and peered over them, "he wouldn't know blue beans if the sack was open. You went to the seminary."

"Going to a female seminary's like going to a nunnery. If I had it to do over, I'd go to Antioch in Yellow Springs. There's women teachers there, and they have absolutely equal rights with men. I hope we can find something like that in California for the girls."

"What do you mean, 'equal rights'?"

"Take me," Dinky tapped her head, "I'm as good a teacher as any man and better than some I've met. In Ohio, I get $50 a month, the men get $60."

"Women are absolutely everybody's doormat." Katherine knew. "Especially wives. There's absolutely no difference between wives and slaves. Men think of a wife as chattel. They can beat her, anything they want. They're worse than animals when it comes to sex. At least animals…"

"…school pay, that's alright, I guess…" Christina's quick words and pained expression anticipated, and correctly so, the twins having crept downstairs to listen just out of sight.

"But it's important for men to be top dog. They ain't happy otherwise. Whereas with most women it ain't so important." She had to work at keeping her face bland. "Besides, somebody's got to stay home and have babies."

"Did you ever think God could be a woman?" Katherine asked.

Christina had had enough. "You've got more book learning than you've got sense, Katherine Marchion!"

The profound indignation on her mother's face set Dinky jiggling with laughter. "I'll leave my 'Literary World' subscription come here, ma," she said when she could. "Let me know how you like it."

T W E N T Y - T W O

I
F I WAS A FISH, *we'd all have a fry,* Christina told herself wist-
fully, wishing Jean Paul were boarding the Albany train with
her, wishing she were going upriver instead of down. It'd been
42 years since she'd been upriver.

The Frenchman who came out of the woods at harvest festival
smelled of saddle leather and whiskey. Lean as a wolf he was,
with the dark and roving eye of a hunter. When he touched her
hand, it was like the time she was drawing water from the yard
pump and lightning hit the creek. Dancing with him was like
swinging on a star. But instead of demanding a kiss, he asked her
to marry him. Why? she never knew why.

The ceremony took place in the church yard in Economy,
deep in the Pennsylvania hill country. She wore the same grown
she'd worn to the dance and braided her hair on top of her head
like a great lady. Arriving early with her parents, seeing the
Frenchman seated on a stump smoking his pipe, turned her weak
in the knees. She'd feared being jilted, now she faced a future of
a different kind, something with no pattern at all. Seized with a
queer abandon, she undid her hair as she walked away from the
wagon, the honey-colored cascade falling to well below her
waist.

Curious family and friends came from miles around to counsel quietly with her parents, who confessed shamefacedly they'd had no say in the sad affair. How many Indian wives did the stranger have? Christina could see the question in their faces. And why he was turning the blanket for a white woman taller than he and not the least plump?

Heavy beard trimmed close, dark hair held back in a red ribbon, the doomed man waited patiently for the ceremony to put itself together, assuming his place when told. Christina was struck by his aloneness, no friends about to buck him up, no trappings of any kind, not even a horse. Struck too by the realization that her father was right. There was no farm in New York, no rich parents.

And still she said "I do."

The minister closed the bible. Jean Paul pecked lightly at his bride's cheek and said something in his own language, and they left in a shower of barley seed and good wishes. But not before the young, single girls kissed the groom and whispered things in Christina's ears that made her blush.

North and east the newlyweds walked through the colored woods out of Pennsylvania and up along the lake waters. Like her husband, Christina packed her blankets and extra clothing on her back. And unlike her husband, never wanted the journey to end. The days like wine under bright Indian-summer skies, the nights full of the nakedness of their bodies skin to skin, all their secrets unveiled in the soft whorl of animal furs.

"Before ever I saw you I dreamed of a woman such as you. I was afraid you would not have me, poor unlearned trapper, a nobody, and you so beautiful. What is it you want of me? how can I ever repay you, *ma belle sans peur et sans reproche?*"

"Oh no, Jean Paul, you are a wonderful person, you're not a nobody, don't ever say that. I love you so much. I can't believe you're not interested in my father's farm. It's my dowry. The men who walked out with me always spoke of it."

"And how many trappers do you walk out with?"

"Well, none." She laughed at his silliness. "Economy is very civilized."

"There! you have it! The men of your acquaintance (he made them sound like round heels) are afraid to speak of more. Yes! afraid. It takes a Frenchman to bed a queen!"

(The only really bad memory—she never dwelled on it, indeed had mostly forgotten it happened—was his trying to leave her behind in one village after another. He must hurry north alone, he said, do his trapping. And she must wait. He would come back in the spring. But she slept with one eye open, and when he left their bed, she dressed and followed. In time he recognized the foolish cruelty for what it was and put it aside.)

Upon reaching Canada, Jean Paul bought two poor horses and an old saddle from the Indians. He could not go home afoot, he said. Four weeks after leaving Economy, on a quiet well-shaded street a mile north of the river, he drew rein at the Chateau Marchion signpost.

Christina gazed in disbelief at the noble three-story, white clapboard surrounded by lawn and flowers. "Go tell them first," she begged when he came around to help her from the saddle. But Jean Paul wouldn't hear of it. Warn his family ahead of time? of what?

When her feet touched the ground, he kissed her hard on the mouth and scolded, "Ah, Christina, you are a witch! Right here in the open street before my birthplace you would seduce me!" Christina's face flamed bright pink, and Jean Paul added softly, "come, ma *beaux yeux*. They will love you as I love you."

Their boots sounded hollow on the planking. Borders of

bright daisies waved them on. A large mahogany peat bucket holding umbrellas propped the door ajar. Christina entered as if in a dream, a dream that disintegrated when she saw the ragamuffin in the narrow looking-glass in the foyer. Dirty face, hair uncombed, shirtwaist gapping open. Mortified, she did up the button and, licking on her fingers, washed her cheeks. And followed her husband into an unbelievably beautiful room dominated by a large white table. On the far side two white staircases curved down hame-like.

"Wait here," Jean Paul ordered and sprinted up the stairs.

The table sat on a wool rug patterned with red-and-gold flowers. In the center was a starched circle of lace and in the center of the lace a golden candelabra. Tall glass-door cabinets occupied the corners of the room. Large rusty-colored tapestries of men astride jumping horses decorated the white walls.

Christina felt a small spring tighten deep inside. She'd been far more comfortable thinking her husband a liar.

A very American looking woman, alerted by the muddy-hocked horses at the hitches, hurried into the room. Her loose bob of chestnut hair resembled a large, windblown cap, her arms were full of orange and purple gladiolus.

Christina stood speechless, fingers splayed against her trail-soiled skirts.

Her eye caught by the knobby gold wedding band partially wrapped with twine, Rebecca Marchion lay the cuttings on the table. Her father's ring, on this woman's hand?

"Madame Marchion?" The words floated down the stairway, impatiently, imperiously.

Rebeccah smiled even as her eyes filled with tears. "Is it me he calls for, or you?" Thus did Jean Paul find them, hugging and crying at the same time.

"Hey, *mon dieux!* everybody crying! Here, here, you cannot cry! I make the introductions. Mama, my wife, Christina

Marchion. Christina, my mama, Rebeccah Marchion. Yes and where is papa, eh? And dinner? I am starving." Hugely pleased with his surprise he gathered the women against him and headed for the kitchen.

Samuel Marchion, arriving home late that afternoon, found the imposing stature of his new daughter-in-law rather astonishing. His sons had always preferred the *bona petite* dames. He kissed the American *poulet* lightly on each cheek, solemnly welcoming her to the City of Montreal and the Family of Marchion. And looking into her eyes, smiled. Ah, that was it. Those beautiful hazel eyes flecked with gold. A Marchion had no hope against them. He himself was living proof.

Delighting in his new role as tutor, Jean Paul overwhelmed his bride with the hustle and bustle of Canada's major shipping port. Ten wild and crazy days the newlyweds ricocheted about in the *beau monde* of the Ville-Marie de Montreal. A trip to the parliament building to hear cousin so-and-so speak, then off to the race track across from Mount Royal. A wild ride downstream through a flotilla of ocean-going freighters and small inland-hopping vessels to test a rebuilt steam engine, followed by an overnight visit to Hawkesbury to inspect a new lumber mill. Several visits to museums to view artifacts collected by Jean Paul in his travels amongst the Indians. A sightseeing jaunt to the bluffs overlooking the St. Lawrence. A steady round of obligatory suppers.

Abruptly it was over. "We leave tomorrow," Jean Paul announced and off he went alone to the city to busy himself with the business of leaving.

Left to her own devices, Christina wandered about the common rooms of the chateau, encountering servants who, conversing in French, turned their backs to the *roturier*.

And eventually finding herself in the kitchen. Two over-large Russian stoves anchored opposite ends of the room. Open

cupboards displayed enormous collections of tin-glazed earthen-
ware, delicate bone china, and redware. Wide work counters
with cabinetry above and flour bins showed off brightly-painted
canisters and bread boxes and stacks of round spice boxes. Low
shelving in the middle of the room accommodated grinders,
presses, pots, and pans.

Opening on the kitchen was a large dark pantry full of more
kitchenware. An outside door and a short, covered walk led to
a buttery—cool and damp, smelling of fresh milk and faintly
soured butter. Beyond the buttery was the washroom, where
deep sinks laddered with washboards were joined by the
strangest washing machine Christina had ever seen.

Sitting frog-like off by itself, the large, yellow barrel rested
at a tilt on a nest of wheels. A lever rolled the barrel around,
another lever tipped it up and down. She was fiddling with the
contraption when she heard her mother-in-law's voice out in the
yard.

"Ah, *cheri*, it is better than I dared hope. He was so wild.
Sometimes when he came home from the woods, I hardly knew
him."

"That's where a young man belongs, in the woods." Samuel's
voice.

"He is forty-one years old!"

"So?"

"What is it about her you don't like?"

"She's a farmer's daughter!"

"So was I."

"But you came here with me, she is taking him back."

"Samuel! his brothers are there!"

"But he's no farmer, Rebeccah. That's why we gave him the
woodlot and the orchard in the first place. And why in twenty
years he hasn't touched either. He hasn't even got a shed to live
in!"

"What goes around comes around. You were living at home…"

"…I didn't need a house, I was never in town.…"

"…neither did Jean Paul need a shed, he was never in New York."

The argument faded. Christina remained where she was, working the lever on the clothes washer, watching the wheels come together, wondering what kind of a grand house Jean Paul would build her.

One last supper out and home early. They were in the bedroom. She was curled on the couch, the pale welkin gown, a gift from Rebeccah, puffing about her like harebell petals. She had eaten too much, again. Breast of duckling in cider sauce, biscuits with lemon-pear butter, fig and raspberry tarts, all sorts of little side dishes. Jean Paul wanted her clothes off, but she was hardly in the mood.

"I'm stuffed, and now I'm getting cold. Jean Paul! what are you doing?"

"If you get cold enough maybe you will come to bed."

"How can you stay so skinny?"

"By not staying here, why do you think I go off into the woods?"

She had pleased him mightily that evening, joining in, quite unexpectedly, on a conversation having to do with bulls. One of the men was complaining about having a bull that wouldn't stay home.

"Bulls ain't smart enough to come back when they got business to home," she had observed.

Whereupon Jean Paul sent her off to fetch some brandy and made a show of looking down at his nose at her when she left, but he found her candor, or maybe it was the subject, rather exciting.

Christina arched her back, wishing his fingers were warmer. "Now you don't need to go into the woods," she whispered, embarrassed by her forwardness.

"Yes, I will. Does that bother you?"

"Oh, I guess not. Long as you're true."

"In my way, yes."

Something in his voice… She turned around, shaking the loosened gown to the floor and surveying him indignantly, hands on hips. "Well, that's a terrible thing to say!"

"What did you expect of a Frenchman?" He lolled back, obviously enjoying what he was seeing.

"Are you poking fun?" She worked the fastenings of her corset hesitantly, aware that the game was slipping away.

"Surely you're the one who is poking fun." Jean Paul became instantly scornful and hardly happy. "Do I think it necessary to ask you if you will be faithful?"

Christina stamped her foot in exasperation. "I know that you're true, I was just…talking. I don't care…I mean…I do care, of course, and I know you would never…misbehave." Her voice thickened, the German coming out, as it did when she got excited.

"You don't know what you mean, so I will tell you. I choose you to be my wife. I will care for your needs and you will care for mine. There is nothing else that concerns you. I do not know you are so spoiled and foolish."

"I ain't spoiled!" Her voice rose. "I try real hard to do everything right!"

"What is it, then, that doesn't please you?" The words as cool as wind over ice. "That makes you so unhappy as to pick a fight?"

"Nothing! I'm cold and I'm tired," her mouth trembled, "but I ain't unhappy."

"Then two things you will remember from now on, Madame Marchion." Jean Paul pushed himself off the couch and placed his hands lightly on his wife's naked shoulders. In his boots he was nearly as tall as she. "The first is that we will know children and grandchildren together. The second is that good wives are made by good husbands," his smile forgave her tempers, "and I intend to be a very good husband. Finish undressing and get in the bed. But first," he touched the lobe of her ear and the hollow between her breasts, "put on the perfume I bought you today in the market. It pleases me."

Early in October, in a cold rain bringing down the last of the faded leaves, Jean Paul loaded the horses onto the ferry that crossed the St. Lawrence between Montreal and the portage path around the Chambly Rapids to Fort Edward. In the few minutes remaining, Rebeccah found a pair of woolen wristlets in her bourse, prompting Samuel to throw up his hands and threaten to leave immediately for home to see if there were anything left.

"Do you see what happens when you give up your freedom, my son?" Samuel made a show of shaking out a white hem-stitched handkerchief and wiping at his tears. "Instead of one pack horse, you now have three, all so loaded with gifts for your nieces and nephews and linens for your new wife that you must carry your own bedroll behind your saddle. And now comes the worst part, now you must begin immediately to build your house in a foreign country! and to finish it in the dead of winter! And what do you get for all your troubles? my old wristlets thrown in as an afterthought!"

"Don't pay your father any mind," Rebeccah smiled prettily at her son, "these wristlets are brand new. Besides, they're for Christina."

◈

Her magic *chevalier*. (She read the word in a book and it fit her
Frenchman just right.) Shortly after their house went up—a
salt-box affair with two bedrooms upstairs and one down, where
the rocky soil at the edge of the orchard climbed upward under
oak and hickory—Jean Paul went hunting for a month. She was
sure he was lost. His brothers knew otherwise. Angrily stopping
to inquire with closed faces if she needed anything.

She'd long ago forgotten how he explained his absence, or
if he even tried. She just remembered the hat sailing into the
kitchen and landing with a soft plop on the floor.

She got used to it eventually, his needing to reward himself
for raising buildings, gathering and selling apples, erecting a
cider mill, harvesting timber, having babies. They reached an
understanding of a sort. He made a living off his trapping and
the farm, she put up a big garden. He told breathtaking adventure stories, she never asked for details. The boys went with him
as soon as they could walk, and upon their return threw their
hats in the door the same as he.

And also, she felt certain, when they got older, slept with
squaws.

For years the splendor that was Montreal transformed their
Christmases with warm clothing and blankets. Twice Jean Paul
took his sons to Canada, they still talked about those trips. Then
poor Rebeccah died unexpectedly of pleurisy.

Samuel secluded himself for nearly a year, during which time
his principal camp and a large tract of timber suffered a devas-
tating fire. He next took up residence at a religious commune
called Mount Lebanon near Albany, New York, so as to be near
his three sons. Swearing himself to a life of sexual continence,
the gentle ascetic signed away all he owned to the commune
except for a $1,000 cheque to each of his sons.

With his cheque, Jean Paul bought a new, 50-inch solid-tooth, circular cross-cut saw and a long-tug farm harness with white mountings, and she bought a banquet lamp trimmed with an 18-inch fancy silk shade. They hid what was left in the rainy-day box behind the kitchen clock.

Alive, he filled her world like a genie let out of a bottle. But a crayon portrait made by an itinerant artist on their 34th anniversary showed a tall woman more flab than muscle and a short, white-haired man holding a pipe. The picture shocked her. She wanted to burn it.

Instead, she tacked it up in a shadowy corner of their bedroom. When Jean Paul died, she was glad she kept it. But in her heart, her Frenchman regained his narrow good looks, dark eyes level with hers, and often, at the edges of sleep, his strong, young-man's hands closed over her own.

Couldn't he dance though, and sing those French songs! As babies, Walker and Jed went to sleep, but Dinky refused. The louder her father sang through his nose, the louder Dinky howled. It was too bad Jean Paul never got to know Dinky's children or Mun. He would have liked Mun, who liked being outdoors himself and who probably, truth be known, slept with squaws too.

Christina pushed the thought away. At least Jean Paul had lived long enough to see Walker's children. Dear Walker, working every day from dawn to dark, taking care of his farm and his parents' farm and his in-laws' farm. And Katherine.

("I don't think your mother likes me." Katherine had said right after her marriage to Walker.

"Oh, ma likes you good enough," Dinky replied. "She always feels sorry for Walker."

"Why's that?"

"I don't know, I guess 'cause Walker always feels sorry for hisself.")

Christina sighed around the catch in her throat and said aloud, "...so many problems, and he tries so hard."

"Who are you talking about, ma?"

The older woman started, the present roaring back, colliding with the train's rhythmic sashaying and knock-knock-knocking at the ties.

"Oh...I was just thinking about Walker, he works so hard."

"Maybe he needs a vacation." Dinky yawned. "I can't get over how much the valley's filling up with sheep. Look over there, now there's another farm turned into a gentleman's estate."

TWENTY-THREE

NEW YORK, NEW YORK. Thursday afternoon late. Nothing moves except to hurry, no buildings rise except to shut out the sky.

At Grand Central Station the Maine Brigade boards a carriage for the Hotel St. Nicholas and, reaching Broadway, enters a narrow canyon—walls looming ahead like slowly opening doors plastered top to bottom with enormous playbills. Dreadful beasts leap forth. Gigantic hands offer pills as big as wagon wheels. Eye-rocking rivers pour off the rims. Beneath the huge shout of words, the people rush about like angry ants.

"Outoftheway, outoftheway," cries the foot traffic.

"Hurryhurryhurry," shout the street barkers.

Rising above the sea of confusion like a partially submerged fortress is the Hotel St. Nicholas. Dressed in a red uniform, a tall black man made taller by his high hat ceremoniously opens the windowed doors on a lobby overflowing with seashore paintings, potted witches' tongues, and upholstered lounges situated between enormous pink-marble columns. At the marble-topped desk, the attendant bangs on a bell. Red-clad callboys trot up with a luggage cart.

Four flights up is "The Green Room." Green satin-canopied beds flank a window seat overlooking Broadway. Green satin drapes heap gracefully on a green-flowered carpet. Placed just so amid the clutter of oriental natural-wicker furniture, a beveled mirror greets the travelers with their own images. Positioned discreetly out of sight behind a green opaque curtain is a solid oak commode.

A short rest and it's back downstairs to the ladies-only parlor, where a parlor maid pours lemon-flavored water to cleanse the palette. Fresh-cut ferns billow from large alabaster floor urns. Powdered women awash in silk and satin occupy eggshell-enameled wicker fainting couches. Cups full, the twins make their way carefully toward the couches, and the women elect to faint elsewhere.

Supper is served at seven sharp in the ladies-only section of the gilded dining room. French *pot-au-feu* followed by chicken *marengo* followed by *creme renversee*. On a table covered with ivory linen and set with pink roses in cut-glass vases.

"What do I owe?" Christina asked when Dinky signed a slip of paper adding the cost of the meal to the accommodations.

"Relax and enjoy yourself."

But Christina could not relax, particularly over the little bits of strange food. Later, a chamber maid confided that rooms alone cost $2.50 a night and that rich families stayed in the marble palace for months at a time.

An early Friday morning stroll (if one could call the constant jostling with never an apology from the preoccupied faces a stroll) took the brigade up the sunny side of Broadway. Soon enough they found themselves pushing along with no less effort than everyone else.

Broadway seemed to be remaking itself. Giant hoists bearing furniture and crates creaked bug-like up and down the immense buildings. At ground level, carpenters pounded away beneath open upstairs signs, and armorers closed rivets in exposed girders. Stacks of new lumber waited everywhere for old brick and stone to be torn down and hauled off.

Carriage, omnibus, and wagon teams by the thousands clopped up and down the bricks. Youngsters hawked newspapers. Vendors rattled toys. Large, bright wooden posters sidled by. Shop owners blew whistles and yelled hoarsely for attention. Stilt walkers bobbed overhead like whooping cranes, dropping leaflets that fell in a gentle rain off the flat brim of Christina's hollyhock hat.

The ears failed, as did the nose—the street's uproar fading along with the sweet-sour-garbage stink of the city.

Coming to where rails entered the street, the brigade wedged itself into the last seat on a horse-drawn car. The mercantile pursuits of downtown gave way to tall houses with American flags stretched between them—the red, white, and blue colors waltzing gracefully back and forth in the small breeze. Butchers' wagons advertising home delivery dashed in and out the alleys. Enormous coaches swerved past, laden with passengers reading newspapers or looking about impatiently. Policemen in warm woolens stopped traffic to escort magnificently dressed women from one sidewalk to another. Trailing behind the women came servants bearing parcels.

At Union Square the sightseers gave up the car to walk around the massive fountain, the twins coming close enough to the frosty tiers to wet their faces and dresses. From here, they strolled down to Washington Square to take lemonade in the tent-like shade of the trees and watch a detachment of militia in full dress practicing to fife and drum.

The colorful marionette in charge of the militia looked to be held together by his white belts. A crisscross of white belts held the carbine at his side and the leather cartridge box in the middle of his back. A white belt held up his light blue trousers with the yellow stripe. Gold braid edged the collar and cuffs and tails of his dark blue coat, the shoulders were tipped with metal scales. White plumes and yellow cords adorned the tall leather cap. On the front of the cap a brass sunburst and a silver eagle flashed in the sun.

Brass spurs clicking when he put his heels together, left hand resting on the sword in the polished steel scabbard, right arm swinging up and down woodenly, he turned the marching men this way and that with a steady rat-tat-tat of barked orders.

The twins watched in open-mouthed awe.

"The four yellow chevrons on the arm stand for sergeant," Dinky told them.

It was a beautiful day, grass greening up, trees in full bud. Packs of boisterous children scampered along the paths like loosened goats, followed by nannies pushing baby carriages and calling sternly, futilely, for deportment. Dogs chased squirrels or dug furiously in the damp dirt. A hog snuffled by.

But the twins had more important things to worry about, marched stiffly along, ordering themselves this way and that. And reaching a horse-drawn car, took up their posts. Clang, clang, clang went the bell. Bang, bang, bang went the twins, taking aim herky-jerky at Indians and wild animals.

Next stop for the brigade, WSW Gallery's Great Picture Exhibit, where the large Frederic Church canvas, "Niagara," could be viewed for 50 cents a person.

And after the gallery, Fifth Avenue—New York with its best foot forward. Gone were the paper advertisements of the lower streets, gone too, the hordes of aggrieved Irish and poor Rhenish in their gypsy-like garb. Here, elegant mansions rose unannounced, except for discreet nameplates fastened to wrought-iron gates near the bell pulls. The gutters were cleaner, the bricks still damp from their morning washing, and there were no pigs to be seen. Business houses confined their advertisings to metal and stone. The closest thing to garish was the occasional bright green hem of a well-manicured lawn.

Elaborate street cabs eased by. Olive green Broughams and black Phaetons, silver and bronze appointments catching the sun, window beadwork lowered provocatively, horses well groomed, heads checked high.

Sporty Victorias dashed about importantly, a coach dog in white livery in the rumble. Fast, young ladies sat alone on the high front seats, handling the ribbons over flashing, high-stepping matched pairs and paying no attention whatsoever to how the wind exposed their high-heeled boots and bright red petticoats. Wide-awakes adorned their heads with feathers.

"Now those are liberated women, ma," Dinky observed.

"They're nothing but uppity…" Christina pinched off the word.

On the wharves below South Street, Christina and the twins paid a nickel each to tour that enormous wooden side-wheeler, the *Adriatic,* largest and costliest of the Collins liners. While Dinky took care of a different kind of business.

"Always have more money than what you show," Samuel Marchion warned his youngest son when, at 14, Jean Paul announced a trip overnight to Shawinigan. "Trade your peltry for bread and bed, keep your gold to buy your life."

Handing down the story to his own sons, Jean Paul would empty his pocket and separate the soft luster of nuggets from the metal money. As a young man, he'd worn his gold sewn into a shirt seam. In the Matagami Lake region, the little cache bought him a fast horse when the *bourgeois* ordered him off to jail for poaching. In Buffalo, it saved the life of a Delaware boy being dragged through the mud and filth of the street for butchering a settler's cow. In the Olomane settlement, the gold paid for a new rifle after the old piece was lost in a river spill. The Olomane rifle, inlaid with pressed silver picturing a bear bringing down an elk, belonged to Walker now.

Oh, Jean Paul gave his sons plenty of advice alright, with never a thought to the little girl sitting nearby, dolls in her lap, storing the stories unthinkingly as the vine bends to the sun.

In the commercial district's gold-exchange office, Dinky paid five silver dollars for two gold quarter-eagles. At the armorer's next door she paid $10 for a brace of Derringer pistols small enough to be carried comfortably in her coat pockets.

Reunited, the brigade pooled their walking-around money to purchase gifts for Julia. A slim new work by John Greenleaf Whittier entitled *The Panorama and Other Poems* in a bookstore on Ann Street. And on Broadway, two novelties—a roll of Gayetty's Medicated Paper for the toilet and a can of condensed milk.

Returning to the Hotel St. Nicholas, they passed theaters whose blaring music and waving flags proved sore temptation. But Dinky pronounced neither Rousseau's "Emile" nor Davenant's "The Unfortunate Lovers" suitable for children.

New York was a drummer by day and a hussy by night, making her own after-dark light with gaslight. That evening, from the window seat in the green room, the brigade watched as richly attired ladies passed beneath the street lamps in bursts of gay color to collect like moths at the entrances to brightly lit stores.

A distant thunder rolled down the man-made canyon, the kind of thunder made by a parade. And here came a golden pony with red plumes in its harness. Behind the pony, on a low cart painted with the words, BARNUM & BAILEY CIRCUS, was a colossal drum. Two midgets in silvery suits took turns whopping the drum, the long tassels on their drumsticks flying about their heads like shooting stars. Next came a white Cinderella coach drawn by zebras. A man dressed neck to toe in a red sequined suit sat on the high coach seat. A monkey similarly dressed sat beside him. Periodically the fellow doffed a tall silvery hat, exposing a bald pate and a rim of curly hair.

"That's the great P. T. Barnum!" Christina whispered.

A drum-and-bugle corp marched past playing "Yankee Doodle." People clapped and whistled. Fireworks exploded in the sky. Now the bands themselves filled the street, the enormous over-the-shoulder bass horns setting the ears to vibrating with their big, fat sounds. The clowns came, squeezing bicycle horns and throwing candy.

What a grand, grand parade! With the best yet to come.

The street emptied itself of all but a man in silvery robes blowing on a long horn. Behind the herald loomed a long line of tall circus wagons swaying majestically to the stately march of giant Clydes. The horses' dark manes and tails twinkled as if sprinkled with stars, their powerful hooves scrunched the candy thrown on the bricks.

A curlicued banner announced the contents of each huge wagon. In one wagon, bright birds and large monkeys moved restlessly behind a leather lattice-work. Others displayed tigers, wild boars, great apes, bears, and magnificently maned lions behind bars. Still others, boarded over, were decorated with colorful pictures of toothy snakes and alligators. Thus did the creatures ferreted from the dark regions of the world parade by in their wooden boxes—gladiators, knights, kings, queens, and jesters bowing and waving from the broad rooftops.

Oh, how exhilarating! how wonderfully magical! The senses reeled!

Early Saturday morning the brigade boarded the Eastern Express for Massachusetts. New York with all its hustle and bustle, its hopeful poor, its successful rich, departing the skyline in a noiseless puff of smoke.

T W E N T Y - F O U R

S MOKE AND CINDERS pour through the open windows of the crowded steam cars. A brassbound conductor picks up ticket markers from the clips above the seats and remarks on the day's unseasonable warmth. A rosy-cheeked newsbutcher calls what sounds like "candy-cigarettes-cigars-newspapers-magazines." The newsbutcher wears a starched blue uniform and a cap with a brass nameplate and winks at the female passengers. The twins giggle every time he passes.

An important-looking man with a plug hat and sideburns leans over his gold-headed cane to introduce himself to Christina. He is the president of the line, and he apologizes for the lack of private accommodations for the ladies and promises that they will not be troubled with cigar smoke, the Express having fortuitously provided a smoker to which gentlemen can repair to light up and play a rubber of whist.

Eight hours later, the dark outside the coach window is punctured by the gaslight of the Boston depot. Two blocks off Causeway Street, the hotel room is nothing fancy—two beds with a water closet at the end of the hall. But rest is the ticket now.

By 9 a.m. Sunday the brigade is onboard another express, this time the Portland, heading up the North Shore. Ignoring all the best enticements of a newsbutcher even brasher than the previous day's agent, Anne and Emily sit quietly reading Puck and

Judge comics and nibbling on cheese sandwiches made up in the Boston depot. If they never see another soda pop or eat another crackerjack, it will be too soon.

A light fog, drifting off the bay, made the rails shiny and created a lumpy cocoon for the cars to rumble through. Inside the day coach, the engine whistle sounded flat, like a snooping cat being shook out of mischief, and the potbellied stove at the end of the car put out a modicum of warmth along with the smell of coal smoke. Christina rented a blanket and pillow for a penny apiece and commandeered two empty seats. Dinky filled out souvenir postcards for Mun and Katherine and unrolled the Sunday Tribune.

Horace Greeley was all in a lather about the Dred Scott case, predicting succession if the suit were denied before the Supreme Court. Jayhawkers in Kansas and Missouri were busy as usual, waging their own antislavery war.

A headline forecasting overland coach service from the Missouri River to San Francisco by 1858 caught Dinky's eye.

Now wouldn't that be the ultimate in decadence! to see the West from the comfort of a coach instead of a creaky, old-fashioned wagon train. But she had no regrets in choosing the desert route over the ocean. There was nothing to see on the ocean, plus it cost more and took longer, in addition to being definitely more dangerous.

Munching on checkerberry wafers, the tart taste biting her tongue agreeably, Dinky leafed through a new Harper's New Monthly Magazine and settled on the "Song of the Hoops." All in all, it was the nicest day of the journey thus far. Travel always did agree with her.

The Express arrived in Portland at 3 a.m. Monday morning, six hours late, owing to a large bovine creature having wedged itself under the front truck of the tender. Christina was so stiff that she had to be helped down the train steps and into a waiting carriage. Rain and weariness blurred the streets. The hotel appeared in vignettes—dim lanterns, a sleepy clerk who said the trains were always late, long corridors, cool white bed sheets.

The brigade slept Monday away and that evening took supper in an eatery across the street. Early Tuesday morning, ready to do Houlton, Dinky walked down to the stage office. The planks were slick with heavy frost. Commercial Street, a raw, new thoroughfare being built on a landfill, was a sea of frozen mud. But the air had a spring zippiness to it. Tantalized by glimpses of enormous bow-roofed houses up the nearer height of land, Dinky wondered if there might be time for a short stroll that direction before the stage left.

And where are you today, my dear Mun. Won't it be handy to live with no snow and no ice. We'll only come home to visit, and then only in the summer.

She returned not so sanguine. Houlton was 260 miles inland, four days by coach.

"Four days! What was I thinking of to do New York City?! We should have come straight across to Boston from Albany."

"There's no reason to beat yourself up," Christina said. "I ain't that tired no more."

Dinky refused to be consoled. "I had no idea getting around in Maine would be this hard. Good grief, it's part of the Union!"

Four white dray horses in black-nickel harness pull away from the barn at a smart trot, setting the Concord swaying on its leather thoroughbraces. Nine passengers crowd together on the horsehair seats, six more ride the roof. The climbing sun shines hot, the mud flies.

Out of sight of the station, the driver stops cracking his whip. The horses slow to a dull plod.

"Dinky, you forgot to tell us about Portland," Christina said cheerfully.

Dinky continued to stare out the window, her answer as glum as her face. "It has a port that never freezes." End of lesson, indeed of all lessons having to do with the Pine Tree State.

The blackened hills outside Portland resembled a battlefield—trees slashed and burned-over for miles. Here and there a huge trunk stood off alone, like Wayne's legion at the Battle of Fallen Timbers.

It was a relief to reach the woods, drifted deep with dirty snow. Or would have been, had the woods ever stopped, which they never did except to burp up rivers and occasional villages with impossible-to-pronounce names.

Approaching and leaving the settlements, the horses displayed real interest in their surroundings. As did the passengers, some of whom exchanged themselves for other passengers. But the excitement was short-lived, the trace quickly tunneling its way back into the trees, the horses resuming their dull plod. Covered bridges over roaring waters soon lost their charm, as did the tippedy-tippedy-tick of iron-wrapped wheels over marsh planking.

Augusta on the Kennebec, 65 miles above Portland, was another Portland, only larger and without the ocean's inviting skyline. Evening dusk and chimney smoke filled the streets.

The next day's coach was smaller and decidedly less comfortable. Unpadded wooden seats designed for six passengers held eight, the only windows were in the doors. The crowding and solid walls did, however, lend a welcome warmth when the cold rains fell.

Hour after hour, the coach bounced north, up and down the forested heights of land, stopping on average of every 12 miles to change horses, the passengers praying that nature's call be not too urgent in the meantime, and being terribly grateful for anyone else's having to yell out the door for a halt. Day after day of trees, trees, trees, through cheerful bits of sunshine and seas of dark fog, jouncing over the corduroyed, root-scored paths, from one strange sounding place to another.

Bangor on the Penobscot, Passadumkeag, Mattawamkeag, Macwahoc on the Molunkus.

The standoffish manners of the coach's occupants left the brigade taciturn and bearish in turn. The constant bumping left them seasick. Every day they woke to sore muscles and dreary breakfasts of cold grits and milk followed eight hours later by cold meat and gravy over hard bread.

Adding insult to injury were the mean sleeping rooms—no locks on the doors, chamber pots full, damp wind through the keyholes, poor stubs of candle, low slatted beds with horsehair mats that every night had to be remade to shake out the bugs.

A most unpleasant journey, but not impossible. Life, like the Big Woods, went on.

"See you Wednesday, March 4, Thursday at the very latest," Dinky had written from New York.

Wednesday, Julia was aflutter with anticipation. Hope for the best, prepare for the worst, that was her motto. Whatever else, Jed's family would know her as a lady to the manor born.

By Friday she was bored with the whole idea. Come Saturday, anticipation well curdled, she watched from behind curtained windows as the town carriage deposited a dusty huddle of people at the end of the front walk—watched and stomped her foot and busied herself in the furthest pantry. Not until after her guests mittened on the door and were answered by the housekeeper, did she favor them with a greeting.

The visiting, ill begun, bumped but barely along. Positioning themselves like loons on opposite shores of the same lake, the occupants of the Clare residence seemed unable to progress beyond the sparsest of civilities.

Old people depressed Cyrus. How unfair to be forced to have one for a house guest, particularly a long, tall Sally with the hawk eyes of an old madam.

Christina thought the doctor a jackanapes. Why anybody with a slack belly and hands that never turned a tap should act so god-awful important was a mystery to her.

Dinky took interminable walks, sailing through the house with a breezy, "Now mind your Aunt Julia," to the twins who, after one cold, wet walk through misty glens, protested vociferously at ever taking another.

"Go out to the barn and play with Yellow Cat," Julia told them.

But Yellow Cat ran and hid, so the twins played tag with the geese and rode double on the pony. And after being dumped several times, came inside to entertain themselves—eventually discovering the Meissen collection of porcelain soldiers which, when marched up and down the stairs, made a clicking spur-like sound.

"I've had to lock up virtually the whole house." Julia was in Bettina's kitchen, pacing angrily back and forth. "Why in blue blazes aren't they in boarding school instead of running around my house like chickens with their heads cut off?"

"I just don't know."

"Their minds and their nails are *totally* neglected, they never put their grubby little hands in dishwater, their hair looks like brush piles, they play outside in their good dresses."

"Oh dear," Bettina moaned and groaned dutifully. "My goodness."

"What's worse, they refuse, absolutely *refuse*, to eat anything that tastes of buckwheat. As for having a nice dessert, forget that! Any dessert baked for supper, the little monsters eat BEFORE supper." Julia bent over to accommodate a small cramp. "They eat crackers in bed, they use the burying door."

"Oh, good lord!" Bettina protested with genuine alarm. "That is bad luck."

"Bad luck!" Julia picked up a cutting board and swung it at an imaginary seat. "I'll give them a dose of bad luck!"

Of Julia, Dinky wrote Katherine,

> She is beautiful, but when did Jed not fall in love with beautiful women? Her hair is blue-black and her complexion is porcelain. She is huge with child and sews all the time, but is really not too domestic. I'm sure you will approve. Fortunately they have a housekeeper as a well as a neighbor boy to do chores. The house is very large, two stories and wooden. It was built by Julia's great grandfather in the 1700s. Two of the rooms are used by Dr. Clare for his practice. He is retired, but he still sees people occasionally. He is a spoiled old curmudgeon, as Julia herself can be, I suspect, when not on her better behavior. Her mother died in childbirth.
>
> The rest of the downstairs is like a museum with cabinets full of unused dishes, a spinet no one plays, a large spinning wheel just for decoration and lots of books with the most beautiful prints in them. The only fireplace is in the keeping room but it's never lit. All the inside walls are painted white even in the kitchen. In the library a marble statue of Hercules' labor with Diomede absolutely fascinates Anne and Emily as you can well imagine. The house creaks and groans as big old houses do and they are sure it is haunted and love scaring themselves with things.

To Mun she wrote

> The length of time since being gone from you is beginning to be felt awfully. I seem unable to function without you. First I fail to check the time from Portland to here, it was four days(!) Poor mother. Then I miswrite the

ticket cost as $2.50 when it was $25.00, of course I didn't tell her. Once here I discover I completely failed to account for Jed's spending the winter in a logging camp. However, we may still get to see him. Dr. Clare says the logs will be brought downstream much earlier than usual on account of the light snowfall. Julia is sure he will come directly home instead of going to Bangor where the mills are because of the baby.

Houlton is surprisingly civilized considering what we went through to get here and Julia's not at all the kind of woman I thought Jed would marry. Her family is very well-educated and well-to-do and can open all sorts of doors for him. He'll probably end up like my grandfather Marchion who made loads of money in Canada timber. Just eight months more, my sweet, and I will be in your arms and you will be with your beautiful children.

Abruptly, the household thawed.

For Christina, it was when she overheard a conversation in the doctor's office regarding the impossibility of knowing a baby's sex prior to its birth.

"It's not such a mystery, she said, sticking her head in the open doorway. "I could always tell. Put wheat and barley seeds in a bowl of pee. If the wheat sprouts, it's a boy. If both sprout, it's a girl."

Cyrus' visitor lowered his glasses to peer at the intruder. "That theory has been disproved."

"By who?" Christina lowered her own glasses. "I don't think so." The doctor's face said she should go away.

Which Christina did, but not before adding, "If you need me, I'll be around." After that, she rather enjoyed sparing with the old geezer.

For Dinky, the thaw came when she met Sigvald Proulx.

"Is Julia here?" The man who knocked at the back screen brushed a lock of wavy ash-blonde hair off his poet's face. On the small porch his Viking body looked out of place.

"Sigvald!" Julia waddled across the kitchen. "Come in. I heard you were home." She took the tapered sinuous hands in her own. "Sit down, dear cousin, have some cake. Tell us about Washington. Meet Jed's sister." This last without turning her gaze aside. "Sigvald is an aide to Maine's Senator French."

Unfortunately, Sigvald couldn't stay. He was just going by. Some other time. He favored each woman with an absorbing look from deep-set, Norman blue eyes, and was off across the back lot into the woods, a shotgun under his arm.

Unbuttoning the top of her shirt waist, Dinky fanned the ruffled edge against her throat. "That has got to be the most beautiful man I ever saw!"

"Dinky!" Julia protested, an uncertain tilt to her head. "You're married!"

"But I'm not dead." Dinky jabbed a fork in her cake. "Good Lord! I've got to eat something!"

"I can not believe you!"

"He's gorgeous!"

Julia eased herself into a chair, not sure what was expected of her. "I think so too."

Dinky lifted her fork, sighting along it. "I saw him first."

That night, with everyone else in bed, Julia brought downstairs the letter received from Salt Lake City. "It was opened before, do you think her husband is jealous and she wants Jed to rescue her again?"

"Oh no." Dinky was reading the letter. "I'm sure not." She read it twice. "They have so little in common, I think she's just trying to find something to talk about."

"Then why write at all?"

"Why not? He was good to her."

Julia studied her nails and toyed with a pretty pout. "Did he love her?"

Dinky shrugged. "Enough to go back after her. But rescuing
Ellen from the Mexicans was like going off to the crusades. You
go and slay the infidels then you come home, all grown up, and
get on with your life."

"But he did marry her."

"Because of ma. The idea of them living in sin with Jeremy
was simply out of the question."

"You liked her?"

"Oh, indeed! She's got a lot of sand in her, as pa would say.
Her father was a fur hunter, her mother left him for a Mormonite.
So there she was, the daughter of a wild mountain man being
raised in a little fundamentalist sect. Talk about a duck out of
water."

"And your mother liked her."

"*Au contraire.*" Dinky laughed softly. "She hates Ellen. It was
the Indian thing. She hates Indians. Pa spent so much time with
them. I mean, like weeks! Ma kept them shooed away from the
house, but they were always hanging around the barns wanting
leathers mended on the treadle and horses shod. Then along
comes Ellen, the Indians are literally her chosen people, she's
got all these stories and a half-breed son. But don't get me
wrong, ma loves Jeremy like her own. It broke her heart when
Ellen took him away."

"And Katherine?"

"Thought Ellen was the cat's hat, at first. Wanted her to
speak to suffrage groups about surviving the wilderness and how
women are as capable as men and should get to vote." Dinky
made a face of mock amazement and lifted the air with her
hands. "It was all supposed to tie in somehow. But Ellen liked
living in the wilderness, and she didn't care whether women
voted or not. They drove each other wild with their logic."

"How do you feel about Indians?"

"Oh…I don't give them much thought, they sure stoled a lot

of apples. When pa died, Ellen cut herself like Indians do. I thought Ma would have a stroke. That's when Jed put Ellen on the cars for Virginia and hasn't been home since."

"Jed told me they'd already decided to separate when your father died."

"I didn't know that, but I'm not surprised. Jed was miserable, he hates farming. Ellen liked it..." Dinky hesitated, searching for the right words. "The only thing they really had in common was feeling responsible for each other. They were terribly kind to each other, like they were trying to make up for messing up."

"Still and all," Julia folded the letter back into its envelope, "there's something odd about this letter, I can feel it."

"I don't feel a thing." Dinky raised herself to give her sister-in-law a gentle hug. "But one thing I do know for sure. Jed and Ellen didn't love each other the way love was meant to be. Which is why mother and I have darkened your door, and why Katherine and Walker soon will. Because we know in our bones that Jed is finally happy."

Julia poured cold milk in the top of a double boiler and shaved chocolate over the milk. "He never talks about Walker, do they look alike? You don't look like Jed, but I can hear him in your voice."

"I don't look like anybody in my family, I'm sure I'm adopted. As for Walker, he and Jed aren't anything alike. Jed was born knowing about woods, Walker was born knowing about dirt. They aren't very nice to be around when they're around each other. But Walker's really very sweet and gentle otherwise."

"I'm sure he is," Julia observed, thoughts stalled elsewhere. She refilled the firebox and placed two mugs in the warming oven. The junk popped and cracked. She slid the double boiler over the stove lids and, having savored her surprise as long as humanly possible, said, "Perhaps there's something I should tell you about your pa's Indians."

The fur hat hit the piano keys with a PING! and fell to the floor. Anne brushed back the leg skirt and looked up into her uncle's bearded face. His surprise mirrored her own.

A confusion of greetings filled the room. People rushed about. Emily crawled from beneath the piano. "Go upstairs," someone told her, "get your grandmother."

Christina was sound asleep. She put on her glasses, looked in the mirror, poked at her hair. And coming downstairs, reached the last step just as Yam, standing in the front doorway, tucked his chin to light his pipe. The profile, dark against the light, came at her like a fist.

Later, in the patients' room.

"Why didn't you tell ma when Julia first told you?" Jed asked his sister. They were standing on either side of the narrow iron bed.

"Why didn't *you* tell her?" Dinky shot back. "It's called *writing*. Civilized people do it all the time!" Brother and sister glared at each other

"It's all water under the bridge." Julia smoothed Christina's forehead and patted the dry hair. "But one thing I do know, Yam must *not* come back in this house. Our mother *hates* Indians." Julia's mouth snapped shut like a purse.

Reassured by Dr. Clare's pronouncement of no immediate danger, everyone wandered off to visit in hushed tones in the kitchen. Later, hearing his mother stir, Jed went in alone. Christina began to cry and, hugging him, told him how much he looked like his pa. "I thought you was Jean Paul come to get me," she confessed, crying. "Getting old is such a nuisance." She hugged her son again.

No one, then or afterward, thought to ask the twins what they were doing under the piano with the paring knife with the sharp point.

T W E N T Y - F I V E

I T TOOK THE TWINS TWO DAYS to find Yam. He was standing beside a small green lake at the edge of the woods. They crept up on him, and when they got close, he twisted around and made a loud whoop that like to scared them to death.

"What are you doing?" Emily asked, stepping free of her tree.

"Riding a horse."

The girls giggled. Anne opened her fist on a mashed cookie. "Are you hungry?"

The Indian pointed at the fish on the ground. The twins examined the perch, holding it this way and that, making the scales turn different colors in the sun.

Dinky was ready to go home. She and Jed talked endlessly about the West, she could hardly stand not to be off and away, as if hurrying herself she could hurry the calendar. She didn't ask about Yam, and Jed, sensing her discomfort, didn't mention the Indian.

But then, she decided to bite the bullet. "So where's your friend, I haven't seen him since we got here."

"He's around, he sleeps in the barn, you wanna talk to him?"

"Sure, if you promise he won't scalp me."

Jed looked at his sister in disbelief.

"I'm sorry, I was trying to be funny. I don't have anything against Indians, it's just…I don't like to think of our pa with a squaw. I know it happened but….oh, well, what the hell. If you wanna believe he's our brother, he's our brother. Walker will just die. Does he understand English?"

"Dinky."

The tone in Jed's voice, the look on his face, made Dinky ashamed. She'd no idea how much he wanted another brother.

"Alright, she was pushing up imaginary sleeves, the way boys did before duking it out. "Bring him on. We'll get to the bottom of this."

Jed found his nieces and Yam out at the fish fry. "Would you take a walk with my sister this afternoon?" he inquired in a quiet aside.

Yam smiled inside his mouth. First he was showing the youngsters how to clean and fry fish, now he was taking the white woman about. The man who called him "brother" certainly did need a brother.

The woods were marshy with occasional patches of snow. Dinky and Yam walked down an old tote road that kept to higher ground, and Dinky did most of the talking, the Indian answering in monosyllables or with his hands. Other than determining what she would have guessed anyway under the circumstances, that Yam was a pleasant person, Dinky could get nothing out of the visit. They were almost back to the house, she was trying to find a suitable cap for the abortive attempt by describing the Marchion upriver farm.

"What did your father look like?" Yam interrupted to ask.

"Well, he…you don't think we're related, do you. Not really."

"I have a father."

"And you don't want to be related?…none of this is your idea?"

Leaning forward, Yam eyed her intently as if searching for something.

"Maybe Jed's just got a wild hare," Dinky observed, amused.

The Indian continued to study her silently.

"Oh, dear, I don't know what to say. We're nice people, and you and I *are* the same height, for what that's worth." She ran a hand along an imaginary line from her head to Yam's. "Don't get me wrong, I don't care a bit if you're Jed's brother, our brother. Besides, he needs a friend in the woods. I guess everybody does." She felt like a fool.

The Indian smiled and stepped back. A familiar smile, a familiar stance. Dinky stared at the wiry figure with its firm, slightly challenging expression, and felt the hair rise on the nape of her neck. Lord help them all! this really could be their brother!

She turned away, confused. "Do you mind so much if Jed's right? We are really the *nicest* people."

Yam didn't answer.

Collecting herself, Dinky took the Indian's arm and walked on. "Tell me, why are you here if you don't believe us?"

"It is work."

"No, it's something more," she patted his chest, "something you know too. I can feel it, here in your heart."

Which did not surprise Yam. She was patting the cross under his shirt.

That evening Dinky told Jed, "I think you're right. Walker will never buy it, and I don't think Yam will. He says he has a father. But I would have done just what you did, collected him up. He may be ours, and if so, we are his, for better or for worse."

Two days later the Marchions hosted a neighborhood *bon voyage* party for the brigade. A cold, blustery March night banged around the old Clare residence. Inside, warmed by goodwill and hot stoves and the tantalizing aromas of cassia cinnamon and flowery marjoram, the evening felt like the first party of summer.

It also felt like a welcome-home celebration for Houlton's congressional aide. Holding forth in his rich baritone voice, Sigvald captivated his listeners with the doings in the nation's capital. As for a civil war between the States, there would be none. True, the attack on Massachusetts' Senator Sumner had galvanized opinion on both sides of the issue. True, Sigvald had never seen the public mind deeper and more dangerous, but the violence was proving an unexpected boon.

"How so?" Dinky asked.

"Nobody wants bloodshed, particularly at the highest levels where they were forced to witness it." Sigvald put his long fingers together prayerfully and pointed them at Dinky. "With Sumner off to Europe for his health, the Tribune and other antislavery newspapers will cease to exploit the affair, and reasonable men will prevail."

"But the problem of slavery remains." She was enjoying the exchange, hoping her face didn't look as warm as it felt.

"Of course," Sigvald's agreement was dazzling, "but not for the North, unless we make it our problem. Have you ever noticed, with all our fine talk about freeing the slave, nobody talks about feeding him? At least in the South he's cared for. With time and access to northern machinery, the South will gladly disavow its peculiar institution. Trust me on this."

"I'm not so sure," Dinky argued, struggling to sound at least half-way intelligent. "The black man has no rights that a white man has to respect."

"That will change, the northern courts will see to it. And the line between the North and South will be obliterated." Sigvald nodded in self-agreement. "But it takes time. Northern industrialists depend heavily on their southern counterparts, who in turn depend on their stock of slaves.

The South has over two million slaves worth over a billion dollars to their masters. Even though 70 percent of Southerners don't own slaves, the institution is so embedded in their lives that if Washington moves too abruptly, everybody will go to war. Unfortunately, the Abolitionist Movement has probably done more harm than good. Now slave owners are forbidding their slaves being taught to read or write."

"I'm an Abolitionist," Dinky confessed with a smile. "I don't feel I have any choice."

"Scratch us and we all are," Sigvald allowed with sweetest agreement. "Even Buchanan. The President is definitely committed to settling the African problem once and for all. He is very concerned that it be kept out of the West."

"But the Kansas-Nebraska Act…"

"…that vote crossed party lines."

"Hey, you two," Julia lifted the piano lid, "enough!" She pounded out the opening notes of "Vilikins and his Dinah" and singing filled the house. The tooraloo tune was followed by songs about mountains and waters, lost loves and turtle doves, little children and sad-eyed farm boys.

"What was that new song we heard in New York, ma?" Dinky asked, "the one the coloreds were singing around the lamp post."

Christina closed her eyes, thinking back to the hotel balcony overlooking Broadway. The parade was gone and the street was relatively quiet, that's when they heard the singing. In the prompting silence she began slowly pulling the notes together. "Brother, will you meet me by…" she stopped, and started again.

> Brother, will you meet me by…Canaan's happy shore?
> Brother, will you meet me by…Canaan's happy shore?
> Brother, will you meet me by…

Dinky's voice joined her mother's

> …Canaan's happy shore?
> To watch the Jordan roll.

Everybody joined in for a second go-round and then a third, the piano player (Julia having long since abandoned that chore) picking out the notes.

The next day, Wednesday, March 18. Promising to return and inviting one and all to New York and California, the brigade folded itself into the Bangor coach.

Not seeing Yam, Dinky told Jed with a wink, "Tell what's-his-name good-bye for us." And gave her brother a hard squeeze. "You used to be all arms and legs, but you're looking better all the time. I'll be thinking of you out on the Trail. Don't you wish you was going with us?"

"Oh, yeah. I really miss the desert. All that wind, no trees, no clean water. You're gonna love it."

"I love you, brother." She pressed her hands against his cheekbones. "And I'm so glad for you."

"Me too, little sister." Jed rested his forehead against Dinky's hair and breathed softly, "Be careful."

That night, Julia produced the letter. "You don't care that I opened it."

"Hell, no."

"I'm dying to know what you think." Jed was sitting on the bed, Julia leaned against him, the top of her robe open.

"Love it."

"About the letter. I shouldn't have read it, but I couldn't help it."

Absently fingering the tip of breast pressed against his ear, Jed shook open the page.

"Who's Phoebe?" Julia asked. "You never told me about her."

But Jed was silent, reading.

Jedrich Cyrus, J.C. for short, was born Tuesday afternoon, March 24, 1857. Assisted by a midwife, the birth was easy enough, considering it was a first child. A good baby—seven pounds, eight ounces—healthy in every respect except for the shortened Achilles tendon in the left leg.

"This is one of life's gentler birth defects," Cyrus told the dismayed parents.

Jed refused to believe the tendon would not lengthen with exercise. Daily he gently worked the tiny heel back and forth. Preparing to leave for Bangor to settle his accounts, he advised Julia to continue the exercise. When he returned, he thought the foot better. Sitting with the baby on his lap, he said as much.

Dr. Clare would not allow the deception.

"J. C. will never be able to walk properly without a properly built shoe, much less run or carry heavy loads. He must learn a profession if he is to keep a roof over his head, develop his mind. He can not do it with his muscle." Cyrus put his arm around Jed's shoulders. "Son, this little man has everything in him you do. Don't you *ever* worry about him."

After the doctor left the room, Jed told the boy a story.

"When I was little, your Uncle Walker and me and your grandpa, we used to mule logs and sometimes a big deer or bear outta the woods. Your grandpa would tie three ropes to what we was pulling and tie the other ends to sticks. And we'd pull and pull on our sticks. Over the rough ground we'd go, pulling so hard, knocking into each other, falling down. Grandpa was learning…"

"Jed…" Julia put her fingers against her husband's mouth, but he kept on talking to the baby.

"…us to work teams, you see, so's we'd know what it was like…for the horses have room…" He was crying, the tears tracking down his cheeks.

"J. C. will go into the woods with you." Julia patted her tears and Jed's with a square of lace-hemmed cotton. "We'll buy him a pair of calked Elk River boots with capped toes, and he'll ride a horse, one of those fancy Morgans you're always talking about. But he'll also go off to schools and libraries and explore more worlds than you or I ever dreamed of. He'll have dirt on his boots, I promise you, but he'll have stardust too."

T W E N T Y - S I X

S AN FRANCISCO. March 1857. The third floor of the
Merchants Exchange Building floats dreamily above the
bay fog, set aglow by the lowering sun. In the room where
the waiters come and go, dark-suited men accompanied by
heavily powered women take their supper. The men's high
collars are set off with loosely tied, fine-muslin cravats. The
women are awash in deep-colored dresses, their hair pulled back
severely and cleverly rolled under an evening-dress wreath of
flowers at the nape of the neck.

The exception is that beauty there by the window, golden
locks piled high. In the ethereal light, her hair takes on a pink
cast. It's the dress, a Mediterranean drape of dusty pink gauze
gathered at the waist with a sash of the same fabric. Adding no
small charm to the picture is the *au naturale* heart-shaped face,
the delicate rainbow halftones resembling those of an Amans
portrait.

The angel's companion, a slender aristocrat of average height,
is a pleasant-faced, unassuming European in his thirties with
close-trimmed mustache and carefully parted brown hair.
Obviously dazzled by what he is seeing, he nevertheless has the
good grace to be discomforted by the room's attentiveness.

With courtly demeanor he puts down his glass of burgundy,
smoothes the thin mustache rather more than necessary, and
when the raffish creature imitates the gesture, abandons it

completely. Straightening his shoulders, he glances around with a proprietary air—much as a host checking to see that the guests, whose names he can't quite remember, are enjoying themselves.

Lovebirds no doubt, obviously newly migrated and more fun to watch than to hear, the conversation of lovebirds being nothing new in itself.

"Are you sure we can afford this?" Seen closely, the woman is perhaps 28 or 29. Worry clouds the beautiful violet eyes.

"Of course we can't," Nathan returned the nod of a plump matron at a further table, "but attitude is everything."

"I think we're in deep shit."

"Don't be vulgar, and don't assume no one is listening. That waiter approaching, he could be our contact."

"To what?"

"I have a feeling about San Francisco." Nathan picked up the menu, the waiter retreated. "There's money here, lots of it."

"Including mine. I tell you, Nathan, I don't have anything left to hock."

"I know that." His tone said he did know.

"You bastard! If you've been in my jewelry again, I'll kill you!"

Nathan's clear eyes filled with alarm. He fished out his watch and got immediately to his feet. "You're right, my dear," he said in a carrying voice, "it is later than I thought if we are to be at the Parrott's by seven." And they were gone, taking with them not a small piece of the room's ambiance.

A sandy wind streams off the dunes that separate Washerwoman's Lagoon from the Pacific Ocean. Half-buried trash litters the street in the front of the tenements. Inside, the cramped quarters smell of fish. Calico nailed against the beams and joists makes the room seem almost cozy. Nathan strops a

knife while Daphne sits with her back to him. He has changed
into an old pair of pants and an overshirt, but she refuses to take
off the pink dress. Between them on the table, a silvery bass
waits beside a handful of wilted mint.

"You like fish."

"Liked." Daphne waved an open bottle of German Cologne
over her head. "When we had it once a week."

"We have it once a week."

"Don't be funny, you fool! I'm tired of the essentials of life,
I want the decencies!" Daphne's lower lip trembled.

A kind of sorrowful understanding filled Nathan's face. As a
rule she loved these exercises—seeing and being seen in all the
best places—but funds were low, resulting in their brief appearances resembling those of pop-up figures in the ball-throwing
booth at a fair.

"Change your clothes, my angel on an ash heap, or that dress
will smell like a fish. After supper, we'll get out of this pig sty
and take a walk along the water."

"In the fog?! I'd rather go to the Jenny Lind, except I look
like a frump. You and your goddamned props! I don't care what
it smells like, I am *never* wearing this again, *it's a bed sheet!*"

"No one knew. Patience, Daphne, patience. We're about to
hit. I can feel it."

He leaned over the bass to kiss her, but she would not be
solaced. "The least you could have done is brought what was left
of the wine bottle with us!"

The next day.

Nestled at the bottom of a hill studded with scraggly plants
tended by Chinamen, was a tall Victorian house calling itself
The Collectibles.

As agreed upon, Nathan arrived at exactly ten o'clock the

next morning—Daphne's perfectly matched Paria pearls, a gift
from an enamored Venezuelan President Monagas, wrapped in a
handkerchief in his coat pocket. Unfortunately, the shop door
was locked. A sign in the window directed those wishing to
recover their consignments to address the Fallsington residence
on Rincon Hill.

Disappointed, Nathan bought a Picayune from a passing
newsboy and looked around for a bench.

Dollops of black cloud sailed overhead, forcing him into a
nearer doorway to wait out the shower. The sun broke through,
the damp boardwalks steamed merrily. Classifieds underarm, he
set off for another hock shop, prodded by the thought that
Daphne was probably right at that moment playing with her
jewelry—she carried around more loot than a Venetian free-
booter and, once missed, the Paria pearls were sure to become
her favorite.

It was a day made for walking in a city made for walking—
the foot traffic cheerful as wrens, the air sweet with the wild
rosemary that girdled the oil street lamps.

Except for one bleak nob, severely scarred by a quarry, the
wooden city poured molasses-like over and between the hills,
reaching out even into the harbor itself on long docks. Large,
ornate homes reflecting other-world temples and fortresses rose
El Dorado-like over Everyman's theater and church, over the
inevitable big-city pockmarks of recent fires, over the dwellings
of the working man and his entertainments.

The wharves were a study in contrasts. In the harbor, large
ocean-going vessels rotted away. On the beaches, a golden fringe
of banks, factories, and warehouses, stoutly encased in granite
blocks from China and the Sierra, vied with each other for
attention—here a soaring Italian arch, there a Classic sculpture,
a Gothic face, or a startling *ménage à trois*.

Away from the wharves, there was a hint of the serene

grandeur of Paris. But the streets, where lately planked, were cleaner than those of Paris, perhaps because of the more-frequent rains. Unfortunately, street grading and the proliferation of charcoal pots had consumed most of the greenery, but that would return.

Little more than a decade ago this sprawl had been a remote Mexican outpost called Yerba Buena. Then along came America, rattling her sabers, filling the beaches with guns, beheading the Mexican Empire without firing a shot. Behind the soldiers came an avalanche of gold rushers, burying the little outpost, along with its little mission down the bay, under a nineteenth-century metropolis.

These things Nathan had learned while employed at the Hotel des Bains on the Lido near Venice from the discarded newspapers of wealthy vacationers, *nouveaux riches* whose permanent address was San Francisco's International Hotel and whose conversation consisted solely of where, on the hills overlooking the bay, to build their mansions.

Experiencing the remarkable city for himself, Nathan found the claims of superior climate and scenery not the least exaggerated.

Enjoying himself, he arrived at the intersection of Market and Second Streets below South Park. And the sign pointing the way to Rincon Hill. And when he did, he remembered the address in The Collectibles window. Which gave him pause.

He had a theory about such things. If, for instance, he went to dress in black and found a button missing, and replaced the button only to find a hem out, he put away the suit and wore another color.

In this case, The Collectible had been closed. Intending to go elsewhere, he now found himself in the vicinity of the contents of the old shop. A location which would be of interest only to consignors.

Coincidences coming in a string like this reminded him of statues he had read about somewhere—huge prehistoric stone heads all lined up and facing out to sea, as if watching for something.

Taking a seat on a sidewalk bench, he rechecked the crude visitor's map handed out on the *Panama*. They'd been in San Francisco two months, and the map was getting worn. He made a mental note to get another, and pulled from his waistcoat a little deck of calling cards, absently sorting through them. Selecting one, he rested his gaze on the sky. The last time he was in The Collectibles the owner had been uncrating some goods...

...unpacking paintings separated one from another by burlap.

The shop's owner shook his head. "Emigrant paintings. They get all hopped up about something they see out there and think that automatic makes 'em an artist."

But then the man came across some he liked. Nodding, pursing his lips. "Looks European, not the old stuff but the new. Yes sir." The light wasn't very good, but Nathan noticed a legend on the back of one of the boards and told the owner who, turning it over, read aloud, "LDS—Only for the money" and a name.

Nathan squeezed his eyes shut. The name, *what was the name?*

A footman answered the knock of the bronzed-horse head, accepted the proffered card, and rang for the butler. The butler allowed entry into an anteroom colored a sickly yellow by its overhead dome of amber-glass skylights, and rang for a maid, who relieved Nathan of his hat and cane. The butler then summoned Mr. Fallsington's secretary.

Nathan was polite, but firm. The Collectibles inventory was here? He would like to pick up his client's paintings.

"Nathaniel Lafitte, Investments Lawyer," the secretary read aloud and, placing the card on a bamboo table beside a slim, leather-covered notebook, picked up the notebook and glanced at the names. "I don't see you."

"What?" Masking his enjoyment—there is nothing like a British accent filled to the brim with British disdain—Nathan frowned and glanced around. The library doors were partially open, revealing a sense of something amiss, a tufted sofa at an odd angle.

"Oh. My client's name is Jones."

The secretary couldn't find a Jones either.

Not that it mattered to the lawyer. "I'll know the works when I see them." Nathan walked purposefully into the library. A pile of crates resembling the emptyings of a trash wagon occupied the center of the marble floor. Sofas and chairs had been shoved together in front of the cold fireplace. Velvet paintings of women parading *au naturale* were everywhere propped—against the furniture, the fireplace, the surrounding walls.

Nathan turned his attention to the crates, shaking one and hearing what sounded like dishes. And moving on. More dish sounds. Lifting the scrap of packing on a stack of gilded, scrolled frames, he stared down at another nude.

The secretary popped the calling card noisily with a fingernail. "I'm afraid you'll have to leave."

Nathan could see why. "I'm sure you've had it up to here with artisans." A brief, sympathetic smile. He quickly sorted through the gilded frames and let the stack fall back as if unclean. "My client is a Mormonite…"

"I don't…"

"...one of 15 wives. The husband does all the paperwork. And, unfortunately for my client, from time to time forgets her name, which is logical, I suppose." The confession, along with the assumption, totally impassive.

"Fifteen! Are they moronic?"

Nathan laughed despite himself. "My client isn't." Abruptly he changed the subject. "Do you mind? I've a rock in my shoe." He was easing himself into the clutter. "The artist is an illegitimate descendent of Fragonard, her work always sells well."

Settled on the back of a large plaster frog, he removed the offending shoe, shook it and felt inside. "The money is returned, less my fee, with a Mormon courier."

"Who buys her paintings?" the secretary asked.

"I never deal with the public. The only reason I am here today is that I have no choice. If you will bear with me but a few minutes longer, I'll be out of your hair." He returned the shoe and gingerly put his weight into it.

"Who's her father?"

"An architect at the Ecole des Beaux Arts." The lawyer reached inside another broken crate and, touching what felt like antlers, moved on. The adjacent paper-wrapped bundle turned out to be school bags.

"Maybe Mr. Fallsington should see them."

"I don't think so." Nathan flicked a scornful glance at the nudes.

"Those women go to his establishments," the secretary explained. "He buys good art for the missus, some I've recommended myself. Don't take anything away," she gave the butler a see-to-it snap of her chin, "until I get back."

Michael Fallsington won The Collectibles inventory in a card game—the owner of the shop covered a $5,000 bet with it. Big Mike screamed like a scalded hog, the owner swore and be damned the barroom nudes were worth every penny, and Big Mike laid down an ace-high royal flush. The next day Big Mike sent a gardener for the inventory, now his wife was screaming like a scalded hog. Downstairs, he told that story and laughed.

"Mr. Fallsington, there's a lawyer come to pick up some paintings. I think you should see them first."

"Any tits showing?" Swathed in cigar smoke, Big Mike sent a laugh around the table, scattered with money and bottles of brandy bash, and kept dealing. "Give him what he wans."

One of the players lurched to his feet. "You just lost two of them nudes to me!" A limber man with curly black hair greying at the temples, dark eyes slightly out of focus.

"Shee-it! Uergin, I forgot. Sit down." Big Mike swore roundly and ordered the secretary, "pay the man for the nudes."

Uergin stayed on his feet, bumping into the table, backing into his chair, tipping it over. And high-stepped determinedly up the stairs.

Heaping profanity on the deserter's head, the poker club followed.

The inventory filled the library floor—packing canvases and paper strewn about as if by a whirlwind, crates laid over on their side, contents spewed out. Big Mike stared. Jeez! he'd forgotten how much crap there was! "C'mon, goddamit!" He wallowed toward the feast of female pulchritude in front of the fireplace. "Take your pick, did I ever lie to you?" His voice, and those of the men following him, going on without Uergin, frozen in front of a little row of chairs.

On the chairs, neatly placed side-by-side in the midst of the upheaval, sat three paintings.

A stolid-faced farmer. A group of pioneer women on the trail, the sunset glowing orange and gold on their faces. Two children posing as grown-ups—an older boy in a great coat, a little girl trailing an over-large dress and wearing a large blue-stone necklace.

Defined not by lines but by blurry streaks and splashes of color. Unframed, on oak panels.

"Those yours?" Uergin asked the man standing beside the chairs.

Lightly dusting the works with his handkerchief, Nathan answered distractedly, "My client's."

"Mr. Fallsington!" the secretary called sharply to her employer, realizing the richly colored wood was about to slip away.

"How much?" Uergin asked.

"Originally $500," Nathan observed ruefully. "But obviously not now, with these scratches on the frames..." His voice faded. A wad of bills had appeared in the gambler's hand.

"You should of been there, Daph. He went white. I owned him."

"You shoulda got more." Money was an aphrodisiac to Daphne, just to see it left her quivering. Stories that began without it lost her attention immediately, if they ever had it. But money spread even on the ricketiest table—as now, on the pieced-together apple crates—made her drool.

"No use killing the goose," Nathan said, unable to keep from sounding smug.

Abandoning the bed scattered with summer jewelry, Daphne draped a striped-cotton-hose-encased leg over her clever fellow. "Phoebe Taggart!" She worked her tongue into Nathan's ear and stroked the back of his neck, her freshly applied Swan Down Powder wrinkling his nose. "What an utterly ugly name! What did the pictures look like?"

"To tell you the truth, I hardly noticed. Except the backs."

"Oh, Nate!" She slid down over him, squeezing his knee between her legs.

"I knew if I stayed steady…"

"…you're always *so steady!* What did the house look like?"

"Like a bank vault with a Greek portico."

"Ohhhh." Daphne was having trouble breathing. Brushing the appliqued straps off her shoulders, she rubbed her bare breasts against Nathan's face, forcing him to brace himself, heels dug into a rotting floorboard, to avoid slipping to the floor before the story was done.

"The man never flinched. The only thing he said was, did I have any more." With some difficulty, Nathan fished a card out of his coat pocket

CONRAD UERGIN, ESQ.
Lucky Lady Gaming Est.
(*next door to Auction Lunch*)
San Francisco

and went to toss it with the money, only Daphne grabbed the card and kissed it, and kissed Nathan—a hungry, promising kiss.

"Oh, darling, hold me! hold me!"

Despite himself, Nathan slid out of the legless sofa on top of her.

The next morning, he returned to the neighborhood of The Collectibles, while Daphne paid a call on the financial district, more precisely on the saloon a few doors down from the Miners Exchange Bank. But first she went shopping, with totally predictable results.

"Daphne, you look lovely."

"No thanks to your measly allowance. I had a terrible time getting the price down." She was sitting in the center of the legless sofa, the radiance in her face taking the drabness out of the room. Her new dress, hoops billowed to either side like half-furled sails, was a silken grey paisley.

Definitely not her color. And what was that on the sleeves?

Dead bugs? Curious, Nathan came closer. Brown yarn tied in knots. Now he could see into the glued-open turkey wing pinned in her hair.

"You saw Mr. Uergin?" He was having trouble keeping a straight face.

"Of course, *and* his fancy women with their diamond choker necklaces *and* their fancy Parisian gowns. On our way to the inner office—which is paneled and carpeted, with crystal chandeliers, the inner door is padded with red velvet, the French mahogany chairs are padded red too—where we viewed the pictures, which the workmen are already hanging." Catching her breath, Daphne leaned forward slightly, gesturing acceptance of applause due.

Grinning, Nathan clapped his hands. "How did you handle him?"

"Up front, of course. I explained I understood he bought some paintings which were out of the ordinary, and asked if I might see them."

"What do you think?"

"It's a very dangerous game. Why did you call him a goose? I can see his teeth in his eyes." Her own eyes widened in alarm.

Made uncomfortable by her reaction, Nathan reminded himself she was just wanting the fellow to be dangerous. "What about the paintings."

"Well…" Incredulity showed on her face.

"They don't do anything for me either. And unfortunately, I have no idea where they came from. According to a neighbor, the shop's owner is off to Volcano to dig for gold."

"Salt Lake City, wherever that is." Oblivious to the disappointment in Nathan's face, Daphne rubbed her fingers toward him.

Nathan took out his purse and shook out twenty $50 bills.

"Let's visit that duke in Cuba." She was spreading the money out fan-like.

"Dōn, Daphne. Dōn." He unpinned the turkey wing from her hair. "There's more where that came from, you know."

"I know," she purred. "Conrad told me so."

"Let's not talk business anymore," Nathan breathed in her ear. She wouldn't be happy until they spent some time high on the hog. "I've got a surprise. I've bought stage tickets for a little jaunt up to Napa. How'd you like to hobnob with the Nabobs at Byron Springs for awhile? It's about 70 miles northeast of here."

"Hobnob with the Nabobs? That is so sweet! You have such a dear way with words."

"When we get back, we'll pay a personal visit to Mrs. Taggart." Nathan closed the fan of money and put it back in his purse. "See what she's got, buy it wholesale. Salt Lake's quite the curiosity, a regular Kubla Khan. Tall white mountains overlooking a blue lake surrounded by a green valley. People call it the City of Brothers-in-law."

Daphne's looked blank, but interested.

"The rich men take all the wives they want. It's illegal as hell, but so remote no one cares."

"Well, we could go there, I guess," Daphne sighed bravely, "as long as I don't have to be anybody's wife." And unable to repress a delicious shiver of anticipation, added, "I always enjoy a boat trip, of course."

"Of course," Nathan stopped sucking on her little finger long enough to say.

"And," she pouted prettily, "I shall want to visit the States, too."

"Later. Right now the prairies aren't safe, the Indian's becoming increasingly belligerent."

"You said that in New Mexico, and I never saw one mad Indian."

"Last year the Indians in New Mexico and Texas attacked the American Army 11 times. Five more times since the first of this year. As for their atrocities on unescorted travelers, the papers are full of the gory details." He gave her nose a tweak that said she was a silly one, but he didn't care. "Actually, for now, the States aren't any safer than the prairies. They're about to go to war."

"With who?"

"Whom, Daphne, with whom."

"Don't tell me my business! I'll remember the right words when I have to. So who's America going to fight?"

"Herself. If you'd read the papers, you'd know. It's only a matter of time."

At that very minute a brawl broke loose outside. Rolling down the nearer dune came a giant tumbleweed gone mad— Chinese and Chileans going at it tooth and toenail, hats popping, arms and legs flailing.

Watching out the glassless window, Nathan laughed and added knowingly, "All things considered, Utah Territory's probably the safest place in America right now."

TWENTY-SEVEN

T HE LETTER SMELLED FAINTLY of roses. Julia took a deep
breath and slipped a knife under the wax, loosening a
shower of pale, dry petals.

Apr. 14. 1857. Dear Maine Family...I am here in this
place called Independence? Do you remember writing that
Jed, so long ago? What a thrill your letter aroused in me and
now I am writing you from the very same dot. As planned
we took the cars to St. Louis and came by steamer to here,
crossing the Mississippi we used a bridge 1,535 feet long.
There is much talk of violence in Kansas and general
agreement that travel is safer on the water.

Our party up from Arkansas was here when we got here,
what a joy for the girls to know their cousins. The Millers
remind me so much of Mun he doesn't seem so far away.
The captain's name is Alex Fancher and he has been to
California before. We keep our belongings with the
Camerons, in-laws to the Millers, they have 5 children and
4 wagons.

Independence is like the Troy fair only 100 times bigger
and wilder like a bedlam. The variety of goods is staggering,
the tightest pinchwad is undone. I bought sun goggles
37.5¢, extra needles 15¢, a good tent with oilcloth floor and
India rubber air mattress $5.50. That leaves me $266.83 in
hand for Stockton not figuring what we spend along the
way.

Tomorrow it's ho for California...

Written above the Little Vermilion near the junction of the
Independence Road with the Fort Riley-Fort Leavenworth Road.

Dear Mama…every morning soon as "light thickens and
the crow makes wing to the rooky wood" Will Cameron
calls out "up and moving" and so that has become our
watch word. Kansas is certainly the most beautiful country,
waist-high flowers to carpet our every view and grass up 10
feet high but the thunder storms are enough to wreck the
nerves of Hercules and rattlesnakes are as thick as leaves on
trees. Even so I can hear Walker singing "here a farm, there
a farm, everywhere a farm."

We have come about 120 miles and yesterday passed tiny
St. Marys log village which has a Catholic mission and will
not reach another building until Fort Kearny on the Platte.
We are now entering what is called Pawnee territory and
understand they are too busy fighting with their neighbors
to bother the road traffic. Too bad it's not the same with the
mosquitoes. They're thick as flakes in a snowstorm.

Our household goods include carpets, featherbeds,
blankets and comforters to give you an idea of the variety.
Several people have brought little rocking chairs and can be
seen rocking beside their fires at the end of the day. Every
family has several milk cows, mostly Durhams each with
its own bell. You can imagine what a fairylike touch the
chiming gives the morning fog as we journey through our
strange new world.

These are men of commercial wealth, farmers and
businessmen mostly from the northwest of Arkansas.
Slavery is the reason they are leaving the States, they don't
doubt there will be a war over the issue. They are devout
Methodists and never travel on Sunday and carry only
enough alcohol for medicinal purposes. Every morning and
night some fellow tries to blow the trumpet to assemble the
camp to hear the preaching. I am sure you will approve but
I dare say you would laugh to hear our minister, he starts out
in English but it is so murdered you would not call it that
and then he warms up and spits out Dutch as fast as he can
work his tongue so it is always interesting.

We have nursing mothers and many pregnant women who would not be making the trek if they had the slightest concern about the road so you must not worry over Lymund's being too young. I am becoming good friends with one of Mun's cousins who will have her 4th baby on the trail, her name is Malinda Scott. Sadly she can neither read nor write, the curse of the frontier wife.

We have plentiful stores of all kinds including desiccated vegetables, ugh, for our health and Jamaican coffee which we drink out of big enameled cups.

We have been hearing wolves and seeing packs of them through the trees. The first time they started up some in the party thought it was the laugher of children on a big romp.

In the evening when we are too tired to make our own music we have a phonograph and opera records and a sheriff who tells bug-bear stories and spins exciting tales of the old days. We even have portable bathtubs. Thus do we wend our way west surviving (ha ha) the hardships of the trail...

Below Fort Kearny, she pressed sage in her letter.

Dear Walker and Katherine...We have reached the Platte river which is not much of a river but more just a spreading puddle of water. The flag pole at Fort Kearny saluted our march this afternoon and every mile adds something to it. There are large numbers of fires across on the Iowa road but we hold to the south and the twain shall not meet until we reach the mountains.

You will not be surprised to learn we women have divided our skirts, there is nothing worse than a long skirt to catch on sticker bushes and under the wagon wheels. It has bid fair to rain all day and tonight there is a lunar rainbow...

Fort Kearny, May 17.

Dear Maine family...picked up our very welcome letters which are a treat to pour over on this dreary Sunday. Our little fort has three quite nice two story frame houses and the rest are sod. A lone soldier is on guard unmindful of the drizzle pacing back and forth to halt at certain points. The fort is a real work horse out here at the gateway to the prairies and mounted soldiers come and go all hours. We have a very kindly feeling for these men as we hear constantly of indian and Mormon troubles. We are camped near the front gate and last night late a single rider came in at a run. What dire message did he carry I wonder and from what lonely outpost.

It is quite pleasant to have a few days to cool our heels. This afternoon it hailed stones as big as hazelnuts but the wagon tops have two thicknesses of covering so nothing inside gets wet. Pawnee indians are everywhere, they have no regular clothing but wrap themselves in very unsanitary looking blankets which they keep in place with no pins or strings I can see. They are peddling dried meat to the emigrants but were sold out before we knew it was to be had.

Captain Smith the commander warns us to keep a sharp eye out for indians but we are well armed with Texas rifles and will stand ourselves well in a rub.

The following letters were written on the road above Fort Kearny.

Dear Walker and Katherine…We have reached a land scalped by wind. We put sweet oil on our skin and the dust sticks and we look all floured up. Now I want you to remember to save all my letters and I shall do the same with yours for our grandchildren…

Dear Mama…We are in good spirits but that was not true a week ago when all the children came down with the measles. The little epidemic played out with no adults stricken and so all is back to normal.

For several days we have seen <u>handcarts</u> across the river. A rider went over and reports mostly women pulling between the shafts of their carts like draught animals. They are Mormons and except for their leader speak no English. Some hobble along on crutches others holding on to their companions. I can not even imagine such suffering. Their leader asked if we could spare flour so we sent over a horse loaded with flour and rice and tins of hard bread and some bacon, also a sundry packet with jams and bonnets.

It is hard to describe the great reach of empty land all about us. Every afternoon enormous thunderheads make up and roll around long into the night, sometimes we get the full load and other times we are happy to be spectators on a fireworks dance so far away we can't hear the thunder.

Today we saw that wonderful curiosity the jackrabbit. It has long ears like a mule and ricochets around like a bouncing ball. There are numerous dead work animals in the road and many more left behind to sink or swim. Like abandoned dogs they limp sadly behind our wagons as best they can before stopping to rest and wait for someone else to come along…

May 25. Dear Maine family…diarrhea has struck along with hard chills but we tell ourselves it is not the dreaded cholera and budge along as best we can. We did lay over one day and 500 teams passed us…

It is now June 10 and we are back to complaining of mosquitoes and dust and heat and wind. We have the north fork to our right having crossed the south fork and navigated the gorge of Ash hollow.

It is now June 14, a Sunday. The graves are increasing, poor sojourners caught by the elephant. There is something peculiarly affecting about a burial on these lonely plains. The newer ones generally have a board for a sign or a split stick with a paper, but there is no way to turn the whole of the road into a properly tended cemetery and so people do what they can and let the coyotes and ants and birds take care of the last sad rites. The quarantined wagons fly red flags to signal sickness…

Finally saw some buffalo and shot one but had a terrible

time getting the oxen near enough to drag it back to camp...

Dear Mama...We stopped early to explore chimney rock yesterday and the most wonderful thing happened, I spotted Jed's name(!) in what looked to be chalk. There it was in bold letters J. Marchion and the date 6.29.46. I was so thrilled. I scratched mine nearby just as bold...

My dearest husband...I write knowing full well I may well be in Stockton before this letter but unable not to because I want to hear your voice and see your eyes looking into mine so much I can hardly bear it.

We have seen all the wonderful landmarks you speak of, they are like little clicks on our survey instrument. Yesterday and today the fog is very bad and this morning we passed a camp laying by to look for a man lost, they were blowing horns and banging on tubs. The poor man was on our minds all day, it is hard to imagine anything worse than being lost from one's own kind out here.

Our road is quite muddy and there are puddles everywhere. My dearest darling how I would adore keeping your feet warm tonight. My heart is so full of you I wake in the middle of the night and feel you with me...

The following letters were written while at Fort Laramie and posted there together with the letters written earlier.

Dear Maine family...we are here in this place called Fort Laramie and have spit in the elephant's eye. The Oregon Trail is proving not so pleasant as imagined and the emigrant park here near the fort is no different. The ground is littered with carcasses and piles of garbage and worse.

Dear Mama...I am very pleased to read all the news from there and to learn you are feeling well. Now you have to remember you must not worry about us. Our companions are quiet mannered and look out for each other and make sure everyone is safe in at night. Our captain's son Kit Fancher is named after Kit Carson. He has a fine stable of stick horses and lets the girls take their pick. When broken they are buried in the road with their own little mound and split stick. As for Lymund he is completely spoiled and may never recover. Most of the trains in here at the fort are quiet and ordinary like us but some are very noisy with ridiculous displays of fire-arms and drunkenness.

There are rooms for let but they are nothing more than robes thrown down on the floor so we continue to sleep in our little blue tent and put up with the ground and its familiar bugs. My air mattress does not hold air but at least I don't have to press it flat in the morning. Tomorrow it's away to the mysterious mountains...

Dearest Mun...I hear you calling my name in the west wind, I hear you calling Lymund, Annie, Emily when the meadowlark sings. Do stay safe and be careful, we are coming my dearest darling, we are coming soon soon and you will dance with your daughters and kiss Lymund's little downy head and we will talk and talk and talk...

Letter posted from Seminoe's trading post, Devil's Gate.

Dear Maine family...today dark-bellied clouds are dragging their shadows across the land. We are beside the Sweetwater having left our old friend the Platte and are grown tough and brown as old boots. The road is littered with many treasures. Our captain calls them leeverites. One day we saw a beautiful sewing basket with colored threads spread about, another day fine blue china in the sand with the cups unbroken but we leave it all right there, afraid of the proverbial straw.

We celebrated the 4th of July with shooting rifles and making a bonfire to reaffirm that indeed we are still Americans although far beyond the bounds of our country. Last night we made camp in a hurry and this morning found we had built our fire on top of a grave. This post is no longer

in operation but there is a box here marked U.S. mail,
Y.X. Express, so I shall give it a try…
    p.s. happy 29th birthday Jed

Last crossing of the Sweetwater.

Dear Walker and Katherine…our pass over the summit
of the Rocky Mountains is high and wide, this is as close as
we come to the grand kings with their eternal snows but we
see them quite clearly off to the north and also feel their
chill. Their beauty staggers the eye. The men have been
wearing two coats and we women wrap ourselves in
blankets as we walk and keep the children in the wagons.
There is ice in the ruts but fortunately no wind. We have
crossed this river 9 times. How amazing to be out here in
the middle of nowhere sending letters home, this is coming
to you from a mail station run by Mormons…

Letters posted July 20 from Fort Bridger.

July 18. Dear Mama…one of the teamsters gave the
twins an old horse to ride but it has become so thin on the
poor pasture that they lead it everywhere to save it for
California. The whole country abounds with wolves and
vinegarish sagebrush.
    Found a solid ball of crickets today. They were large
yellowish brown and were clinging together to keep warm.
The ball was over a foot in diameter and we had to wonder
who had the best of it, the ones on the outside or the ones
in the middle…

Dear Maine family…we have scrambled over the pass
and are on the Pacific side of the mountains. The water is
very bad, many animals are lost to it and the stench is
terrible. We lost 4 oxen.
    We are a grotesque rabble to look at with our hair all
covered with dirt and out faces the same. Our clothing is
in fringes with countless patches and heavily soiled. Our
bonnets are strange assortments of rags pieced together,

some of the men wear bonnets too, their hats having long blown away. Most of us are barefooted and not even stickers bother us.

Our lips crack and bleed and we force ourselves not to lick them. Today we nooned where several large oxen recently died and sat on the carcasses to have our lunch so nothing bothers us anymore. Malinda and I went fishing and caught two fryers. I like her so much, she is my best friend on the journey but her husband Henry is a worrier and spoils the trip for his family...

Dear Walker and Katherine...Fort Bridger is barren and windswept and surrounded by sage. How wonderful it will be to see a real lake instead of a mirage and replenish our food supply which is getting rather meager. We are looking forward to seeing Brigham in his stronghold and hope to persuade Ellen to give us a tour of his beehive...

T W E N T Y - E I G H T

San Francisco. Friday, July 24, 1857. The California stage for Napa was loading. Daphne wanted the filth swept off the floor, but no one would listen.

At ten sharp the matched team of white mules bowled away from its station by the bay and, whips cracking overhead, headed up the north road on the run. Reboarding at the last second Nathan hooked his arm through an overhand strap and fell into a seat, realizing as he did that some lout had used his newspaper for a floor mat. He stared ruefully about at the unkempt minerly types sharing the coach and turned his attention out the window, his well-polished boots smearing the headlines on the Golden Era.

Troops March on Utah
Big Daddy Out
Military Department Declared

Six hundred miles to the east, in Utah Territory, some 2,587 of the faithful were camped out at Big Cottonwood Creek for a three-day celebration of the tenth anniversary of the arrival of the Saints in Salt Lake Valley. A brass howitzer opened the festivities at 10:15 a.m. with three rounds that ricocheted like

thunder. The Army of Israel was the first group to appear—
50 boys ranging from 10 to 12 years old. Marching briskly across
the newly-raked field in their new uniforms, the boys paused
before Brigham's platform to hear themselves called the Hope
of Israel. Jeremy got to blow the ram's horn, his family clapped
loudly, and George proudly saluted his son with his hat.

Next came the light infantry, followed by heavily mounted
lancers, followed by the life guards. Introducing each group, six
bands played joyously.

At noon, taking dinner in his tent with Heber, Brigham was
surprised by the unexpected arrival of missionaries thought to
be in the States. Bishop Smoot and Elder Stoddard, just 20 days
from the Missouri River, exhaustion showing in their faces,
carried terrible news.

While crossing the prairie east of the mountains on their way
to the States, they had encountered 2,500 American soldiers.
The American officer with whom they spoke said he was recon-
noitering the country for hostiles, but the missionaries were
skeptical. For such a large force to be searching for Indians
seemed highly unlikely. The missionaries' skepticism increased
when, several days afterward, they came on a large number of
freight wagons whose destination the drivers were not given to
know.

Reaching Kansas City, they hurried to the freight offices of
William Russell, who informed them the trains were intended
for GSL City, that Alfred Cumming had been appointed governor to replace Brigham, and that all mail from the States to
Utah Territory was being cut off.

Delivered of their horrific message, the shaken missionaries
turned aside to wipe wet eyes.

"God is in control." Brigham's calm words belied the tremendous roar of excitement that filled him. "Tell no one your news
until after the celebrations here are done." Watching the couri-

ers walk their lathered horses away, he asked Heber, "What d'you think?"

Heber hesitated. He couldn't see the Prophet's face, but 32 years of memories had honed his instincts razor sharp. "I find it perfectly delightful to contemplate," the response high and sing-song, "2,500 soldiers, did they say? a new governor did they say? I suggest you give my wives a week, 10 days just to be sure."

Brigham spun around in a dancer's sword step, stuck his hand out and, lower lip drawn tight over his jaw, ground a thumb into his open palm.

The next morning, Brigham sent for George. Listening with carefully tended concern to the news already heard the previous evening from Judson Stoddard, George found the President's assumed titles taking their place in his thoughts like little pop-up soldiers.

Prophet, Seer, Revelator, President, Governor of Utah, earthly Vicar of the heavenly Savior, Commander-in-Chief of the Militia, Superintendent of Indian Affairs. What else does he call himself?

"The Lord reigns and rules!" Brigham shouted, running over with the Spirit. "He has delivered the wicked, lying, soulless courters of prosecution to the faithful, who will give them back so much they will not know what to do with it!!"

Ten minutes, 20 minutes, raining down the scourings of the chamber pot on the nasty Gentiles' heads as if the whole congregation sat there in the tent instead of one lowly bishop.

Behind the mask that was his face, George's thoughts moved drunkenly. *He's celebrating the American Army's approach, now why would he do that?*

"…my pay as Governor and Superintendent of Indian Affairs will be cut off…"

Feeling for the hook, George jerked imperceptibly. Brigham always came round-about to what he wanted.

"...nor do I want that filthy succoring. I fight best with my back to the wall. But the Legion needs help if we are to keep the stinking devils from killing us. I've notified our people in San Bernardino and Carson to buy all the guns and ammunition they can get their hands on and come on the run. I'll need $50,000 immediately."

George's nod was perfunctory, a wedge for his own words. "This was bound to happen, what with the Gentile officials spreading their poor, rotten-hearted curses. However, we mustn't lose sight of the fact that you continue to be the Territory's spiritual leader. As such, your power will continue to be recognized in Washington. The Americans will pay to use our warehouses, and the profits will be enormous."

Which was the truth. What amazed George was that the American President would commit such a financial blunder. "This kind of cash-flow will soon rectify any shortfall incurred by strengthening the Legion," he concluded.

"Goddamn you, George!" Brigham roared, bringing his hard, red face close. "You never bite anymore, do you?" Straightening, the President laced his thick fingers together and pressed them against the top of his thin, sandy hair.

Something in the action reminded George queerly of their age difference. Brigham was 56, nine years younger but not as healthy. All last year the Prophet had complained of dizziness and ringing in the ears. More than once, leeches had been applied.

Brigham relaxed his arms. "You're right, the Americans will pay. Dearly. We'll begin by letting the rabble cool their heels outside the Valley this winter. Double that transfer. A hundred thousand to open the ball. The Americans will pay us back, but first they must pay the piper, AND I AM THE PIPER!" Brigham opened his mouth wide and pressed a thumb and forefinger against the corners. And despite some effort not to, began to laugh.

George should have joined in, but was unable to. Brigham waved his bishop off, the sound of laughter following George out the tent and down the path to the boweries.

Sunday afternoon, July 26, 40 miles above San Francisco on the promenade deck of the commodious Bryon Springs Hotel. A lovely summer's day, but not for that woman over there, the large woman dressed all in black. The long fringe from her sleeves and overskirt trails down the sides of the sea-green wicker lounge. Partially hidden under the folds of her jowls is a five-strand necklace of large, fresh-water pearls. Pressed to her eyes is a black silk handkerchief.

"Poor Mme. de**," a steward confided to Nathan. "Her husband and her only son tied down the safety valve on their steamship and blew themselves to pieces in a race to Sacramento."

The compassion shown the estimable Mme. de** by the Laffites was touching. And healing. So much so that after four days of tea and sympathy, when Daphne announced she was packing to leave, Mme. de** begged the couple stay to the end of summer.

Whereupon, taking the older woman into her confidence, Daphne tearfully, but bravely, bared her soul. Due to the death of her dear father-in-law, recently deceased of an incurable disease caught while hunting lions in the wilds of Africa, which is why her dear husband felt a vacation necessary in the first place, the Laffite export business banking accounts were temporarily frozen, pending settlement of the estate.

"We have spent all we can prudently afford for now." Shame flushed Daphne's lovely face.

The poignant confession rendered Mme. de** temporarily speechless. Did not the naive child realize that audits were necessary in the banking business? There was nothing to be ashamed of.

"Please, dear friend, stay," Mme. de** pleaded in her scratchy voice. "The room and board are mere trifles, I'll have them added to my voucher."

But Daphne would not take charity! Absolutely!! The very thought was repugnant.

"Oh, please, child, don't be offended. Consider it a loan. Pay me back when you like, but don't carry on so. I can buy anything I want except companionship, and you have given me that, you and your sweet husband, including me in your walks as you have, and at your table. You have such very jubilant personalities, and it is so hard to be alone, so very hard." She burst into tears. "You have no idea."

That evening, the trio treated themselves to a six-liter bottle of cabernet sauvignon to celebrate their being able to stay together awhile longer.

It would be six weeks before the dreaded telegram arrived, urging the Laffites' immediate return to San Francisco. In the meantime, Daphne would bravely sign over $10,000 worth of rare paintings held by the Laffite family—a figure approximately $2,000 in excess of the tab carried by Mme. de**.

Causing Mme. de** to complain forcefully more than once, "I don't in the least need these notes. You really must be more careful, my dear, about just signing things away."

As the Laffites prepared to depart for San Francisco, their munificent benefactor offered to accompany them, herself having powerful friends on Montgomery Street, but was relieved to hear (selfishly so, she felt, but she was becoming *quite* comfortable at the sulfur springs and starting to enjoy wearing bright clothing again) that the young couple anticipated no trouble and should return in time to take the fall colors.

T W E N T Y - N I N E

FORT KEARNY, Nebraska Territory. Wednesday afternoon,
July 29.
Lt. Elisah G. Marshall, Commanding Officer, tossed
the newly arrived dispatch in the file box and sat contemplating
the knots in the floorboards. Depending on his mood, they could
look like cannon smokes. Right now they looked like horse
droppings. The lieutenant's eyes went out of focus. Dobytown.

The soldier bellied up to a stack of gingersnaps and a bottle of
tanglefoot in the Dobytown saloon acted like he didn't hear.

"Sergeant Reeves," the orderly said again, "C.O. wants you at
headquarters."

"Later."

"Now."

"You didn't find me."

"There's only two places you can be, here and Dogtown."

Layers of smoke and the stench of sour-mash fouled the air.
A chair being carried overhead through the crowd bumped the
ceiling. Loose dirt trickled down.

The red-headed sergeant fished a rat turd out of his cup.
"What about?"

The orderly shrugged.

Charlie sighed and answered his own question. "Utah
Territory."

The C.O.'s words exactly, along with something about a few good men. "As you know, sergeant, the region is being made a Military Department. I'd be interested in hearing your evaluation of the situation."

"Begging your pardon, sir, I'm on short time." A rugged, large-framed man with big hands. Stern faced. Direct, honest blue eyes.

Not for the first time the lieutenant wondered where men like these came from. Men who thought in straight lines, who got done whatever they put their mind to. Or died trying. God help the country if the politicians north and south put men like these to fighting each other.

"I haven't forgotten why you're not in the field, sergeant. Have a seat. Have a cigar. Permission to speak freely."

In the waiting silence, Charlie cleared his throat. "Well, sir, with the infantry and batteries not leaving Leavenworth until the 18th past, I figure that makes 'em wintering at Fort Laramie."

"I'm not referring to the Army's orders so much as Mormon mentality. Will they understand our motives are peaceful?"

"I never met a Mormon yet didn't think everybody and his dog was after 'em."

The proffered cigar lay on the desk. The lieutenant drew deeply on his own cigar and held it out as a light.

"I have word from General Harney that a quartermaster department representative is to be sent through ahead of the Army. Capt. Stewart Van Vliet will investigate supplies and arrange for provisioning and housing in the basin. He's to leave Fort Leavenworth 30 July with orders to be in Salt Lake City in 25 days. There should be no problems in the desert, with Sumner keeping the Cheyenne under the gun. What I want to know is, what will happen in Salt Lake City?"

Charlie had his eyes closed, enjoying his cigar. "They'll burn theirselves out so we can't make use of what they got. Starting with Bridger's."

"We're sending 2,500 men to that region. Our intelligence indicates the provisioning of a large force will make their farmers rich. They have more than adequate stock and grass to sell. It's important to remember what we're doing is establishing a fort in the midst of a civilized people, not opening a frontier."

The sergeant opened his eyes. "You're gonna give 'em another governor. They think the one they got's God."

"No mention is being made of a replacement for Young."

"Shit! Begging your pardon, sir. But I know. If I know, he knows. He'll never let the captain's escort into the city."

Lieutenant Marshall studied the row of Presidential peace-council medals in the dusty little display case on his desk. It was too bad Utah hadn't been made a Military District back when New Mexico and the Pacific Departments were formed. The place was becoming a foreign monarchy and extremely danger-ous for outsiders.

The problem was in the timing. The batteries weren't prepared. The men hadn't drilled together, the horses imported from Ohio and Missouri wouldn't take the field like horses raised together.

Worse than that was the desertion rate. Many of the compa-nies were half-full. Faced with the isolation of a winter campaign in the desert, soldiers were deserting by the hundreds. The 5th Infantry alone had lost over 200 men by desertion since leaving Florida and was suffering from the scurvy to boot. The ranks were being refilled with raw recruits who scarcely spoke English and who had absolutely no understanding of military discipline.

The C.O. absently tapped first one end of his pencil then the other. Foreigners fighting foreigners, that's what it boiled down to. Utah was full of them. Religion made their foreigners soldiers.

Sixteen dollars a month and freedom from religion didn't

have quite the same ring for the States recruit fresh off the turnip wagon.

"It's essential the Utah Expedition go smoothly. It only takes a few loose cannon to blow everybody out of the water. Whatever the moral persuasions of the Territory's inhabitants, however deplorable or revolting to the public sentiment, it is not up to us to interfere beyond enforcing the law." Concern flickered on the lieutenant's face and gave way to an habitual expression of courtesy.

"You were with Colonel Steptoe in '54 when he canvassed the situation in the Valley with regard to Gunnison's survey party. What would you do, sergeant, if you were in Van Vliet's shoes?"

"Leave the escort at Ham's Fork on the Green, find me some Mormons to travel in with, there's plenty on the road."

"You think that'll get Brigham's cooperation?"

"Nope, but at least the captain won't get hisself blowed up."

"Let's hope you're wrong about the cooperation."

"Yes, sir." It was raining, a soft, late afternoon rain that washed down Powell's trees and blotted out the fort's other sounds.

"Van Vliet should be here in 10 days with a detachment from the infantry. He may require additional support." Lt. Marshall located the dispatch and read, "'Men selected for this service are to be repeatedly admonished never to comment upon or ridicule anything they may either see or hear, and to treat the inhabitants of Utah with kindness and consideration. They should be men of high bearing, intelligence and devotion.'"

The C.O. looked up. He'd long ago come to the conclusion that he had an obligation, in the spirit of *noblesse oblige,* to make the Army a better place for the enlisted man. It was like wishing in one hand and shitting in the other. Still, he kept the commitment.

"You're 35 years old. A good number of those years in the Army, with just one complaint. That's pretty good, soldier. Damn good. If it becomes necessary to send someone from this post with the quartermaster, I want a sergeant I can count on. We're talking about another tour of duty for the length of the Expedition only. And a 30-day leave, 10 now and 20 when you get back. As you know, pay is extra for service beyond the Rocky Mountains."

The sergeant made a polite, denying smile. "I never lost anything in Utah, sir."

The C.O. lowered his voice. "The Army has a lot of Southern sympathizers among the officers. Heth, Stuart, Lee, McCowan, May, Chilton. Perhaps as many as a third. If there is a war, they'll resign their commissions and offer their services to the Confederate government. It will be easier than ever before to promote good enlisted men. You're from Ohio, that makes you a Northerner."

"Yes, sir."

"In 1854 Colonel Steptoe commended you for…" the C.O. picked up another paper "'…character, wisdom and discretion…' Do this for me, sergeant, and if the South bolts the Union, I guarantee you a commission as a second lieutenant."

THIRTY

CHARLIE SIGNED ON the hand-ruled line, drew a $20 partial and a four-day pass and caught a ride on the Overland to St. Joe.

"The boys are gonna prowl around Utah for awhile, jerk Brigham's chain," he told Sarah, who cried.

He'd met her in 1843 in a little backwater bar outside Fort Gibson, Oklahoma Territory. He was 21 and drunk. She was 20 or 16, whatever entered her mind, and hotter than a fresh-fucked fox in a forest fire. She wanted to get married, and the next morning, cold sober, he told her he couldn't get married without his C.O.'s permission. She didn't care, she didn't want to be a laundress anyway. But near as he remembered the previous evening, someone calling himself a deacon *had* married them for five dollars.

Three years later, stationed at Fort Leavenworth, he ran into her in St. Joe. They had a Mexican stand-off. She wasn't just anyone's fancy woman. She was a high-born Cherokee with a pedigree (sometimes she admitted to being part Irish, but this wasn't one of those times), and she had her commitments.

But if it would make him feel good, let the American soldier put his money down. She'd be his when he was in town and make a prayer for him every day.

Shortly afterward, he was assigned escort duty to the Great Lakes, and after that it was the prairies. The next time he saw her, she'd gotten herself out from behind the red-curtained windows below Robidoux Row and into an old man's bed on Penn Street.

"What was your name again?" she asked.

A couple of years after that, and a letter caught up with him. The old man had died and left Sarah a run-down carriage house. Sweet Charlie should write once in awhile, let her know how he was getting on. She'd fix up a room, her blue-eyed soldier boy could keep his things there when he was in town.

She didn't mention money, but what the hell, he sent her a couple of bucks anyway.

Almost 15 years they'd been dancing around the May pole. She used to be sleek and honey-voiced. Now she was fat, what she called her Indian hair was shot through with grey, and she had a settled, guileless look about her. And a lingering smolder that could still make a man look twice.

Walking out at dusk to watch the fireflies, they talked about what the sergeant was going to do with the rest of his life, eventually finding themselves—like ships passing in the night—on the other's shore.

The hell with it, Charlie told her, the Army was too busy to come looking for him. He was tired of living alone. They'd go to California. What did she think?

The Army owed him, that's what Sarah thought. Besides, being an officer's wife had a certain ring to it.

They had a nice time after that. One day they took a loaf of squash bread and a jug of wine and rode around the city on excursion carriages. The Missouri was shifting its banks, coming in against the wharves. From the bluff above, they watched the river, like an enormous brown snake, suck up a long row of hastily emptied Robidoux warehouses.

Sitting under the black oak trees at the free Independence Picnic in the park, they listened to Hannibal and St. Joseph officials describe their new railroad. A tall, angular lawyer in a black stovepipe hat stepped up to the podium. His name was Abe Lincoln, and he spoke of how the peoples' iron horses were steaming westward.

Watching the lawyer, Sarah saw cannons exploding over his head. Charlie said ice cream and fried frogs' legs on top of red wine did that to him sometimes too.

When her soldier boy left, Sarah held her skirt against her face and refused to be solaced. Charlie thought about that a lot, dozing in the corner of the stage back to Fort Kearny. That even now he was her only man he had no conceit. But for some reason he believed that her straying and playing occurred no more often, and for no better reason, than his own occasional dallies.

He wondered if she might have fallen in love with him. He wondered why he'd signed up for the Expedition. The company of animals and men wasn't much of a life, particularly in the Army. Bad food, long hours, bad policies.

As for the Army making him an officer, he was peeing into the wind if he believed that. Trouble was, away from the Army he was bored. The last time he got out, back in '50, he'd made good money clearing and filling land for a railroad yard in Hannibal, Missouri. But three years of living in a shack alongside the river, with only occasional visits from Sarah, and he'd reenlisted.

He had to have something more important to do on his watch than move dirt around.

Late July in Houlton.

Black flies and mosquitoes are about gone. The setting sun has moved well north of Mount Katahdin, and the Meduxnekeag is low enough that the more nimble-footed can cross without getting their rolled-up trousers wet. Daisies and buttercups bloom at the edges of the yards, potatoes bloom in the gardens. Flower baskets hanging from the piazza of the Snell House brim over with asters and goldenrod.

Seated beneath one of the baskets, the Marchions sort through the morning's news, lean together and laugh. It was Jed's idea to have lunch. Julia has arrived with a surprise—a natty, green-striped silk tie and matching handkerchief.

"I'll wear it if you will first," Jed whispered against her ear. "Tonight."

Julia turned her face aside from the sinewy pile of material on the red oilcloth. "It looks so 'jungle-ish' in the sun."

"I'll show you how to tie it. Unfortunately, I won't be able to wear it in public."

"Jed!"

"JULia! It says in my contract…"

"…what contract?…"

"…that under no circumstances is the new foreman in charge of fitting up a factory for the manufacture of…" he stirred the silken material with an idle finger and smiled wickedly "…comfortable beds with delicately turned legs for the people of Houlton to make babies in, that under no circumstances is that foreman ever to wear green-and-white striped ties, much less blow his nose on green and…"

"…you went to work for Shep Cary?!" Julia squealed. "Oh, dear! You won't have to go back into the woods?"

"Not like before, not all winter."

Thrilled, Julia was absolutely thrilled. Her first inclination was to rise to her feet, tap the water glass with a spoon, and make an announcement the way the men did when calling attention to a profitable luncheon transaction. She settled instead for provoking a titter from the serving girls by kissing her husband soundly on the mouth.

T H I R T Y - O N E

ON MONDAY THE 3rd of August 1857 the ditches bordering the streets of the city by the salt lake ran with blood. Headless skeletons hung in the trees, vultures with empty eye sockets perched on the ridge poles of the houses. A wind from a different land made the bones go clack, clack, clack, and ruffled the bloody-edged feathers.

But the only person who might have noticed was sitting at a desk in San Francisco, under a collection of emigrant paintings.

Cooling his heels in the outer room of Brigham's private office, George scarcely listened to the conversation issuing through the open door. Two elders were reviewing the tremendous beating they'd given an apostate for telling emigrants stopped over in the city what damned rascals the Mormons were. The bishop loosened his collar tiredly, the afternoon was late and he had an evening meeting with the stockholders in the dry goods and grocery cooperative.

When the elders left, their high spirits lingered in Brigham. "Come in, come in!" the President cried. "It's not easy holding the people down, Brother Harris, not easy at all. They bite hard on the bit." With a flourish, he whisked the $50,000 draft from George's hand.

"Hell is yawning and sending forth its devils and their imps—what for? to destroy the Kingdom of God upon the earth—*but they cannot do it!* Woe, woe to those men who come here to unlawfully meddle with me and this people."

That Brigham did not sit down told George their business was over. Leaving the outer office, the bishop met Porter Rockwell coming in. Greasy Port, hair looped and tied like an Indian's, dung on his boots. As a younger man, the grey-eyed chief of the Danites had been beefy and physically overpowering. But the years were gaunting him, draining the fat off his cabbage face and giving his stocky body a specter-like stoop. Why keep a killer on the payroll? George wondered. In the early days maybe. But even then, Port couldn't save Joseph Smith's life.

The Danite stuck out his hand and George grasped it weakly, aware he was behaving like a fish. Outside in the sun, the sky was soft and low, the air yellowish with the tinge of wood smoke. George shook back his shoulders and wiped his hand on his coat. Something lurked in Port, something evil looked out from the shadows.

But much more worrisome at the moment was Brigham's continuing transfer of church funds "in trust of the Trustee," up to $150,000 in less than two weeks.

"They's here, down on the public graze, a good 140 of 'em or better." Porter flipped a chair about and straddled it as he would a saddle. "Sixty good heavy wagons. Good big ox teams. Near 100 top-notch mules and horses, a good-looking racing mare with only one eye." His grin widened in the telling. "Over 700 head of cattle, fine milk stock, buggies, hacks, three fancy carriages, one with carved elks' heads on the doors. Add 'er up…" he licked a dinner crumb out of the corner of his lips, "…you're looking at $100,000, plus whatever's hidden in the hounds."

Too excited to remain still, the scout stood and put his foot on the chair rung.

Brigham leaned back in his seat to where he could see the level expanse of what passed for lawn outside the open window. This time of year the brittle grasses looked like hog's hide. The church leader massaged his armpit absently.

"The Christian world does not have the religion that Jesus and his apostles taught. If this were not the Kingdom of God on earth, do you think for one minute the world would be arrayed against us? When we first came here, all I asked was 10 years. Ten measly years! After that, I swore I'd ask no odds of Uncle Sam or the devil. We got our 10 years, Port, and no one's slipped the bow on old Brigham's neck yet. Now I say, so help me Joseph Smith, in 12 years I'll be President of the United States or dictate who shall!"

Porter sat down heavily, retreating into his usual gloom. He didn't like to be preached at. He'd heard all this before. At Big Cottonwood Lake last summer when Brigham declared war on the United States. A dozen times since in the Bowery.

"So it don't matter where we start," he answered, voice low and fathoming.

Invariably the sound touched Brigham like a harp struck in an empty room. "It matters to the Lord."

"Ain't that why he's sending 'em along now?" Like Heber, Port knew the value of the coin he exchanged. Only in Port's case it was not the wit to amuse, but the utter tick-bird-like disregard for his own safety. Private conversations with the most powerful man in the Kingdom invariably left him cocky and light-headed. He banged his heels on the floor, his mouth twisting in arrogant self-amusement.

The pureness of this most perfect instrument—never doubting, never wavering—humbled Brigham, who kept his head inclined toward the window.

"If it wasn't meant to be," Porter's low monotone continued, "this bitter salt would of stayed west at the cutoff."

Brigham swung around, fixing the Destroying Angel in a stare of ferocious intensity. "The Indians are the sticking point. It's too big a party."

"Goddamn cowards," Porter agreed happily and, leaning forward, rapped the desk with his knuckles. "Ever torch a porky-pine, Brother Brigham? They burn just like coal oil, everywhere they run they set the country on fire. Long as the Lamys got the name, that's all that matters."

Brigham continued to stare at the Danite. All he ever asked for to keep the priests and hellish rabble at bay were soldiers. All he got, except for Port and his little band of police, were farmers. He'd given the Saints a Kingdom to wash in the blood of the Lamb, and they couldn't stomach the blood. Well, like it or not, they were going to have to let go the plow handles and pick up the broadax now—the American Army was on its way! The thought flooded Brigham's face. Shifting his weight, he put his elbows on the desk and rested his forehead against his clasped hands.

"Come back at first light, I'll have the letters ready." He didn't need to see the scout's face to see the sour smile. His own insides felt as if he'd doused them with vinegar. When he looked up, Porter was gone.

Alone and restless, Brigham put on his straw hat and left the office through a private door. On a side porch several wives were working on a big pile of cucumbers. The smell of turnips boiling followed him into the yard and up the hill to a small white house. In it lived the only wife that didn't live in the Beehive House. The first wife.

Brigham hesitated outside the windowed door. The crone sat alone, hunched over a scrap of sewing by a cold stove. Her hair was all but gone, and several large moles disfigured her neck. How old she was becoming! he'd have to move in one of the younger wives to take care of her. He was on the verge of quitting the door when Mary Ann gave a start and looked up wide-eyed.

The look changed Brigham's mind. Her desperate gratefulness would be soothing. He came inside and, opening the bible on the table, began to read aloud.

In the large Harris mansion on State Road, Dinky was delighted to find her former sister-in-law so amply provided for and looking so well. That Jed was the first person Ellen asked about scarcely surprised Dinky. Jed was the same way, wanting to know, when he saw her in Houlton, if she'd heard from Ellen. They couldn't live together, but they had a deep need to know the other lived well.

George came home at 6 p.m.

"Fair with me," was how Jed had described his former employer. "But he sure did think he was God's gift to the world."

"An arrogant churchman," Ellen had called George years before her marriage to him. "Always using God to get what he wants." Even after settling in Salt Lake City, Ellen wrote only of her husband that he worked too hard.

Now, meeting for herself the gentle aging bear with his droopy eyes and droopy jowls, Dinky was at once in love. Later, walking past where the bishop sat, she kissed the top of his bald head and whispered, "I always wanted to kiss a saint."

Immediately after supper the travelers retired upstairs to the large room Phoebe called her studio—the room originally planned as a playroom before George discovered he couldn't stand not to have his children playing downstairs. Easels and paint boxes had been pushed aside, and a makeshift bed and thick feather floor mats made up.

Later, carrying cups and a pot of warm milk, Ellen was struck by the room's transience. The sleeping children, the scatter of unfamiliar belongings, provided an altogether perfect foil for the billowy artwork that commanded the walls. She felt as if she were in another world, a place in time she'd never been.

Dinky lay propped against the bed pillows in her print night-shirt, her new calico dress with its tight sleeves (and faint but unmistakable smell of wagon mold) spread over the sideboard, her new Sunday shoes beneath. On the bed table, half-hidden in the folds of a lace handkerchief, was a silver-backed brush.

Moved to tears by the wistful homage in the finery, Ellen sat at the foot of the bed and massaged the bare callused feet. Dear Dinky, so loyal and so loving.

Please, pray God, let California be everything she dreams of. Let it be as beautiful as they say and warm and healthy for them all.

She studied the children, brown as Indians. Seeing Jed in their features. Wanting to see Jed. The sharp longing disappeared as quickly as it had come.

She returned downstairs happier than she'd been in a long time. The nearer city retreated, the outside world flowing in, full of its greater mysteries and promises. They would visit Dinky in California, it wasn't that far. Jeremy and Nancy could see a different part of the world, Phoebe could sell her paintings there.

Noticing Jeremy bent over his desk—an ornate cherry wood affair in the corner of the dining room—Ellen set the tray down and lit the lamp. Jeremy closed his arms over his paper, and she playfully pulled the paper free. "What are you working on?"

A pencil drawing. Covered wagons surrounded by headless bodies, arms and legs sticking out at grotesque angles, dripping blood where hands and feet should have been, privates exposed, women's breasts jutting up like pointed mountains, a sky filled with loose heads staring jack-o-lantern-like.

"Jeremy George!! for god's sake! what is this?!"

Jeremy tried to pull the paper free. "Nothing."

"You are ten years old!" Ellen's voice rose. "There is absolutely no excuse for this!"

"It's Gentiles," the boy said defensively.

"What kind of excuse is that? Look at me, Jeremy!"

The boy stuck his thumbnail between his front teeth, and Ellen smacked his forearm against the table. Still, he wouldn't look up. She crumpled the drawing, threw it on the floor and, taking the second thought, retrieved the drawing and marched Jeremy by the ear to where George sat asleep on the front-room sofa.

"Do something, I don't care what you do!"

George sighed and, after one glance at the picture, didn't look again. He pushed himself to his feet and lifted the fly swatter off its nail hook by the door, and he and Jeremy went out and sat in the front-porch swing.

"Did you show your picture to the company?"

"No, sir."

"That was considerate of you, it would have scared them. I hope the Indians don't do that, don't you?"

"Yes, sir."

Jeremy sat with his hands dangling between his knees. George wanted to take those little-boy hands and hold them in his own. His children's fingers had always fascinated him, they were so fragile. Instead he patted Jeremy shyly on the knee.

"I've been wanting to talk to you. I…you know…about Morris."

Jeremy tilted his head back, staring out across his cheeks at the darkening city. His eyes slid side to side suspiciously. He was practicing for his part in "The Missouri Persecutions," a role he liked. The cursed leader of the Sectarians was very haughty and, truth be known, Jeremy in his natural state was a little haughty.

"Do you remember," George asked jovially, "when your mother sent you to the butcher for fresh bacon and you came back with green bacon, and she got so mad because it cost $2.00 a pound and it wasn't fresh? Remember? You said it said 'fresh,' but she said the labels must of got mixed up? So down we all marched to the butcher's, remember that? and here was all these chunks of bacon and every one labeled 'fresh,' and every one with green edges." The bishop laughed with genuine warmth. "So after that we always said, 'never mind what the label says.'"

A whine came close and he shook the swatter.

"What I'm getting at is, maybe that's not a very good start, but…alright, what I'm getting at is, just wipe the slate clean of everything but the word 'labels.' Alright? Think about the church. Sometimes the church is like the butcher, it gets carried away and labels everything a sin. Like…" George took a deep, grim breath, "…masturbation. Now, that's not a sin."

Up and down the street the lanterns were being lit. The outlines of the houses faded, the inside lights glowing like little clumps of firebugs.

"I think Morris masturbated, all boys do." George tried to sound casual. "And that's nobody's business. But as a matter of fact I believe Morris was telling the truth about counting his quarters."

That's what Morris said he was doing on the street corner that day, counting his money. He had five quarters in his pocket, and he was counting them when the block teacher walked by and thought he was playing with himself and told Morris' parents, who whipped him when he got home even though he said he was only counting his money.

Morris' father was one of the clerks who regularly rode out to tally emigration charges on the overseas converts prior to the converts being admitted to the city. That this important position should be the least besmirched by a filthy act done by *his own son!* made Brother Morris *sick to his stomach!*

Sunday morning at sacrament meeting, Morris bore testimony to the truth of the church's wisdom in forbidding self-gratification. Except he did manage to tell everybody first that he was really counting his money. But, if he had been doing IT, which he never would, he certainly never would do IT again. Then the elder in charge of the meeting had all the boys raise their hands and swear that *they would never never* engage in the vicious habit that was the devil's way of cozening the weak-minded into unspeakable sin.

That afternoon, at priesthood meeting, the Deacon's Quorum voted in the affirmative on Brother Morris' request to deny his son the privilege of passing the sacrament for a year. That night, in his grandfather's barn, Morris hung himself.

Morris was 14 years old, he lived right down the block, he was the one who taught Jeremy how to play catch.

"Masturbation is just something men do." George tried to relax, tried to put together the words his own father, a part-time minister, might have used. But for the life of him, he couldn't remember the religion of his youth being the least interested in that part of a young boy's anatomy. He really doubted Jeremy even knew the meaning of the word.

"You know how male animals hump up when they get excited, man isn't any different. But man has a higher mind. He thinks how he would look in front of children and women, so he waits till dark. That's the safest, to make sure no one sees. And it's a good idea to use a little rag if you're in bed."

"Do you do it?" Jeremy lowered his head to a normal plane.

"You remember when I went to England? I did then. That's because it's a sin to have sex with a woman you aren't married to, and your mother wasn't with me." George was suddenly conscious of having left out something crucial. They hadn't yet talked about "sex with a woman." Screw the details.

"A man has to relieve himself, or else he turns sour and mean. You know how crazy penned bulls and stallions get."

"Does President Brigham do it?"

"Not now probably, but I'm sure he did. A title don't mean anything when it comes to that." Despite himself, George began to chuckle. Jeremy looked up, and his father said, "I don't know about Heber, though. Maybe he never did do it, he can get pretty crazy sometimes."

Jeremy made saucer eyes. "Yeah."

"There's nothing wrong with relieving yourself. All those scary stories about God hating you and making you blind? that's just little kids' stories, even if big kids use 'em. God has better things to do with his time."

George waved away some more whiny sounds. "You understand what I'm getting at? A lot of growing up has to do with learning about labels on green bacon."

Jeremy nodded solemnly, and George wanted to hug him. But the moment was too delicate. Then he remembered he was supposed to be talking about Gentiles, but the thing with Morris had been on his mind.

"Anyway, it's the same with Gentiles. Some are good, some are bad. You have to decide for yourself which are which. Now, did you have anything else we should talk about? No? Well, send your mother out."

Ellen didn't know what they were going to do. "You know where that crap comes from? It comes from sitting in church and listening to Brigham and his men always talking about cutting off Gentiles' heads. What are little children to make of such bloodthirstiness? It's not normal. They see beatings every day on the city streets, just because people are Gentiles or apostates. What gives us the right to do that?!"

"It's our city." George sounded cynical. "According to Brigham, God's about to cut the thread between Zion and the States anyway, then we can let in who we want."

Ellen waved her hand past her face. "The Indians didn't think the white men were coming either!"

George made no answer, and she went on. "When Nancy and Jeremy got home, they played so nice with the twins, and Jeremy gave Lymund wheelbarrow rides. Then our own son *sits down and does this!*" She cast about vaguely for the picture and, not seeing it, went on to other things. The swing chains made a steady eeeeek-uuunk.

"Why are children in school in August anyway? They can't play out in the cool of the day because they have homework. And why are we changing the words to the old songs? At the Salt Lake House sale on the Fourth of July, the choir sang 'Yankee Doodle,' and it was all about Heber. 'Brother Heber went to town, riding on a pony. Cut a Gentile up in slices because he was a phony.' Now that is just plain *stupid!*"

"I thought I made it very clear Phoebe was to discontinue selling her paintings in the Salt Lake House," George observed mildly.

"Yes, you did. You know what else I think about? About us only having one paper and it only repeating Brigham's sermons. When I read the newspapers wrapped around the glasses shipped to Kinkeads from California, I realize how much we haven't been told. Did you know that Texas is importing African camels? or that a cable is being laid across the Atlantic Ocean?"

"You've not been in Kinkeads since Brigham imposed his ban, I hope."

"Of course not. But there's a lot going on we don't realize, George. People are leaving ..." she rattled off a string of names "...or trying to, God only knows how many make it, and we kill them for it, George! It's the bald truth. We tell ourselves they're turncoats and so that makes it alright. You don't want to hear that, do you?"

"Hush! Softly, speak softly, such language will cause us both a great deal of trouble."

"Alright, but just tell me, why is the Legion drilling for war! We can't whip the United States Army! What is Brigham thinking of? Do you know that Jeremy is complaining because he's not old enough to drill? Our own Jeremy!" She began to cry, all jangled and wanting settling. "If we could just have more time together, it wouldn't be so bad. You're never home, we never sit out like this."

George opened his eyes and put a hand on Ellen's knee. His fierce wife. Such high hopes she had for this visit from America. For weeks she'd been getting ready. She must be tired. God knows, he was tired. But she *must* be more careful. More than once her conversations in public had been reported, and he'd been obliged to employ all his influence on her behalf.

She hated the Reformation, called it Brigham's wild hare and refused to worry about it. "We've given him too much power," she liked to say. "He thinks he *is* the church."

What she ought to be thinking about, George reminded himself, were the miraculous changes in the once-desolate Valley. How well-ordered everything was. The beautiful streets and houses and fields, the happy foreigners. Prophets good and bad would come and go, but God and his people would prevail.

This thought made George remember something.

It was 1852, the adobe work on the Social Hall was just finished. The women served a community supper to celebrate and were resting over their empty plates when Brigham came in late and wanted fed. He gave his order to Ellen, sitting with a vacant smile on her face—an expression which George long ago learned had nothing whatsoever to do with his wife's state of mind—and Ellen sent the President to the kitchen.

Infuriated, Brigham huffed and pierced the insolent sister

with his eyes, but Ellen wasn't noticing. If the two of them had
been alone, Brigham would have sworn at her, or worse. George
could see the threat in Brigham's face, in the way the President
leaned forward and afterward walked away in a stiff-legged strut.
Every time George remembered the incident, he felt proud.

He used to consider these acts of defiance as giving his wife
courage to come back, as a former apostate, and live in the
Valley. The same with her absolute refusal to wear a temple
garment (which blasphemy, he supposed, by now had spread to
Phoebe). A kind of whistling in the dark of her own solitude.
Gradually, however, he came to realize Ellen did not consider
herself a victim. The Indian sojourn may have stripped her of
her Victorian prudence, but it left her with a fatalistic acceptance of what she must do to survive, and that, by god, was that.
Any terms beside her own were like a foreign language—in one
ear, out the other.

A mosquito landed on his eyelid long enough to bite.
Goddammit! was it asking too much to have a bit of boredom
once in a while? Just coming home after work was like jumping
in cold water and having to swim like mad to keep warm.
Tonight for instance—a house full of Gentiles, Jeremy's homework, Ellen's mindless distresses.

Ellen's problem was she wanted life in the Valley to get back
to the charm of the early days. For her, religion was religion and
a clean house was a clean house. That the two should overlap
was unthinkable. She was, George was sure, continuing to buy
her straight pins and anything else she wanted wherever she
damn well pleased. As for the once-a-month fast days, she would
have nothing to do with them.

"They make the children listless," she argued. "And they
aren't good for you either. You work such long hours, you need
to be able to think clearly."

At first he tried a quiet observation of the required fast day—eating a little at home but not away from home. Gradually he just forgot about the rule. The fasting did save on food, thus enabling the faithful to tithe more, but it wasn't good for them. They already didn't get enough to eat.

With a heavy heart, George put his arm about his contrary wife's shoulders and drew her close. She was the one with blinkers. That the church, like a big, oversize watch dog, now lived inside all the houses was because the people wanted it there.

A midnight storm filled the sky with sound and fury. Driven from her warm bed by an irrational fear of thunder, Ellen moved barefooted through the cold flickering light down the hall to George, who slept on. Lying against him, she cringed at the nearness of the strikes and as always, if the storm lasted long enough, remembered Whonow.

They were on the prairie, she was pregnant with Jeremy and they had gone for a walk. A storm came out of the south, and she crouched under the sage, Whonow looming over her. Lightning popped violently overhead, whirlwinds scattered through the bushes, the grass crackled. But Whonow wouldn't bend down. Finally she took his hand and stood and told herself she wasn't afraid either.

The memory—but it was more than a memory—pulled her downstairs to sit on the porch.

Again and again fiery snakes lit up the distant Sugarloaf Peak. Thunder rolled off like potatoes hitting an empty wagon bed. She saw Jeremy's crumpled drawing and picked it up, and when the rain came in slanted sheets, made her way back through the dark house to drop the paper in the coal bucket.

And climbing the steps to her room, realized something peculiar. Her hand, where it touched the paper, tingled.

T H I R T Y - T W O

BRIGHT AND EARLY TUESDAY MORNING.

Dear Jed and Julia,
    We have reached Ellen. She is the picture of good health
and the same lovely person I remember. Her house is big
and rambling and surrounded by banks of blown rose bushes
and the rooms are full of bright artwork.

Suddenly mindful of Julia's reaction, Dinky divided the
writing paper and begin anew.

Dear Julia and Jed,
    We have reached Salt Lake City and find it to be an
oasis entirely shut in by its brown and barren heights. How
strange to hear the sounds of civilization take up their long
abandoned chorus. We learned at Fort Bridger that our army
is coming to put Brigham aside but it is difficult to see why.
    We have a solid roof over our heads for the first time in
over three months and a table to eat from. George and
Ellen send their love as does Phoebe. The house is full of
her paintings. I bought one for J.C....

To Mun she wrote,

    We are becalmed in Utah. Your most welcome letter
was waiting but nothing from the east, I believe the mail is
shut from that direction owing to the politics of removing
Brigham. By all means, if you get to Sacramento before me
do not hesitate but go immediately and rent a house, I will

do the same if there is no letter waiting at the post office
telling where to find you. We will leave soon as we are
refitted, 3 or 4 days at most. That will put us in Sacramento
by October 3. Today Ellen is taking us on the grand tour.
All my love to my husband and best friend. Dinky

The Harris carriage was approaching the public graze when
Brigham's black coach swept by. Seated beside Brigham was a
woman veiled in black. Apostle Charles Rich sat across from the
couple.

A cold finger touched Ellen's spine.

The Fancher camp was all abuzz. Dignitaries from the
Mormon church had visited the camp to urge the emigrants to
turn south on account of Indians having burned the grass on the
Humboldt route.

"One of them was Brigham!" Malinda reported excitedly.
She'd been standing *right there by the carriage!* "He didn't get out,
but the man who did says we can't buy anything in the city on
account of the war." She had a rolling, drawlly Arkansas accent
and a laugh light and chiming. "'What war?' I says, but he never
answered."

Other voices joined in. The southern towns had large
surpluses of grain, and fresh teams could be secured at some
place called Lehi, less than 30 miles away. To make up for the
inconvenience, the Mormons would waive the toll charges.

"Was that woman one of Brigham wives?" Malinda asked
Ellen.

But Ellen ignored her to climb back into her carriage. "We
have to go," she told Dinky.

"Let's take Malinda with us and drive past Brigham's house,"
Dinky suggested, hiding her own disappointment with a big
smile. The last thing she wanted to do was turn south.

"Some other day," Ellen said shortly, sitting like a wooden Indian in the shadows.

Put off, Malinda stepped back.

"Where does the lower road come out?" Dinky asked, boosting Lymund into place between the twins.

"Maybe you'd like to see one of George's farm houses," Ellen told her.

The carriage moved away. Dinky shot a glance back at Malinda and shrugged her shoulders.

The awkward moment stretched into five. Dinky asked again where the lower road came out.

"Los Angeles. Eventually."

"I don't want to seem argumentative," Dinky said firmly. "But this thing of waiving tolls—I know, from being a surveyor's wife, there aren't supposed to be any tolls on a Territorial Road."

Ellen didn't comment. Two miles out City Creek Road, at the front gate of an unpainted farm house, she pleaded a suddenly remembered chore for the bishop and left the carriage. "Take them up on the grassy knoll," she ordered the driver. "Where the view is good."

Dinky studied Phoebe's face as they drove away, but it was impossible to see through the artist's thick glasses. The children filled up the space with their chatter, the horses' hooves sounded rhythmically on the damp road.

A small, straight woman with a severely afflicted face answered the door. Zilpha Lindsey Harris, dressed all in black, as usual. At 73, George's oldest wife and—because she was sealed to Joseph Smith for eternity—the one most favored by God. Zilpha and Mr. Lindsey came to Utah from Nauvoo in 1849. When Zilpha asked to be sealed to the dead Prophet, her husband up and ran away. Whereupon Brigham made her George's wife by proxy for life. She brought two teams and a house full of furniture to the union.

Once inside the house, Ellen forsook her usual scrutiny to seat herself on a front-room chair and invite Sister Zilpha to do the same.

Zilpha's ears perked. The hated first wife usually referred to her as "Sister Lindsey."

"Brigham took Elenore McLean to a camp of Arkansas emigrants this morning with Apostle Rich." Ellen leaned forward confidentially. "Apostle Rich told the emigrants there wasn't any food here for sale. I was wondering why, since the city warehouses are bulging."

Electrified by the news, Zilpha snickered and hugged herself. "So he took her this morning."

"Why?"

"The dirty American devils are coming to conquer the Saints and make us live in Babylon's chains." Zilpha's watery blue eyes swept the ceiling.

"The American Army is merely escorting Brigham's replacement here. That's all."

"And you want him replaced!" In a move reminiscent of her childhood, Zilpha fiddled briefly with her shoe strings, as if to remove her shoe and swat the intruder.

"Good Christ! It's nothing to me. Although it would be nice to have a governor who cared enough to build a hospital instead of another expensive church building for his wives to sleep in." Ellen's words raised the specter of Constance, clutching so long, incontinent and incoherent, at the brink of eternity. The first wife had parceled out the care of Constance to George's outside wives—none of whom complained louder than Zilpha at the church's not having a hospital.

"Don't you dare blaspheme in this house!" The older woman

shook her finger under Ellen's nose and, casting about for the last word, whispered, "Two kings cannot sit on one throne!"

"Oh, I agree. Something exciting is going on. Let's talk about the emigrant train from Arkansas. Why would the President take Elenore to that camp?"

"It's a secret."

"I need to know what the secret is," Ellen pressed gently.

"Ask our husband."

"Oh, he never discusses church business at home. I'm willing to grant a reasonable favor in return."

"Like what?"

"What do you want?"

"I'm tired of milking a cow."

"Alright, I'll find a place for the cow this winter."

"Forever."

"Zilpha!"

"I want a colored servant."

"That's out," Ellen answered firmly.

"I guess I could settle for having the carriage…not the buggy!… whenever I want it. Along with a driver."

"I said 'reasonable.'"

"Well, short of letting our dear husband cut your throat…you did hear about that unfaithful woman on the Tooele Road didn't you? In order not to be doomed in eternity and stand always with the angels, she consented to pay the penalty of her error. Her husband helped her make her offering of blood." The prickly voice sounded positively chirpy. "It was a great burden off his shoulders…and his children's. He preached last Sunday at evening service most joyfully."

Ellen smothered her snarl in a smile. "You can have the carriage one day a month. Now, why did Brigham take Elenore McLean to see the Arkansas emigrants?"

"The riches of the ungodly are to be consecrated to the

House of Israel. It's doctrine." Settling back, Zilpha loosed a blustery litany. "Missouri drove us out to starve. We asked for help and Haun's Mill was our answer. Just this spring poor Parley was hunted down like a dog in Arkansas. It's bad to have an unpaid debt. So we'll pay back, with usury," her voice climbed the scale, "and send the God-hating Gentiles cross lots to Hell!"

"Parley Pratt was an idiot. He should have kept his pecker in his pocket. He already had 11 wives. What did he expect?"

Zilpha's crushed velvet face closed up like a prune.

Be careful. Ellen took a deep breath. "So the Lord's mad at some people in Arkansas and Missouri…"

"…don't forget Carthage Jail…"

"…and Illinois. So what?"

"What about the servant?"

Ellen had enough. She was half-way out the screen door when Zilpha called, "Are you still gonna come get the cow?"

"What did Elenore tell you?"

"Sister Elenore McComb McLean Young to you, missy. And I ain't telling you out there on the porch."

"I haven't got all day." Angry at herself for being unable to walk away, Ellen returned to the front room.

Zilpha clapped her hands to her mouth. Abruptly her hands flew open. Charged to the point of bursting by the dark secrets, she began to sing to the air of "Loch Lomand,"

> In thy mountain retreat,
> God will strengthen thy feet
> On the necks of the foes thou shalt tread

Toe tapping, elbows angled like cup handles, body twisting side to side.

> And their silver and gold, as the Prophets foretold
> Shall be brought to adorn thy fair head.

Catching her breath, she made a cat's cream smile. "The blood of the martyrs is to be avenged. The children are very excited about it."

Ellen sat looking into middle space. Zilpha's son taught in the ward's only schoolhouse, not counting Brigham's private school. That's where Jeremy was taking his picture. "You're not telling me anything I don't hear all the time in the Bowery."

"The emigrants are to be fed the same bread as we got in the States," Zilpha spit out, fired by the other's refusal to take her seriously. "The Destroying Angel left yesterday for Provo with special orders for Apostle Smith. Joseph's nephew is to persuade the brethren in the southern settlements that the Arkansas mobocrats deserve to be destroyed. Blow their religion red-hot, so's to put their mind at ease about the rest of the orders."

"Mmmmm, interesting." Keeping her face smooth, Ellen concentrated on Zilpha's white starched cap, from which no loose hairs protruded. Was the favored wife, whom George called a week older than coal, becoming bald?

"The rest of the orders?"

"No one is to talk to the emigrants, or sell them so much as a swarmy sack of flour. Anyone who does will be put out of the way."

"Zilpha! You don't know what you're saying. Apostle Rich himself promised there'd be food and teams available on the southern route."

"He lied for the Lord."

Beyond Cedar City across to the Mojave River was a good 60-day wagon journey. Without fresh stock and food, a train would have to grub its living from the desert. Bad weather could make that impossible. Ellen said as much, conversationally.

"Oh, it'll be impossible alright."

"The American Army's coming. There will be retribution if we harm that train, Brigham will go to jail."

"Oh no! no!" Zilpha chortled. "Not against the lambs of Zion. The Lamanites are to serve as the Lord's battle axe." She grinned and flapped her arms as if to fly away. "The men who killed Parley Pratt will be all alone in the wilderness, all alone. And what's more, Brother Boyle's to be at the Mojave Crossing with a mail-sack key to intercept any letters they send west asking for help."

"So they're to be robbed?"

"They're to be used up," Zilpha chanted softly, deep in revelation. "The arrows of the Almighty are to drink their blood. Not a grease spot is to be found. Except the little children under eight. They will be spared. No innocent blood will be shed."

An upstart of wind, catching the unlatched screen door, flung it against the house. Ellen jumped to her feet. "That's enough! Stop this gibberish immediately."

She walked nervously into the kitchen and stared out the window. Lake showers were cooling the air. In an upland corner of yard, a patch of cherry-pie flowers was opening—the pleasant scent from the grayish-white blossoms lending a sharp contrast to what she was feeling.

"How dare you even story about such a thing," she protested, keeping her back to the mean-spirited little creature in the other room.

"The angels have been watching over the train ever since it left Fort Smith, Arkansas," Zilpha revealed, so warmed by the thought that she rubbed her parched hands together. "We all prayed the President would be led to do something. But first, Elenore must identify the men who killed Parley."

"You don't know if she did?" Ellen stood in the kitchen doorway to ask.

"I know," Zilpha covered her heart, "in here."

"Why doesn't Brigham just lock them up and charge them? We lock up people for a lot less."

"I'm telling you, *a decree has been passed, there is to be blood atonement!* We'll snatch off their heads like chickens in a barnyard."

"What you are telling me, sister dear, is that the Arkansas people are to be robbed and murdered and everything blamed on Elenore McLean."

"Put it however you want." Zilpha tilted her chin waggishly. "The Lord has promised to avenge us of our enemies. The Lion of the Lord hears and obeys." She made a bony fist and punched the air in front of her nose. "He socks 'em away."

"Zilpha, are you telling me the truth? Because if you're lying, it will go hard with you. I'll have you moved in with someone else, and all your furniture will stay here."

"And if I am telling the truth," Zilpha replied sweetly, "then you'll know your turn's coming. The Land of the Honey Bee ain't for women who won't share."

Ellen shrugged. George hadn't been in the Lindsey house in years, and never in Zilpha's bed. Looking around, she noticed a clay bowl resting on an uncovered pedestal table. "Put a scarf under that bowl. I'll send Jeremy for the cow. As long as it doesn't inconvenience the bishop, you may use the carriage as I promised."

"It's worth more," Zilpha whined. "What I told you's worth a colored servant! And don't bring the cow back."

Leaving the house, Ellen tripped on a loose porch step and fell. And scrambling quickly to her feet, walked home, skirts held high over the puddles and dirty piles of hail left from the previous evening's downpour. Along the way she met a long file of men, young and old, on parade, rifles to the shoulder. Seeing her, the soldiers stepped a little smarter. There is nothing like a pretty woman to make a man pick up his feet, even if that pretty face is full of anger. Indeed, whose face these days was not!

Elenore McLean drove up the road alone in a small run-about, her face a dreary stare down the road. Was Brigham's latest wife going to visit Zilpha? Ellen wondered, and called to her, but Elenore, lost in thought, didn't answer.

The Harris buggy preceded the mistress of the house home by a hair. The horse stood blowing at the railing. Dinky and the children were in the kitchen with Phoebe.

Ellen sent everyone else out of the room and, in a low voice, told Dinky there was talk of the Arkansas emigrants being executed in some lonely dell by Indians for the murder of a church apostle. Her tone suggested skepticism. She *was* skeptical. But ridiculous as the possibility appeared, Dinky had no choice but to take precaution.

Dinky stared in disbelief.

"The woman with Brigham was Elenore McLean from Arkansas. Apostle Parley Pratt stoled Elenore and her children from her husband, Hector McLean. Hector shot Parley seven times and then stabbed him to death in Arkansas." Despite herself, Ellen's voice began to shake. "Now the church is going to use that as an excuse to destroy the train. That's what George's wife says, and we don't have any choice but to act accordingly."

"I'll talk with Mr. Fancher tomorrow," Dinky said quietly, torn between what she was being told and what she was seeing.

"Yes," Ellen agreed firmly, relief in her voice. "Tell him he must take the north road, either that or wait till there's more traffic on the south road. He mustn't go down south alone. If you can't convince him, you'll have to stay here and catch another train, there are trains coming in every day."

"You go with me."

Ellen's features froze. "I can't."

"Why not?"

"It's not safe. It could cause George trouble."

"Let's talk to George then, and get his opinion."

Ellen shook her head. "He won't believe me."

"It's difficult for *me* to believe you, particularly when you won't talk to Mr. Fancher *or* your husband." Dinky felt her initial shock dissolving. Everything was all right, the problem was in Ellen's head.

"I promise I'll talk with Mr. Fancher. I don't know what he'll do, but I'll tell you right now, I'm not sure I'll leave the train no matter how he decides. It's a long ways, yet, from here to California, and I'd rather travel with friends and family."

"If Jed were here, he'd tell you the possibility of attack is very real," Ellen argued, desperate to put a face on her fears. "So would Uergin. The Indians are particularly thick below the Corridor."

Dinky's steady expression crumpled in embarrassment. Uergin and Jed and Ellen had come west together in '46. From Jed's endless stories of the guide, Dinky had fashioned a shadowy, romantic figure. Now she was reading that same fascination in Ellen's face.

In desperation, Ellen found Phoebe out in the hen house with the children and brought the artist back to the kitchen.

"Yes," Phoebe agreed reluctantly, hearing the gossip. "That Zilpha's kinda gulchy."

"Phoebe! you're not listening," Ellen cried, growing increasingly strident. "Listen to me! There's to be an attack by Indians! They're all to be killed!"

The enormity of the accusation left Phoebe speechless.

Watching Phoebe, Dinky's dismay turned to alarm. She hugged Ellen carefully as she would a deranged person—to comfort, but not to be close—thanked her for her concern and insisted on returning to the camp that very night.

And off went the little family who just the day before had arrived in such a clatter of joy.

The first thing Ellen did, after the horribly painful good-bye, was pour herself a glass of whiskey. "Feed the children in the kitchen," she told Phoebe.

Moved to tears by the bright, scattered anger, Phoebe didn't argue.

Sitting alone in the dining room, waiting for George, Ellen brushed mindlessly at the dried mud on her shirt.

A bitter argument followed George's arrival. Concentrating on his food, the bishop hunched his shoulders against the storm. He'd issued no orders waiving the toll on the southern route, but Brigham certainly could have. As for Zilpha, she was crazy, always had been. He would look into her gossip, but there was nothing to worry about. Absolutely nothing. Greedy as Brigham was, he was not stupid. He would never sanction an attack on a wagon train of innocent people.

"They won't be innocent people! Not if Elenore identified them as Parley's killers. And, of course, the fact that they're a very rich train helps.

"George, don't get that look on your face. Please, just listen. Why was it so important that they go south? important enough to bring Brigham to their camp. And why would anybody down the Corridor sell them anything if they'd been refused here?"

Ellen's voice broke in exhaustion. "I know Zilpha's crazy, but she believes what she's saying. Please, you must do something."

George bowed his head. All day he solved problems, at night he deserved to rest. "They can go around to the Gentile merchants, there are trades that can be worked out for church grain, and they can still go north."

"Yes, of course!" Relief and hope flooded Ellen's face. "It would take time, but they have time, and they have money. Oh, George, that is so obvious, why didn't I think of it? I don't suppose you'd consider telling them yourself in the morning?"

"Absolutely not."

"You could be careful how you worded it, you could just say…"

"…it is not necessary to say anything, Sister Ellen. These people are not in danger!" His voice had a rasp to it. "You're always pounding on Brigham, trying to make him worse than he is. And then you believe it, and then it gets worse because you want it to."

"That's not true!"

"Yes, it is true and I'm tired of it. Can't you be grateful for what you've got? do you always have to be tearing things down? Stop thinking about Brigham, you're making yourself sick. Find something else to think about. I absolutely will not have any more of it! Absolutely will not!"

Ellen ran her fingers through the hair over her temples. She felt despicably guilty, George looked so weary. Leaving her chair she stood near him, trying to press his head against her stomach, but he resisted and went on savagely chewing his meat. So she climbed the stairs to the studio with its empty clutter of beds and began folding the quilts. And folding them, felt as if she were tumbling in space, weightless and lost.

A piece of paper under Dinky's pillow caught her eye, a scrap of unfinished letter saying lovely things about her hostess. Reading the paper at the window in the waning light, Ellen wondered what Dinky would tell Jed now.

And who would read that letter?

THIRTY-THREE

WEDNESDAY MORNING. No sooner had the hired man returned from delivering George to the office than Ellen ordered out the buggy. Driving alone toward the river, she was startled by a rider emerging from the mists near the public ground—Joseph Henderson, the son of George's wife, Appella. According to Appella, the boy had recently returned from San Francisco with a bride who took one look at the extra wives in the city and went home.

"Good morning, Aunt Ellen."

"Are you spying on these people?"

"Ain't you glad to see me?" Joseph edged his horse against the buggy horse. A compact, good-looking youth, with his mother's olive skin and thick eyebrows.

"You shouldn't be in the Danites. They're a gang of thugs. You want to be a soldier, join the Legion."

"No offense, Aunt Ellen," taking hold of the bridle in courteous fashion, Joseph pulled the buggy horse around, "but the Legion's a bunch of old women."

"Use your common sense," Ellen hauled back on the reins, "that's why God gave it to you." She slashed down hard with the whip. The saddle horse jumped high and away, leaving the guard sprawled in the mud, his new California hat, with its all-too-familiar white Danite cord, under his boots.

The visitor wore blue velvet and introduced herself as the wife of George Harris, Presiding Bishop of the Church and Trustee in Charge of the Church of Jesus Christ of Latter-Day Saints General Tithing Office and Storehouse. Tangled in the reddish-black curls that hung to her waist was a blue velvet ribbon. A braid of fine gold chains fastened her cape at the shoulder. Bunched at her throat was a white silk scarf embroidered with tiny seed pearls.

Alex Fancher, a tall lean man with dark, weather-beaten complexion, would have believed her if she'd claimed to be the queen of Spain.

What road was the train taking to the coast? she wanted to know. Learning Fancher favored the Corridor and planned to leave immediately, the bishop's wife ordered him not to leave the city without supplies and to wait for the added protection of other trains. Gentile merchants would sell him whatever he needed. She handed over a list of names and addresses. The Gentile merchants also had yards that could be rented, the cost in hay and time would be well worth it.

Glancing up only infrequently at the woman's strong-boned face with its full mouth and satiny skin, Fancher addressed his concerns to the dirt. The men who visited the park yesterday promised plenty of supplies and good water further south. As for buying from the Gentiles—he stumbled over the word—maybe those merchants would jack up the prices pretty good.

"My husband feels it would be wiser to go through the Gentile merchants, even if the price is higher. He says there is not that much surplus food to the south and he should know." The lie colored Ellen's face.

Fancher made a gesture of uncertainty. "It ain't a question of money. Sure and we'd like to save what we could. I guess we could talk to these people." He glanced at the list of merchants. Behind him, the wagons were being loaded. "Problem is," he leveled his dark green eyes, "I don't know who's telling the truth here. Let me ask you, lady, what's it to you?"

"Mrs. Miller talked with you?"

"Yes."

"You didn't believe her?"

"Like I say, I don't know what to think. These was church men that come here."

"You must trust me. *You must not leave the city without everything you need to reach California.*"

"Lord knows, I ain't happy about any of this." The captain eyed a nearby ox, gaunt and trail-weary. "You suppose your merchants would sell us some draught horses?"

"Yes, there's no doubt..."

"...ELLEN! what are you doing here?" Returning from the United States Post Office in the Emporium, Dinky was horrified at what she was seeing. "Leave these people alone!" She took the demented woman by the arm and tried to draw her off.

"Listen to me!" Ellen jerked free, her voice harsh. "I've lived in Utah Territory seven years. And I've learned one thing if nothing else—there is *always* a reason for what Brigham does. You dare not leave here without supplies. The men outside the park with white cords around their hats? they're our Destroying Angels. The Gentile merchants can't come to you, *you have to go to them!*"

"Go home, please, and rest," Dinky pleaded. "You're embarrassing me. Now, PLEASE!"

"I'm embarrassing you?" Ellen's voice thinned. "Would to God that's all you had to worry about. Look, forget about the Corridor. Just forget it. You shouldn't even go there. Buy what you can from the Gentiles here in the city and head for the main road. There'll be grass enough, you'll make it, people will help."

Henry Scott was listening. He crowded close, as if to ask a question.

"I think we should get her out of here," Dinky murmured sotto voce to the captain and took one of Ellen's arms. Fancher took the other.

"The Indians are very bad on the lower road," Ellen called loudly, noticing Henry and throwing caution to the wind. "Do you know why? Because we pay them to be. We divide the goods with them. We've been using Indians to kill people for years. Gentiles and apostates. They leave, and afterward their things show up for sale in the city. One of my husband's wives wears a petticoat with bloodstains on it."

She was being escorted to the buggy. Now Fancher was helping her up the step and into the seat.

Tears filled Ellen's eyes. She turned to look down on Dinky, whose own face was white with anger.

"Alright, Dinky, you win, let's hope you keep winning." Ellen's voice broke and she took a deep breath. "There's an Indian Farm at Corn Creek south of Fillmore. The agent's name is Garland Hurt. He's a federal officer, he might have something to sell." She drew a paper out of her purse and handed it down. "These people live in Cedar City. They were with the Harris train. They know Jed."

Blindly unwrapping the reins, she gathered them in. She couldn't stop shaking. The buggy pulled away, and the silent mist seeped close. Momentarily isolated, Dinky unfolded the paper. It was an I.O.U. dated 1851 for $100 payable to Bishop George Harris from Emil and Verity James. On the bottom of the note was written, "paid in full, August 5, 1857, Ellen Harris."

The elder in charge of the post office, arriving at Brigham's office just before noon, handed over the following:

August 4, '57. Dearest brother and sister. It is with extreme
pain that I relate the following. This morning while touring
the city Ellen bailed out of the carriage and we saw no more
of her until late this afternoon when she walked home. She
was extremely agitated and looked as if she might have
fallen. She insisted we were in danger of being murdered by
indians if we take the southern road as the Mormons advise.
It was very frightening and made no sense. She got Phoebe
to agree but I could see Phoebe was as unnerved as I was.
I was strongly reminded of the night she cut herself up after
pa died. It was so bizarre I had no choice but to get the
children out of the house and return here to the camp. I feel
sorry for her family, they are all so sweet. Will write later.
Much love. Dinky.

Lips pursed, Brigham tore the poisonous letter into succes-
sively smaller squares and tossed it in the trash accumulating in
the unlit fireplace.

Afterward, he instructed his clerk to send a shoat to the
postal reader, compliments of the Presidency.

At 2:30 the afternoon of Wednesday, August 5, 1857, after
just one day's rest on the public graze beside the River Jordan,
the work animals of the Fancher party went under the yoke.

Malinda Scott, nearing her ninth month, climbed heavily
into the wagon and wiped her wet face with her skirt. The bitter
argument between her husband and her brothers had come to
blows, and the man who joined her on the seat was badly
skinned. Her parents were crying for her, as were relatives and
friends. As was Dinky.

The train started up, 57 wagons swaying and lurching slowly
south through Salt Lake City, headed for Lehi and the good
grass and water.

Three wagons stayed behind, those of the unyielding, belligerent Henry Scott and two other emigrant families, who, after

buying food staples from the Gentile merchants, stubbornly set out north around the lake, making for the main California road.

T H I R T Y - F O U R

WHEN LIEUTENANT J.E.B. STUART, First Cavalry Quartermaster, bought horse equipments for the Utah Expedition, he chose horses from the north of America. Tough Dutch-Thoroughbred-German-French-Morgan-Puritan hybrids with their superior size and training. These horses— remounts for the dragoons and batteries, as well as a sufficient number of draught animals to replace those which should die or be broken down on the march—were already on their way to Forts Leavenworth and Kearny.

The Mexicans also had *caballos* for sale—the small shaggy Mexican *caballitos* just coming on with the blood of their North American conquerors. But polite inquiry in Washington by the Mexican delegate as to the availability of contracts, resulted in equally polite regrets from Quartermaster General Sidney Jesup. The American Army had horses sufficient to get to Utah and would secure replacements there.

Calculating that the *americanos* over-estimated how much cooperation the United States would get from the citizens of Utah Territory, Mexican officials alerted the settlements to the north of the *Jornada de Muerto* as to the possibility of a market for Spanish *caballos* crossed with *americano* stock developing in the near future.

Alfredo Luna, horse dealer out of Ciudad, Monterrey, perked his ears. His best *caballos* came from Eduardo Ledyard in the

Mora country of New Mexico, who covered his mares with a fine Morgan stallion.

Gambling on the outcome, Alfredo moved his operations to Las Vegas and let it be known at Fort Union and at the Albuquerque garrison that he had *caballos* for the Department of Utah and would deliver them.

He had never seen the Yuta lands, but his uncles trailed horses and mules there in the '30s and '40s—trading their worn-out stock for Ute children and experiencing no trouble to speak of in the red-rock country. True, now that the Mormons had their own noose around the Ute's neck, foreigners were not so safe. The Mormons, or their Ute friends—it was all the same to the man who stood the loss—would gladly pick a *mexicano* clean as a rack of ribs if given the opportunity. But *no hay atajo sin trabajo*. Such a foothold in the American market might not come around again.

◈

I left Fort Leavenworth July 30th, and reached Fort Kearney in nine travelling days...At Fort Kearney I was detained one day by the changes I had to make....

— Captain Van Vliet
1857 journey entry

One of those changes was the addition of a sergeant. The captain and his 10th Infantry escort then departed the fort August 10, pushing up the hot, dusty road beside the South Platte as fast as the six-mule wagons could proceed. The escort reached Beauvais' Crossing, and Van Vliet made the north landing with his sergeant and three men.

The sluggish August river was a mile wide and more sandbar than water. Returning to the south shore, the sergeant ordered the teams unhooked and driven across to beat down and level the quicksand bottoms. Settled in the shade of a storm-battered cottonwood, Van Vliet sorted idly through his dispatch case, his fingers closing over a slim metal flask. At this rate, the crossing could take the rest of the day.

The mules were put back in the hitch, soldiers on horseback were stationed between the sandbars. One by one, the wagons entered the water—one soldier riding ahead of each wagon with a rope tied to the lead mule, two soldiers riding off-side to keep the teams from drifting downstream. The wagons came in roughly 50 yards apart, pausing on the sandbars and going on, with no more than three wagons anywhere in the water at one time.

Watching his mules work, Charlie thought about how some things never changed. Men dragged their spoils back and forth across the desert, thinking to make life easier. But the rivers always ran the same, always had to be crossed.

The day was hot as the hubs of hell.

Van Vliet sharpened a pencil with his knife and counted his blessings. He was traveling with old soldiers used to moving from 1,500 to 3,000 miles every summer through Indian country, constantly on the alert, getting by with little transportation, little forage save what grew naturally, and generally on short rations, depending on the abundance of game The men's appearance and that of the mules, the short time necessary to put up the tents, the lightning speed with which they were stuck, folded and placed in the wagons, the lack of confusion and the quietness on every hand—left no room for complaint.

Men like these had some style about them, knew what they had to do and did it cheerfully. Ruminating, the captain heard the sergeant's voice above the river voices and smiled wryly. His sergeant hardly sounded like a cheerful man.

The lightest load came in, the hospital supplies. In the middle of the river the off-leader caught a hoof in an underwater snag and tried to back out, stepping over the chain and going down. Sand and water boiled over the animal. The wagon listed and began digging in, a muddy current easing across the hindboard. The wheelers and swing team braced themselves, wall-eyed.

Charlie unhooked the leaders, leaving the small mule named Tyler to find its own way out of the river. But was too late to save Tyler's teammate. Tippecanoe bobbed gently up and down like a buoy, long ears for once uncaring. After all the wagons were across, someone would go downriver and retrieve the harness.

A hot and heavy August afternoon in Maine. School-age children stoop over the blueberries, faces and hands smeared with blueberry juice.

"The yield is down," an older girl explains to no one in particular, wielding her berry rake with great efficiency. "Too much fog on the bees last spring. And rain. Bees won't work in a fog."

One of the little boys drops down on his back. "I got a fog on me," he cries. "I can't work no more." All the little boys fall down.

Nothing better spelled ambition than a young man who, having married well, displayed a vigorous penchant for using his new capital as a floor and not as a roof. Overnight, the Houlton community's acceptance of Dr. Clare's son-in-law moved from courteous to cordial. As Shep Cary's foreman, Jed was recognized by bankers and freighters. At the local barbershop, the care of his hair was taken away from the apprentice and given to Mr. Leek, the proprietor, who cut only certain individuals.

Ennobled by a sudden awareness of one's responsibilities to

the society in which one has been nurtured, Julia volunteered to organize the Thanksgiving-basket program for the needy—a favorite missionary project of Susanna Cary's. In addition, Julia graciously agreed to oversee the renovation of a large stall in the Clare barn to store the many books being collected by the Forest Club in the hopes of opening a free library.

She also arranged with her cousin in Sherman to put Yam to work as a handyman for the Traveler's Inn. To her dubious husband, Julia explained that not only did the Sherman position have possibilities, it placed Yam nearer Molunkus and his common-law wife.

In less than a week the feckless Indian was back. He stopped by the construction site on the mill road, and Jed sent him home with a load of junk wood.

A blueberry pie sat on the kitchen counter. Yam cut a piece with the butcher knife, juggled and blew on the sweet, and opened his mouth wide. That's when he heard the funny little noise. Dripping blueberry juice on the rugs, he catwalked through the house.

A tortured tangle swayed drunkenly in the parlor shadows. Swooning, moaning, Julia opened her eyes. Seeing over Sigvald's shoulder, to her utter disbelief, Yam's smeared face. Quick as a cat she dodged around her cousin and came at the Indian.

"Shoo! shoo! you filthy thing!" She shook her apron. "Get out of here, get out and stay out!"

By the time Jed came home that night, Julia's anger had scarcely abated. "Why isn't Yam in Sherman?"

"Got tired." Jed splashed water over his face and neck from the kitchen basin.

"Got tired!" Julia's face flushed with anger. "He can't do that! Does he want to be treated like a white man or not?!"

"What he wants is his own business. Hand me a towel."

"What he wants is to be lazy and eat here every chance he

gets, and gobble and grunt. He refuses to learn by example, he can't talk, and he wears those dirty leather...hides!" She cleared her throat with the word.

"Yam don't bother no one, your pa likes him."

"My father is being courteous. Here, don't drip on the floor!" Julia jammed the towel against his hands. "Bettina says Yam is a bad influence on the baby."

"J.C. is four months old for chrissake!"

"Good manners begin at the cradle and don't swear." Why couldn't he wash in the laundry room? "I will *not* have Yam around J.C. and that's final."

"I don't care what you do." Jed sat down heavily at the table and rested his chin on his hand. It'd been a long day. A log, jamming in the slip, had snapped the pulley. The new man on the filing machine put the wrong edge on the band saw. And there was a rush order for 10,000 surveyor stakes that he didn't have wood for.

"Call your pa and let's eat."

Dr. Clare was coming, his cane tap-tapping on the hallway floor.

"Jed, don't be angry," Julia whispered. "I know Yam *claims* to be your half-brother, but...but I just don't think so. He is very, very primitive. He belongs to a stone-age culture. His brain..."

Jed threw up his hands. "...it's your kitchen. Yam don't need to eat here."

The next night he was saying, "There's some folks in from Toronto with timber leases around Lake Simcoe. They'll be here for supper tomorrow, along with Yam."

"But we have an agreement!"

"We'll hire extra help."

"I'm not talking about extra help, I'm talking about Yam."

"This is business. We don't need J.C. at the table anyway."

"And you don't need me either!"

"Yes, I do, if Carys come."

"You are not…you're certainly NOT going to seat Carys at the same table with that savage!"

"What's wrong with you? Shep Cary sees Yam most every day. Just calm down and remember, Yam may be primitive but so is that Saugeen country. There's a lot Yam knows."

Julia took a deep breath and, annoyance scooting sideways like a bubble of mercury, said, "You're right, of course. I am being foolish. I won't mention it again."

Men! Her father, her uncles, the old dowagers made silly by her smiles, the young suitors made bold. Julia understood them all, and what she understood most was winning.

The boys sent off to the Meduxnekeag early the next morning brought down the bird skimming the meadow grasses with one shot. Boys shooting birds was not so unusual—white boys, particularly, had no religion when it came to killing living creatures. But what they had chosen this day was the Great Eagle—the bird of Tirawa the Creator.

Yam put down his fishing pole and walked over to visit with the shooters.

Julia was in the kitchen when the Indian came through the back door. Her father was asleep, Jed was at the mill. She felt no need to explain any of this to Yam, it was obvious what he wanted to talk about and she was ready.

"You serve me the Great Eagle to eat?" Yam drew himself very straight, making himself little taller than she.

You're still a little man no matter how straight you stand, Julia scorned silently and said, "White people like fried chicken." An unwilled smile puckered her face. "Or whatever passes for it. You want to be with white people? learn how to eat."

The next thing she knew, Yam had his arms around her and

was kissing her. She twisted violently, futilely, and bit the Indian savagely on the lip. She could taste the blood, still he persisted. She banged her head into his, unmindful of the pain, and he let go and stood back.

"Now you've done it, Yam!" Her mouth was bloody, the hands gripping the back of the chair shook. "You won't be safe in Houlton, you won't be safe anywhere in St. John country. Jed will kill you. You'll have to run away."

Yam's face was as hard as a rock. Blood trickled down his chin. "I will tell my brother." He was halfway down the front walk before Julia collected her wits enough to follow.

"Do you want Jed to kill you?!" she shrieked. "Get out of Houlton or I'll tell him myself. Do you hear me? YAM! Listen to me! Stop!" Victory was turning to ashes in her mouth. "Don't you dare tell him anything. Yam! damn you, NO!"

Yam turned around and came back. " 'No' what?"

Julia stared bug-eyed. Her face, except for the smear of blood, was white. Not for the first time, the Indian thought how ugly she was.

"Supper's at seven," she said hoarsely.

"What is to eat?"

"Mutton."

"You understand I know how to eat?"

"Yes! you bastard! you fucking pain-in-the-ass bastard! I hate you. I hate you, Yam. You understand that?"

Shaking with fury, she stomped back to the garden and began pulling the supper carrots, banging them against the ground to knock off the dirt. One, a long Golden Lad, she hesitated over, rubbing it with her thumb, feeling Sigvald against her stomach. Her cousin, beautiful, beautiful cousin, so well-read, such a deep golden voice…

Then she remembered Yam, the Indian's remark about knowing how to eat, and heaved the carrot as far as she could.

T H I R T Y - F I V E

Elders, never love your wives one hair's breadth more than
they adorn the gospel; never love them so but that you can
leave them at a moment's warning without shedding a tear.

— President Young,
  Bowery service, Salt Lake City

I F EVER A MAN LIVED THE GOSPEL it was Porter Rockwell. The
church was his only mistress. For the church Porter drove his
wives like horses to their tasks, for her he cleaned his guns and
sharpened his knives.

If ever a man hated Porter Rockwell it was the Apostle
George A. Smith, Joseph Smith's nephew and heir apparent to
the throne. The reason was simple enough. Porter hated the
nephew, hated all Joseph Smith's relatives, starting with the
Prophet's widow.

When seceding Mormons in Nauvoo turned on their
Prophet, Joseph fled across the Mississippi to Montrose, Iowa.
This appearance of cowardice deeply humiliated Emma Smith,
who wrote her husband a cruel and indignant letter likening the
Prophet to the shepherd who left his sheep in danger and fled.
Come back, she begged. Governor Ford will keep you safe, she
promised.

Heeding his wife's urgings, Joseph returned to Illinois, only
to be detained and killed in the Carthage jail. The night of the

massacre, people in Nauvoo were awaken by the sound of hooves on cobblestones and Porter's frantic screams, "Joseph is killed, they have killed Joseph!"

Spurring his lathered horse up on the lawn outside the Prophet's mansion, Porter hurled accusations at Emma that she had betrayed her husband with a Judas letter.

Upstairs a candle was lit. The Elect Lady drew back the bedroom curtain and raised the sash, not understanding what she was hearing. And then heard, indeed could not help but hear, Porter swearing to avenge Joseph's blood as long as there was one descendant of the murderers left upon the earth.

After hounding Emma out of the church, the Danite assumed the title of the Hound of Heaven. Too shrewd to openly countenance the pursuit, Brigham laid Porter's derangement to grief and counseled that it would pass. Those nephews of Joseph who remained in the church learned to live with the dementia the way one learns to live with a neighbor's barking dog.

The first thing Porter did on reaching Provot, 45 miles to the south, was order the Apostle George A. Smith to drape his windows and empty the house of people.

The General Commander of the Iron County Militia expected news from GSL City as to how to react to the approaching Army. What he did not expect, and in no way welcomed, was a visit from the Chief of the Secret Police of the Kingdom of Deseret.

"What are you doing here?" George A. asked, finishing his breakfast without offering so much as a crumb. Nor did he have to, Porter helping himself to the food on the hastily quitted plates.

"Keeping you in line." Porter pulled two letters from his coat and flipped one across the table. "You're being sent south. You're to leave immediately, horseback."

The mission sounded like a punishment, which George A.

acknowledged ruefully to himself, it was for an old fat man, considering the hot August sun already beating down. Not even the thought of Parowan and the wife who waited there, or the other wives in the other towns, had any appeal in this kind of weather.

"I'll leave any damn way I please."

"It will be your responsibility to alert the faithful to the approach of the United States soldiers." Porter wadded up a corner of the tablecloth and wiped his greasy fingers and mouth. "You will tour every settlement in the area, muster and drill the troops and…"

"…I know my business, you jackanapes!" George A. snarled and opened the letter marked "military orders." Commanders were to get themselves ready to march to any part of the Territory at a moment's notice, equip their men for a winter campaign and prepare for a long siege. Every able-bodied man was to be called into service.

The apostle's face showed no emotion. The Saints were constantly being curried first one direction then the other by Brigham and his counselors. As for the new appointee, that news had long since arrived. It meant nothing. Brigham would cripple his replacement politically, and life would go on as usual. Utah was too isolated for the outcome to be otherwise.

"Something new's come up." Porter tipped his head back with a snicker. A rugged, mastiff-like English ruffian. "The Lord sent Parley Pratt's murderers into the city yesterday and directed Brigham to send 'em south without supplies." He paused to pick at his teeth with the second letter, and continued his instructions.

"You're to make that known in your travels—no supplies, no fresh teams for outsiders. Anyone disobeys will answer to General Authority. The Prophet's cutting the thread between Zion and the States, say that too."

"Is it true?"

Porter lowered his chin, and the apostle felt a small glow of

satisfaction. The second letter hit the table. "This'ns' for Jacob
Hamblin," Porter said. "To be delivered personally by you. It
stays sealed."

"Do tell, and how many people have you showed it to
already?"

Fastidiously avoiding the wet, stained corner, George A.
placed both letters in a tin box on the nearer shelf. And pouring
himself the last of the coffee, observed casually, "I'm surprised
you'd ride all this way in this weather, when there are others you
can send. Do you really miss Joseph so much you have to keep
reminding yourself of what he looked like?"

Porter stared, sorting through the words.

Getting heavily to his feet, the man ordained by his church
as the Entablature of Truth flung wide the back door. "Good day,
Brother Rockwell." He had not ordered the policeman's horse
taken into the shade and watered, and the poor brute stood
head-down in the bare yard.

"Sit down, I ain't through," Porter ordered, his face resuming
its usual goading, accusatory anger.

"I am."

Porter pulled the pistol from his waistband. "Not before I tell
you the stories."

A week later, far to the south at Jacob's Hamblin's mountain
ranch, the missionary and George A. sat alone in the front
room, the second letter open on the table between them.

President's Office
Great Salt Lake City
August 4, 1857.

Elder Jacob Hamblin,
    You are hereby appointed to succeed Elder R. C. Allen
(who I have released as President of the Santa Clara Indian

Mission). I wish you to enter upon the duties of your calling immediately.

Continue the conciliatory policy towards the Indians, which I have ever recommended, and seek by works of righteousness to obtain their love and confidence, for they must learn that they have either got to help us or the United States will kill us both...

We have an abundance of "news." The Government have a last appointed an entire set of officials for the Territory. These Gentry are to have a body guard of 25 of Uncle's Regulars...There errand is entirely peaceful. The current report is that they somewhat query whether they will hang me with or without trial. There are about 30 others whom they intend to deal with. They will then proclaim a general jubilee and afford means and protection to those who wish to go back to the States. We feel first rate about all this and think every circumstance but proves the hastening of Zion's redemption...

Do not permit the brethren to part with their guns or ammunition, but save them against the hour of need...

your Fellow Laborer in the Gospel of Salvation
Brigham Young

At first blush, Jacob thought the new appointment due to the ineptness of Elder R.C. Allen, the current president of the southern mission. Elder Allen controlled the Indians well enough, but his control over his wife was another story. The minutes of the Women's Relief Society in Harmony revealed Sister Allen to be opposed to the relocation of Paiute children with church-approved families.

"What consolation is it to the Indian mother," Sister Allen had argued, "whether her daughters are sold to the Mexican slavers or given as slaves to the Saints?"

It was time, yes indeed, for the President of the Santa Clara Indian Mission to take up new orders somewhere else, and take his big-mouthed wife with him.

Jacob said as much, but then George A. revealed the true intent of Brigham's guarded letter. The Prophet's eye was upon a train of emigrants from Carroll County, Arkansas, a very rich train. As atonement for the murder of Parley Pratt, these Gentiles were to be used up.

"What's more, our people won't be selling the Arkansas dogs so much as a cup of weevily flour. And they won't want to." Leaving the impression the stories sprang from his own inventiveness, George A. recited Porter's stories. Done, he leaned back in his chair and, grasping his hands together, fingers made knobby with gold rings, stretched his sore back.

"By the time the killers of Parley Pratt reach Cedar City, our people will be praying for a massacre. We'll be contacting all the tribes. Your duty is to persuade the Santa Clara Mission Indians to help. They gotta know they gotta get ready for war and obey everything we tell 'em."

"Does Brigham realize the Indians are cowardly about attacking large groups of white people?" the missionary asked.

"The old boss knows alright, and he don't anticipate no trouble. The Iron Military District boys'll go in with 'em."

"Brigham's calling out the militia?" Jacob was surprised.

"Hell, brother!" the militia commander squealed. "He's closing the Territory!"

Jacob felt a sudden trembling in his breast. At last Zion was to have its own country! Instead of federal judges, Washington would have to send diplomats to Utah Territory. Godless Gentiles would no longer hold office.

The churchmen hugged each other and quickly stepped back. George A. had tears in his eyes. Much as he loathed Brigham's messenger, the message itself was sweet to repeat.

T H I R T Y - S I X

THE TRIBAL CHIEFS ALSO FOUND the message sweet. How many horses? How many guns?

"Half," the missionary promised.

The meeting took place in the Santa Clara Indian Mission yard. The wagon canvas that served for a canopy sagged in the hot, still air. The missionary sat in a chair fashioned from willows, his listeners sat on the dirt in a circle at his feet. The dirt had been swept clean of droppings, and there was a tiny ceremonial fire.

At 38, Jacob was the youngest man in the circle, his voice the strongest. He had a crooked face, and when he said the emigrants owned over 100 horses, the firm mouth became a slanted line.

The meeting did not go smoothly. The fly in the ointment was the Paiute who had ridden in from the Yannawant camp. This Paiute, a stocky boy with a solemn face, was of that special class of runners the chiefs used to relay important messages. He arrived from the Kaibab Plateau just as Chief Tutsegavit was leaving for the meeting called by the missionary, and so was invited to ride along. His name was Dancer.

When Jacob said the mission Indians would get half the Mericats' animals for helping the Moronies, Dancer rose from his place in the shade of the mission building and approached the circle. He had never seen a white man before, nor a man so large, but he was determined not to show fear.

Except for the breechclout, his body was bare. In his hand he carried a many-strand necklace of red-dyed quills, and the first thing he did was to hand the necklace to Chief Tutsegavit. That the runner waited until now, in the solemnity of a meeting, to present the gift, showed that his words were this important.

As an outsider, Dancer had no right to speak ahead of those in the circle, but because Chief Tutsegavit did not object, neither did the other chiefs. And because all the chiefs sat facing the rickety chair, so now Dancer stood beside that chair and spoke thus.

"Chief Naraguts of the Kaibab Paiutes will stop all foreigners from moving further south. Chief Naraguts will kill the foreigners when they came with their cows and wagons to settle like ticks in the ear."

"You have to kill the right foreigners," the missionary explained earnestly, getting hurriedly to his feet. He was a foot taller than the Kaibab Paiute, the flat hat on his head pushed up the canvas ceiling.

"The Mericats. They are your enemy."

Dancer shook his head so hard that his black hair swished across his face, and corrected the missionary. "All white men moving on the rivers that lead to the Mystery River. Chief Naraguts has a big heart for the Mystery River and all its secret places." The way Dancer looked at the missionary, and afterward ignored him, showed no respect, no respect at all.

Jacob tapped his chest with his thumb. "Good, honest," he said. He pointed at his hired man, sitting a little back behind the circle. "Thales Haskell good white man." He arched his arm against the northern sky. "All Saints good, do not need killed." Now he was pointing eastward. "All Mericats bad, need killed."

The old men nodded their dirty white heads. Many times

Jacob wished that his lot were cast among a more cleanly people, instead of among the loathsome diggers. But he did not let his disappointment affect his labors in the Lord's vineyard.

"If you obey the Great Spirit, we will help you against your enemies, and we will keep you from want and sickness." He spoke clearly, but kindly. The tone of his voice said that he knew life was not easy for his Indian charges.

"If you do not help us, the Mericats will come over the desert and KILL ALL OF US! The Mericats will steal the hides from your tents, they will take your women, they will take your babies. They have many things you need, many horses, many guns. You can take their things away and use them in your own camps. You can use their guns and ammunition to hunt your meat with. This is what the Great Spirit wants you to do."

The Lord's instrument stopped talking. He hoped the old men would now smoke the pipe. But it was not to be. The chiefs wanted to hear what Chief Naraguts would say to Jacob's words, and so they looked again at Dancer.

Nostrils flared, lip curled as a dog snarls, Jacob turned on the boy. But Dancer did not care. To have journeyed so far from home using the maps in his head made him very proud, and he was not about to be put off by a puff toad.

Speaking slowly, signing where necessary, this is what the runner said.

"The white man is stealing the wintering grounds of the People to the north, covering up the fish-trap places and the camping grounds and forcing the People up into the mountains to starve. It is not Chief Naraguts' wish to object to the treaties that allow these thefts—these treaties have already been made by the chiefs of the Tonaquint and Parouse. But starting with now and in all the days to come, no white man's wagons will be permitted on the drainages above the Mystery River. Chief

Naraguts will do this and asks all the People everywhere to work
together to do this also."

Speaking, Dancer cleared his throat even as Chief Naraguts,
in spelling out the message to the runner, had cleared his own
throat.

Jacob fished Brigham's letter out of his coat pocket and waved
it in the chiefs' faces.

But the messenger would not stop talking. "Listen to me,"
Dancer insisted. He had come to the most important part. The
chiefs did not look at the paper fluttering before them, and
Dancer talked on.

"Chief Naraguts had a dream. In his dream, men with light
hair and white skins made buffalo paunches of the Mystery
River, tying it off with stick and stone hoops. These evil men
put poison in the paunches to make the People sicken. Then
they took away the flesh of the People and kept it."

Dancer stopped talking, his eyes accusing the missionary, as
if the missionary himself were guilty.

Jacob opened his mouth, but Chief Tutsegavit put his hand in
the air. Now the pipe would be smoked. This took a long time,
and during this time Dancer left the men gathered in the shade
of the canopy and returned to the shade of the mission building.

Finally, Chief Tutsegavit signaled the Paiute back. The chief
did not rise, but continued to sit on the ground. He was an old
man, he did not need to be tall to gain attention the way the
young bucks did.

The chief interpreted Chief Naraguts' dream to mean the
white men must not build any more dams like that built two
seasons before on the Tonaquint—the river the foreigners called
the Santa Clara. After that dam was built, the Tonaquint dried
up. Chief Tutsegavit did not understand that it was the Great
Spirit who made the river dry up until he heard Chief Naraguts'
dream.

Now Chief Tutsegavit knew what happened to the Tonaquint and that such would happen on the Mystery River. To dam a river was to kill it.

Was there any more to say? Chief Tutsegavit asked Dancer.

Dancer nodded. "In return for stopping the white man from building his villages on the rivers beyond the Tonaquint, the Kaibab chief will let the tribes who live above the Mystery River hunt as far south as they wish—the Moqui, the Paiute, the Navaho, will not stand in their way."

Jacob made a hard laugh that took in the circle and, getting to his feet, carelessly swung the chair aside, almost hitting Dancer's leg. The narrowed, hazel eyes locked in on the black Indian eyes.

"You left out the Apache, you little bastard." The missionary laughed again. He stood so close that the hot iron nails in his boots pressed the runner's bare toes. "I'll tell you what I think. You Kaibab boys have had that empty country all to yourselves too long as it is, and there still ain't no trade fairs going on. Now the Saints are here and the Saints are gonna be here forever, as long as the wind and the sun. You sign any treaties, you sign 'em with us."

The white man was standing too close to use gestures, and Dancer did not understand the meaning of all the words, still he caught the gest.

"On Mountain Lying Down there is enough food," Dancer insisted. "Or Chief Naraguts would not make this promise."

Jacob's reply was soft and menacing. "I'll remember that, Lamanite." Turning back to the circle, the missionary ground the toe of his boot against Dancer's toes, but the runner didn't wince.

Instructed by Chief Naraguts to pay close attention to the names of the white men he met, Dancer did not think it would be at all hard to remember the missionary Jacob Hamblin.

The tribal chiefs agreed to all Jacob asked. And to all that Chief Naraguts asked.

"We do not want the white man to enter on the Mystery River," they told the missionary, who answered that no white men lived along the Virgin River—the river the Indian called the Parouse—nor on the plateaus overlooking the Mystery River.

Dancer thought the missionary should say more, that he should make a promise never to go to the Mystery River, but it was not a runner's place to press a demand. And now the chiefs were asking again, how many horses and guns.

And Jacob was wondering how to stop the pesky Paiute from causing more trouble. Reluctantly, he extended an invitation that Brigham had not authorized.

"I will take all the chiefs north to Salt Lake City, where you can talk directly to the god your god gave Utah to—the Great White Governor Brigham Young himself."

Chief Tutsegavit wanted Dancer to accompany the party and so relay Chief Naraguts' message to this god. But the missionary would not permit it. Only important chiefs were allowed to visit the Great White Governor.

THIRTY-SEVEN

T HE MORMON CORRIDOR, a montage of golden fields, vitrescent river pastures, and fruitful gardens.

Lulled by the serenity, the Fancher party arrives in Lehi with high hopes, despite having earlier been denied supplies in the Mormon forts of Big Cottonwood and Little Cottonwood. In Lehi, two men in a shiny black wagon with the words LDS Church in white letters on the side sell the company a load of fresh produce for $35 and report no replacement animals available.

American Fork…nothing for sale. Battle Creek…nothing for sale.

In Provot, nearly 50 miles down the road, the largest settlement reached since leaving Salt Lake City, the main street is strangely empty. A stack of newspapers, freshly smelling of printer's ink, sits on a bench near where Fancher stops his wagon. He is reading a copy when several riders approach.

"I hope you wasn't planning on buying anything here." The rider who asked was missing his lower left arm and wore his coat sleeve pinned up.

"That's just what I'm gonna do," Fancher bridled. "Who wants to know?"

"Elder George Washington Bean of the Church of Jesus Christ of Latter-day Saints. There's nothing for sale in Provot, you folks best move on." The churchman spoke in a monotone, as if announcing a train departure.

"You got any Gentile merchants here?" Fancher asked, turning his attention back to The Territorial Enquirer. Beneath an item announcing the engagement of the Provot bishop's only daughter to the Dramatic Association's talented scenery painter, was a large advertisement for draft mules.

"The only Gentile merchants are around the upper lake," the elder replied primly and rode off with his retinue.

The Arkansas families were going from store to store, the street so quiet Fancher could hear their boots on the boardwalks, their fists on the locked doors. And listening, swore softly to himself. If there were none but men in his company, he'd handle things differently. As it was, he had no choice but to pull in his horns.

A parade of young drummers moved alongside the wagons. In the midst of the hubbub, a man with maddened hair hurried up to present Fancher with a small white card.

WILLIAM ALLEN ADEN
Scenic Painter

A young Giuseppe Verdi of a fellow despite the English name and disheveled London suit. Deep, dark eyes under a wide brow, square face, rather flat nose, medium-height dock-worker's body. Mr. Aden wanted passage out of the Territory and, learning that the train lacked supplies, was scarcely dissuaded.

"You gotta talk their lingo," the artist stated firmly above the roll of the drums. "I'll gladly help."

"You can start with those goddamned drums," Fancher snapped.

Having circled the parked wagons once and forced some of the yoked cattle to their feet, the band was preparing to do so again. Will strode purposely toward the boy with the biggest drum, leaned close and growled through clenched teeth, "Go home right now or I'll break both your arms and legs, and then I'll break your drum."

The boy marched away immediately, taking his jeering companions with him.

"I need supplies." Fancher handed over a roll of paper bills. "Let's see what you can do about that."

What Will did was simple enough. Walking along the line of wagons, coming to a spring wagon, he motioned the driver into a nearby alley and led the way around to the back of the Provot Mercantile. The wagon returned loaded with 50-lb sacks of flour, potatoes, dried beans, and a large assortment of bundled, fresh vegetables. A crowd was gathering across from the train. A knot of old people assembled in the middle of the street to lift their brave, ruined voices in a church hymn. Now all the onlookers were singing.

"Do it again," Fancher ordered Will. "Take a buggy, catch up with us."

The Arkansas men urged their worn animals off the ground, and the company walked slowly out of Provot to the sound of the offertory. In the meantime, Will motioned a buggy out of the line-up and eased down the alley as before—the mercantile's owner being only too happy to join in the singing outside his front door, while clerks tended to the business of business on the back dock.

With the buggy full of supplies, Will directed the driver to a row of clay apartments where the artist picked up a bulging portmanteau and a large newspaper-wrapped packet. The buggy then made its way south, somewhat circuitously, toward the main road.

Will Aden was on what he called his grand tour. "An irreplaceable rite of passage, the only way to properly round out one's education," he explained with ever-renewed optimism.

"Next year, after collecting the necessary letters of recommendation, I shall be off across the pond to Paris. Then it's south through France and across the Alps and down the boot to finish in Rome, the center of civilization. Two years from now, I shall visit the palaces and spice markets of Istanbul, where I shall haggle for jade in Hong Kong's Kowloon market."

He called himself a winter saint, having spent the winter in Salt Lake City with no intention of taking up permanent residence. Born in Tennessee, 19 years old, he'd traveled up the Overland Trail sketching as he went and planned to sell the sketches to Harper's New Monthly. In the meantime, he kept the wolf from the door by painting scenery and signs.

He had a fine voice, and entertained his new companions with ditties learned in the Mormon capital, including one written by Heber Kimble.

> Brigham Young was a Mormon bold,
> And a leader of the roaring rams,
> And a shepherd of a heap of pretty little sheep,
> And a nice fold of pretty little lambs,
> And he lived with his five and forty wives,
> In the city of the great Salt Lake
> Where they woo and coo as pretty doves do,
> And cackle like ducks to a drake.

What he didn't mention, scarcely seeing the need, was his brief engagement to the Provot bishop's daughter—an engagement immediately followed by the promise of a whittling job by the Melchisedec priesthood if he didn't renounce Luther immediately and embrace the God of Mormon. Making the timely appearance of the Fancher train in Provot most fortuitous.

And what more charming traveling companion than Editha Anne ("Dinky" he immediately eschewed). A delightful creature, Editha Anne. Well educated, bright. Ah, yes, a rare piece of good fortune indeed.

In the face of hostility at Springville, and further on, in the beautiful valley of Spanish Fork, and further still, on Peteetneet Creek, where the Lord's chosen lined the road to holler curses and throw stones, Will exuded the optimism of a young man in love. What the hell, kill another cow.

One day a grain wagon, traveling ahead of the company, broke down, the wheel careening off into a ditch. The wagon was full of ground corn, and the farmer hauling it home agreed to sell the whole load for a double eagle and the wheel put back on its axle. The farmer had only one eye, the other having been crudely sewn shut, and only one complete hand, the other lacking several fingers. While the Fancher party was unloading the grain, a rider came up and called the farmer aside.

The farmer could be heard swearing something about full granaries and no skin off anybody's teeth. The rider continued to argue, and the farmer walked over to the emigrant unloading the wagon, asked for the shovel, and threw it at the heckler. The man rode off, the farmer retrieved the shovel, the unloading went on.

The next day several dozen boys, afoot and horseback, blocked the road. The boys wanted money, $10 a wagon. One of the boys waved a pistol, the others brandished sticks.

"Put your firearm down," Fancher told the boy with the pistol. "Before someone gets hurt."

The boy leveled the weapon and shot a hole in the dirt. Fancher jammed his hat down on his head and ordered the wagons turned around. Damned if he would fight children. The American Army was on its way. If he had to winter in Salt Lake, the Army'd see to it he had food.

The next morning, bright and early, here came Elder George Washington Bean riding hell-bent-for-leather, coat flapping, shirttail out, tie gone along with his derby hat. Behind the elder rode a large body of men looking equally as disheveled and unhappy.

Why had the wagons reversed their course? Hearing the reason, Elder Bean was full of apologies. Stammering and stuttering, he called the ruffians a terrible reflection on the Saints. The company must not return to Salt Lake City! There was plenty of food at Buttermilk Fort. Plenty of food. The folks at Buttermilk Fort were expecting the wagons, it wouldn't be a good idea to disappoint them, it might cause trouble for other trains coming down the Corridor. It was very important to try to get along. Very important. The elder was truly sorry. Those bad bad boys would be severely reprimanded for their prank, severely reprimanded, yes sir!

Turning his horse just so, George Washington Bean dropped the looped reins over the saddle horn and stuck out his hand.

"How much further to the Buttermilk place?" Fancher asked, ignoring the gesture.

"Not far, not far at all," Elder Bean said sincerely. And hurried off down the road, retinue in tow, ostensibly to find and punish the offenders.

So Fancher turned the train again. Lord, but he'd be glad to be shut of Mormon country!

That the Corridor was not totally without amenities gave the Arkansawers some comfort. Grass was adequate and water plentiful, there was an abundance of red currants and an occasional luckless deer. But only Will Aden took any lasting pleasure in the creak of the slow-turning, iron-wrapped wheels that measured the long road south.

Walking out together each day through the scalding sunshine, watching the sunset fires ripple through ghostly cloud corridors, the sign painter and his lady reached a common ground strewn with poetry and proverbs.

"'Tis distance lends enchantment to the view, and robes the

mountain in its azure hue,'" Will reminded Dinky infectiously. "Look around you. The wind up-gathering the clouds, the hoarse croaking of the solitary raven under the burnished sky, the desert lark singing its heart out from its lonely perch in the sage, the distant mountains with their lofty vistas. The only deserts are deserts of the mind."

I've been too long from Mun, Dinky told herself. *That's why, when I'm with you, Will, I don't notice the wind.*

"Your eyes are warm as black olives, Editha Anne," Will whispered. "Your elegance endearing."

"My heart leaps up when I behold Will Aden stepping out so bold," Dinky replied lightly.

On Dinky's 23rd birthday, Mun's relatives gave her a handbag made of leather strips woven together. Everybody sang "Happy Birthday," and there were sugar cookies.

At the edge of Salt Creek, what looked to be an invitation turned into another insult. A banner proclaiming PARLEY P. PRATT DAY hung above long tables loaded with produce. The air was thick with the smell of roasted meat. The wagons stopped, the Arkansas women walked over with bright expectant faces, and came back empty-handed.

For once, Will was silent. Having assumed the actions of the Corridor's residents to be reflective of their attitude toward emigrants in general, now he wasn't so sure. All that work, preparing the food, setting up the tables, just to be rude? It didn't make sense.

"Do you believe her now?" Will asked, referring to the story Dinky had told him about an incident in Salt Lake City.

"Yes. I wish with all my heart I'd listened to Ellen. I pray every night that she's wrong about the Indians. If all we have to put up with is mean people, we can do that."

"I think so, too," Will told her, his smile infectious. "And speaking for myself, I'm very glad you came through Provot when you did." *In more ways than one.*

Down the long sweep of valley the land grew increasingly barren and sterile. Alkaline flats dotted the sagebrush pastures, foot-deep alkaline dust boiled into the faces of the yoked cattle, choking them. Seen through the dust, the sun was a golden globe. Hard by on the east rose mountains smoky with haze and streaked with an occasional slant of long, grey far-away rain. To the west lay an ocean of dry desert mist dotted with occasional rocky upthrusts.

The more Dinky saw of the countryside, the more she hated it. "It must be the isolation and dreary sameness," she observed, pointing out the fright in the faces of the Mormons who lined the main road as it passed through the tiny settlements. "It's turning their minds."

"What can you expect of people who live where fashion does not reach?" Will asked knowingly.

"I think they're hungry," Dinky said. "Particularly the children. It breaks my heart the way they huddle so close together and act so wistful, like they wish they could go with us."

"Maybe they do, children like to see new things."

Quoting Keats as he walked, the artist pointed out the various evidences for the theory that they were traveling along the edge of an ancient lake. The only time he'd been on a boat was to go around about the Horn to California. But *veni, vidi, vici!* and the same with Utah Territory.

It seemed impossible for him to be serious. Dinky told him so, called him a gentle soul, and stuck a sprig of sage in his lapel.

Work-cattle used up, supplies down to a nubbin, the Fancher company grew increasingly weary and worn. The world was strangely out of plumb, and on their poor diet it was hard to think clearly what to do about it. Should they wait for another train? and if so, how long and where? Could the Mormon priests be shamed into releasing supplies? Should riders be sent ahead into San Bernardino to bring back food and extra horses? Were the Indians to be a problem, as the bishop's wife had warned?

In the end, the California dreamers simply kept going, conserving their animals' strength as best they could, reassuring themselves that every mile south took them that much closer to the ocean.

Saturday, August 21. Above Buttermilk Fort, the supposed place of welcome some 110 miles below Salt Lake City, small boys appeared out of nowhere to pelt the wagon canvases with rotten eggs and ripe tomatoes. In the fort itself, men stood guard with rifles.

But that night, some miles down the road, something sharply different occurred. Alerted by the dogs, the night watch saw a solitary wagon take shape in the silky starlight. A woman called softly. The watch approached cautiously, and the woman handed him a straw basket full of eggs and a roll of soft, cloth-wrapped cheese.

At Fillmore, after dark, a man came pulling a child's wagon full of potatoes.

Wednesday, August 25. Garland Hurt's Indian farm at Corn Creek. Dr. Hurt was the only federal agent left in the Territory. Unfortunately the agent was away, but his kindly Pah-Vant Indians sold the train all the corn that could be spared, 30 bushels. The train lay over a day and a night, and during that time three white men rode into the fort's yard—Missionary Jacob Hamblin, his assistant Brother Thales, and Apostle George A. Smith— followed by 12 Indians, short, bandy-legged nomads with dark, dried-apple faces. When the missionary explained that the chiefs were being shepherded north to meet Brigham Young in an effort to keep the road safe, the emigrants felt a great relief.

Asked about the Corridor's lack of charity, the missionary apologized and explained kindly, "It ain't meanness, it's the boastful and hateful remarks of the Gentiles that keep our people bulled up."

"We shouldn't all be tarred with the same stick," an Arkansawer observed.

"I know that." Jacob grimaced and shook his head. "I tell them so myself." Surveying the party's weak stock, he seemed genuinely concerned. On a piece of paper he drew a single sloping curve of line connecting the words "Corn Creek" at the top, "Cedar City" toward the middle, and "Beaver Mts" at the bottom. Directly beside Beaver Mts, he made an "X" for meadows.

"Better lay over here a week or so in these meadows, rest up before taking on the Mojave. The road goes right by my house, the meadows is some four miles further. I'll be back by the time you get there."

Asked about replacement animals, the missionary said, "I got work stock for sale."

A true humanitarian that Jacob Hamblin. As for the Thales boy, he smiled shyly when not keeping his head ducked. Only George A. (having what the Arkansawers laughingly described as orders from headquarters) smiled not at all. The missionary and his party lingered less than an hour at the Indian farm. During that time, the savages walked between the wagons and fingered the bedding and utensils. The hawk's bells tied to their leggings jingled, and their foreign mutter of words sounded of excitement.

On the 26th of August, convinced they had at last shaken the fanaticism of the upper basin, the Arkansas company left Corn Creek.

T H I R T Y - E I G H T

THE MEN LOOKING FOR the Fancher train had pushed their horses too hard in the hot sun. The horses stood on splayed, trembling legs, blood dripping from their noses. Three of the men went immediately to stripping the animals and finding them a place to roll.

The fourth, a lanky jug-eared fellow, planted himself belligerently in front of Alex Fancher.

"Name's Powers, out of Little Rock." His voice sounded parched. "And you're a dumb ass." He took off his felt hat, slapped it against his thigh, and put it back in place, using two hands as if battening down a hatch.

"You boys doctored the drinking well at Corn Creek Sloughs, killed upwards of 60 cows and a couple of Injuns. Lucky my outfit's still north of there, or some of them cattle coulda been mine. Like to ask you to stave it from here on out." The worried man was having trouble keeping his temper, his red-rimmed eyes jumped about and he snapped the fronts of his faded red suspenders repeatedly.

"You got the wrong train, mister." Fancher sounded disgusted.

"Yeah? Your oxen's named Brigham Young and Kimball. When you ain't cursin' 'em, you're bragging about shootin' Joe Smith or else singing songs about coming back with the Army to burn down Mormon town. Now tell me I got the wrong train!"

"You got the wrong train. Good Christ! That'd be like

marching through South Carolina beatin' the drum for Dred Scott. Who'd be crazy enough to do that?"

"You would, that's who!" Powers waggled his finger under the captain's nose. "Yours is the first train down here this season, the only one's ahead of us. And I'm telling you here and now, throw any more poison out, do *anything* that causes me any trouble, and I'm gonna job you full a' holes!"

"And I'm tellin' you, I don't know what the hell you're talkin' about."

"Somebody in this train does." Powers looked around expectantly, chin out, braced for a fight. "Where's them no-good Helltown Greasers?"

Watching the jinglebrain, Fancher felt himself caught in one of those whirling, stalking winds that spring up out of nowhere. "We ain't got a Puke Stater one. Whoever it is you're looking for, mister, they ain't with us."

Will Cameron drifted over.

"Man here's looking for some Missouri boys," Fancher said by way of introduction. "They's supposed to poisoned a well."

"Ain't seen 'em," Cameron answered, distracted by the bright yellow corn being poured on the ground for the riders' horses.

"Goddamn!" Powers exploded shrilly. "Acting dumb ain't gonna cut it!"

Cameron jerked his head around.

"Now maybe you boys didn't mean to poison that water. I'll give you that. Maybe you just lost an animal in it, and that's what done the trick."

"We never lost a damn thing in it," Cameron said.

"Listen to me!" Powers pleaded. "You got Mormons following after you like copperheads. We damn near got shot riding up on 'em. They give us one hour."

"To do what?"

"What we come here for, you dumb ass! Talk some sense into your heads. One hour. Any more 'n we can't leave at all."

"Sounds like it's you got the problem," Cameron observed.

Powers stared slack-jawed. He'd left Salt Lake City planning to join this train, what a mistake that would have been! In every settlement the story was the same—the Fancher train was looking for a fight, there was going to be a terrible calamity. Thinking it over, Powers continued to stare.

Fancher leaned forward, the vein in his temple pulsing visibly. "Let me tell you something, pilgrim. Ever' goddamned Mormon I see I smile real big and offer him a potful of money, and I can't buy a damn thing. Right now I got 40 days rations, that's half what I need. We're eatin' our stock cows and feeding our California seed to the work cattle. Now the goddamned Mormons, they don't have to refit us if they don't want to, but *they can't stop us from using a Territory road! That is the last straw!* I got 50 good men to tie to if they try. You go back and tell your friends that! Tell em' they're baitin' the wrong bear!"

Powers took a deep breath and returned doggedly to his task. "If I gotta spell it out, I will, goddammit! Stop turning your stock loose on the fields, stop poppin' off chickens' heads. We met a preacher on the road says you boys call the Mormon women whores and the men swamp hogs. Stop with all that!"

Fancher was done arguing. He shoved his hands deep in his pockets and walked away. Powers threw the saddle back on his horse and rode off with his friends. Cameron, dropping to his knees, worked at collecting the scattered corn.

Fifty miles below Corn Creek, at Beaver, the mountains shut out the sky both east and west. The emigrants attempted to buy hay for their oxen from a stack beside a beaver pond and, having no luck, herded their gaunt animals out on the grasses beyond the river. That night two men, driving by, rolled a barrel of green tomatoes sweetened in sorghum off a wagon into the road ruts and placed a sack of flour and a crate of chickens beside the barrel. The emigrants called their thanks. Hats pulled close, the good Samaritans drove off without replying.

At a walled city with the words PAROWAN spelled out in white-washed rocks on the hillside, and the words FORT LOUISA burned into the signpost, heavy log gates closed off the main road. One by one, the wagons turned and jolted downhill through the sage toward the water.

When Dinky realized what was happening, she turned on Will Cameron and declared angrily, "There is some shit I will not eat!" And marching up to the gates, pounded on the leather-laced gate poles with her fists.

A voice from the other side warned her away, and she cast about for a stick and used that. A man with a long beard pushed open the gates a crack. There was a religious service going on inside, no one could come in.

Through the crack, Dinky could see a good many men and horses milling about. "You can't shut us off a public highway!" she yelled, her face in the gatekeeper's face. "I happen to know the United States Government paid $25,000 in gold coin for surveying and opening this road in 1854. My husband is with the Bureau of Topographical Engineers, and we are United States citizens, legally passing through a United States Territory!"

The greybeard leaned forward, lips drawn back over rotten teeth, aimed a stream of tobacco juice at the Gentile whore's pantaloons, and pushed the gate shut.

But Parowan was not a town without mercy, as witnessed by the poorly dressed Parowan farmers who carried sacks of produce down to the emigrant wagons.

Peeking through portholes in the western wall, spotting the

traitors, church elders ordered their bishop's son, "Go outside and stop them!"

So Brother Lewis ran out the gates and, not being a husky fellow, made a bee-line for the smallest of the Mormon farmers, an Englishman bearing cabbages. But even as Brother Lewis held a bowie knife to the Englishman's throat and recited the order forbidding trading with the enemy, the rest of the farmers persisted—Brother Lewis being only one man and having his hands full with the feisty Englishman.

For the first time since leaving Fort Bridger, the Arkansawers were able to stand openly in the sunshine to buy food.

Elder Sam Jackson sold the emigrants a small measure of wheat, Bishop William Leany a modest quantity of onions. This latter sale was due to Bishop Leany's having recognized Will Aden as the son of a Mr. Aden who had earlier befriended Isaac while on a mission in the States. Another of the Mormon farmers traded an Arkansas woman a large cheese for a bed quilt.

However, the company was not allowed to have their Indian corn ground at the Parowan gristmill, the first mill struck since leaving Corn Creek. Church Authority forbid it, the miller said.

The next day being Sunday, the extra-large tent purchased in Fort Smith for Methodist ablutions was set up in the midst of the Arkansas wagons. Whereupon Will, being Will, decided a walk-about would do as well and invited Editha Anne to join him. Which was a mistake.

Dinky refused to make a religion of her agnosticism, particularly now, and launched a stern sermoning. The children, hers as well as the 43 others, were reassured by routine. Just as their parents were reassured by prayers and hymn singing. And although not very comfortable with other people's definitions of God, still she recognized that something *did* exist, some higher intelligence. A higher power, if you will. Otherwise, what lifted man out of the primordial mud and...

"...enough, enough! cease and desist!" Will put his hands over his ears. "I am undone. Tomorrow I renounce all my renunciations and become a monk." And off he went alone to admire the beauty and peacefulness of the countryside. To listen to the birds and watch the paired yellow butterflies dip and glide over the green grasses and sketch a halfhearted waterfall setting its pebbly basin asparkle in the sun.

Monday, August 31. Some 20 miles further, outside Cedar City.

In a countryside awash in rolling benches dark with cedar, a Mormon bishop sold the emigrants 50 bushels of tithing wheat and ground it, along with their corn, at his mill. The bishop had direct, bright blue eyes and a ready smile, his name was John D. Lee.

"Lose a few, win a few," Alex Fancher remarked to his brother. The captain would have waxed less philosophical had he known of the punishments meted out by the priesthood back in the walled city of Parowan.

For giving comfort and aid to the enemy, Good Samaritan William Leany lay that very moment near death, beaten with a heavy oak cane. Samuel Jackson had been excommunicated, his stock and cleared lands confiscated by the church. As for the Saint who traded cheese for the accursed bed quilt, that man had simply vanished.

THIRTY-NINE

I N THE CREEK PASTURES BELOW Cedar City the emigrant children were running and laughing, there were sounds of pans being unpacked. Dinky drew a bucket of water and surrendered it to Will, who walked with her back to the wagons.

"Don't your friend's friends live in Cedar City?" Will asked.

"That's what she said."

"Are you going to look them up?"

"Are you kidding? I'd as soon look up a shark."

"I think you should consider it."

"The shark?" Dinky brushed an ant off Will's shoulder. "I couldn't find the James' anyway. Nobody talks to us, remember? except to spit."

"Anyone would be glad to receive a note that big paid in full."

Dinky made a face. "Ellen can take care of her own business. If I never see another Mormon as long as I live, I'll be happy." She glanced at Will's profile and closed her eyes.

"A friend is a friend, wherever you find them," Will said.

Enjoying the cheery sunshine, Will busied himself exploring the cluster of queer stick houses that was Cedar City. From the lip of a shallow, three-sided amphitheater, he saw where a flat rock, trailed by deep, ragged furrows, had been dragged into the center of the bowl. Small children, giggling and behaving as small children everywhere, sat on the edges of the raw furrows like crows on a fence. Up the sides of the bowl, folks were seating themselves on the grass.

No one was paying him any mind and, reassured by this democracy, the artist spread his coattails and settled down expectantly, sketch pad in hand. The growing crowd seemed evenly divided between families and numerous men in the company of other men—English and Danes for the most part— so fretful, faces so long, that Will was half a mind to ask who died. Gradually the overheard conversations sorted themselves into raucous accusations against America, the words spit out as if pieces of lemon.

Now where did that come from? Will wondered, his own parents being terribly proud to call themselves Americans.

A dark-suited man, beard tucked inside his coat, hopped unceremoniously upon the rock platform, his opening remarks floating clearly and sweetly into Will's ear.

"Brothers and Sisters, the devil is among us." The amphitheater lent the admonishment an echoey, jangled sound, as if attended by a chorus of high-pitched voices.

The man at Will's elbow nodded sharply and hollered his agreement.

Will made an approving face and braced himself for the onslaught. Growing up outside Kingsport with the sons of Hardshell Baptists, he'd attended enough camp meetings to know how to act around people who prayed to a God of Vengeance.

The meeting lasted a good hour, during which time the United States Army got a fine blowing up, along with President Buchanan, whom the preacher called "puke-annie." The more the preacher rained down curses on the enemies of the church, sending them cross lots to hell with their throats cut, the more excited became his listeners, responding like strings on a fiddle to every indictment.

"Tell it, Brother Haight," they begged repeatedly. "Tell it how it is."

Brother Haight responded with thrilling atrocities which, if loud groans and curses were any measurement, were wonderfully received. Vivid descriptions of the bloody wrath of God caused the devout to cheer. Demands for obedience to the priesthood made them tremble. When, pointing his finger at perdition and feeling the heat of hell-fires through his boots, Brother Haight did a little dance step, his listeners clapped.

Bowing deeply to the east, the good brother brushed the seat of his pants. Raising up, he heaved an imaginary wad in that direction. The men in the audience guffawed loudly.

"Feed the Gentiles the same bread they fed you!" Brother Haight ordered on a stirring note. "Defend Zion with your last ounce of strength, your last drop of blood."

Head thrown back, grandiloquent and preening, the holy man beseeched the heavens, "Our Father, avenge the wrongs of thy people upon their enemies. Pour out upon them the wrath which thou hast in store for them. That they may be used up and not a grease spot of them remain."

"Wives," now he was caressing the audience, his fingers spread wide, "heed my words, OBEY COUNSEL. Let a woman rise up in rebellion against her husband that lives his religion, and I promise her sorrow and woe."

The Saints sucked in their breath and looked sideways at each other, sharing unspoken thoughts. But Brother Haight, checking his timepiece, elaborated no further.

"Parents, this afternoon spend time with these innocent little children." The churchman leaned forward, opening his arms wide to the children lining the furrows. "Rehearse to the children your sufferings and the sufferings of your family and the church while in the States. Tell them," his voice rose dolefully, "of the murder of our Prophets and Saints, how we was robbed and plundered and driven here to the mountains. Do this so they will NEVER FORGET WHAT THEY MUST DO TO THE ENEMIES OF GOD TO PRESERVE HIS KINGDOM!!

Meanwhile, out at the emigrant camp, a knot of armed men calling themselves the Iron District Militia had marched into the midst of the parked Arkansas wagons. The emigrants had not paid Bishop Lee enough for his tithing wheat. They owed Bishop Lee a cow. And by the way, where was their safe-conduct pass? No Gentiles could travel the common road without a safe-conduct pass.

"Get the goddamn hell outta here," Fancher ordered the militia.

"You can't do that," the man in charge screamed. "You can't profane the name of God! You murderers of Parley Pratt!" The affronted man began to shake violently and wave his revolver around.

Several of the emigrants lifted their rifles. In the confusion, a burley fellow took the one-eyed mare off her picket line. Emigrant Josiah Miller picked up his bull whip, and the thief let go the halter rope.

A Mormon long in the tooth, with a flowing mane of yellowed hair, strode purposefully across the open ground to where Fancher stood. The people couldn't be controlled, the train needed to move on as soon as possible.

Back on the flat rock, Bishop Haight was concluding the meeting. "Remember what I tell you and the day will be spent most pleasantly and profitably by all." He closed his worn bible and slapped it against his open palm. "A special indignation meeting of the High Council will be held immediately in the church."

Worshippers straggled away. The sky was pale with too much

heat. Off to the west, a sun dog shaped a piece of colored haze. The sun dog looked like a scrap of painter's rag. Sitting alone on the warm grasses, making himself aware of these things, Will tried to shake the sermon from his ears. For hostility and virulence and bawdy obscenities, he'd never heard the beat.

Eventually he resumed his stroll toward the storefronts. Which led to another kind of awareness. Although Cedar City was the largest settlement encountered since leaving the lower lake, its houses could in no way accommodate all the people represented by the numerous teams and saddle horses seen on the street and up the little side-alleys.

"What's the occasion?" he asked a passerby and was immediately surrounded by pop-eyed men who wanted to know just who in hell he was.

Will's jaw dropped open. He spit out his full name and, in an unfortunate flash of prudence, admitted to studying on being a Mormon. Whereupon he found himself grabbed by his shirt front and rushed backwards into a wall so hard that he saw stars.

"You ain't no Mormon!" his assailant charged. "That's a fuckin' Gentile name. You better study a little harder. You're a SAINT! Or gonna be." The bully looked around at his friends and laughed. "That is, if we let you." This last made everybody laugh, even Will.

The men walked off, except for one hanging back with a piece of boast. "You're on the right side here, brother. You seen them wagons outside town? Them's ourn, soon as the Injuns do their business."

"What do you mean?" Will rubbed the back of his head and noticed blood on his hand. As did his informant, who sidled away.

A bucktoothed woman approached with several small children in tow. Will made his voice as abject as possible. "Sister, could you tell me, please, where Brother Emil and Sister Verity James live?"

The woman paused. One of the children was ambling too near a tied horse. "Do you want me to cut your head off?" she asked, snatching the child back by its hair, and told Will, "Out the California road toward Pinto. Hog farm. You can't miss it." She gestured at a ragged bowery across the street. "He's over there right now."

Will glanced at the people in the leafy shadows. "Which one's James?" he asked, but before the woman could answer, a man, hatless and gasping for breath, came running up.

"Trouble with the emigrants!" he shouted. "Trouble! Trouble!"

A sudden surge of people brandishing various weapons flooded the street and moved as one toward the creek.

"Stop!" Will yelled over and over. "What's happening? What's going on?"

No one heard him. Howls and curses and hysterical screams filled the air. The angry hornets' nest swirled downhill, through a willowy marsh, and out on the sage. Will could see Fancher standing in the open with an old man—the old man's hands upraised as if to push back the crowd. Behind the pair fanned the Arkansas boys, rifles at the ready.

Moving closer, the artist caught Fancher's words, tinny in the distance. "Just tell me the charges, that's all I ask."

"Let's hear the charges, brother," Will urged the man beside him. "It's the Christian thing to do." Another serious miscalculation.

Without warning, the Mormon swung around and slammed a rifle stock against Will's arm. The blow knocked the artist down, a searing pain shot into his shoulder. He cried out and felt himself being jerked to his feet.

"We're no damn Christians here!" the attacker cried.

The old Mormon with the yellowed white hair was walking alone toward the mob, and the mob was milling around him. Ignored, Will slipped back to camp.

"Do you play chess?"

"No!" Dinky was jerking the little blue tent free of its pegs and wagging it up. "And I'm not in the mood to learn. I wonder why that is!"

"In chess, tactics is what you do when there's something to do." Wincing, the injured shoulder resisting, Will pulled the pegs from the ground and dropped them in their little sack. "Strategy is what you do when there's nothing to do."

"Stop pestering me! I'm not leaving this train!" Dinky threw her tent in the Cameron wagon, grabbed the peg sack out of Will's hand and threw it after the tent. Pandemonium reigned. Oxen being hurried into the yoke, men shouting orders, women shouting for children, horses neighing, dogs barking.

A man, working at dismantling a stove, dropped a hot lid. The lid thudded to the ground and rolled toward Dinky. She kicked it over and kept walking toward where the children were being herded together, Will hard on her heels.

"Tactics, my love, tactics. Right now there's still time to do something. *You've got to leave the train!*"

"We'll go on to the meadows, we'll be just fine. You leave if that's what you want."

"Fancher'll be lucky if he makes it to the meadows without a fight, if there even is such a place. Just hold onto your shoelaces and wait here until things calm down, there'll be other trains."

Dinky put her hands over her ears.

Stepping in front of her, Will took hold of her wrists and drew them down. "This isn't the weather, this didn't just *happen*. These are *not* the random acts of ignorant prejudice. It's a conspiracy. Remember who the missionary was with? *Indians*.

Remember the way they walked around, fingering the harnesses
and the iron kettles? remember? like they were going to buy it?
and they are, with arrows."

"Will! we're carrying enough guns to open an arsenal!"

"Alright, alright. Say Hamblin told the truth, that there is
meadows. What if he isn't back from Salt Lake City? What if
you can't buy any stock?"

"We're almost out of Mormon country."

"That's right. Almost to the desert with used-up cattle.
They're pulling five, maybe six miles a day. Figure it out, that
makes San Bernardino over two months away, and we've got a
month's rations at…"

"…stop scaring yourself."

"Look around you, look at the faces. These people are scared.
Now by God you've got friends here, use them!"

"Friends!"

"That I.O.U. makes you their friend. Tell them you decided
to become a Mormon, tell them anything."

"NO!" She'd reached the children, sorting through them,
scooping up Lymund. The twins clung to her skirts, eyes wide.

"Editha Anne, you've got to listen to me!"

"Stay away from me!"

"The Indians are going to attack the train, and the Mormons
are going to let them."

"We'll shoot them!"

"Yes, we will, and I think we'll make it. But not all of us. You
have three little children. *You can not afford to go to Corinth!*"

Dinky bit at her lower lip, shredding a flake of dry skin. "It's
cowardly. All they've done is bully us. Mun's waiting in
California."

"Write him a letter."

Dinky held her hand against her mouth. What to do? What

in the world to do? Everything she could dredge up said *don't stop! don't stay here!*

Will took hold of her free hand and kissed the rough palm. "If I thought for a minute I could keep you safe, I'd never let you leave."

"Oh, Will Aden, such a romantic," Dinky keened. "I just… I can't…"

But Will was done arguing. "When you get to the James', whatever you do, don't act afraid, don't let on you know anything."

"I don't know anything!"

"Good, remember that." He gripped her shoulders hard, almost shaking her. "Use your intellect, forget your heart. Tactics, my love, tactics."

"Where do James live?"

"Out this road, toward a city called Pinto. We'll know the house when we get there, it's a hog farm." He cupped her face in his hands and stole a kiss. "Get your things ready."

Next the artist hunted up Fancher.

"They act like they own this goddamn country," Fancher groused, despaired.

"I think they're going to let the Indians attack pretty quick now," Will told him.

"That'll be a fight they won't soon forget. We left the States primed for Indians. You seen an Injun yet you was scared of?"

"I talked Mrs. Miller into leaving the train. She knows people here."

The captain didn't answer. He was counting the loose horses being brought off the grass, the number was short.

"I'm scared of the Mormons, Mr. Fancher, real scared." Will stepped in front of the captain. "I was in Cedar City and heard crazy talk. I think we ought to give ourselves up."

"For what? We ain't done nothing!"

"That's it! Let them see all we are is emigrants with no axe to grind, and they may cool down. We're safer in jail, if they want to put us in jail, than we are hightailing it out there. *There are no due processes of law out there!*" Will waved his arm at the afternoon sun. "You won't be able to get that far before dark anyway. We'll stay here, stand trial, pay whatever they want."

"The hell with that!" Fancher was walking away. "You stay. I'm going to the meadows."

The artist followed, tripped over a wagon tongue, falling hard, and scrambled to his feet.

"Call a meeting," he begged. "For god's sake, man! vote on it. It's a trap! The Mormons think they're getting the wagons. The Indians must think they're getting something too. Don't leave here. Out there anything can happen. Call a meeting, let me talk to the company. Please listen to me!"

"Son," the captain wheeled to look Will straight in the eye, "we can handle Indians."

"Yes, sir. But what if the Mormons give them guns?"

"Don't matter." Fancher took hold of a box his wife was struggling to lift into the wagon, threw it in and turned back for another. "They can't shoot worth a damn."

F O R T Y

ITHIN THE HOUR the Arkansas party was once more on the move, plodding drearily through the fragrant cedars. A short distance west of Cedar City the California road passed between two winding sheets fastened in the trees. The sheets hadn't been there long, they were too clean. When Dinky walked beneath the sheets, a loose corner brushed her hair.

Once, long ago, as a young woman in Economy, Pennsylvania, Christina Marchion had seen a winding sheet being prepared for two babes lost in the woods. When she sang the song about the babes, Dinky would cry and ask all sorts of questions. And now the winding sheet was in Dinky's hair. She stepped quickly past, but in the press of wheels against the earth could still hear her mother singing,

> Do you remember, a long time ago, two poor little children
>   whose names I don't know
> were stolen away one bright summer's day,
> and left in the wood so I've heard people say.
> And when it was night, so sad was their plight,
> the sun had gone down and the moon gave no light,
>   and they sobbed and they sighed,
>   and they bitterly cried,
> and the poor little things just laid down and died.
> And when they were dead, the robin so red, brought
>   strawberry leaves

and over them spread, and all the night long,
   he sang them this song,
poor babes in the wood, poor babes in the wood.

Two miles further and she could smell the ripe stench of the hog farm. She'd wanted Will's information to be wrong. Now she realized why. Here, in the narrow lane opening through the trees to the left, was her Armageddon.

Will stopped the Cameron wagon and helped Dinky drag her bundles out. The wagon started up, restarting the line. Standing with her children beside the road, watching people and animals dog by, Dinky felt as if she were outside her body, as if she'd never left the train. Adding to the unreality was the Arkansawers' lack of interest in the forlorn cast-offs.

We are tireder than we know we are, Dinky realized, surprised.

Then Mary Dunlap was walking back to thrust a book into Dinky's hands. The book's cardboard cover was covered with pale green cloth decorated with a border of neat white stitches.

"It's poetry I wrote," Mary explained with a quick smile. "All about the little ones' adventures, it'll be something for them to read when they get big."

"I have friends here," Dinky offered hollowly. "I'm going to stay and visit awhile."

But Mary hurried off without answering, as if late for an appointment.

Wanting desperately to anchor herself, Dinky wadded Will's shirt sleeve in her fist. "I don't think I can do this." Her voice shook. "I'm afraid, don't leave me here alone."

Will smiled at her as if the summer's afternoon were just that, a afternoon made for lovers and easy living. "And what if they only have one bedroom?" he asked. "Then I'd have to be your husband." He put his arms around her and nuzzled her hair. "My dearest rose of the desert, tonight when the sparks from the campfires have become stars, I shall be sorry once again I am not."

The last of the wagons creaked by. Dinky kissed Will soundly on the mouth, tasting the salt in his tears.

Then he was breaking free and walking away.

"Don't forget," she called gaily. "If anything goes wrong, I'll be watching for you."

In answer, the artist waved jauntily over his shoulder. He could see his beautiful Cassiopeia standing there, the twins waving their stick horses, Lymund frowning, hands on hips. But didn't turn around. She had a husband waiting for her, and he had Paris.

A pole gate on a rock-fenced pen admitted the refugees into a sour-smelling yard rooted bare of anything but old cedars. Large mud holes, accompanied by swarms of mosquitoes and hogs, pockmarked the yard. Several hogs trotted up snuffling, and Dinky rocked them off. The pen ran uphill to include a two-story pole barn and badly-listing pole corral and a further scatter of low, red adobe buildings.

White curtains showed in the windows of one of the buildings. Dinky made her way that direction, reaching the door just as a man hobbled around the corner of the barn and stopped short. A small man with a large bandage on his foot, arm hitched over a crutch and tattered shirt fluttering in the wind.

"Mr. James?" Dinky called. There was no response. "If you're Mr. James, I have a note for you from Salt Lake City from Bishop Harris."

"Verity!" the man yelled, and was answered distantly. "Someone's to the house!"

The woman who came on the run had been butchering chickens. She carried the chickens by their legs, the severed necks staining the white feathers red and splattering blood everywhere. Nearing Dinky, she lay the birds on the ground and wiped her hands on her bloodied apron. A thin woman, medium height, with pale brown eyes. One of the headless chickens hopped up and began flopping around, and the twins chased after it.

"Are you Mrs. James?" Dinky asked and, getting no answer, added, "I'm Jed Marchion's sister." The name triggered no response. "I have a note from Ellen Harris in Salt Lake City."

"Emil!" It was Verity's turn to yell. "Better get up here. She wants information."

"What kind?" A snuffy fellow, Emil stood waiting for an answer, but Verity, busy with pushing her brindled hair into its Chinese topknot, had resumed her scrutiny of the visitors.

Several piglets wandered close, and Lymund tried to free his hand from his mother's. Emil approached, walking gingerly. One of his eyes was squinted shut. He was followed by an enormous boar.

"Couldn't we visit inside?" Dinky asked. *Was there no one in the whole Territory who could manage a civil greeting?!* "Rest assured, I'll make it worth your while."

Emil nodded at Verity. Verity gathered up the chickens, the runaway having toppled over, and everyone trooped inside. The packed earth floor was polished hard with wear. On either side of a comfortably large, low-ceilinged kitchen, thick-walled doorways opened on what appeared to be bedrooms.

The kitchen walls looked to have been recently plastered over. Built-in cupboards displayed wooden doors painted dark blue. A deal table accompanied by two similarly painted blue chairs occupied the center of the room. Water heating in a bucket on the cookstove steamed gently. A row of small peaches, sitting on a counter fashioned from wagon boards nailed on stout chunks of wood, blushed as if glowing from within.

Verity plopped a chicken in the hot water and doused it around by the legs, and fed the firebox. Emil took off his hat and mopped his bald head and mutton-chop sideburns with a hand towel.

"I was with the company that just left Cedar City," Dinky explained, fighting a sense of tremendous depression. "This is Anne and Emily, they're four now, and Lymund, he's two. They're very good children, no trouble at all." She opened her bag and, suddenly mindful of her alibi, sat down. "I'm not feeling well. Ellen Harris is a relative of mine. She said to contact you if I were unable to go out on the desert."

She loosened the drawstring on the little leather sack she carried for good luck—it'd been her father's, he kept his tobacco in it—and withdrew the two gold quarter eagles purchased on the wharves in New York City.

"I'd like to stay here and rest awhile, and secure passage on to San Bernardino with another train."

Emil fingered his mouth. Verity, her own face solemn, tested the chicken's feathers and pulled the bird out of the hot water.

Pawing through her bag a second time, Dinky found the note marked paid and laid it on the table. "Ellen said to give you this note." If anything, the paper made the James that much more distrustful. They went immediately outside and out of earshot, Verity strewing chicken feathers to either side as she walked.

A clock ticked on the mantle. The house seemed clean enough. Above the smell of wet chicken feathers was the smell of hog wallow. Flies buzzed in and out the open doorway.

The twins shared the remaining chair, Lymund squatted to consider a jar of pickled pig's feet. In the rather dark room, the children's hair shone as if lit with sunshine.

"I hope this is a good idea," Dinky said with a smile that was more like a grimace, her stomach in knots.

"This place stinks." Anne held her nose.

"Like grandpa's pig pen," Emily agreed. "Only worse."

A Maltese cat resembling a twisted piece of frayed rope wandered by, tail straight in the air. Anne grabbed the cat and put it on her lap, and both girls petted it. Lymund grabbed a foot, and the cat jumped down and ran away.

Verity came back alone, laid the naked chicken in a pan of cold water on the counter, checked the firebox, and doused the second chicken in the hot water. Was anyone hungry? She directed her words at the children.

Lymund was thirsty. Verity filled a dipper from one of the buckets on the floor under a towel, and the iron taste puckered the little boy's face.

The second chicken was plucked and committed to the cold water.

"The chickens are for supper," Verity told the twins. She opened a cupboard door and pulled out bread and headcheese.

Emil came in. Verity set out one tin plate, and Dinky got to her feet, as did the twins. Emil sat down, and no one sat in the empty chair. But then Lymund helped himself to it.

Eating, Emil carefully brushed the crumbs off the table into his hand, and dropped the crumbs on the floor. And almost as an afterthought, slid the golden eagles off the table into his pocket.

Becoming restless, Lymund wanted to go outside, and Verity asked if the hogs would eat him.

"No," Emil said. "He's too big. Let him play outside next to the door." And asked Lymund, "You frown all the time don't you, boy, that mean you're thinking?"

Lymund smiled shyly and stepped outside.

Verity filled a jar of milk from the other bucket under the towel. Stirring the clots of cream with his spoon, Emil relaxed. "I guess I'm gonna have to scare up some more chairs," he told the girls.

Dinky shook silently with relief. Verity too acted relieved. She smiled openly at the children.

"So, how's that Mister Jed doing?" the hog farmer asked, meeting Dinky's eyes for the first time.

FORTY-ONE

THE JAMES VIEWED DINKY as through a pane of glass, but not so her pretty little towheads. Supper that evening was a festive affair, with every word uttered by the children met with rapt attention. Jogging their stories with mention of Maine and the wind-up soldier in Washington Square, Dinky steered clear of any mention of the Arkansas company—and, wolfing down the fried chicken, tried not to think of the thin soup and fried mush being made do with somewhere out on the dark road.

Seated on his mother's lap, Lymund fell suddenly into his own lap, straightened, eyes glazed, and took another drink of milk.

Verity jumped up, upsetting her chair. "Sakes alive! shame on us for keeping that youngster up past his bedtime."

Resting on posts driven into the dirt floor was a narrow bed piled high with clothing. Working together, Verity and Dinky cleared the bed and tightened the rope netting. The straw mattress was puffed and repositioned, and the canvas sheet tucked tight. Quilts were laid out. A second straw-filled mattress was unrolled on the floor and covered with a handwoven woolen blanket.

"There now," Verity crowed. "That's everything we got."

The next morning, reticence evaporating, Verity ranged from being instructive to plain ebullient.

"...when first we come here, all we had was pig weeds and wheat, couldn't eat any hogs. Still can't 'cept at special times. But now we got us enough to put on the dog a little, and we got a cow and some fruit trees, and civilized fruit this summer for the first time..."

"...folks with big families, those kids still grow up like coyotes, but we help each other. That's how Emil got hurt. He was over on the Santa Clara hauling corn, and one of the horses caught its bridle under the wagon tongue and pulled off the bridle, and the team got to running. They ran over a wood pile and threw him out and the wheel caught his foot..."

Not given to irrational exuberance, the master of the house kept mostly to himself and, when asked to watch for emigrant trains headed for California, replied curtly, "Ain't none."

That same Tuesday, 260 miles to the north, the first wife of Bishop George Harris was busy doing what she did the first day of every month—collecting the household receipts from the bishop's six outside residences. Because these houses also served as short-term hostelries for newly-migrated Saints, each house was assigned two boxes. One box for the transient's tithes, the second box for the household's routine receipts. The resultant eight wooden boxes, each the size of a sewing drawer, required the use of both seats and made collection day the one day the first wife ordered out the conveyance for herself alone.

The large carriage was a comfortable beast—its seats being covered with sheep's hide and the turned-down wool lending a springy effect. But rather strange looking. To save money and set a good example, George had ordered the door paneling swabbed with boiled linseed oil instead of paint. The frugality never caught on, leaving the Harris carriage—its naked woodenness resembling an oak lowboy on wheels—the only one of its kind in the city.

Making her rounds, absorbed in her figures, Ellen heard the driver say, "Morning, Elder Hamblin," and looked out the open window into the missionary's burned, wind-chapped face.

Jacob raised his hat, as did young Thales. The bishop's first wife nodded and noticed the Indians in their old, curled-up saddles, grey splayed feet swinging free of the wooden stirrups. Noticed the heavy turquoise necklaces.

That the white woman recognized them for chiefs, the Indians saw in her face and made their own faces open and proud.

"Don't you think that's odd?" Ellen asked Phoebe later. "Twelve chiefs together, headed for the President's office?"

"Why, it *is* odd." Phoebe stopped folding the wash.

"It's probably not anything…" Ellen was carrying the traveling office into the dining room, her words fading and returning "…newspaper logs all the trains through the city…no way Brigham can make one vanish."

"We'll just see." Phoebe dropped the sheet she was folding. "I'll go right away and get a copy. What day?"

"The first week in August." Watching Phoebe scoot out the door, Ellen had to laugh. If Phoebe'd been painting, there'd be no getting her attention. As it was, she'd stop by the Prophet's Block, visit George in the Tithing Offices, and stroll past Brigham's palace, none of the wasted time having a fig to do with the Fancher party.

Struggling to turn her thoughts aside from what was clearly becoming a neurosis, Ellen arranged the money and notes from each of the residences on the dining room table for George to review. Next, she returned the boxes, empty now except for their up-to-date inventory sheets, to their specially built cabinet. She had designed the bookkeeping system herself, ordering what she needed from the cabinet maker, and was proud of how well it worked.

She concentrated on Nancy's being in regular school in the fall and Jeremy's beginning his priesthood training and needing a new black suit. She concentrated on getting the beet seed and flax seed taken care of and the garden turned. But nothing worked for long. Over and over again, like straw thrown against the wind, thoughts of Dinky returned, and she had to remind herself that other trains had since taken the southern route. The emigrants would look after each other, no one would starve.

Behind the cloistered walls fronting on South Temple Street a very private meeting was taking place—delayed somewhat by the suspicions of the gatekeeper who refused to let the visitors pass until Brigham could be located.

Jacob had worried that the Prophet would see the missionary's bringing the chiefs north as letting the cat out of the bag, but Brigham left no doubt as to his pleasure.

"Let God do his work," the President admonished sternly, giving Jacob a warm hug. "That the Lamanites ride openly through the city means God is expecting great things of them." He immediately sent for Dimick Huntington, the church interpreter. And ordered his wives to their rooms—the women, made timid by the appearance of the ferocious savages within the sanctity of the palace, quickly doing as told.

Leading the strange parade of field commanders into the dining room, Brigham took his usual place at the head of the long table. The curious Indians wandered about until marshaled into chairs by the missionary. Dimick arrived, breathless. Like a golden sword a lengthening shaft of sunlight fell on Brigham. Jacob moved to draw the drapes, but the President waved him back. Ready at last, the missionary and the church interpreter at either elbow, the Great White Governor faced his loyal red brothers.

Tutsegavit, head chief of the Yannawants and the Piede chief over six Piede bands, along with Moquetas and Big Bill. Kanosh from the Nephi region, chief of the Pah-Vants, treacherous as the best of them, still wearing Gunnison's medals on his shirt four years later, still taking credit for the massacre on the Sevier. Toshob, chief of the Uintah and White River Utes, looking more like a Chinese warlord than an Indian. Ammon, chief of the San Petes and brother to the hawk, Walkara. Jackson, chief of the Santa Claras, along with a brother whose name Brigham did not bother to remember. Four other lesser chiefs with still lesser names.

Wily, treacherous dusty-grey men of the desert. Broad, flat faces, some darker than others, cruel eyes.

The meeting lasted an hour. The room reeked of horse and unwashed bodies. Intent on his message, the Great White Governor kept the disgust out of his face. Poor lost Lamanites, it would seem impossible for them ever to become white and delightsome. Some of them weren't even very brave, despite their evil looks, not when it came to fighting white men. But they would learn. Enough guns and victories would teach them everything they needed to know about killing the enemies of the Church.

Brigham's words are simple. Let the Indian help the Saint and together they will rid the mountains and plains of the Mericats. The Great Spirit and the Great God of the Saints will help the Lamanites do this.

The chiefs do not understand who the Lamanites are.

The Lamanites are the seed of the Great White Chief Joseph. The Lamanites are children of the greatest prophet of all the gods. The Lamanites are brothers of the Saints.

Speaking thus, the Great White Governor smiled often and drew circles in the air that included everyone at the table.

The Indians remained impassive.

Brigham gave up and concentrated instead on who the Mericats were.

The Mericats were bad white people who hated the Indian. The Mericats hated the Saints. The Saints loved the Indian, the tribes of the Piede, the Desert, the Santa Clara, the Rio Virgin, the Harmony. The Indians must remember this and not take things that belonged to the Saints. Just take Mericat things. The Indian missionaries would tell the Indians who the Mericats were. The Indians must remember they were the battle axe of the Lord. As long as they did not bother the things belonging to the Saints, the Saints would not bother them.

"You are to have all the cattle that go to California over the south route for helping us," Brigham revealed, leaning back in his chair to hook his thumbs in his pockets.

This revelation opened the chiefs' eyes wide.

"You have told us not to steal," Huntington translated from their various mutterings.

"So I have," Brigham agreed. "But now the Mericats have come to fight us and you, for when they kill us, then they will kill you."

At the end of the hour, 11 of the chiefs were sent off with the interpreter to the horse pasture east of town, where each chief was to take his pick of two of the church's stock of war horses.

Chief Kanosh, Brigham kept back another quarter of an hour. And confided—Jacob interpreting when necessary, Kanosh speaking some English—that the very rich train to be shared as a sign of the Saints' friendship would be ready in seven or eight days.

The train would be isolated in the mountain meadows near

where the missionary built his summer house. This is where the Indians should strike.

Cedar City was 35 miles to the east of the meadows, the rock fort of Santa Clara a good 20 miles to the west. In addition to being isolated, the broad, open meadows would hold the train in the open. The surrounding hills would provide plenty of cover for attackers.

Indian farmer John Lee would be at the meadows. Lee would tell the Indians what to do. The Indians could have all the livestock. On no account were the Indians to burn the wagons. Or carry off any papers.

Kanosh looked puzzled.

"Papers don't mean nothing to Indians," Jacob explained softly.

Chief Kanosh wanted to know if the Saints would put on war paint as before. Yes, Brigham assured him, the Saints would do that. The President refilled the water glasses and confided something else. A very small train was traveling 10 days behind the big train. If the Indians acted with honor in the meadows, they could plunder the cattle from this train too.

After the meeting, Jacob took Kanosh down to Brigham's horse barn where young Thales was shoeing the missionary horses. The finest of the church's horses were here, and Kanosh was given his pick of one horse, along with a mule loaded with provisions, before being taken out to the horse pasture to meet with the rest of his tribesmen. The entire party was then herded onto the south road. There would be other gifts of friendship as well, as time went by. But for now, the Indians must hurry home.

With the Indians out of their hair, Jacob and Thales returned to Brigham's office.

The church leader was working at the desk that faced the west. Triumph flickered in his rugged farmer's features. "A spirit seems to be taking possession of the Indians to assist Israel, I can hardly restrain them from exterminating the Americans." Stretching out his hands, catching the missionaries' hands in his own hard grip, the Prophet bowed his head.

"The southern corridor to the Pacific Ocean is closing. No one knows when it will open again. A year, two, ten. But when that time comes, when that glorious time comes, the Lord who lodged us here in this desolate outpost will spread us like watermelon vines across the face of the earth. The Saints will sit on the throne that is America and trail their nets through the waters of all the oceans, and the scales will be lifted from our peoples' eyes and they will see the heavenly road that is being opened for them to the celestial kingdoms."

Brigham raised his head, released his brothers' hands, and settled back, drained by the terrible responsibilities of discharging God's duties. Didn't Jacob have a family in Tooele? he asked, making a visible effort to relax. And didn't Thales' sister live at Little Cottonwood? Good! While in the region, the two should take the opportunity to visit their families, and also take a wife. Particularly the younger women adapted more easily to the rigorous demands of life in the desert. The couples could then return to the city for the ceremony, and afterward travel to the Santa Clara Mission together in the same wagon. Leisurely, taking time to acquaint their new wives with the countryside.

The President smiled a warm, caring smile and opened his appointment book. "I anticipate the American Army will soon find a way to make a nuisance of itself, but for this important matter, I could arrange to be free early next week, say on the eighth, Tuesday, for a marriage ceremony in my own sealing room."

Jacob beamed with undisguised pleasure. A healthy young girl would turn the otherwise monotonous journey into a most pleasurable conquest. Even more important, the long stay in the region would keep him away from the bloodletting in the south. Much as the missionary might agree with giving up the Fancher company, the last place he wanted to be when the massacre took place was on his own ranch.

Red-faced, Thales stuttered a thanks which Brigham accepted gravely, hiding his amusement. Jacob's assistant had only recently taken his first wife, a love match as Brigham recalled. Well, that was alright. The new wife would have to learn sooner or later about sharing her husband, just as Thales himself would learn that added responsibility could have its pleasant asides.

FORTY-TWO

THE DESERET NEWS did not list the Fancher company as having been camped near the city on August 3. Ellen stared off into space. The paper routinely cleaned up Brigham's discourses before printing them. Were there other things tidied up as well? Should she go see Albert Carrington? Ask the editor if he'd been told to omit the Fancher train? Would he admit to it if he had?

The house smelled pleasantly of chocolate. By the time the children got home, there would be warm chocolate cake waiting with hot chocolate syrup poured over it. Returning to the paper, remembering the smells and troubles of food cooked in the open, Ellen read further, coming at length to the news item,

> The Apostle George A. Smith departed from Provot Aug. 4 with general orders for the southern military districts.

A sudden weakness washed over her. She cried out and pushed the heel of her hand hard against her teeth. *Zilpha was right. Oh my God! Oh dear God! Please let Dinky leave that train!*

Friday, September 4. The wagons that have rolled 2,000 miles across the face of the continent reach high, broad meadows perhaps five miles long and a mile wide, surrounded by a chain of low hills.

Near where the ground sinks downward to a large spring, the train stops. The minister gives thanks for having made it to the edge of Utah Territory, he also gives thanks for the honest, old missionary who invited them to rest here in this place of peace and beauty.

Proceeding with utmost despatch, Captain Van Vliet reached Ham's Fork in the Green River Valley Saturday, September 5, with all wagons intact but at least half of his animals unserviceable.

That the losses were not greater was due to his sergeant. The captain commented favorably on the sergeant's actions in his journal, but made no mention of his appreciation to the soldier. A man who liked mules well enough to think like one, didn't want to hear it.

Over 100 contractors' wagons loaded with supplies were camped at Ham's Fork. The teamsters reported the countryside quiet as a nunnery, the Mormons coming around regularly to take what peeks they could under the canvases, but never raising a gun.

On the face of it, the remaining 143 miles posed no threat. Nevertheless, choosing discretion over valor, the captain left his wagons and escort behind and continued on with two Mormons traveling to GSL City from the recently abandoned settlement on Deer Creek.

Sunday in Cedar City.

Readying the wagon for church, Emil told Miz Miller (he refused to call her Dinky) to stay home and, if anyone came into the yard, to go immediately to the house. That Verity was left behind to enforce the order was painfully obvious.

Sensing an impending clash of wills with Verity, Dinky tried hard to hold onto the spontaneity of the previous week. Fortunately, the hog farm received no company, and she and the children did not have to be shooed inside.

That night, Emil off to a church meeting, she tested her boundaries.

"Let's walk to the city tomorrow." Lightly as whipped egg whites.

"You shouldn't go there for awhile."

"Why?"

"Well…there could be hard feelings. What with your Army coming to wage a war of extermination against us."

"Verity, don't be silly. Of course they're not."

"And too, maybe I shouldn't say it, but that train you run away from? they stirred up a lot of bad feeling. Boasting the way they did about driving the Saints out of the States. They's murderers in among 'em, the ones killed Apostle Pratt. You probably didn't know that."

"No, I didn't know that," Dinky made no effort to hide her amusement, "but I doubt it, I didn't meet anyone…"

"…they carry the very pistol killed Joseph and his brother. Why, they even named their oxen 'Brigham' and 'Heber.' Wouldn't you think they'd of had more sense?"

Dinky's answering laughter angered the older woman.

"Ain't nothing to laugh about! Everywhere they gone they

caused trouble. Snapped heads off chickens, poisoned a spring and killed a bunch of cattle. Now you don't wanna go laughing about things like that, missy…"

"…Verity…"

"…times are hard down here…"

"…stop this garbage! This is all garbage. None of it's true. *I was there.* We couldn't buy food. We couldn't buy fresh stock. We had to throw trash out of the road so we could get by. Do you think we're crazy? that we'd add to our woes by riling up the very people who could help us? We offered good money, we even tried to trade livestock for food, nothing would work. What you're telling me is garbage. *It didn't happen!*"

"Bishop Haight says it did."

"I don't care what he says. He wasn't there and I'll tell him so, and anyone else who asks!"

The angry words turned Verity's face white. "No, you won't! Don't you dare! It would go hard with us, we'll be used up. We can't go against counsel." She started to shake. "Don't you dare do this to us after all we done for you. We took you in! Please!"

"Calm down, now calm down. I'm not about to get you in trouble. We're just here visiting from the States. We won't tell anyone how we got here, we just dropped out of the sky."

"You don't understand," Verity clutched at Dinky's wrist, "it's a sin to aid the enemy. We can't allow infidels to occupy our holy places."

"What enemy? What *are* you afraid of?"

"You're not supposed to be here. You don't have a pass."

"Nobody told us anything about a pass." Bewildered by the deep vein of fear she had tapped, Dinky softened her words to little more than a whisper. "Maybe God wants us here. Maybe you could tell yourself this was meant to be."

Verity covered her ears and squinched her eyes shut.

Afraid Verity might run outside, Dinky bowed her head,

fighting to control her irritation. While teaching in the wilds of Ohio, she'd met up with women driven gulchy by solitude and hard work. Met up with them, but never had to live with them. Verity opened her eyes. Dinky covered the older woman's cold, thin hands with her own and drew them down to the table. "We're good help, aren't we? even if we do eat you out of house and home." She tried to sound merry.

Verity hunched her shoulders, her eyes clinging to the younger woman's face. "Alright," she answered tumultuously. "You can go to town, just wait till everything's done."

"What's everything?"

"Your country will be broken to pieces, then it'll all calm down and we can live together in the Garden like the lion and the lamb."

"My country *is* your country, Verity. We're all in this together. I think I better not wait, don't you..." ever so lightly "...it could be quite awhile."

"Well..."

Watching the distraught woman fight off her demons, Dinky realized they had reached the wall. Either Verity took the jump, or she and the children remained prisoners. Or worse, got thrown out on their ear.

"Alright, you can be my sister." Verity breathed so deeply that her whole body shook. "But don't forget, *you can't tell no one you come with the Arkansas company!*"

"I won't, I promise."

What Verity told Emil, Dinky didn't know. The hog farmer was late coming in and left the next morning before breakfast. Morning chores done, women and children walked to Cedar City, Verity keeping pace in watchdog fashion.

Several storekeepers remarked on Dinky's being new in those parts. Dinky gave answer that she was Verity's sister.

Verity didn't say anything. But once more back home,

became almost giddy. In short order she and the twins were
rolling sugared pine pitch into snakes and cutting the snakes
into cough drops and telling stories.

My daughters are building my bridges, Dinky thought wryly,
watching the small fingers shaping the warm pitch. And remembered Mun. He was standing at the bed looking at the twins.
Little, red wiggly miracles. "These are the children who will look
after us in our old age?" he'd asked, drawing her head against his
shoulder, and they had laughed and laughed.

What a funny picture the memory made. And what a sharp,
deep pain.

F O R T Y - T H R E E

ONDAY MORNING in the meadows. A brisk wind sweeps the high grasses, awash in the smells of fresh coffee and toasted cornmeal. The strange actions of the Mormon fanatics seem far away and California very near.

Only Will is not sanguine. One minute he is bitterly regretting having left Editha Anne behind, the next minute looking fearfully about the pastoral countryside. He can't get Cedar City out of his head. He has never seen such moral confusion in a people as a whole. Nor felt such hatred in the masses. It was as if all the hostility met along the Corridor were condensed into a shiny drop of poison hanging over his head.

He holds his coffee mug under his face and tries to lose himself in the warm, rank odor. A big wolf trots into the open and pauses to look back. Keeping an eye on the startled wolf, Will fishes for the ground with his cup.

A shot rings out, a child topples over, a woman screams.

In the sudden barrage of gunfire, the emigrants struggle to shove the heavy wagons together. The bullets sound around them like angry bees. The marksmen are in the ravine below the sunken spring, and they are very good. In minutes, seven people are dead and 22 wounded. None of the half-dozen night horses are hit.

The wagon circle closes, the shooting stops, the only thing to

be heard are the screams. The sound does not trouble the
Indians, but some of the Mormon soldiers cover their ears.

A half hour goes by. A bullet finds a pickle crock, and pickles
slide out on the ground. A second bullet pings off an iron wheel.
The attack has shifted and comes now from behind the stones
along the crest of hill to the north. Frantically working to save
the wounded and throw up entrenchments, the emigrants
hunker closer to their bloodied patch of earth.

Anticipation keen, poisoned arrows readied along with war
attire, the Indians wait in their camps for word. Late Monday
morning that word comes.

Samuel Knight, a farmer from the Santa Clara, rode into the
Yannawant camp waving a paper and yelling excitedly. The
paper was signed by the White Governor and ordered Chief
Tutsegavit to go and help whip the emigrants.

Thirty miles to the east a messenger rode into Chief Jackson's
camp with a similar letter ordering the emigrants to be killed.
On the Virgin, Indian interpreter Huntington delivered the
same letter to a Pah-Ute chief named Touche.

Chief Tutsegavit and his Piedes were the first to arrive in
th meadows. The inside wheels of the wounded train had been
sunk into the earth, making the wagons look as if they had all
slid sideways into the same mud hole. Painted Mormons milled
about, whooping and yelling and shooting their guns.

One of the riders directed Chief Tutsegavit to a small spring
at the entrance to a canyon a mile and a quarter to the northwest where the Mormons were camped. The Indians built their
fires nearby, and the Mormons gave them guns and powder.

The Lower Virgin and Muddy tribes arrived, along with Chief
Ammon leading a large band of Piedes from the Beaver country.
In no time over 200 savages were riding around, hollering and
shooting their new guns.

Dancer did not participate, but observed with great interest the actions of the weapons that imitated the flash-and-noise water sacks of the sky.

The Mormons ordered the Indians to stop shooting at rocks and bushes. "Charge the wagons!" they ordered, prodding their red friends with loud scolding cries of "A-i-i-i! A-i-i-i!"

Chief Ammon ran dodging and screeching through the grasses on foot, carrying his new rifle within 200 yards of the corralled wagons. And got killed for his trouble. The Indians immediately lost interest in counting coup by courting Mericat guns. The guns were too long. The chiefs wanted to fire the wagons instead.

This stupidity made the Mormons furious, and they promised if anything burned, the sumbitch Injuns would be sent home empty-handed.

The following day, Tuesday, September 8, Brigham married Jacob Hamblin to 16-year-old Priscilla Leavitt, and Thales Haskell to Margaret Edwards, a young girl newly arrived from Wales who spoke no English. And again suggested that the newlyweds take their time returning to the south.

Captain Van Vliet arrived in the Valley. The lake was beautifully calm, like some huge piece of flattened silver. Beneath the blue sky, small silvery clouds rested like halos on the encircling mountain tops. The well-ordered streets, the deep greenery with its border of golden fields of grain, made the tranquillity almost palatable.

God has to have a hand in this, the captain told himself, *or it wouldn't be so perfect.*

Quartered in the residence of the Honorable W. H. Hooper, Mormon Secretary for Utah, the captain rested and reviewed his notes.

Brigham called that evening, accompanied by a large delegation of dignitaries. The meeting was exceedingly cordial. So rounded were Brigham's words, despite their dark recitation of past atrocities committed against the Saints, that his pronouncement on what would happen to the approaching Army—"the troops now on the march for Utah shall not enter the Great Salt Lake Valley"—sounded more like an invitation to the dance than to a war.

The lesser dignitaries were equally as affable—their chorus of ascent or descent as called for, equally as cheerful. Van Vliet felt as if he had entered another country, as if he were meeting with a titled head on the same footing as the American President himself.

Late that evening, taking a pipe alone in the Hooper yard, the captain was struck by the serenity and beauty of the Valley by starlight.

He would have been surprised to learn that under those same stars, approaching from the very direction in which he was looking, an express rider was barreling north with a letter from Commander Isaac C. Haight notifying Brigham of the destruction of Parley Pratt's murderers. Under orders to complete the 270-mile trip in 100 hours, James Haslam also carried orders from Commander Haight for fresh, fast horses as needed along the way.

Wednesday in the meadows.

The people who have been working under shelter of darkness to care for each other, return to their hiding places. Sunshine seeps into the camp and slides down into the trenches.

There are 118 people left alive. Fortunately, the emigrants collected water for cooking shortly before the siege began. They are good on staples for maybe another week. Good on ammunition. Good on meat, figuring a horse every two nights. There is plenty of fuel in the furniture, plenty of medicine.

These and other long, desperate thoughts fill the wagon captain's head. He tries not to think of the dead, buried one on top of another in a common grave, and prays instead for the living, most especially for the wounded. Directing his prayers toward the deep blue trough overhead. And praying thus, tries not to hear their cries of anguish.

He recalls the warnings sent by the Lord to Joseph, and asks the Lord's forgiveness in turning a deaf ear to the warnings he himself received. The memory of those unheeded warnings hammers at him. Still he has hope. He knows Indians. They will wear down. In the meantime, someone will come along the main road.

Concealed behind their stones on the hill, the snipers resume their fire. Not heavy, more like the intermittent fall of large hail-stones at the edge of a storm. In sight of the wagons, but well out of range, the Indians visit amongst themselves, congregating in little knots.

Repeatedly, angrily, the Mormons urge the savages to stop playing games and attack. But the Indians counsel patience. The Mericats are trapped like foxes on open ground with no water. The man who wears the eagle's feathers is the man who has patience.

This cowardice incenses the Mormons, and weary of the mess they have gotten themselves into, they argue violently with each other. Shoving breaks out, rifle shots are exchanged.

Such preening and bulling amongst the Moronies puzzles the Indians and makes them not a little nervous. Will the Moronies stop killing their own kind and start shooting the Indians?

And where are the promised animals? How many animals are there? Where are the animals? Over and over the Indians ask where the animals are. Over and over their painted friends answer that the stock is penned in the missionary's corrals.

The sun shifts away, up the dirt walls. With help from her two older sons, Hampton and William, Eliza Fancher works to move her husband to the other side of the trench where he can have the light awhile longer. Alex can feel the bullets grind in his shoulder and pelvis, and grits his teeth.

"You're gonna have to dig new latrines," he tells the boys. "Make 'em deep enough we can throw dirt on 'em and keep usin' 'em."

At 9 a.m. sharp this same morning, Captain Van Vliet met with Governor Young a second time—a business meeting in the Social Hall. A U.S. Military Academy graduate and ten years a captain, Van Vliet knew how to handle men with little formal education. He was exceedingly careful not to rub salt in the Mormon leader's face. Nevertheless, push had now come to shove.

"It is my duty to inform you that Utah is now a Military Department. Troops numbering 2,500 are on their way here to take up suitable position. The United States Government requests assistance in securing the necessary supplies of grain and other articles of forage and subsistence. From 50,000 to 75,000 bushels of oats, corn or barley; 1,000 tons of hay; some 150,000 to 200,000 feet of assorted lumber. All articles to be purchased on the open market at fair market prices.

"In addition, the Government wishes to purchase 50 cords of dry wood to be taken up by the Army wagons as they pass through the city to the site of the new camp, a site which the Government will welcome the guidance of the Mormons in choosing."

Having thus gently, but firmly, stated his mission, the captain made the official presentation of the letter addressed to "President Brigham Young, of the Society of the Mormons," and signed "Wm S. Harney, Colonel, 2nd Dragoons, & Brt. Brig Genl, Commanding."

Brigham accepted the missive gravely, securing it in his coat pocket unread. Nevertheless, Van Vliet couldn't help but notice that there was something of the farm animal way back in the secretive grayish-blue eyes.

The meeting in the Social Hall was followed by a tour of Brigham's private orchard, vineyard, and garden. A second tour visited the barnyard and numerous sheds crammed full with carriages and farm implements.

The power of the Mormon church as manifested in its leader was not lost on the captain, who made dutiful note to that effect in his ledger.

Shrouded by descending twilight, three of the caged emigrants flee the meadows in a desperate bid for help. One, hunched over the back of a big horse running flat out, passes near Dancer.

You are a brave man, Dancer tells the drum of hooves, *what do you ask as you ride for your life?*

The rifle tied to Will's saddle is loaded, as is the heavy revolver tied to his waist. These are not his weapons. His own small pistol is in his coat pocket. Clinging like a burr, he breathes a prayer as Peter Huff's black gelding bunches and stretches beneath him.

> *My poor darling, I leave this desperate hell on earth*
> *where death waits as surely as it waited in Babylon for*
> *Alexander. But not to fly to your arms, my dearest.*

*I who am not a soldier am now entrusted with the
soldier's most sacred duty. Pray there is a wagon train
close behind us. If not, pray that in Cedar City there is
at least one brave man who will spread the alarm and
raise the siege. My dear maid of Athens, I leave behind
me a place of death and horror such as you have never
seen. If I die out here, at least I will die a free man.
Remember me.*

◈

Thursday morning in Salt Lake City.

Having expressed a desire to see the domestic workings of
what he called the governor's "peculiar institution," the captain
was accommodated with a tour that revealed the finishing and
furnishing of Brigham's Beehive and Lion mansions from garret
to cellar. Numerous of the great one's wives and children were
introduced.

The lavish displays of splendor, the multitude of well-dressed
wives and servants, the fine multi-storied buildings, served well
to underscore that the only thing separating this Prophet from a
Moroccan Sultan was the geography.

Afternoon plans called for Secretary Hooper and Territorial
Surveyor General J. W. Fox to accompany Brigham and their
American guest to the potential site for the new American mili-
tary reservation in Rush Valley. As the entourage passed the
church buildings, cloistered behind their walls, a clerk ran up to
Brigham's carriage with a note.

"I'm afraid I'll have to cancel," Brigham said and gestured
offhand toward the horse tied at the railing—a white brute
blackened with sweat-streaked dirt.

Long accustomed to the priority held by messengers, Van
Vliet accepted his host's apologies without a second thought.

In his office, Brigham questioned James in a low voice. *Everything.* He needed to know *everything.*

James was dog tired. The attack started Monday, there was a lot of shooting, the Indians were there. The boy's words were almost incoherent. A clerk brought sliced beef on bread and a glass of buttermilk.

"Go ahead and eat," Brigham said and added conversationally, "Right now I'm being entertained by the Government's representative. As soon our good captain leaves, we'll shut the door behind him. With a bang!"

James munched away obediently and began to doze off.

"Rest, my boy. You've earned it. There's no hurry. I've ordered a fresh horse and saddle bags well packed with food, but you can take your time returning. If the fighting started Monday morning, it's already over. I told the American Army I will not hold the Indian's wrist. Now they'll see what I mean."

"They won't fight," James whispered, more asleep than awake.

"What?!"

"The Indians, they ain't doin' nothin'."

"THEY'VE GOT TO FIGHT! THE LORD WILL NOT BE MOCKED!"

James jerked and dropped the glass of buttermilk on the floor.

Brigham slammed the desk with his fist and shouted, "You tell our boys the Territory is CLOSED! Those wagons aren't going anywhere!"

At that very second, someone turned the knob on the outside door.

Grabbing James by the shoulder, Brigham jerked the exhausted messenger from his chair.

Hamilton Gray Park was on the porch. The employee saw the door flung open and, hopping aside, saw a man dressed for a long ride stumble with weariness through the doorway. A greatly troubled President followed close behind, his face suffused with worry.

And this is what Hamilton Gray Park heard.

"Brother Haslem, I want you to ride for dear life, ride day and night, spare no horse flesh. That company must be protected if it takes L.D. Saints in Iron County to do it."

"Company?" James was confused.

Hamilton followed the two men out through the gate to the plank walk where a fresh horse stood at the railing, and heard Brigham say again, loudly and with much feeling, "Brother Haslam, I charge you to ride for dear life, ride day and night. That company must be protected from the Indians if it takes every L.D. Saint in Iron County to do it."

As the sound of flying hooves faded down South Temple Street, the President turned on Hamilton. "Go inside and write down everything you heard and saw."

Brother Park did as ordered, sitting at one of the President's desks and writing everything out on a ZCMI order blank. Stopping often to ask how to spell a word.

Brigham grimaced to read the finished sheet—Brother Park could hardly write—and handed the paper back. After receiving instruction in the addition of a few more lines, the employee was sent off on a fool's errand. Alone in the office, Brigham drew out a clean sheet of writing paper.

President's Office
Great Salt Lake City

Sept. 10, 1857
Elder Isaac C. Haight:
   Dear Brother, your note of the 7th inst. is to hand. Capt. Van Vliet, Acting Commissary, is here, having come in advance of the army to procure necessaries for them...They cannot get here this season without we help them. So you see that the Lord has answered our prayers and again

averted the blow designed for our heads. In regard to the
emigration trains passing through our settlements, we must
not interfere with them until they are first notified to keep
away. You must not meddle with them. The Indians we
expect will do as they please but you should try and preserve
good feelings with them…

All is well with us. May the Lord bless you and all the
Saints forever.

Your Brother in the gospel of Christ.

Placing this letter with the witness by Hamilton, Brigham
locked both papers away. Only then did he allow himself to
relax, scratching his ear and his arm—the bugs were terrible this
time of year, all that water. And every bit of it controlled by the
church. The thought caused the Prophet to smile.

The Americans would come around, they had no choice.
In the meantime, closing the Territory would give the faithful
something to chew on. As for the Paiute and the Piede, they
would pay for their betrayal. Down through all the centuries
they would pay dearly.

At this same hour, Mormon sharpshooters bring down the last of
the horses remaining in the Fancher camp.

The emigrants draw up a paper addressed to all good people
everywhere, including the Masons, Odd Fellows, Baptists and
Methodists of the States, asking for their help, and if time ran
out, for their justice. Every man, woman, and child signs the
plea. That night three more men leave on foot, bound for
California.

FORTY-FOUR

DAWN, FRIDAY.

From the wounded camp comes the sound of music. "The Lord My Shepherd Is." "Abide with Me." "Nearer My God to Thee." "Father, How Long?" Women and children's voices rising above the heavier timbre of the men's.

"They're singing their death song," Chief Tutsegavit tells Dancer.

An Indian whoops, a rifle sounds. The cool, clear air begins to be fouled with gun powder. The singing goes on awhile longer and fades away.

Day five in the meadows.

Far to the north, taking his usual early-morning stroll, woolen overcoat open over a grey homespun suit, Brigham saw that the mountain tops were white with snow. Burning bitter brush and mahogany bushes speckled the lower slopes. All about him beneath the picture-perfect heights was the picture-perfect town. The realization that he and he alone was responsible for its existence lifted the Prophet's chin and lightened his step.

⬧

In Tutsegavit's camp the Piedes were leisurely preparing for
another day of white-man watching when Jacob Hamblin
arrived. Having crossed paths with James Haslam below Provot
and learned of the diggers' betrayal, the missionary left his new
bride in the care of Thales and hurried south. He was not
painted, but wore clothing which, because of its unusual green
color, Dancer decided must have magic powers.

Jacob did not smoke the pipe, he did not even get down off
his horse. Consumed with a scorching rage, he called the Indians
cowards, women afraid of their shadow. *They were all going to
burn in hell for disobeying the Great Spirit!! Nothing would be
given them if they did not do as ordered. RIGHT NOW! THEY
MUST DO SOMETHING RIGHT NOW!*

The miles of trail dust had dried out his throat. When he
yelled, it was like seed pods rattling. His glance fell on the
Kaibab runner, and Dancer wrinkled his nose and spit on the
ground.

A young warrior, tired of being called a coward, rode out from
the trees shooting, and got shot from his horse. No more Indians
rode out, it didn't matter what the missionary called them.

Three baggage wagons attended by a large group of riders
arrived at the Moronies' camp. In the meeting that followed,
Dancer counted over 50 white men. First the men formed a
hollow square and listened to speeches from their leaders. Next
they got down on their knees and bowed their heads to hold
hands and listen to yet another speech.

That done, the Moronie leaders met with the Indian leaders
and afterward marched their soldiers off double-file toward the
meadows. Realizing there was at last to be a fight, Dancer followed Chief Tutsegavit to the crest of hill north of the wagons,

where Moronie snipers had earlier positioned themselves. The snipers were gone, replaced by a large number of Indians.

The Moronie soldiers stopped in full view of the wagons and made a show of holding up their guns. Now two men Dancer recognized as Indian farmer Lee and the man called Haight, faces scrubbed free of paint, were walking across the open grasses waving a white flag. The Mericat men stepped free of their wagons and stood tall, rifles at the ready, and a little girl dressed in white walked out from the corral. Reaching the flag bearers, the child returned with them to the corral.

"The Moronies are pretending to be friends," Chief Tutsegavit said, watching the flag bearers talk with the Mericats outside the encircled wagons. "They speak things that aren't true. They'll tell the Mericats all we want is the wagons." He smiled sagely. "What we'll do with wagons, I don't know. I think the Moronies want the wagons."

Indian farmer Lee disappeared inside the wagon circle.

Dancer looked around the meadow. Not an Indian was to be seen.

"We can't show ourselves until the time comes," Tutsegavit explained.

At last, Haight walked back to the trees alone, and Dancer decided the Mericats would not let the Indian farmer go. The afternoon shadows were long, and many of the Indians, including Chief Tutsegavit, were sound asleep in the deep grass when two baggage wagons came out of the trees.

Dancer woke Tutsegavit, who, seeing the wagons enter the corral, nodded in self-agreement. One of the wagons reappeared and headed for the trees. "All the guns are in that wagon," Tutsegavit said. "Now they can't shoot."

"Will we attack now?" Dancer asked.

"No." Tutsegavit grinned. "Not until the little colored snake they've let into their blankets strikes."

Now the second baggage wagon was leaving the emigrant corral and returning to the trees. Dancer knew the driver of this second wagon for Samuel Knight, the messenger who had ordered the Piedes to the meadows.

Tutsegavit nodded again. "The crippled Mericats are in this wagon. They will all die. All little children no older than seven summers are here too. They will live. If they are eight summers," the Piede chief made a sideways motion with his forefinger, "they aren't here. The Moronies don't want them." He shook his head, confused by the logic.

Now the women were coming out, sheltering the older children with an arm across the shoulders. The Moronie who led the women toward the trees walked very fast, and so the women and children walked fast too, looking around fearfully like a band of sheep, the breezes stirring their clothing and hair. It occurred to Dancer that they were looking for Indians.

"The Moronies want the Indian to kill them." The chief pointed at the group and sighed audibly. "I don't think I'll do this."

The women and older children were in the middle of the open meadow beyond the shelter of their circled wagons. The Mormon baggage wagon carrying the young children and the wounded was several hundred yards from the trees.

Now Moronies were hurrying out of those trees on foot. They gathered at the corral of wagons, and the Mericats came out— one at a time, empty-handed.

Chief Tutsegavit made a tsk-tsk-tsk sound. Here was the heart of the matter. With the bulls coming out, the slaughter would begin.

As each Mericat man came into the open, a Moronie holding a rifle stepped forward to walk beside him, as if to protect him.

Dancer glanced at Tutsegavit, but the chief, intent on what he was seeing, was silent.

Side-by-side the two columns moved out on the grasses, and Chief Kanosh could hear the Mericats thanking the Moronies for saving them. How glad they were. How thankful. Kanosh thought this very funny and told the warriors nearby who told others, the little story bringing amusement to all who heard it.

"The Moronies walking with the Mericats have paint on their faces," Dancer observed, surprised. "Why do Mericats trust them?"

"They're under the spell of Moronies' god," Tutsegavit explained. "But he doesn't protect us. Don't go where you can get shot, I have no one to send to Chief Naraguts in your place."

The double row of men had marched about a quarter of a mile, when a Mormon hiding in the bushes stood up, surrounded by a dozen Indians.

"HALT!!" the Mormon yelled. "DO YOUR DUTY!" he yelled.

Swinging around, each Mormon soldier fired point-blank at the unarmed man standing nearest him, a distance of about 20 feet. The volley triggered a hideous beseeching and moaning, which in turn released from the little hills overlooking the meadows a swarm of Indians whose whooping and yelling added to the frightful howls of betrayal and agony.

The baggage wagon had not yet reached the trees. Stray bullets ripped through the canvas. A large ball struck three-year-old Louisa Dunlap below the elbow, breaking both bones and cutting the little girl's arm in half. Two other children were similarly mangled.

An older boy crying "Pa! Pa! Pa!" ran toward the wagon and managed to grab hold of the box. Samuel clubbed the boy over the head, almost hitting Chief Kanosh, who, jumping up on the seat, ripped open the canvas flap and screeched at the terrified passengers.

A Moronie hoisted himself on the back step of the wagon

and tore open the back canvas flap. "Lord, my God," the soldier cried, "receive their spirits, it is for thy Kingdom that I do this." Poking his rifle against the huddle of wounded men, he killed two emigrants with one shot.

Kanosh raised his fist in a salute to the Moronie, even as the soldier, turning away, vomited over himself.

A large woman, calling frantically, ran heavily into the melee, and a Moronie shot her in the back.

Dancer had never in his life seen such a big fight. The frenzy reminded him of red ants swarming over a dung beetle, trying to drag itself away.

Looking about, he spied dark horsemen waiting as he himself had waited on foot, many times, at the edge of a rabbit hunt. But instead of clubs, these executioners used rifles, picking off the Mericats being helped toward the trees by their women. The terrified little knots made easy targets. The children, squealing and dodging like rabbits, offered more of a challenge.

Dancer saw Jacob Hamblin's half-Indian son lead two white girls into a ravine and, shortly afterward, come out of the ravine alone. Expecting to find the girls tied up, Dancer worked his way through the brush, determined to let them go. But the poor little sparrows had their throats cut.

Long ago, Spanish slavers, wandering through the Southwest, stole women and children from the Paiute and the Piede. Hard on the heels of the Spanish came the Utes and Mexicans, also searching for slaves, primarily young girls. For this reason, less than one-half the children born to the river and plateau tribes grew up in their own band. For this reason also, there were not enough women to go around. Such was the history of his people as Dancer knew it. To waste even one woman or child was incomprehensible to the Kaibab runner. His most sacred prayer was for a wife and child.

Filled with sorrow, Dancer straightened the little sparrows and, taking a handful of dirt, sprinkled it over them, commending their spirits to the one who made them.

Out on the bloody meadow grasses, the Indians were balking at killing women and children. One Indian, told to kill two girls who looked alike, spoke of much evil coming from such foolishness. As a result, the Moronies shot the twins.

A third baggage wagon was brought into the meadows, and soldiers began transferring the children from the wagon bearing the wounded to this wagon. The crazed children kicked and screamed, and the soldiers grew as hysterical as their prizes.

Get 'em outta here!" they yelled at each other. "COVER THEIR HEADS AN' GET 'EM OUTTA HERE!" Running wild-eyed, banging into one another as they ran, the soldiers chased the children down and carried them to the third wagon. Some of the youngsters escaped and had to be caught again, so soldiers sat inside the wagon while other soldiers brought ropes. Eventually this third wagon, filled with shrieks, rolled off to the Hamblin ranch.

In the meantime, soldiers stalking the groans and pleadings of the wounded shot every emigrant with a spark of life.

The killing fields grew silent. It seemed to Dancer that the gunfire had gone on a long time, but it wasn't even dark yet.

The dead were quickly stripped naked and their clothing thrown in piles. The shoelaces of their shoes were tied together and the shoes also thrown into piles. The baggage wagon carrying the emigrant guns was brought back, and shoes and clothing thrown on top of the weapons.

Once more, the soldiers gathered before their leaders. Chief Kanosh, easing close, reported overhearing that the Moronies' god was very pleased and would make the Moronies rich and happy.

The Indians started looting the wagons, putting an abrupt end to Moronie prayers of thanksgiving. A soldier ordered the Indians back to their camp and promised there would be beef for their supper.

Another soldier, fearing that the emigrants who had earlier escaped would return with help, countermanded the order. "Stay here and shoot anyone who does not identify himself as Moronie."

"This we do, we are battle axe of Lord!" Chief Kanosh agreed in English and happily fired a hole in a wagon box.

A fresh argument broke out between those soldiers wanting the Indians to stay, and those wanting the Indians to return to their camp. The soldiers looked around for Jacob Hamblin to settle the issue, but the missionary was gone. As were all the Moronie leaders. It was almost dark. Finally, someone got hold of the situation. The Indians could stay and guard the meadows, but *could not go inside the wagons!* The wagons belonged to the Moronies. If the Indians wanted to scalp the Mericats, that was alright.

Leaving three soldiers behind to guard the emigrant wagons from the dirty red thieves, the remainder of the Moronies rode quickly away with their loaded baggage wagon.

As soon as their friends were out of sight, the Moronie guards ran and hid.

The first thing the Indians did was to build a fire in the center of the wagon corral. Squirreled away in the rocks, the frightened guards shook with fury, thinking the stupid diggers planned to burn the wagons.

But the Indians didn't want to burn the wagons, they wanted to dance. Searching for something to wear, they hacked away at the canvases and threw out all manner of curious things that, smashing and tinkling, made a wonderful lot of noise. Once sat-

isfied, they began to dance. A clever fellow ripped open a pillow
and danced in the scatter of feathers, and soon everyone was
dancing in a scatter of feathers.

The celebrants did not, however, trifle with the naked bodies.
Indifferent to the horror of the scene, they were not indifferent
to the fierce, low cry of wind through the woods ringing the
meadows. These spirits they did not wish to anger further.

The wagon that had carried the wounded and little children
away from the corral, its traces now empty, sat off alone under a
silent ocean of stars. Using a burning pitch knot to survey the
interior, the Indians realized the Moronies had overlooked stripping these bodies, and helped themselves to the blood-soaked
blankets and several small sacks of gold coins.

Returning to the fire, they piled the blankets high with sugar
and molasses sacks and tins of honey. They then tied the
unwieldy packs on their ponies, secured the bright coins in their
weapon cases, and rode off to the spring at the canyon entrance.

The Moronie campground was empty of tents. As promised,
six drawn beeves lay on the Indian campground. The tame meat
was tough and tasteless, but the diners didn't care. The sweet
food unrolled from the new blankets made it a feast.

Captain Van Vliet returned from Rush Valley.

Except for being close to fine wood, the site was entirely
unsuitable for a military encampment, containing as it did little
grass and being much exposed to the cold winds of winter. In
addition, the distance from the city, between 40 and 45 miles,
would require teams four days to go there and return.

That evening in the Globe, the captain partook of a sumptu-
ous supper attended by the usual phalanx of dignitaries. After

supper, Brigham spoke of the apocalyptic landscape that existed in the Valley before the Saints' arrival.

In reply, the captain expressed warm gratitude for his former and present acquaintance and associations with the Saints. He closed his remarks with, "My prayer should ever be that the Angel of Peace should extend his wings over Utah."

The scythe face of the moon rises over Jacob Hamblin's home, where 20 newly orphaned children cling to each other. Over the large pile of clothing and shoes in the corral. Over the pole barn where heaps of jewelry and coins glow dully in the light of a candle guttering on a tin plate.

Over the Indian camp where warriors with full bellies rest.

Over the meadows where idle wagons creak gently in the wind, lanterns unlit as they have been for the past four nights. Over the cold reach of empty arms.

Slow but steady the new moon rises, holding the old moon in her arms.

Wild animals pause uneasily and trot on by. The breezes sigh. The night birds cry.

FORTY-FIVE

IN THE FARMHOUSE where the survivors of the Siege of
Sevastopol have been taken, the white-faced children are
stripped of their stained clothing and washed, two at a time,
in the tin tub by the front room stove. The water grows redder
and redder, but is not replaced. There is not that much hot water,
or time. And there are so many children.

Clean and dressed in cast-offs, the children sit on blankets
on the dirt floor. They can hear the leaders of the massacre, put
in high spirits by the business in the barn, gather in the kitchen.
The children don't understand the laughter, and wonder if
somehow they have misunderstood what's happening.

The kitchen door opens and a man speaks with the women
in the room. The door closes. One of the missionary's wives get
a child to its feet and leads it by the hand into the kitchen. The
child, returns, and another is led in.

In the kitchen the smell of cedar burning in the stove mingles
pleasantly with the smell of warm spice cake. The waiting men are
lacing their coffee with clots of cream spooned from a bowl in the
middle of the plank table. The table is scattered with cake crumbs.
One by one, white-faced and exhausted, those children who are
old enough to talk answer their interrogators in soft whimpers,
gladly sharing shards of memory. Sometimes they eye the crumbs.
One of the men pushes a raisin across the table with his fork at a
little towheaded boy, who, after some hesitation, eats it.

Waiting her turn, seven-year-old Rebeccah Dunlap realizes something amiss. Those children who talk a great deal do not return to the front room. Instead, there is the further sound of a door opening and closing, and then the next child is sent for. Fearing for her younger sisters, Rebeccah warns all the children yet to be questioned to be quiet when they get in the kitchen, or they will not be able to come back to the front room.

Rebeccah's turn comes. Does she remember what the white man said who came into the Fancher camp before the attack? Did she see who killed her father? her mother? Did she see any white men shoot at the emigrants? Does she remember anything about seeing anyone hide papers or money or anything at all anywhere around the wagons?

Straight Rebeccah sits in the wooden chair. And doesn't remember a thing.

Not even, Jacob prompts her, running up to him and begging him to save her and her sisters?

Yes, she remembers that. But nothing else. She says not a word about seeing anyone die out in the meadow. Not a word about the Indian boy at that very minute saucering his coffee across the table from her—the same boy she saw lead the two Baker sisters into the ravine. Those sisters never came back either.

Her eyes fasten on the back door. That must be the door that is opening and closing. Where are the children who have been taken out that door? She begins to shake like a dog that's been kicked.

"She's in shock," someone says and yells for a blanket.

"Is there anything you want to tell us?" Jacob asks kindly. Rebeccah shakes her head, and says not one word about how earlier, while being bathed, she saw, through the partially open kitchen door, men standing over the sink washing paint off their faces.

FORTY-SIX

THE NEXT MORNING, pausing often to work his pipe, Chief Tutsegavit gave Dancer the message for Chief Naraguts.

"It is true that no foreigners live beside the Parouse River, but their travels back and forth have burdened our land. As many as 5,000 animals feed and water on the pastures in one time of grass to the next. The tribes who live along the Muddy, the Parouse, and the Santa Clara now grow hungry on their once-good lands. The beaver and the ancient cottonwoods are gone and the mountains grow bald. Far to the north where the foreigners build their villages are more white men than any one Indian can stand before and talk to. All the People working together can't stop so many white men.

"The poor Indian is become like the noisy-winged-one on the back of the horse. The horse goes where it wishes. The noisy-winged-one can not stop the horse. It must balance on its perch as best it can, hope the horse will drop dead."

Tutsegavit gestured toward the new blankets, stiff with dried blood, that littered the ground. "The Moronies and the Mericats are twigs off the same tree. They carry the same things about. If they fight each other, they won't fight us. Tell your chief that. Tell him to hold hands with the Moronies if he wishes to sleep in peace."

The Indians returned to the massacre site and carried off all manner of prizes. Tutsegavit gave Dancer a tin box for Chief Naraguts and a silk-lined canvas bag with leather straps that the Kaibab runner could keep for himself.

Riding close-bunched and quiet, expecting the land to shudder and roar and split apart under their feet, Mormon soldiers entered the meadows. When they saw the wagon loads upchucked and the Indians helping themselves, they thought the guards dead. But then the guards came out of hiding and told of having to flee for their lives. And emboldened by the presence of the soldiers, waved their rifles menacingly and yelled at the thieves, "Go bring back what you took away, you dirty thieves." But without Jacob Hamblin and Indian farmer Lee, nothing could be done to make the heathens retrieve their caches.

The Mormons went to work pitching the litter of goods back into the tilted wagons and trying to ignore the carnage.

"Let's go home like men," cried a badly shaken soldier, encountering a dead man looking up at him. "Not like scavengers of the dead."

"God sent us these things," argued another. "Times are hard." Spying a doll with a porcelain face, the soldier secured the doll in his coat pocket.

The corral was policed and the bloodied grasses along the walk of the dead combed. Using shovels and grub axes recruited from the wagons, the white men enlarged the rifle pits earlier dug by the desperate emigrants. And opened a new pit in a steep box wash a quarter-mile distant. Chipping away at the hard dirt, they didn't move or make noise as warriors who had dispatched an enemy, but snapped at each other as camp dogs.

The Indians collected themselves in the shade. The sun stalled overhead. A soldier approached and made a show of weighting a paper with a rock. His loud words and wild gestures told the Indians to search for other papers and promised a horse for any paper found.

The task didn't look very interesting to the Indians, who had yet to see any of the horses already promised.

Another soldier approached and, in much the fashion as the previous soldier, ordered, "Go and drag the bodies out of the brush and deep grass."

Again the Indians declined.

Using their own horses, the Mormons then made of themselves a macabre parade of mummers dragging toppled statues—men to the corral and women and children to the box wash.

"Why do that?" Kanosh asked. "They do not care who they lie down with."

Stupid Indian.

The common pits inside the corral hadn't been enlarged enough. Neither had the box wash pit. The bodies, startling white in the sun, began to pile up. Attacking the earth as if fighting with it, the soldiers renewed their digging. They became red of face and short of breath.

A horseman rode up on the nightmarish scene. "Gather at the spring as soon as you're done," he ordered briskly, seemingly oblivious to what he was seeing, and hurried away with a handkerchief over his nose. No sooner was their savior out of sight, than the grave diggers threw down their shovels and dragged the unburied emigrants back into the brush. And they, too, hurried away.

While waiting at the spring, Mormon leaders cleared an area of undergrowth and there outlined a small square of earth with rocks. The grave diggers showed up, and well-scrubbed, wet hair plastered down, formed a circle around the square. Their leaders stood inside the square— each leader facing a different direction.

Bishop Haight entered the square and, standing in the center, raised his arms. A mantle of sacredness descended, shielding the bishop's listeners from the witches' cauldron brewing in the further meadows.

"You are privileged to…keep your covenant to avenge the blood of the Prophets…Before God…you are never to speak of what happened here…not to each other…and not to anyone else save Brigham Young himself…never!..never!"

That he might prod the eyes of each of the soldiers, the bishop pivoted slowly on his heel as he intoned the sacred orders. "Each man…will place his left hand…on the shoulder of the man nearest…and raise his right hand…to the square…and repeat after me…"

He lost his balance, righted himself, and continued his pivot, his voice growing harsh. "…Any Saint…failing to keep this pledge…will suffer his life to be taken…everything done here… was done in the name of God…and for His glory…Amen."

Sanctified, the Mormons removed to the meadows and, in a sudden whirlwind of activity, harvested the last of their ill-got gains. Oxen earlier run off were brought back and put under the yoke. The Arkansas wagons were pulled out of their makeshift corral formation, and the half-dozen or so buggies that were scattered about were refastened to the wagon rings.

"Where are our horses?" asked the Indians. "What have you done with our horses?" The Mormons ignored their loathsome bedfellows as long as possible, but then an Indian grabbed a bridle, and missionary Hamblin was forced to intervene.

Calling the chiefs together, Jacob pointed at the thin, unused cattle bunched off to one side. "You can only have the cattle. Because you have proved to be so low and cowardly, you can not have any horses."

The broken promise made the chiefs see red.

"White Governor promised Indian all the cattle of this camp and one coming," Kanosh argued loudly in his best English. "And you promised half the horses. White Governor speaks it is good to steal from Mericats. From now Indian will take all Mericat horses and cattle and will not need help."

Crossing his arms against his chest, the chief from the Nephi region commenced strutting back and forth like a prairie cock. "Moronies are cowards for shooting women and children. We no longer wish to be friends with Moronies."

Jacob clenched his jaws. He knew—he'd always known—it didn't work to put savages and militia together. But it wasn't his place to change that. "You do not understand my words." The missionary pointed at the unused cattle. "They are all yours. Come with me to the ranch, we will make a fair division of the horses."

In the midst of the confusion, Dancer ran down a paper blowing in the wind. He was studying on the designs when a Mormon grabbed the paper away, but said nothing about a horse.

Eight days after reaching the meadows, the wagons of the Fancher party trundled out as they had come. Behind the wagons rode the Iron Military District—majors, field and staff officers, troops. Sour-faced men, heads down.

Behind the soldiers came the Indians. Heads high, new clothing rustling. The necks of the Indian ponies displayed all kinds of belts. Flour sifters and musical instruments hung from their saddles.

But the real parade rode south—those warriors who, after everyone else was gone, retrieved their valuable caches and started their loose cattle home—grotesque apparitions laden with goods and dragging long strings of banging, clanging buckets and kettles.

The Kaibab runner was not with either party, having slipped away to the east when the missionary and his murderous half-breed son were not looking.

◈

On this same day Brigham gave Captain Van Vliet the answer for General Harney. The articles of food required by the American Government could at present be procured. However, due to the lateness of the season, among other things, the continuing availability of the food was "too difficult of solution to admit of being determined from the information at present before me…" As for the wood requested, it was available.

◈

Early evening in the holy city.

The lowering sun, peering beneath a lid of black-bellied clouds, gilds the windows of the Heber Kimball home. The yard is full of buggy teams. In the dining room, the luminous-ink scrolls on the nile-green wallpaper gleam like pewter. The long banquette table is spread with white linen, the glasses are spotless, as are the silver appointments.

Dinner is called. Leeks and tomato salad are served, followed by steak *au poivre*, roast chicken, calf's liver, and trout dressed with lime vinegar. Boys in black suits and girls in white starched dresses station themselves along the walls to replace the empty platters and refill the glasses and cups.

The usual round of dignitaries is here, accompanied by lovely women wearing gowns of faille, velvet, and satin. And although each man has only one wife with him, Captain Van Vliet is quite certain that each, like Brigham, also has other wives at home.

These must be the youngest, the captain reflected. *I am seated at a table with withered white-haired men whose religion allows them to marry young women in addition to the aged females they have at home. No wonder they'll go to war to keep Brigham in charge.*

Indeed, it was the women, floating in small seas of color—
apricot, pear-gray, champagne-pink, ice-blue, deep, rich brown—
who gave the dinner its soul. Low necklines reminiscent of
European courts, long hair piled and braided as in France. And
none was more beautiful, in fact the most beautiful woman the
captain had seen since leaving the States, than the woman
seated diagonally from him.

In the candlelight, her loosely piled hair shone like burnished
mahogany, her pale apricot dress, décolletage free of decoration,
was eye-catching to say the least. Her eyes were a magnificent,
dark green. She was older than the others. But where the others
resembled butterflies fixed on pins, there was an awareness in her
expression.

She is seeing the room as I see it, the captain realized, to his
surprise. *And she's seated with the bishop introduced as Harris.
That's interesting. He's always seemed a little uncomfortable in
the meetings, and now here he is with a woman who also seems
different.*

The captain finished his *gigot,* served with white and green
beans, and waved off another helping of steak. Making table
conversation, he became aware that Mrs. Harris was taking an
inordinate interest in what he had to say, and wished she'd
express herself.

The table was cleared and refilled with dishes of lemon tarts,
creme caramels and various fruit cobblers. Each of the men was
given a small glass of amber wine. Brigham rose to speak, waxing
eloquent about the beauty of the Valley, and lamenting,

> ...for the government to array the army against us, is too
> despicable and damnable a thing for any honorable nation
> to do; and God will hold them in derision who do it. The
> United States are sending their armies here to simply hold
> us still until a mob can come and butcher us, as has been
> done before.

Across the table from the captain, Bishop Harris was nodding in agreement with every point the President raised his voice to make.

I'd like to know what you are really thinking, sir. Van Vliet observed silently, and glanced at Mrs. Harris, whose face held a lovely Mona Lisa smile. *And you, my pretty lady, what are you thinking?*

Keeping his own face solemn, Van Vliet allowed himself to relax. That the church, with all its poor-cow lamentations, still kept faith with the sanity of superfluous civilization convinced him that for all their posturing, the Saints had no real intention of going to war.

> Our detractors are liars, bigots, and mercenary politicians of the most corrupt stamp. I and my innocent followers are being defamed and persecuted for their religion's sake. I have broken no law, and under the present state of affairs, I will not suffer myself to be taken by any United States officer, to be killed as they killed Joseph!

Brigham slammed the table with the palm of his hand, catching the girl pouring the wine off-guard and causing her to spill a portion of the pitcher's contents on the table, the dark red stain spreading under the President's plate.

> We are condemned unheard, and forced to an issue with an armed mercenary mob which has been sent against us at the instigation of hireling priests and howling editors who prostitute the truth for filthy lucre's sake!

Groaning inwardly, would the man never relax? Van Vliet repeated what he had earlier made clear in the Social Hall. "It is not the intention of the Government to arrest you, sir, but merely to install a new governor in the Territory."

There. Let him swallow that.

The captain's glance fell again on Mrs. Harris. Who winked at him.

FORTY-SEVEN

SUNDAY FORENOON SERVICE in the Bowery. The large, open-air building, roughly 140 feet wide by 160 feet long, was packed with worshippers. Their deafening songs leapt out at the American sitting with The Twelve on the stand. The President's opening remarks as regards the foreigner in their midst:

> Captain Van Vliet visited us in Winter Quarters…he has always been found to be free and frank, and to be a man that wishes to do right…I understand that he has much influence in the army, through his kind treatment to the soldiers.

were followed by an altogether different assessment of that army's motives.

> …they are organizing their forces to come here, and protect infernal scamps, who are anxious to come and kill whom they please, destroy whom they please, and finally exterminate us.

Seated in the front row of the congregation, George wondered—did the young captain think it an honor to sit up so high with the rulers of the Kingdom? or was the square-faced Dutchman savvy enough to realize he sat there as Brigham's trophy?

At 6 a.m. sharp Monday, September 15, Captain Van Vliet
and Dr. John M. Bernhisel, Utah's delegate to Congress, left
GSL City in a church carriage escorted by Brothers Rockwell,
Jones and Taylor, The next day, acting in his capacity as
Governor of the People of the United States in the Territory of
Utah, Brigham closed the Territory.

> ...Martial law is hereby declared to exist in this Territory
> from and after the publication of this proclamation, and no
> person shall be allowed to pass or repass into or through or
> from the Territory without a permit from the proper
> officer...

Two days later, in the contractors' camp on Ham's Fork,
Porter saluted John Bernhisel one last time, leveled a sneer in
the Gentile's direction, and sawed his horse away. Inwardly
seething, Captain Van Vliet's features remained impassive. His
one chance to save face was to act as if traveling with the Utah
delegate had been his idea.

That evening over supper, the captain was briefed by his
sergeant, who reported conditions quiet.

"Mormons watch everything we do," Charlie said. "Used to
be a man against the sky was an Indian, now it's a Mormon
scout. Makes the contractors nervous."

"I shouldn't wonder, considering they're here entirely unescorted. They can't handle Mormons the way they do Indians,
that's for sure." The captain grimaced. "And neither can we.
It changes the whole Mary Ann. The only thing I got out of
Brigham was a ration of shit. He has everything we need, but
won't turn loose of it till next spring. He says he'll burn his city
if we force the issue. I'm surprised he hasn't burned these pastures. Winter's his friend, the same as it was for Russia in 1812,
when Napoleon got as far as Moscow before being forced to
retreat. The blockheads in Washington didn't learn their history
lessons very well."

"The problem is, if the Army has to winter on this side of the mountain, it'll be root hog," Charlie observed. "There's grass enough, but not much wood."

"The problem is, with General Harney tied up in Kansas and Colonel Johnston not due here before November, we're left with the old lady." The captain's words sounded of exasperation. "If Colonel Alexander gets excited and pees her pants, it's going to be one hell of a winter for the Expedition."

An aide brought two bowls of chocolate pie. The sky emptied itself of light, but not of wind.

"I'm cutting you loose, Reeves. There's no commissions in Washington."

Charlie's features remained impassive.

The captain, knowing what his sergeant was thinking, grinned. "Not here. I'd like you with me through the mountains. I guess that won't break your heart any. After that, I suggest you take a good look at Fort Kearny, see what shakes out."

The American quartermaster and his escort of 10 men got off with the sun the next day, intercepting the Army four days later beside the Sweetwater. Concluding his report to Colonel Alexander, Van Vliet strongly recommended that the Army go no further than the contractors' camp on Ham's Fork.

"However, you do have Brigham's permission to stay the winter at Bridger's, as long as you turn over your weapons to the Utah quartermaster," Van Vliet explained. "Otherwise, he'll order the buildings burned, along with the surrounding pastures."

"Just who in hell does he think he is?!"

"The governor. In that capacity, he's telling me what he will and won't do, and I haven't got any authority to say otherwise."

"Belligerent old coot."

"I told him I'd stop the train on Ham's Fork on my own responsibility."

Colonel Alexander straightened in disbelief.

"But what I really think you should do," Van Vliet said earnestly. "And I can not emphasize this too strongly, is return to Fort Laramie."

"That's out of the question."

"Brigham mentioned the railroad several times in private conversations. Give the man time, colonel. Money talks and bullshit walks."

"I am in utter ignorance of the objects of the Government in sending troops to Utah Territory, or what their conduct should be once they reach there, however…"

"…you can recommend. You're the officer in the field."

"I hardly need you to remind me of that, captain. As I started to say, I have no intention of being held hostage by a terrorist."

"The road in from this side," Van Vliet persisted, "50 miles of it, runs through narrow canyons and over steep mountains. A few men could hold it. Apart from their religion, these are the kind of men you'd want for soldiers. As it is, they're Brigham's soldiers. He'll burn your supplies and scatter your livestock. Should you by some miracle reach the city, he's promised to turn the whole Territory back to the desert—burn every house, cut down every tree, lay waste to every field."

Colonel Alexander shrugged. "He's bluffing."

"At church last Sunday, the speaker, a man called Elder Taylor, asked how many would torch their homes and fields, and every hand shot into the air, I estimate over 4,000 people, making one noise like an animal on the end of a chain. They believe the Army's coming to kill them, and they'll do anything Brigham says."

"Is he off his head?"

"I'm not sure where his grip on reality ends and his belief that he's God's anointed begins, but I suspect he's that combination so frequent in history, half-deceiver and half-fanatic. The Saints are addicted to their religion, and they're enormously capable of anything he asks of them, that kind of power is hard to manage. However, he is shrewd enough to capitalize on Buchanan's mistakes, and fielding an army with winter coming on is a mistake."

"Cumming's been appointed governor of the Territory by the highest authority in the land. He will be installed."

"Yes, sir, he will. But Brigham will remain governor of the people. For that reason, I strongly suggest we wait until spring to go in. The people will not have their back up so. It's a foreign country in there. Many speak no English, they've had absolutely no exposure to democracy, no idea what to expect of their new country. They see themselves as under siege and frequently refer to Sevastopol."

"Maybe it's time they learned."

"Maybe, if it were June instead of September. Fremont Peak's already covered with snow. With no supplies, you'll be like a bug on a snowdrift with its legs cut off."

Colonel Alexnder drummed the little portable writing desk nervously with his fingers and stopped abruptly. "We picked up a Mormon escort at Devil's Gate. I assume they'll be with us till we reach the city, and that they have couriers going back and forth. When it becomes clear we mean business, I'm sure we'll hear a different tune from Brigham."

The officer turned his attention back to his paperwork. "That will be all, captain. I trust you'll have a pleasant trip eastward. Washington is far preferable to the prairies in winter."

A hard, dusty wind rattled the night. In his tent, the canvas breathing against his ear, Charlie thought about the men from the Tenth and the Fifth Infantries camped nearby. A man strapped a pack on his back and marched up a hill to nowhere, for what? The privilege of getting paid $12 a month every two or three months if he were lucky? The privilege of being bored to death on post, or killed in the field and thrown in an unmarked grave?

As sergeant, he was king of his own little ant hill. As a second lieutenant, he'd be back to low man on the totem pole. A little more pay and the opportunity to ride up front and get killed first—in exchange for attending birthday parties for the commander's children and doing the paperwork for the rest of the corps. But at least he'd get a marked grave.

In Cedar City on Thursday the 17th of September, the sun was shining.

"The children and I are walking to the city today," Dinky announced over breakfast.

The James looked at each other. And didn't argue. Or say much of anything else after that. Verity did however, as usual, tag along.

In the little city park, Dinky convinced her shadow to stay behind with the children at the swings and teeter-totter while she walked up to the general store. Passing on the way the meat market with its cardboard MAIL PICKED UP HERE sign in the window, where earlier she'd left a letter addressed to Mun in San Bernardino,

> My dearest husband, We are here in Cedar City visiting my
> sister and hope to be along shortly to the coast. Love, Dinky

Up the street beyond the general store was a church. Curious as to what was inside, she wandered that direction, coming first to the churchyard, busy with a number of people and wagons.

Several men were admiring a large, elegant carriage with carved stag heads. Transfixed, Dinky walked toward them. Passing the Cameron wagon, her hand trailing along the box as if greeting an old friend, she glanced toward the hounds. William Cameron had $3,000 in gold $20-dollar yaller boys in cigar tins secured in a hollowed-out portion of the wagon hounds.

No one was paying any attention to her. A man leading a big grey gelding, newly branded with a cross, turned the animal loose in the church corral, shooing out of the way a number of similarly branded oxen. The horse belonged to the story-telling sheriff, William Wood.

A hat fell out of a box being handed out of a wagon, and Dinky picked it up. A boy's navy blue sailor hat made of broadcloth, a small bronze-colored horse with garnet eyes pinned to the front of the material. Kit Fancher's Sunday hat. The charm and the little boy's stick horse were named…

Seizing on the memory, Dinky reached for the name the way a drowning man, clinging to a stick, closes his eyes on the heaving ocean.

People were busy carrying goods ant-like from the wagons into the church cellar. Joining the line, descending a short row of stairs, Dinky entered a rather large, poorly lit room with coal-oil lanterns spaced the length of long, narrow tables. In the dim light, human shapes could be seen working at the tables. Her eyes adjusting, Dinky realized the shapes were working with piles of goods. The room stank to high heaven of something long dead.

Making space with his elbow on a nearer table, a man upturned a small barrel of jewelry and various toiletry articles, including pearl inlaid hair combs, looking-glass mirrors, and hair pieces. A woman working nearby took off her glasses to put one of the necklaces over her head.

Another woman unfastened a large lace pin from a badly discolored gown, tossed the pin on the table, and dropped the gown on the floor.

"This stuff'll all have to be soaked," she told Dinky, pushing the gown toward a large heap of clothing with her toe.

Dinky turned her back and walked out through the open cellar doorway into the sunshine.

"You can't keep that."

It was the man standing beside a stack of iron machinery parts. He pointed at the hat. "Everything stays for now."

Dinky looked at her hand as if seeing the hat for the first time. A dark stain curled one side of the brim. "Dandy," she said. "That was the name."

The man took the hat away and threw it back in the room.

Verity was genuinely sorry for what Jed's sister had seen. "I didn't know they'd bring the wagons here," she said. Dinky, in shock, didn't realize Verity had already known about the loss of the train.

Emil got home. Indians was all he knew. He didn't know about survivors, didn't know where the attack took place. Dinky was weeping, the stark horror of the scene at the church having set in. Verity, too, was upset, as were the twins and Lymund.

"You ain't doing the dead no damn good nor yourselves either," Emil protested loudly and, failing to put an end to the caterwauling, caught up the horse only a few minutes earlier turned loose and rode away.

Returning for supper in a better mood. There were survivors being cared for by the families in Pinto. Emil didn't know how many, but they were asking for Mrs. Miller. Someone would take her in the morning. She'd have to ride horseback.

The next morning well before dawn, feeling Mun's hand on her shoulder, Dinky woke to see Verity bending over her. Later, taking her chair at breakfast, she thought Verity looked ill.

"Are you alright?" she asked

"Yes! she's alright!" Emil barked.

The room was smoky with strips of liver frying in lard. In

another skillet, last night's beans burbled, the juice hitting the stove with the smell of burnt sugar. Dipped candles made from hog tallow occupied a scatter of tin candlesticks—one on the table and several on the plank countertops.

"Let Verity speak for herself. Are you alright, Verity? I know you didn't want people to know I was here, but it's out of our hands now. I don't have to leave the children, they can go with me, we'll arrange for a wagon. Three children are a handful all by yourself."

"She ain't by herself." Emil looked at Verity and shook his head back and forth like a dog shaking moisture off its mouth. "Tell her."

"I'm alright." Verity busied herself setting out plates. "Go with God, go do what you gotta do. The kids'll be fine here."

They ate breakfast in a silence broken only by the stove noises, and Emil sucking the grease off his fingers. Two men came to the door—Dinky's guards to where the survivors were being cared for. In the lamplight the guards' eyes glowed the color of blood oranges, except for the glass eye, white with a brown dot in the center.

"I'm Mrs. Mun Miller," Dinky said, offering her hand to the nearer of the men. "And I appreciate what you're doing for me."

"Brother Lot." The man, lanky with a hank of dirty blond hanging down his back, glanced at Emil. "Yeah, Brother A. Cross Lot."

The glass eye belonged to the second guard, a man of medium build with dark thin hair and a pockmarked, beefy face. "The Indians call me *Is´takpe*, Bad Eye." He shook Dinky's hand and nudged Emil with his shoulder. "Don't you worry, little lady, we'll get you where you gotta go. Ain't no Injuns gonna bother us."

"When will we be back?" Dinky asked.

"Before supper," Emil answered.

Verity didn't say anything. She'd done up a lunch for the party, she spelled out its contents—sweet bread, cured bacon and raisin cookies. Dinky placed an arm about the older woman's shoulders and, feeling their shake, laid it to Emil's churlishness.

"VERITY!" Emil yelled in his wife's ear. "Look at me!" He'd never married but one wife, they were too expensive. But he sure could, he had the hogs for it. At times like this, the threat was sure there in his eyes. "Sit down!"

Returning to the dark bedroom, Dinky kissed her sleeping children, pulling their blankets close and thanking God for keeping them safe from the Indians.

After Dinky left, Verity hid her face in her hands. Emil was silent for awhile and then resumed his usual bluster. "Now don't you start with me, old woman. The kids is here, ain't they, what more you want? Get up and pour me some coffee."

Which Verity did, picking up the pot and blindly pouring it into the skillet of hot fat.

FORTY-EIGHT

THE COOL DARKNESS smelled of apples. *And why shouldn't it?* Dinky asked herself. *It's the first day of autumn. I'd be in California by now if I'd listened to Ellen, instead of stuck in some godforsaken backwater.*

Remembering the Fancher party, she grew ashamed. All she'd lost was time. Who was asking for her? Mostly likely it was Will, having no family of his own to worry about. The horses reached the dark, still settlement of Cedar City and clip-clopped across a wooden bridge. The pace slowed, now they were climbing. The distant westward mountains turned a dusty pink. The path was narrow and rocky, and Emil's horse stumbled often. Riding behind Dinky, Lot kept hitting the plow horse, making it jerk.

"Stop that!" Dinky complained sharply. "He's doing his best."

"He's gotta keep up."

"If you don't stop, I'll ride last."

The switching stopped.

Will had said the hog farm was out the road to Pinto. That road was also the California road, the Old Spanish Trail. "Why are the survivors up here on this mountain?" Dinky asked. "I thought they were in Pinto."

"This is the nigher trail," Bad Eye said over his shoulder. His horse, in the lightening day, was a blooded sorrel with a nice stepping-out gait.

The most dangerous man rides the fastest horse.

Recalling, for some queer reason, her father's words, Dinky studied the valley below, still in the shadow. Did the road to Pinto split off from the main road beyond the hog farm? A sudden, irrational fear seized her. Arguing with herself, she held her chin high, gasping for breath. Emil set this up, it must be alright. Verity'd been nervous, but Verity was always nervous with Emil in the house.

It must be what I saw at the church, that horrible, horrible thing.

Just that and nothing more. Sanity returned. She was safe. Her children were safe.

I wonder why no one at the church was upset.

Like a wave slapping the side of a boat, the fear returned. The Derringers carried all the way from New York were in her belongings at the James.

My pa would never make that mistake.

The climbing path reached a broad, deep trail that crossed the face of a steep mountain. Thinking about her father, Dinky recalled a phrase that had electrified her as a child.

"Prendre la lune avec les dents!" her father would say in the midst of a story, tapping his palm with a clenched fist. *"Prendre la lune avec les dents!"* Years later, at the seminary, she asked a teacher what the words meant.

"Oh, yes!" the teacher exclaimed with a laugh. "That is very right. Seize the moon with the teeth," and added, when Dinky looked blank, "aim at impossibilities."

A scruff of cedar bordered the trail on the upper side. The lower slope was given over to loose rock. The sun climbed higher, the shadows drew back. And still no road unraveled itself in the basin below, no chimney smoked.

Crossing a shoulder of mountain, the trail reached a bench of forested land—the trees spilling off the bench and down through the lowering rocks for a good half a mile before petering out in the long slide of rocks. Not a wide bench. No sooner had the horses entered the little patch of forest, then the trees were thinning. A buck trotted into the open ground on the far side and paused to look around.

Tactics when I have choices? strategy when I don't? What am I doing here?

Bad Eye stopped, hand in air, and eased his rifle out of the sling. Lot, too, readied his rifle.

The buck took one hesitant step, and another. Bad Eye rested the rifle barrel on a dead tree limb, waited, and pulled the trigger.

And Dinky smacked the sorrel's haunch as hard as possible with her reins.

The horse jumped forward. Caught in the fork of the tree, the rifle smacked Bad Eye's jaw. At the same time, the guard's knee hit a stub of broken branch, the stub jamming itself under his kneecap.

Lot didn't see what happened. One minute he was watching the deer, the next minute Bad Eye was screaming and and the woman's horse was plowing into his horse.

"HOLD ON, HOLD ON," he yelled. "STOP PULLING ON THE REINS!"

Pulling with all her might, Dinky didn't hear anything. Her instincts told her that the plow horse was not really sore-footed, but doing what old horses did sometimes, stumbling along outbound until turned for home.

Once past Lot, she could make a run for it.

Lot had his rifle in one hand, now his other hand was on the plow horse's bridle.

"NO!" Dinky screamed and jerked the rifle free and shot the guard point blank. Lot fell holding onto the bridle. Dinky dropped the rifle, slid to the ground, and scuttled over the bank.

Bad Eye stopped yelling and took a shot. Sliding in loose

rock, Dinky grasped a tree branch. The bullet hit between her fingers, then she was gone. Falling, getting to her feet, scrambling catch-as-catch-can, driven by sheer terror down over the rocks and through the snarl of branches. She reached the dead buck and flung herself across it and came out at the edge of the trees.

Less than a hundred yards below where she stood, the last of the trees were thinning away. Forced into crossing the slide, and not seeing anything large enough to hide behind, she cut back through the trees to the other side of the little forest. And coming out above a hodgepodge of massive boulders, eased into their shadows. Safe, if only for a few seconds.

Face pressed against a cool slab, she made herself stop and get her breath. Then she was on the move again, keeping out of sight of the trees and the overhead trail.

Straight ahead, the boulder field opened. At her feet, a large smooth slab offered a steep chute into another nest of large boulders. Studying the risk, wondering where Lot was, she heard Bad Eye behind her in the cedar.

"Where are you, little girl? Don't be afraid. No one's gonna hurt you. Better come out 'fore the Injuns or rattlers get you. Hey! HEY! I see you now!"

For a split second she thought he really did. Then the voice faded. She leaned forward to where she could see uphill. Bad Eye's horse was watching her over the rim of broken rock. Standing there all alone, ears pricked.

Seize the moon!

Bending low, concentrating on keeping a shield of rocks between herself and the spill of cedar, she shinnied uphill, fighting for breath, putting everything she had into the gamble, skinning her hands and face and tasting blood in her throat.

Bad Eye's horse was standing in the trail, reins dragging. Lying in the sorrel's shadow, blocking the trail back through the trees to Cedar City, was the plow horse. Lot sat at the edge of the trees, his chin on his chest, a rifle across his legs. Immediately above the trail was a shaley, dished-out slope.

Putting together what she was seeing, dragging air into her lungs as quietly as possible, Dinky walked up to the sorrel, gathered the drag of reins up close to the jaw, and walked out on the open face of mountain. Keeping to the rut of the deeply worn trail, keeping the horse between herself and the rocks below.

"John, hey." Bad Eye called from far below, the words floating upward, losing their urgency. "Get that horse, he's getting away."

A good 400 yards from cover, Dinky shrunk inside herself and kept walking. She imagined Bad Eye clawing his way uphill to catch his horse. She imagined herself in Lot's rifle scope.

Drifting up the mountainside on the current, an eagle sailed close enough for her to see its yellow eyes. From far away came the dank of a cast-iron bell. Nobody was behind her.

A hundred yards to go, the iron-shod hooves clinking on the gravel...50 yards...10.

And the path was swinging off the face of mountain and into a saddle of scrub oak.

FORTY-NINE

HOMEWARD BOUND, Dancer took his time. The high mountains east of the meadows were smoky hot and unfamiliar. They were also empty of the murderous whites.

Enjoying himself despite the inconvenience of having to haul about the heavy bag, Dancer dined well. Fish, rabbit, seeds, berries, wild potatoes. Eventually he came to an edge of mountain overlooking the wide, good-traveling swale that opened to the north and south.

The runner knew the lower part of this swale very well—the red-striped hills, the little river of the Roaring Water Canyon. In the southern distance, he could see the massive shoulders of Mountain Lying Down. Once beyond the Parouse, it was a long dry way across Mountain Lying Down to the cool island in the sky that was his home. He prayed the Moronie would never trouble themselves to make such a journey.

Descending the mountain on a narrow, crooked trail, Dancer paused often to study the wide belt of greenery in the bottom of the swale. The day was very hot, and he was getting sleepy. A coyote, working the grasses, came close, hesitated, and trotted away to the north. That's when Dancer saw the horse. It was coming toward him at a great distance, wavering like a tiny brownish flame in the warm, bright haze.

Seeing the horse, Dancer realized the coyote had been Shinawav. He rubbed the dust from his eyes and looked again.

The flame was gone. He hurried downhill through the cedar to a closer overlook. A horse moving that deliberately had to be going somewhere. Sure enough, there it was again, holding to the edge of the trees along the creek. Someone on its back, but not an Indian. This the runner knew instinctively, the distance still being goodly.

The creek turned aside, taking the horse with it. And Dancer moved accordingly. Now he was looking down on the beaver dams. In time the horse came, following the trail around the ponds and again passing from sight, ridden by a woman dressed in white man's clothing.

Knowing what there was to know, Dancer retreated to higher ground and made himself comfortable in the last of the sunlight. Shinawav was the younger brother of the creator gods, Tabut was the older. Tabut wanted a perfect world. Shinawav, appearing as a coyote, acted as a messenger between his older brother and the Paiutes. But Shinawav could also be a mischievous trickster coyote, reversing the work of Tabut to make himself a hero.

That Shinawav told him of the woman could be important. On the other hand, a white woman alone was nothing to worry about. Determined not to cast his lot with the coyote spirit's foolishness, Dancer slept. And woke with his eyes on the dust, as if it had entered his eyelids.

The sun was easing itself away behind the heights. To the north, above the ground that was still in the light, a thin plume of sand soared in the wind.

Keeping his eyes on the sign, Dancer adjusted his moccasins and hung his little water flask around his neck.

The trail south from Cedar City meandered back and forth, little worried by rocks or bogs. A pleasant path shaped and churned to sand by the passage of wild animals, but a hard-traveling road for a woman listening for sounds of pursuit and trying to reach dark.

Dinky fled that pursuit with rage in her heart and with the equally fervent prayer that the James' whole purpose in having her killed was to steal her children. Believing thus, needing to believe, she made herself concentrate on saving the horse and staying beside the water. Water led to water and that lead to people. Sooner or later, somewhere someone would help. In the saddle bags she found a large piece of cactus candy and sucked on it absently. *Please God, don't let there be dogs.*

Sometimes she could smell her father's pipe, as if he rode with her. Hear him singing to himself, working in the orchard picking apples.

> This old horse is a tired old guy.
> It's a hot old trail under a hard old sky.
> Ain't it dry, dry, dry.
> Ain't it dry, dry, dry.

Oh, pa, you don't know dry.

The beaver dams gave way to a steep ravine. Dismounting to push her way through the shrubby thickets of birch, Dinky found what she was looking for. Hoping the woman wouldn't be foolish enough to take the horse into the Parouse, Dancer was hard on her heels. Much of the river was hitched up under the rocky arm of Mountain Lying Down. The horse would kill itself, if not in the deep holes then in the quicksand.

He found the woman standing at the water's edge. Not a very big woman. The horse was dark with sweat. A powerful red horse. Dancer lofted a pebble to fall near the woman's boot. She paid no attention, but another pebble caused the horse to move and the woman to look around.

Her face was badly scratched. Dancer came into the open and

put his hand in the air, palm out. He pointed at the woman, at himself and at the Canyon of the Roaring Water, and walked his fingers upriver. Next he pointed the direction the woman had come, splayed his fingers and waved them upward. And made a line through the air to the ground at his feet. Twice he did this.

Dinky stared at the Indian, thinking she understood, hoping she was right. The river here was about 30 feet wide, swift, but not too deep. Directly across from where she stood rose a wall of mountain too steep for a horse to climb. The river itself disappeared either way into its own narrow canyons.

I have to follow the river upstream, and someone is coming. Is that what he's saying? Pa, let this Indian be like your Indians. She started to lead the horse into the river.

Dancer stopped her and made a chopping gesture at the horse's legs. Moving as fast as possible, he gathered an armload of dry sticks into a pile, as if to start a fire.

Next he undid the horse's cinch. Dinky tried to stop him, and he told her she was being followed, that Shinawav had visited him to tell him about her, and that he had seen the dust of those who were coming. That the little Parouse was full of deep holes and quicksand, and it was only with great difficulty that she could travel up or down, and not with a horse. For this reason, he wanted to drive the horse away, hoping the chasers would try to catch it. For this reason, he gathered wood for a fire, hoping the chasers would think the woman nearby.

Watching the boy's face, Dinky understood only that he was afraid. And that he had a plan. She stepped back, and Dancer finished stripping the horse. Placing his arms around the animal's neck, he asked with all his heart for the horse's great strength and courage, then flew at it with his arms wide.

The red horse was tired, it trotted a few feet and stopped. Dancer tried a second time, with similar results. Giving up, he walked into the river and beckoned at the woman.

God help me! Dinky told herself. *I'm losing everything. First my children, now my horse.* She undid her coat from the saddle, tied the sleeves around her neck and, trapped in a nightmare that wouldn't end, stepped into the cool water.

Immediately she was out of sight of the horse. The crevice resounded with the noise of the hurrying current. The scum-covered rocks were dangerously slick. The water rose to her knees, then to her hips. The crevice closed in like a vise, and opened abruptly to accommodate a side bar. And so it went. Brief parks of sand and thick greenery, but mostly just the river, dark and gloomy in the waning light, filling its entire channel.

That the Parouse was not higher was a great relief to Dancer, who otherwise would have had to fashion a little raft of drift-wood for his heavy bag. But the river passage was a monster for Dinky. Wading into deep holes with water to her armpits, sinking without warning into what she feared could be quicksand, she floundered free and kept going, following blindly where the boy led. All thought of pursuit vanquished by the fear of where she was.

Remembering her babies, she kept going. Miserably alone and frightened, feet aching from being twisted this way and that, telling herself she would rather have this Indian for a guide than the rattlesnakes who called themselves her guards, she kept going.

Shadows filled the Canyon of the Roaring Water and turned the water inky black before Dancer was where he wanted to be. The cove's sand was wet, as were the rocks that sheltered it on three sides. Shaking, Dinky unfolded her coat and made a shawl of it.

From where Dancer crouched, he could see a huge pile of driftwood and a clump of box elders surrounded by a wide, sandy floodplain. The deer were coming down to drink. Little groups of them, appearing at the mouth of a shallow ravine that opened from the south. Nearing the water, the deer nibbled on the dense growth and played, and slowly disappeared into the dusk. Night came on, a fattening moon floated over the abyss. The plum moon.

Dancer gave the woman a handful of seeds. She would be better off without the wet coat around her, but that was her concern. His concern was figuring out what to do next.

He closed his eyes, listening to the Parouse's voice. High water would wash them right out of their little rabbit hole, but there was no whisper of it. Upstream was a thin sheet of water several hundred yards wide and only a few inches deep running over a bed of quicksand. Perhaps it would trap the chasers.

That the chasers came from the north told Dancer they were white men. If there were no Indians with them, they would not know of the good trail leaving the Parouse here to climb onto the back of Mountain Lying Down.

The woman was asleep, jerking in her sleep. Holding a finger against her mouth, Dancer woke her as soon as the moon was out of sight. They entered the river, and he splashed water over the cove's sand to hide their sign. And led the way upstream toward the deer. He needed the deer. He could hide his tracks from a white man, but not from Indian trackers or dogs.

Now he was leaving the river. Several deer got to their feet and milled around, but there was no general alarm. Pussyfooting, lugging his heavy bag, Dancer crossed the open ground and, following a unseen trail through a tangled mass of willows and vines and wild rose bushes, passed into a shallow ravine, his shadow close behind.

The plan didn't work. The deer didn't use the trail of the previous evening, but it didn't matter. Early the next morning a mountain lion, coming to drink, chased the deer across the river. The lion was still at the water when the hounds spotted it. A mile distant the Indian and the woman heard the baying, the sound rising between canyon walls, and began to run. But it wasn't necessary. The lion, crossing as the deer crossed, drew the dogs with it.

F I F T Y

CLIMBING OUT OF THE CANYON, the Indian boy and the white woman pass through a forest of dwarf cedars, in time reaching the foot of vermilion-colored cliffs. More than once, they stop where they might study their back trail, but no one comes, and on they go, in no hurry now, following an ancient trail through a silent, vivid land.

They gather the fruit of the cactus plant, eating it as they would grapes. Gather seeds and winnow out the chaff and roast the seeds in a willow tray along with hot coals, and shake and toss the tray to keep the seeds separated and the coals aglow.

And Dancer explains how his mother grinds the seed into fine flour and makes it into cakes and mush, and he pats his stomach and closes his eyes. And Dinky tries her hand and catches the willow tray on fire, and they both laugh.

But mostly they eat grasshoppers, roasted in a hole in the sand and cooled. And afterward, sleep away from the embers where they will not be easily found. But no one comes.

Three days later, some 60 miles south of the Parouse, they reach Yellow Rock Spring. At this great spring, Dancer has two routes to choose from. The longer has the surer water. The shorter, by 10 or 12 miles, has only rock tanks to hold the rainwater, and then only if it has rained recently. He chooses the shorter, the woman is strong. Drinking all he can, he insists Dinky do the same.

And on they go, the eerie sweep of cliffs and crags and turrets unfolding like a beautiful scarf in the constant shift of shadow.

The first night away from the sunken spring, a wolf howled from a far rim with no one to answer him. Dinky heard an old lobo howling at their fire out of curiosity and loneliness. Dancer heard Tabuts signaling the approach to home.

By late the next afternoon they had not reached water. A hot wind off the rocks forced frequent stops, and finally Dinky could go no further. Despairing of his mistake, Dancer gestured that she should wait and he would go alone and bring back water.

They were resting in the shade of a mesquite thicket. Fishing around in his bag for the last of the jojoba nuts, Dancer turned the bag upside down. That's when the evil spirit that lived in the bag jumped on the woman.

She grabbed Chief Naraguts' tin box and held it against her body, all the while screaming at Dancer. She got right in his face, her own face made ugly and red with anger. Dancer did not want to strike her. This woman could be his. He got up and walked through the sun to another shadow where the crying did not sound so loud. She couldn't keep the tin box, it wasn't his to give, but when he got home, he would burn the bag.

In his camp as many as 20 men might pursue one woman. He would announce, as soon as he arrived, that this woman chose him. He would be good to her, she wouldn't look at anyone else and would stay with him. This would be enough to keep the others away. Otherwise, he'd have to wrestle for her. Most of the men were older and stronger, he had no hope of winning such contests.

She was very brave and not too old to have his children. He'd already killed his first deer and given all the meat away, keeping none for himself. Since then, he'd killed a second deer. When she could be made to understand, he'd tell her this.

Clutching Will's treasured box of oils to her breast, Dinky let go of her prayers. She was with one of the Indians who had attacked the train, there was no one ahead to help her. There were only more Indians. She would go back the way she came. Go back to the river and follow it. Whoever was chasing her would be gone.

Dancer drew close and, when the woman wouldn't look up, got down on one knee to where she could see him and again gestured that she wait there.

As soon as he was out of sight, Dinky left. Taking her time, walking as she had come through the desolation, occasionally spotting their tracks here and there.

I am lost on a giant's chess table, she told herself, watching the clouds sail like purple-bellied rooks across the long vistas.

The thunderheads building in the north caught fire in the last of the sunlight. Settling herself on a smooth slab of rock to watch the tops snuff into darkness, Dinky was past being thirsty. All that was left was a tiny center of awareness of the rock's warmth and the sorrowful drift of wind in her hair.

if only I could stop and get some order in my life Emil Verity I forgive everything you have done to me if you will only take care of my children kiss away their tears and never never be mean....find my ring Mun

She worked the plain gold band from her finger and laid it on the rock.

come put it in your pocket against your heart my dear husband my dear dear Mun

From a tiny waterpocket full of wiggletails, Dancer emptied four mouthfuls into his water container. The last mouthful he swallowed, spitting out pieces of fine rock. Returning to find the woman gone, he scurried back and forth across the dry earth like a lizard, thinking her nearby. But then came to his senses and read the dirt.

It was dusk when he found her. She lay as if asleep, but he couldn't wake her. As he had seen done to babies grown too warm, he poured a little of the water over her face, put his wet fingers in her mouth and rubbed her gums, opened her shirt and rubbed water under her arms, chanting as he worked, the wiggle-tails curling under his fingers.

The water was gone. The woman's eyes remained closed. Head back, Dancer made a great mourning cry to call back the departed spirit.

Clouds poured over the mesa with a sweep of stinging sand. Dancer turned his body against the storm, shielding the woman. He closed up her shirt and fastened the little belt at her waist, all the while pleading with her to stay with him. A fine mist billowed up, followed by rain. Getting to his feet, Dancer took the woman by the arms to drag her to the shelter of the sage.

The last thing he remembered was the lightning squirreling over the rock in little pieces of fire.

Dawn. Little grey clumps of mist everywhere. Dancer saw the clumps against the pale sky and heard a bird cry. It took him a few seconds to realize the lightning had thrown him off the rock. He craned his neck around and, not seeing the woman, jumped up, but his leg wouldn't jump. It collapsed in a ball of fire. Dancer cried out, and tried again, moving crab-like to find the woman head-down off to the side of the rock.

He pulled her to the ground and, realizing she was alive, gave thanks with all his heart. The sun was shining, the waterpockets were full, and they were going home. He told the woman this, and how the spirit that lived in the water wanted her to live.

Dinky rolled over and tried to push herself up. She thought it was still night. Reaching out, she found Dancer's bare foot and patted it.

"Did you kill Will? You don't know any names, do you. I have to go back to the river. You have to take me back to the river. Please."

Dancer pointed happily at a nearby depression. But the woman's open eyes looked past it. That's when Dancer realized her head was swollen and that the back of her hair was matted with blood. Now Dinky was feeling her head and smelling the blood on her hand.

"'Are not the mountains, waves, and skies, a part of me and of my soul, as I of them?'" she asked the boy, sensing she was forgetting something.

They stayed there perhaps an hour, then the Indian was pulling on her hands. Her head hurt terribly. But it was his country. If he said they had to move, they had to move. They went a short distance and stopped, repeating the process over and over again, measuring the earth in slow-motion leaps. Whenever they stopped, Dinky slept and the runner gathered food. He found very little amongst the slick rocks, but enough.

The long night and a slight dizziness caused Dinky some consternation, but the Indian was unfailingly at her elbow and gradually her head felt better.

I must keep walking to remember who I am. I must keep talking.

"How can you see where you're going?" she asked. "It's so dark." Later she said, "Mun never gets lost."

Sometime afterward, speaking slowly so the child at her elbow might understand, she explained, "'Nature chose for a tool not the earthquake or lightning to rend and split asunder, not the stormy torrent or eroding rain, but the tender snow-flowers noiselessly falling through unnumbered centuries.'"

They reach ground covered with fragments of lava. There is no trail here on the lava ground. But the Indian knows every gulch, every rock, every ledge, he knows where the earth hides her water when the rains stay away.

Crossing in and out of the deep ravines at the head of the canyons that run all the way down to the Mystery River, Dancer never hurries his woman, gladly accepting her weight when necessary, leading her on slowly and carefully. She is very weak and mumbles much. Dancer's knee is swollen as big as his new bag.

Thus do they travel south, a tiny knot in the hot, autumn-brown distance.

TO BE CONTINUED

~

A HEMMING UP

THE HISTORY

In telling this story I have tried to use real people in supporting
roles whenever possible, colored in with the history that sur-
rounds them, and to follow that history wherever it may lead.

Colonel Alexander was commonly referred to as "the old lady"
by the men serving under him. However, at the time of his
meeting with Captain Van Vliet beside the Sweetwater, the
colonel truly believed the Mormon militia posed no threat. He
would not have been happy to hear of the captain's promise to
Brigham to stop the American train on Ham's Fork.

The name Tufts, given to the robber in Molunkus, is an oblique
reference to Henry Tufts, a celebrated New England horse thief
and racketeer who often retreated to Maine to hide. The real
Henry Tufts lived to old age and died peacefully. As for those
Salt Lake City residents, the watchmaker Saltus, Jarvis and
Wilson, and the unnamed woodcarver, their stories are found in
early Utah histories and are representative of the reign of terror
unleashed by the Reformation.

Dinky is the only fictional member of the Fancher train. Henry
Scott's distrust of the authorities in Salt Lake City is true. Had it
not been for Henry, described by researchers as belligerent and

unyielding, he and Malinda and the two families with him who took the main California road, would have died in the Meadows.

It appears, from a notation in Jacob Hamblin's unedited diary, that the missionary took the 12 chiefs to see Brigham Young without Brigham's bidding because the Indians were anxious to meet the Great White Chief. The conversation repeated here is taken from Dimick Huntington's record of that meeting.

Brigham's sermons and letters are printed verbatim. His private conversations are largely unknown and are told here as fiction.

The experiences of the Fancher party, from the train's arrival in Salt Lake City down through the Mormon Corridor to Cedar City, are detailed in William Wise's 1976 thoroughly researched but little-known nonfiction work, *Massacre at Mountain Meadows*.

The romantic involvement of a Provo bishop's daughter with Will Aden is fictional, but Will himself was real, a scenery painter who joined the Fancher train in Provo.

Riding under cover of darkness for help, Will was killed at Leachy Springs, some 15 miles from the Meadows, when he stopped to water his horse. Unhappily, Mormon soldiers were at the springs. Challenged by William Stewart, a high priest and member of the Cedar City Council, to explain why he was on the road, Will described the train's situation and told that he was on the way to Cedar City for help. Stewart shot Aden in the back, killing him instantly.

The men with Aden turned back for California and the Spanish Trail. Both Mormons and Indians claim credit for killing them.

Among the three men who left on foot for California the eve of the massacre was a John Baker. Baker's fate is made particularly

interesting by the papers he carried—a letter asking for help
which contained the names of the Fancher company, together
with a book detailing the route and difficulties encountered
along the way, and the conditions in the Meadows.

Both Chief Jackson and Indian missionary Ira Hatch, in
detailed, widely varied accounts, claim credit for killing Baker
and confiscating the papers. Chief Jackson says he gave all the
papers to Jacob Hamblin.

My characterization of Alex Fancher as wounded is based on
speculation by researchers that Fancher must have died or been
seriously wounded during the siege. Otherwise he would not
have turned the train's weapons over to the Mormons.

The "very small train" traveling 10 days behind the Fancher
train, the train whose cattle were promised to the Indians, had
half their cattle run off but suffered no casualties.

With exception of Indian farmer Lee, who was executed for his
role in the carnage, those participants who kept silent escaped
punishment from the Church. A Mormon bishop by the name
of Philip Klingensmith, whose honesty under oath shown a spot-
light on the massacre and the Church's involvement, was forced
into exile. In 1876 Philip told a reporter that

> "I know that the Church will kill me, sooner or later, and I
> am as confident of that fact as I am that I am sitting on this
> rock. It is only a matter of time; but I am going to live as
> long as I can."
>
> – Salt Lake City Daily Tribune, 4 Aug. 1881.

Whether or not the bishop died as he expected is unknown.

The grim interrogation in the Hamblin farmhouse is recorded in
a special report made by U.S. Army Major James H. Carleton
after having interviewed the children.

Albert was the name of the half-breed son of Jacob Hamblin. Several of the emigrant children reported Albert's having killed the girls found in the ravine. The girls' names were Ellinor and Nancy Dunlap.

Jacob Hamblin denied having been in the Meadows at the time of the massacre. I have placed him there because the survivors told of a man in green clothing being at the site. Hamblin often wore green-dyed jeans.

Not one bullet, not one wagon part, not even the most insignificant of papers belonging to what Doctor Brewer, U.S. Army Surgeon, in 1857 described as "probably the finest train that had ever crossed the plains," has ever been located.

In 1859 Major Carlton and his troop of U.S. dragoons found 34 skeletons at the massacre site and buried them. The soldiers marked the grave with a rough stone cairn on which they placed a 24-foot cedar cross. On the top of the cross they wrote, "Vengeance is mine: I will repay, saith the Lord."

Two years later Brigham Young, visiting the meadows, pronounced "Vengeance is mine, and I have taken a little." He then lifted his right arm, and the Mormon men with him destroyed the cairn and the cross.

This bitter chapter in the history of the American West is full of heroes. The Fancher party, brave enough to walk away from their wagons separated from their children—poor, beleaguered emigrants, little dreaming they had delivered themselves into the hands of men who would kill them for God.

Bishop Klingensmith, whose faith in a different kind of God gave him the strength to clear his conscience.

Those lionhearted Mormons who, ignoring orders from their Church, risked life and limb to get food to the doomed party.

The bloodied children who somehow managed to stay quiet and survive.

The courageous historians who continue to embrace the philosophy "damn the torpedoes, full speed ahead" in pressing the Church for the truth.

There are many different dates given for the slaughter at the end of the siege. September 11 is the date given in testimony at both John D. Lee trials. It is also the date used by the California papers who first reported on the massacre.

The number of the people reported in the train varies. The emigrant registers at Fort Kearny and Fort Laramie have disappeared, taking with them the names of the people who had signed on thus far. In addition, with the deliberate destruction of the train's diaries, etc., there is no way to know who might have joined or left the train once it arrived in Utah Territory. A monument placed on the massacre site lists "more than 120 victims."

The number of children saved also varies from account to account, and these accounts are the most bizarre of all. The American Army was not able to enter Utah until 1858. The children (17 of them) were not turned over to the American authorities until June 1859. Not all the children who were spared in the attack were returned to their families. Some were secreted away and grew up in Mormon families. Of these children, those who identified the goods of their families—horses, knives, jewelry, etc.—in the possession of their caretakers, simply disappeared.

THE STORY

In bed with Lady Luck in San Francisco, Conrad Uergin is awash in friends and wealth. And while Phoebe's gentle paintings are a welcome reminder of days gone by, the former trail guide has no plans to return to Salt Lake City. But it was Uergin who paved the way for Ellen and Jed to be together in 1846, Uergin who shepherded Ellen across the Plains in 1850. He won't be forgotten when the chips are down.

The ever-resourceful Nathan and Daphne, their own plans to visit Phoebe sidelined by the Utah War, happily burrow into the City by the Bay and wait for peace to return to Utah Territory. At which time they will waltz into Salt Lake City (Daphne is already anticipating the boating parties) and pluck the artist known as Phoebe Taggart. After all, what could possibly go wrong in that little backwater settlement these cosmopolitan grafters can't handle?

U.S. Army Sergeant Charlie Reeves will leave Captain Van Vliet at Fort Kearny. Alfredo, meanwhile, is busy with his own pursuits. It will fall to these two to change the course of the story.

And Yam, what about Yam? Not to worry. To paraphrase Dinky, "He is ours and we are his, for better or for worse." Yam is the son of the Seneca maiden, Little Bird, and Jean Paul. Jean Paul made Little Bird the gift of his wooden cross, which Yam now wears. The gossip that, by the end of September 1857, is seeping out of Church offices in Salt Lake City will toss Yam like a tumbleweed across the prairies west of the Missouri River.

In the meantime, the ominous silence from those prairies is thought by Dinky's family to be the result of Brigham's decision to close the Territory.

BIBLIOGRAPHY
A SAMPLING

IN TELLING THIS STORY, it has been my endeavor to use nothing but historical fact when these facts are known. Of the several hundred books and periodicals I have read or referred to, a few are listed below. Although early Church leaders privately deplored Brigham's Reformation and the slaughter it led to, official Church policy is to let the stories circulated in 1857 serve as justification for the Mountain Meadows Massacre. However, new information incontrovertibly documented suggests different explanations.

Adjutant General's Office, 1979, Chronological list of actions, &c., with Indians from January 15, 1837 to January, 1891: Old Army Press.

Agnew, S. G., 1974, Garrisons of the Regular U.S. Army, Arizona 1851-1899: Virginia, Council on Abandoned Military Posts.

Arrington, L. J., 1970, Great Basin Kingdom, economic history of the Latter-Day Saints, 1830-1900: Lincoln, Univ. of Neb.

Backus, A. J., 1995, Mountain Meadows witness: Spokane, Arthur H. Clark.

Barry, Louise, 1972, The beginning of the West, 1540-1854: Topeka, Kansas State Hist. Soc.

Brodie, Fawn, No man knows my history, the life of Joseph Smith: New York, Knopf.

Brooks, Juanita, 1950, The Mountain Meadows massacre: Noman, Univ. of Okla., 1970 ed.

———— 1992, John Doyle Lee: Logan, Utah State Univ.

Burton, R. F., 1862, The city of the Saints: New York, Harper & Brothers.

Cannon, T. L., 1959, Temple Square: The crossroads of the West, *in* Utah Hist. Quart., v. 27, no. 3: Salt Lake City, Utah State Hist. Soc.

Chase, A. W., 1880, Dr. A. W. Chase's family medicines: Ann Arbor, Michigan.

Clark, A. C., 1985, From the orange mailbox: Gardiner, Maine, Harpswell.

Crampton, C. G., 1986, Ghosts of Glen Canyon: Salt Lake City, Tower.

———— ed., 1975, Sharlot Hall on the Arizona Strip: Northland Press.

Department of the Army, 1956, American military history 1607-1953: ROTC Manual 145-20, U.S. Govt. Print. Off.

Egan, Ferol, 1970, The El Dorado Trail, *in* American Trails Series: New York, McGraw-Hill.

Frink, Maurice, 1968, Fort Defiance & the Navajos: Boulder, Pruett Press.

Hafen, LeRoy, and Hafen, Ann, eds., 1956, Rufus B. Sage, his letters and papers, 1836-1847: Glendale, Arthur H. Clark.

———1958, The Utah Expedition 1857-1858: Glendale, Arthur H. Clark

Hafen, LeRoy, and Young, F. M., 1938, Fort Laramie and the pageant of the West, 1834·1890: Glendale, Arthur H. Clark.

Hieb, David, 1954, Fort Laramie, national monument: Washington, D. C., Nat'l Park Service Hist. Handb. Ser. 20.

Holt, R. R., 1949, Beneath these red cliffs: Albuquerque, Univ. of New Mexico.

Hungerford, Edward, 1949, Wells Fargo, advancing the American frontier: New York, Bonanza Books.

Ingvard, Henry, 1972, Oregon Trail: Chicago, Rand McNally.

Jackson, W. T., 1952, Wagon roads west: Univ. of Calif.

Lee, John D., 1877, Last confession and statement, *in* The Mormon Kingdom, v. 2: Salt Lake City, Utah Lighthouse Ministry.

Lee, W. S, 1968, Maine: New York, Funk & Wagnalls.

Lotchin, R. W., 1974, San Francisco, 1846-1856: New York Oxford Univ.

Marcy, Randolph, 1859, The prairie traveler: Williamstown, Corner House, 1978 ed.

Mattes, Merrill, 1969, The great Platte River road: Nebraska State Hist. Soc., v. 25.

Moffat, Frances, 1977, Dancing on the brink of the world: New York, G. P. Putnam's Sons.

Nibley, Preston, 1936, Brigham Young, the man and his work: Independence, Missouri, Zion's Printing & Pub.

Peterson, N. M., 1984, People of the Moonshell: Frederick, Colorado, Renaissance House.

Powell, J. W., 1957, The exploration of the Colorado River: Illinois, Univ. of Chicago.

Putnam, C. M., 1958, The story of Houlton: Maine, House of Falmouth.

Rusho, W. L., 1998, Lee's Ferry: Utah, Tower Productions.

Schindler, Harold, 1966, Orrin Porter Rockwell: Salt Lake City, Univ. of Utah.

Simmons, Marc, 1982, Albuquerque: Albuquerque, Univ. of New Mexico.

Smart, Donna, ed, 1997, Mormon midwife, the 1846-1888 diaries of Patty Bartlett Sessions: Logan, Utah, Utah State Univ.

Stegner, Wallace, 1964, The gathering of Zion, in American Trails Series: New York, McGraw-Hill.

Stenhouse, T.B.H., 1873, The Rocky Mountain Saints: New York, D. Appleton.

Stenhouse, Mrs. T.B.H., 1875, Tell it all, the story of a life's experience in Mormonism: Hartford, Worthington.

Wagner, Henry, 1953, The plains and the Rockies, 1800-1865: Columbus, Long's.

Valley of the Great Salt Lake, *in* Utah Hist. Quart., v. 27, no. 3, July 1959.

Wilson, D. R., 1980, Fort Kearny on the Platte: Crossroads Communications.

Wilson, Everett, 1963, Early America at work: Cranbury, Barnes.

Wise, William, 1976, Massacre at Mountain Meadows: New York, Thomas Y. Crowell.

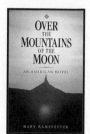

CM

C Lazy Three
PRESS

HISTORICAL FICTION

Over the Mountains of the Moon: An American Novel

By Mary Ramstetter
Softbound, 5½ × 8½", 496 pages, map and bibliography
ISBN 0-9643283-0-5

*First Place Overall Design Winner—Best Design of a Novel
Colorado Independent Publishers Association, 1997*

Vol. I—The West of the American emigrant in the late 1840s. A would-be trapper traps himself in a shadowy love affair. The first wife of a Mormon polygamist clings to shards of past happiness. A Fort Laramie bourgeois philosophizes about the Oregon Trail. Intrigue and betrayal, unexpected partings and surprising reunions pop up like dust devils. Plus dramatic river crossings, Indian captures, and dozens of well-drawn winners and losers from New York to New Mexico intermixed with true historic places and events—an irresistible, page-turning, history-rich experience from start to finish.

☐ Send one copy of *Over the Mountains of the Moon* at the regular price of $14 plus $4 postage, total $18.

☐ Send two or more copies postage-free at $14 each.

Down the Valley of the Shadow: An American Novel

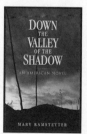

By Mary Ramstetter
Softbound, 5½ × 8½", 488 pages, map and bibliography
ISBN 0-9643283-1-3

Vol. II—The saga begun in *Over the Mountains of the Moon* continues as the friendship between the Marchion and Harris families deepens. In Maine, an Indian puts a face on an old love affair. In San Francisco, a flimflam artist peddling emigrant paintings finds a gold mine in a saloon keeper. While in the heart of the West, the Utah Reformation maims itself with the violent betrayal known as the Mormon Massacre. The steady drumbeat of events makes for a fascinating, history-haunted story.

☐ Send one copy of *Down the Valley of the Shadow* at the regular price of $14 plus $4 postage, total $18.

☐ Send two or more copies postage-free at $14 each.

ORDER BOTH VOLUMES AS A SET

☐ Send both *Over the Mountains of the Moon* and *Down the Valley of the Shadow* postage-free at $24 per set.

C Lazy Three
PRESS

HISTORY

John Gregory Country: Place Names and History of Ralston Buttes Quadrangle, Jefferson County, Colorado

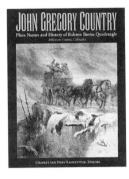

Charles and Mary Ramstetter, Editors
ISBN 0-9643283-2-1
Softbound, 8½ × 11", 280 pages, nearly 200 photographs, quad and location maps, bibliography and index

An amazing collection of every scrap of history known to exist surrounding the first road through the mountains to the fabulous gold strikes in Blackhawk and Central City, Colorado. Richly illustrated with photographs old and new, the book doesn't confine itself to the origin of place names, but ranges across the countryside to show how the dreamers who followed in Gregory's footsteps suffered and coped.

- ☐ Send one copy of *John Gregory Country* at the regular price of $24 plus $4 postage, total $28.
- ☐ Send two copies postage-free for a total cost of $48.
- ☐ Send three or more copies postage-free at a reduced cost of $20 per copy. (_____ copies × $20 per copy)

All are available from your local bookstore, or directly from the publisher
Distributed by Baker & Taylor, Ingram, and Books West

To order directly from the press, send a check or money order to:

C Lazy Three Press
5957 Crawford Gulch
Golden, CO 80403
Telephone 303-277-0134

PLEASE ALLOW 3 TO 4 WEEKS FOR DELIVERY

If you represent a non-profit organization or a business interested in purchasing copies of this book for educational or resale purposes, please write or call the publisher for detailed discount information.